I0577692

CALGARY PUBLIC LIBRARY

MAY - - 2015

MIKE MAIHACK

CLEOPATRA
IN SPACE

BOOK TWO
THE THIEF AND THE SWORD

graphix
AN IMPRINT OF
SCHOLASTIC

Copyright © 2015 by Mike Maihack

All rights reserved. Published by Graphix, an imprint of Scholastic Inc.,
Publishers since 1920. SCHOLASTIC, GRAPHIX, and associated logos are
trademarks and/or registered trademarks of Scholastic Inc.

The publisher does not have any control over and does not assume any
responsibility for author or third-party websites or their content.

No part of this publication may be reproduced, stored in a retrieval system,
or transmitted in any form or by any means, electronic, mechanical,
photocopying, recording, or otherwise, without written permission of the
publisher. For information regarding permission, write to Scholastic Inc.,
Attention: Permissions Department, 557 Broadway, New York, NY 10012.

This book is a work of fiction. Names, characters, places, and incidents
are either the product of the author's imagination or are used fictitiously,
and any resemblance to actual persons, living or dead, business
establishments, events, or locales is entirely coincidental.

Library of Congress Control Number: 2014939603

ISBN 978-0-545-52844-3 (hardcover)
ISBN 978-0-545-52845-0 (paperback)

10 9 8 7 6 5 4 3 2 1   15 16 17 18 19

Printed in China   38
First edition, May 2015
Color flatting by Dan Conner and Kate Carleton
Edited by Cassandra Pelham
Book design by Phil Falco
Creative Director: David Saylor

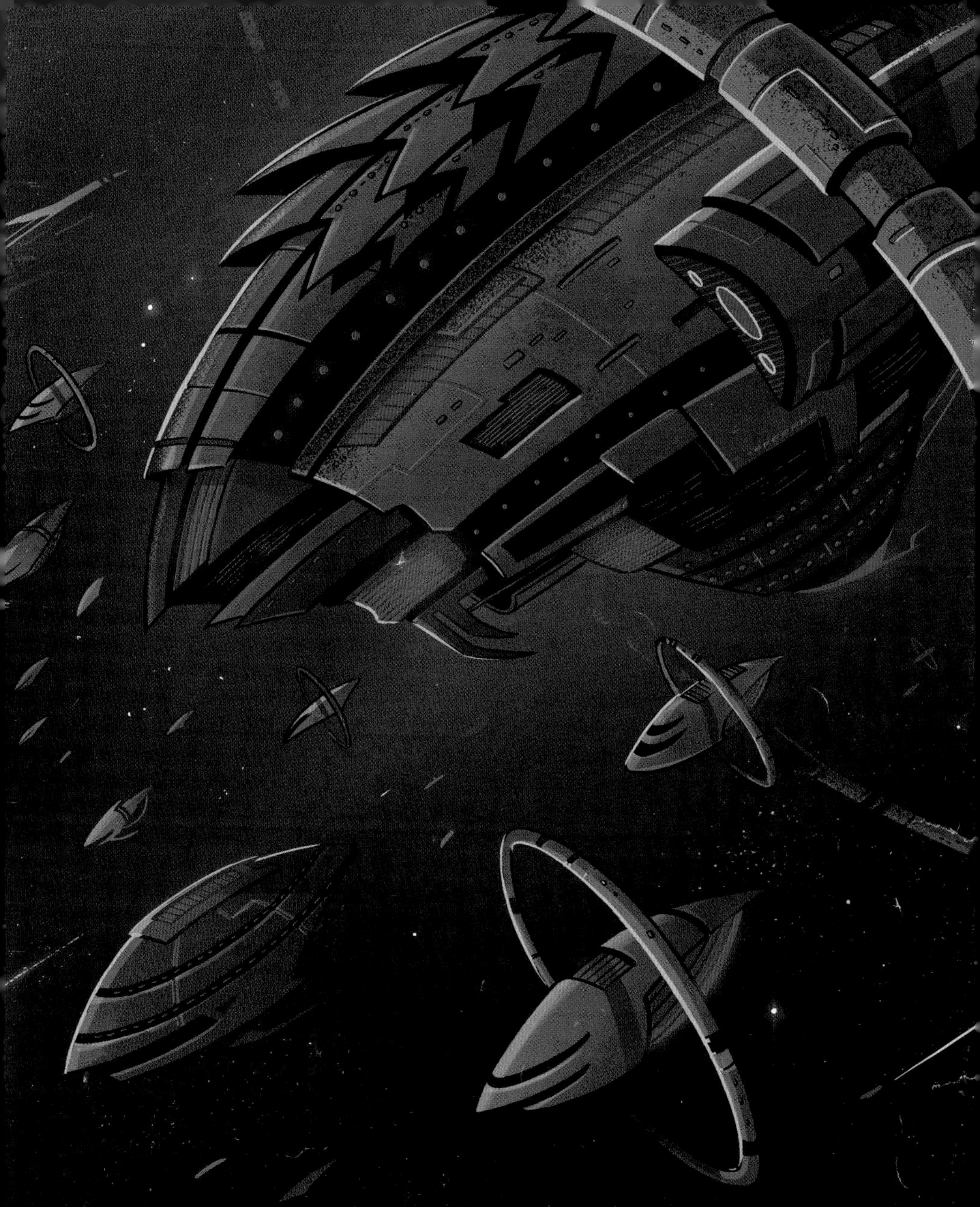

CHAPTER ONE

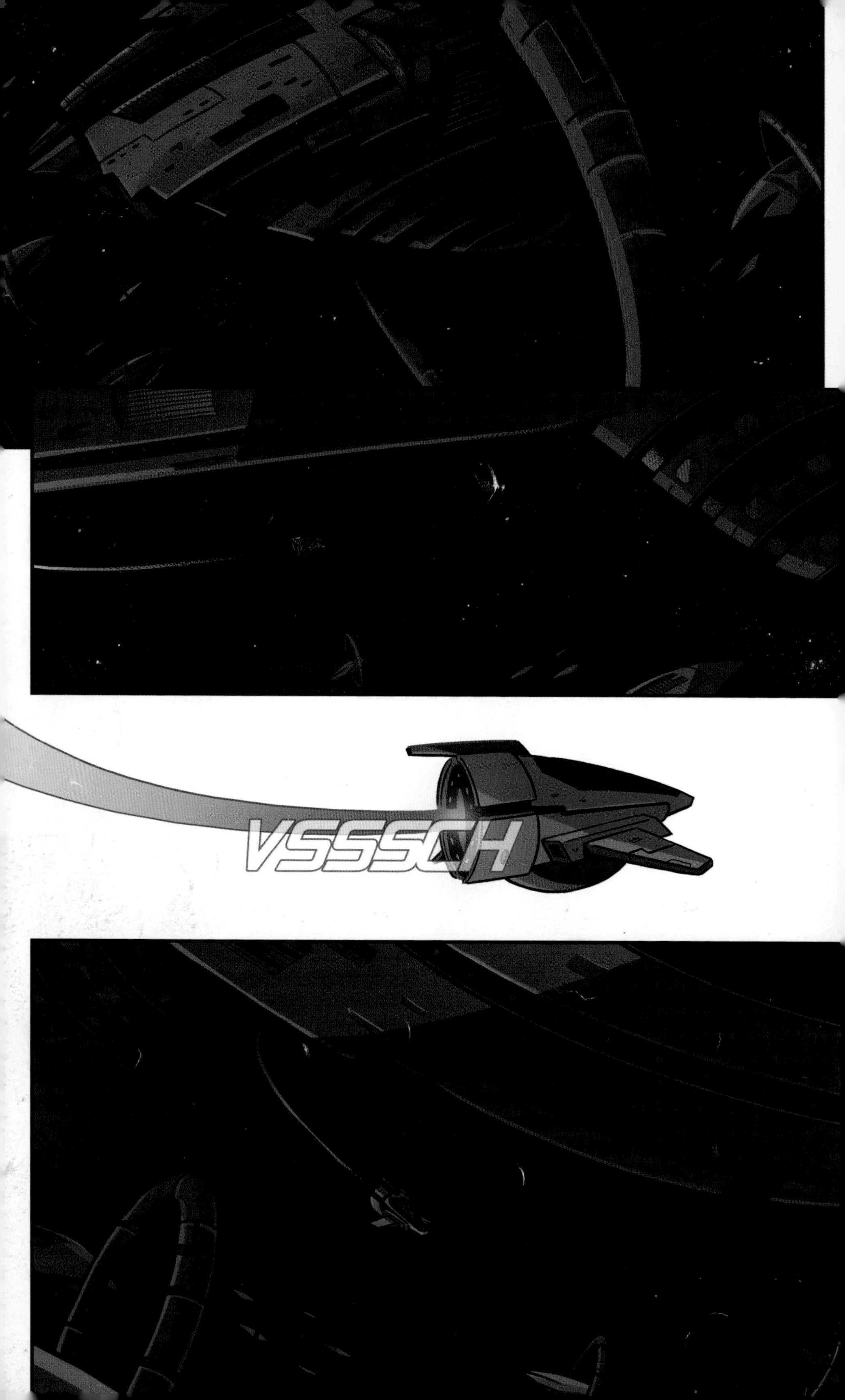
VSSSCH

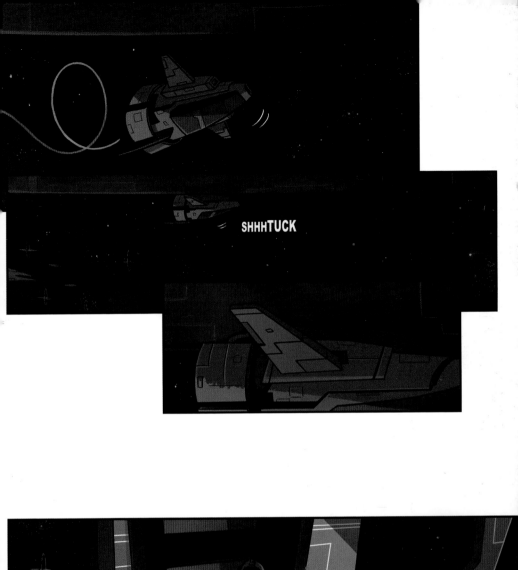

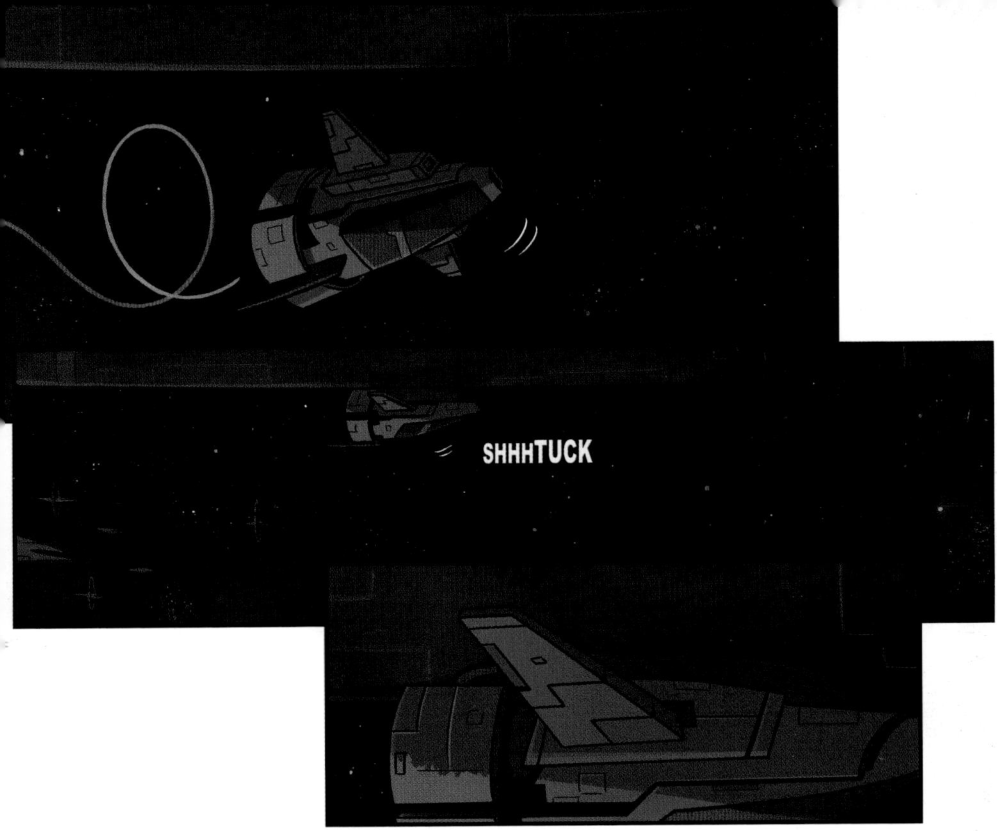
SHHHTUCK

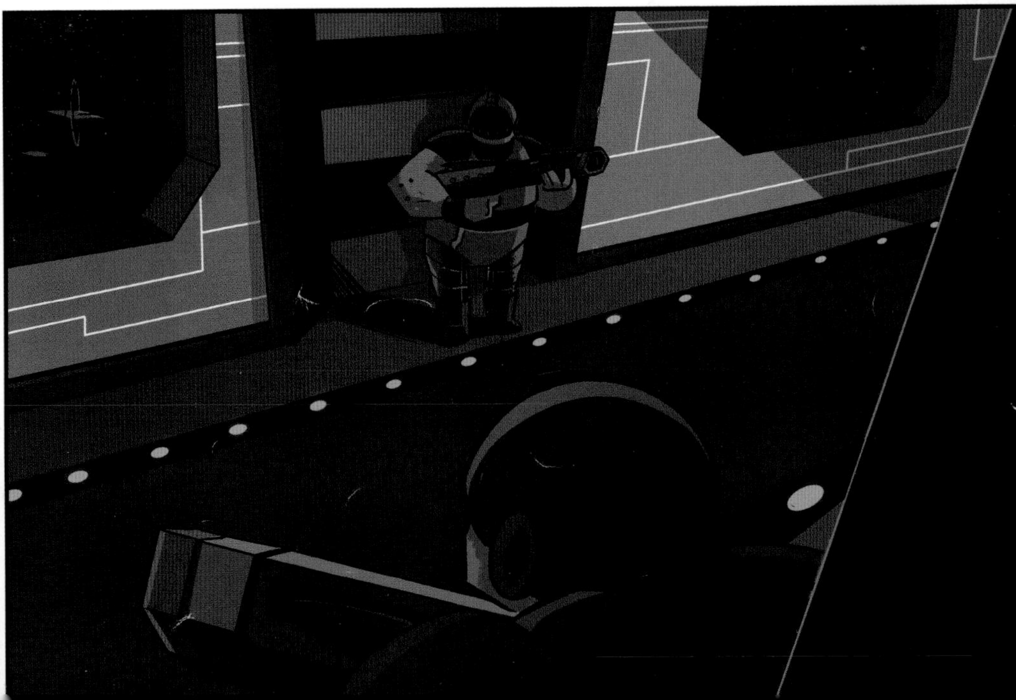

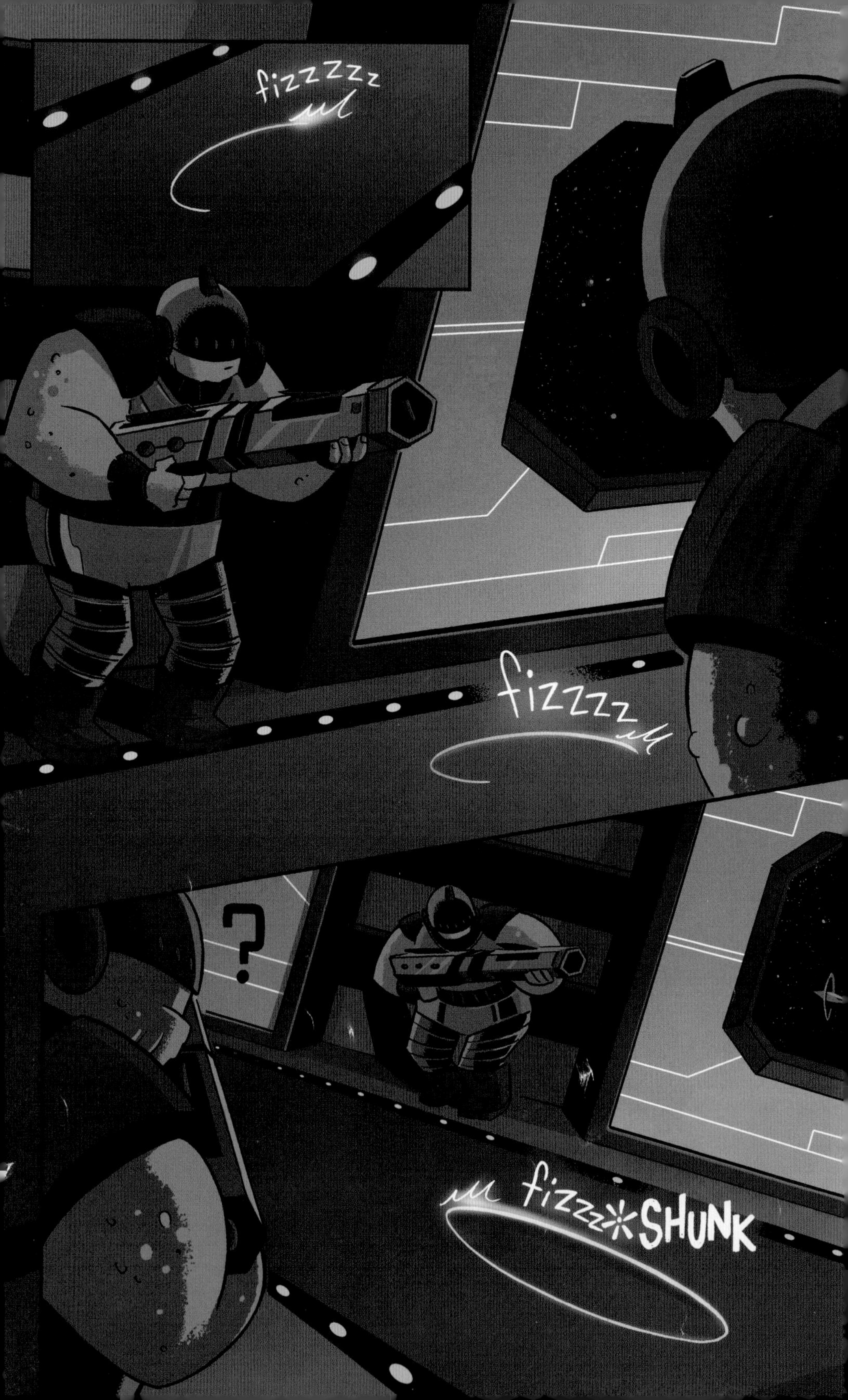
fizzzzzz
fizzzzz
fizzz*SHUNK
?

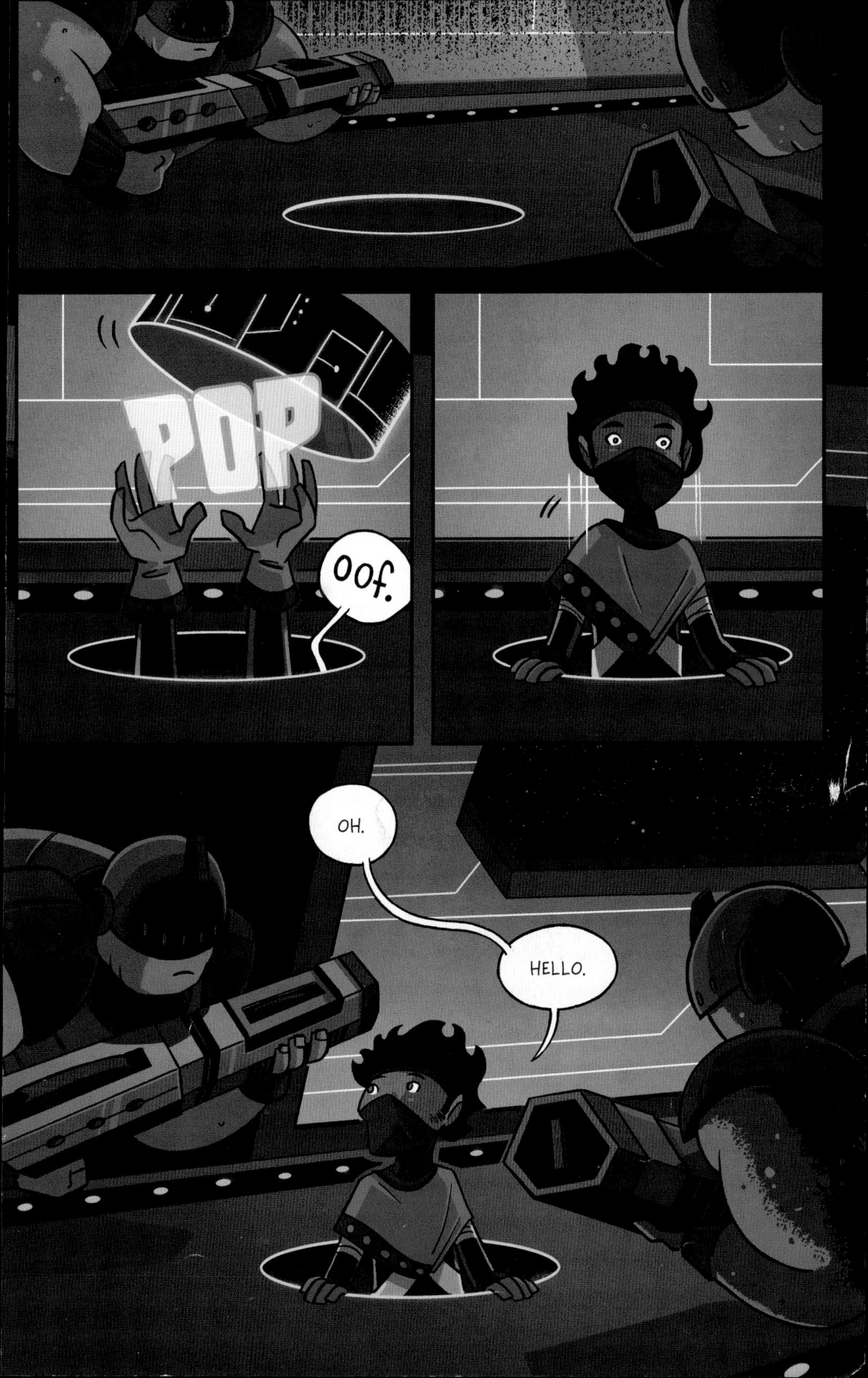
POP
oof.
OH.
HELLO.

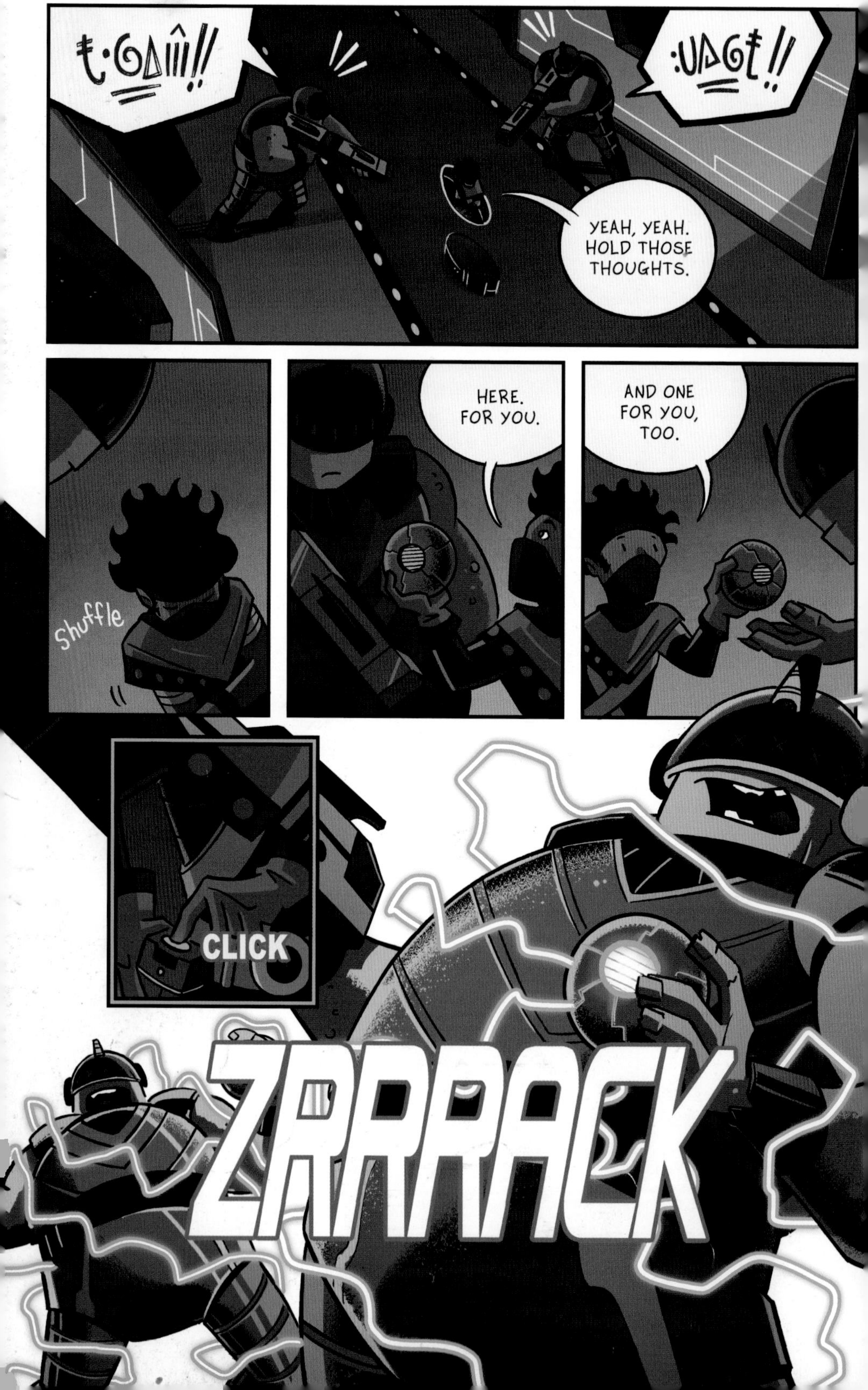

YEAH, YEAH. HOLD THOSE THOUGHTS.
shuffle
HERE. FOR YOU.
AND ONE FOR YOU, TOO.
CLICK
ZRRRRACK

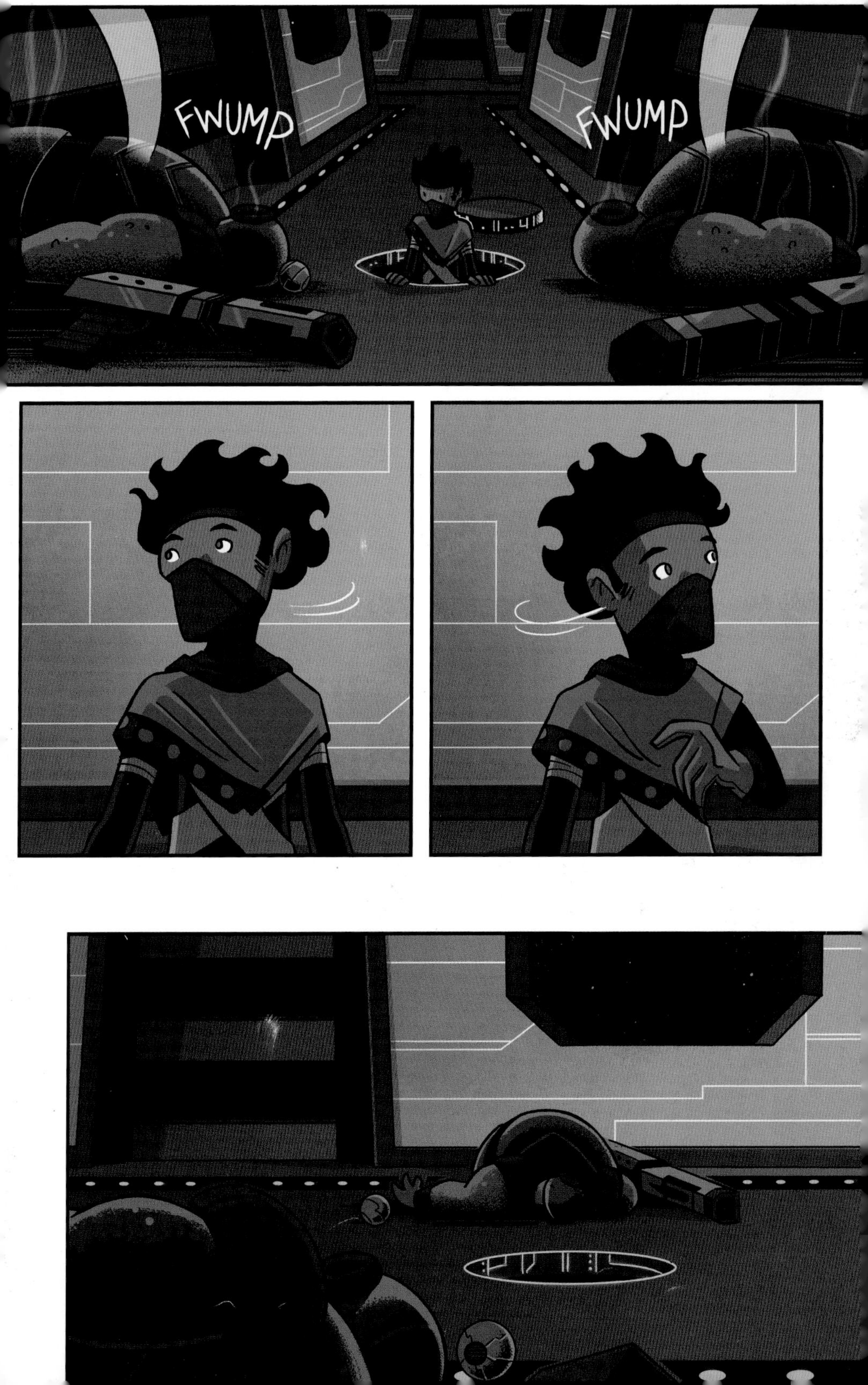
FWUMP
FWUMP

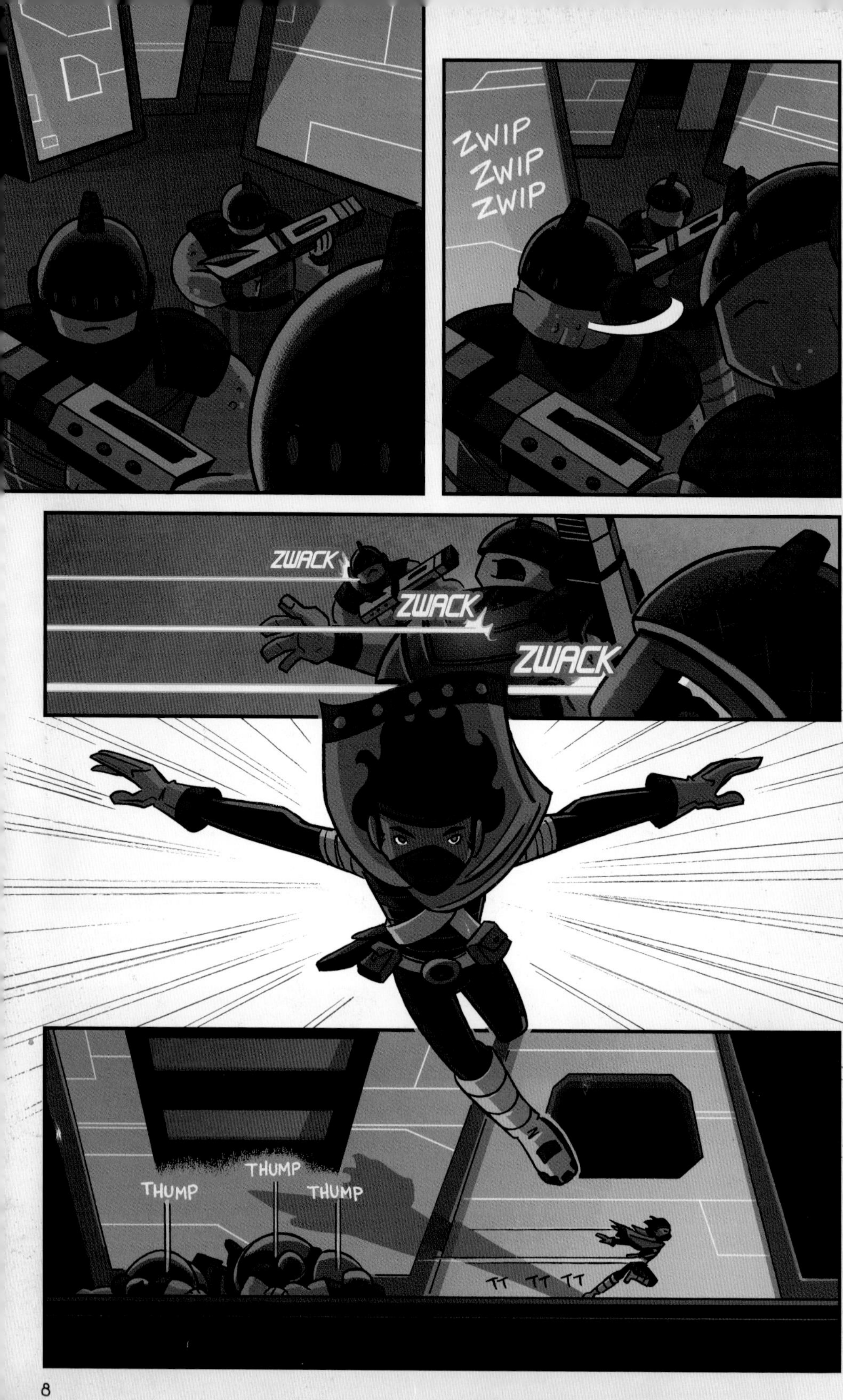

ZWIP
ZWIP
ZWIP
ZWACK
ZWACK
ZWACK
THUMP
THUMP
THUMP
TT TT TT

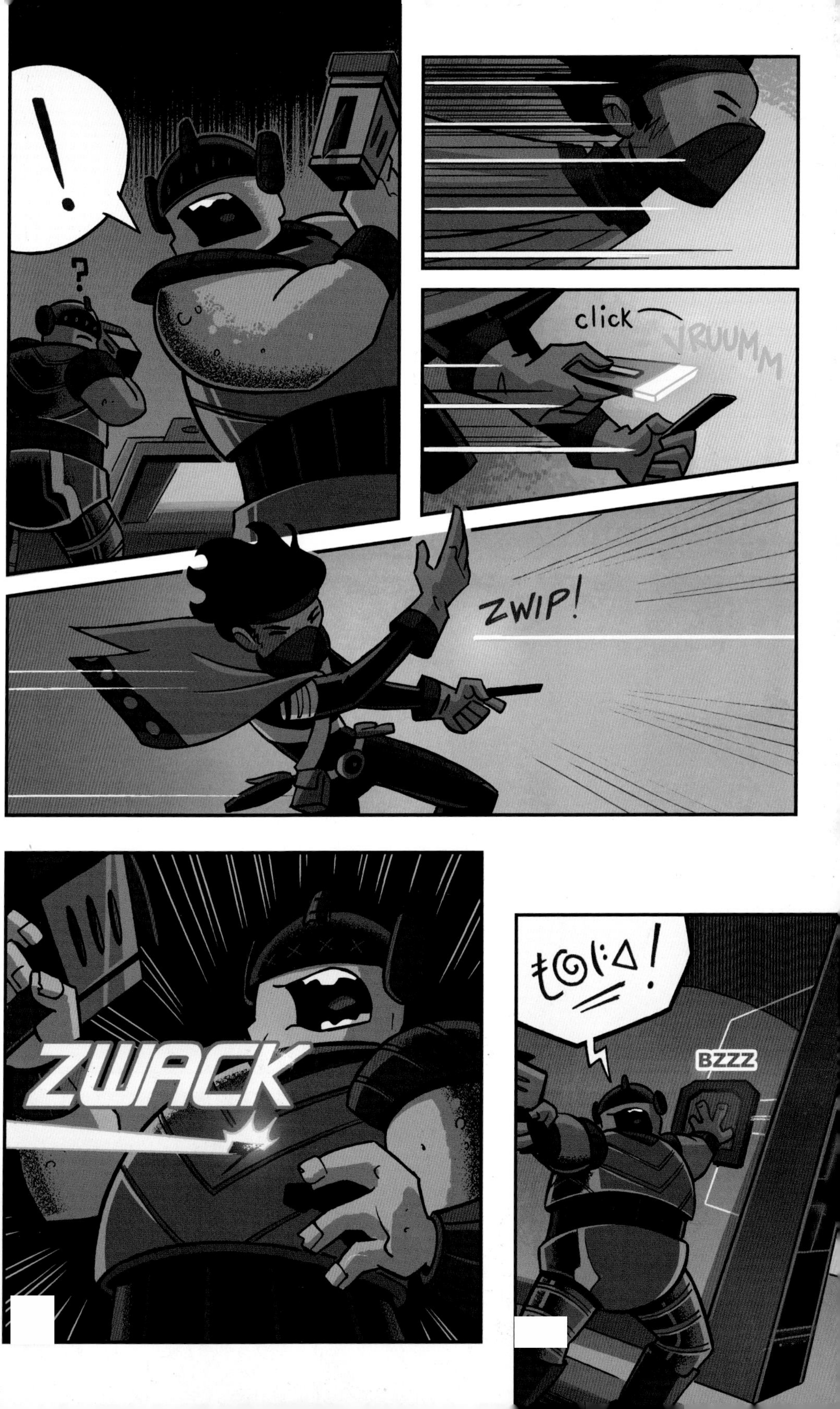
!
?
click
VRUUMM
ZWIP!
ZWACK
BZZZ

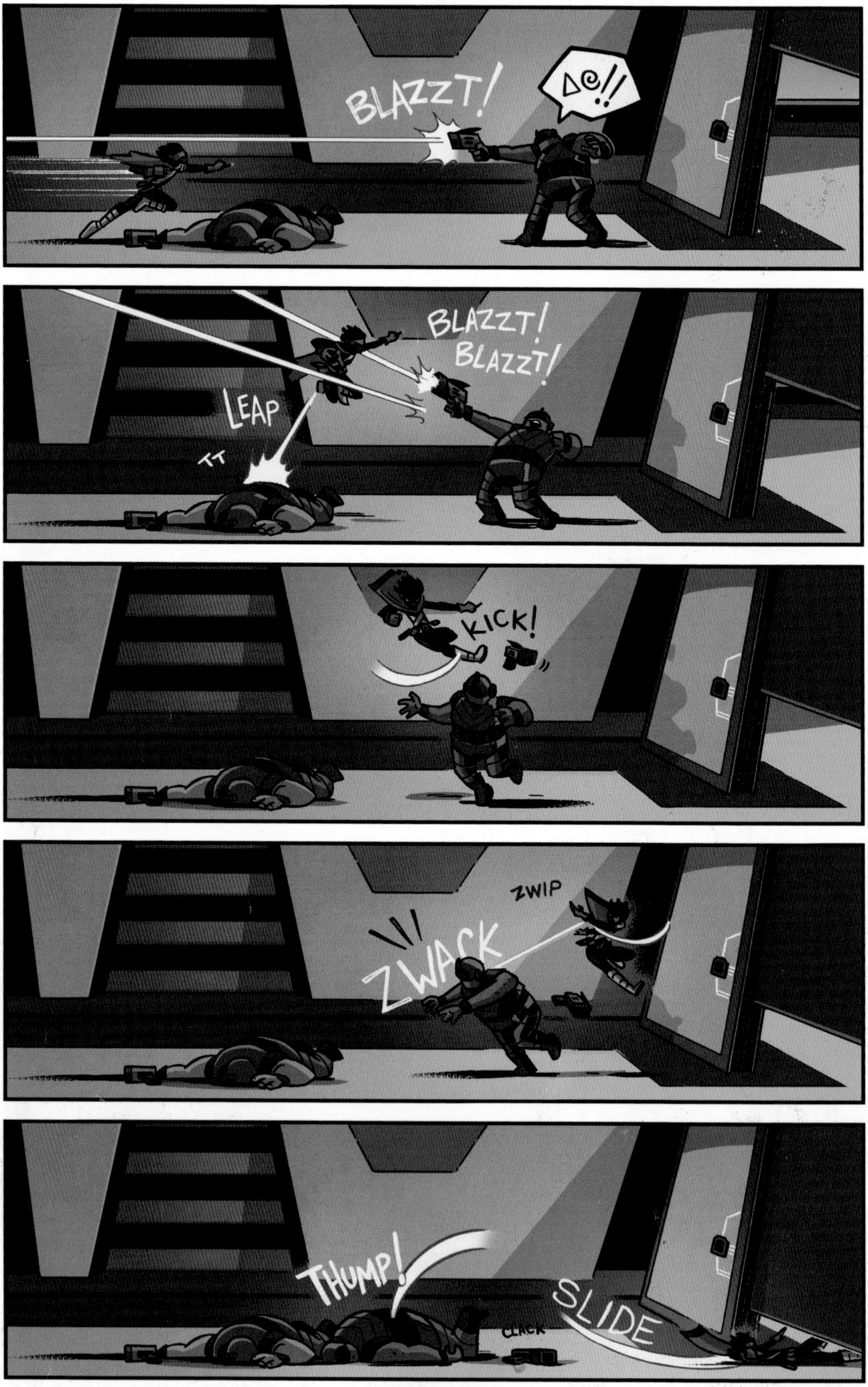
BLAZZT!
BLAZZT!
BLAZZT!
LEAP
KICK!
ZWIP
ZWACK
THUMP!
CLACK
SLIDE

SLAM!

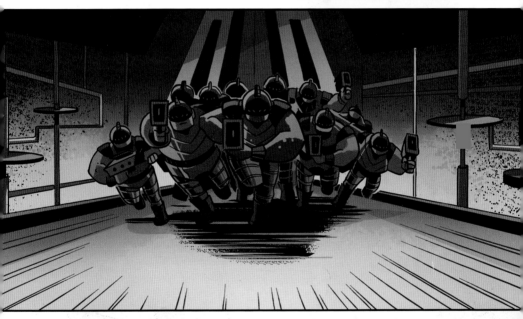

toss

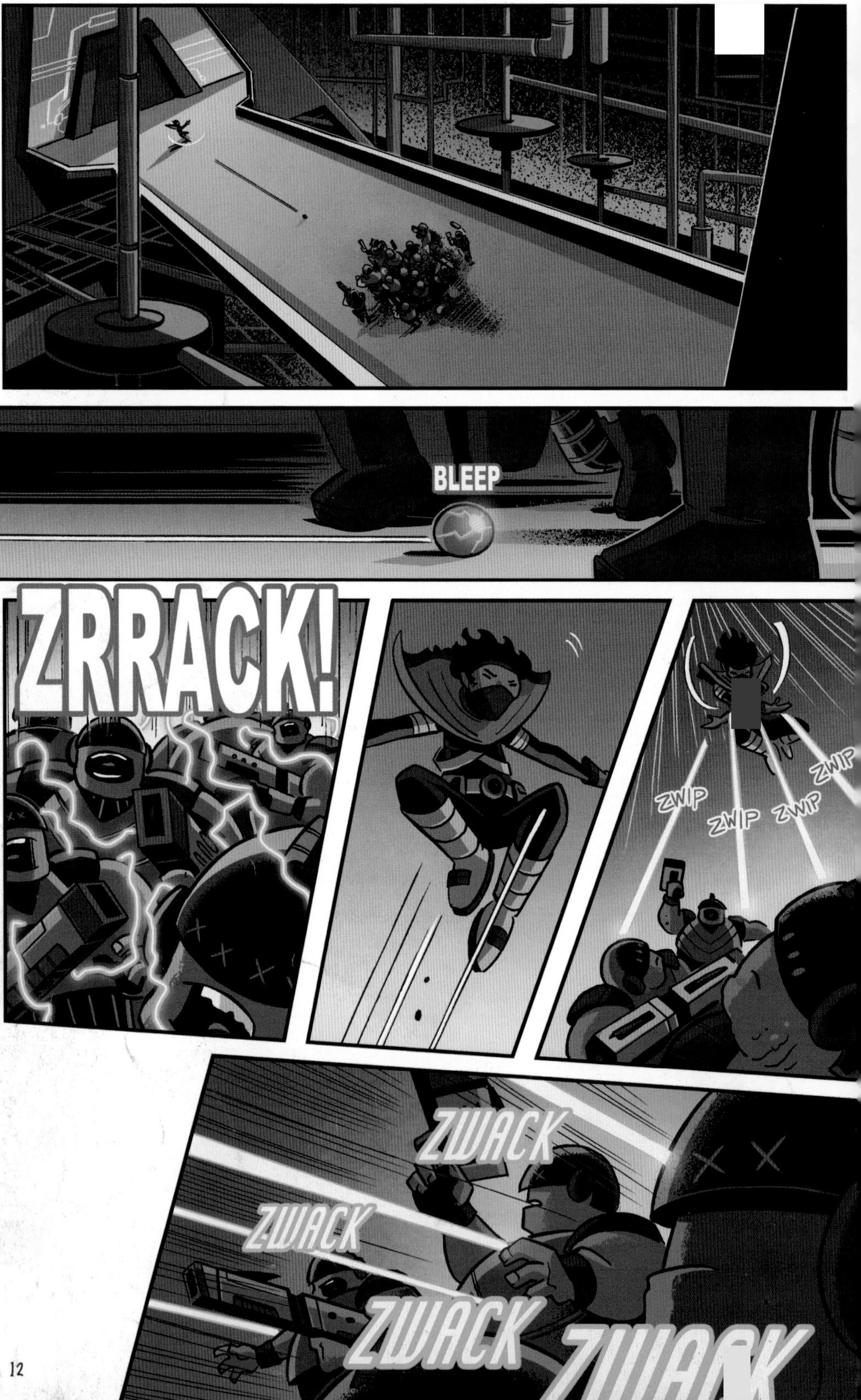
BLEEP
ZRRACK!
ZWIP
ZWIP
ZWIP
ZWIP
ZWACK
ZWACK
ZWACK

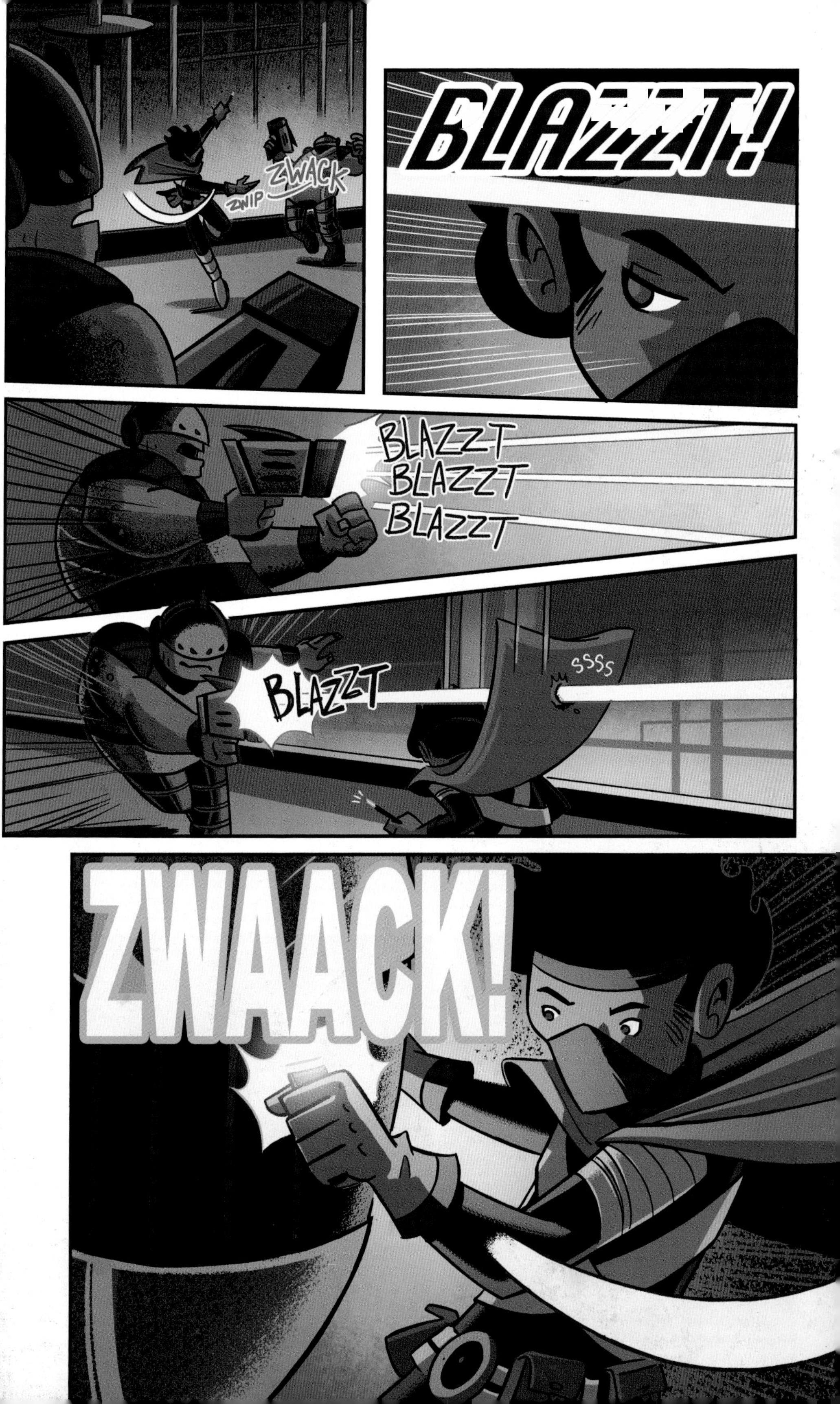
ZWIP
ZWACK
BLAZZZT!
BLAZZT
BLAZZT
BLAZZT
BLAZZT
SSSS
ZWAACK!

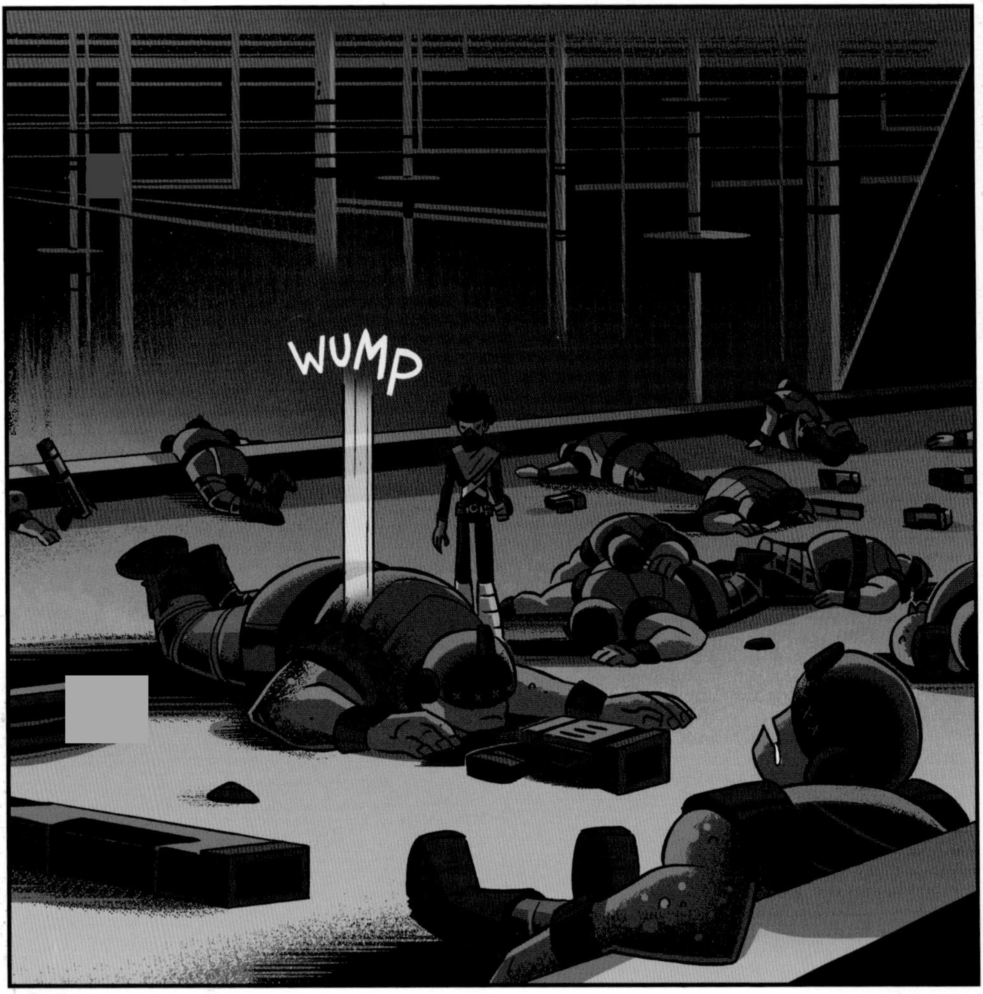
WUMP

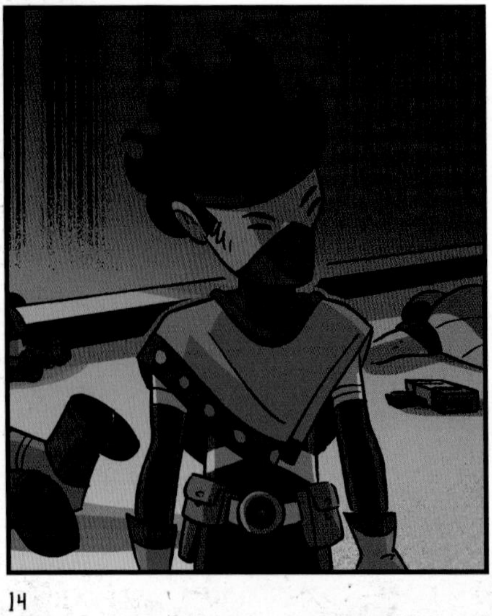

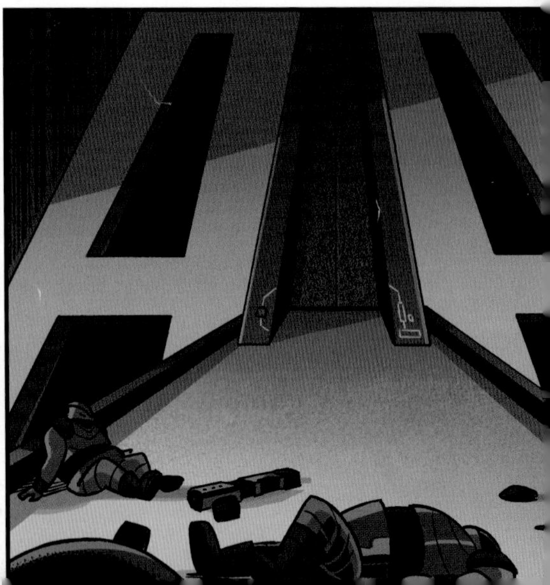

DRAAAAAG

huff.

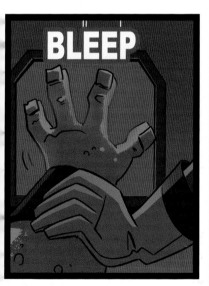

BLEEP

BRRUMMM

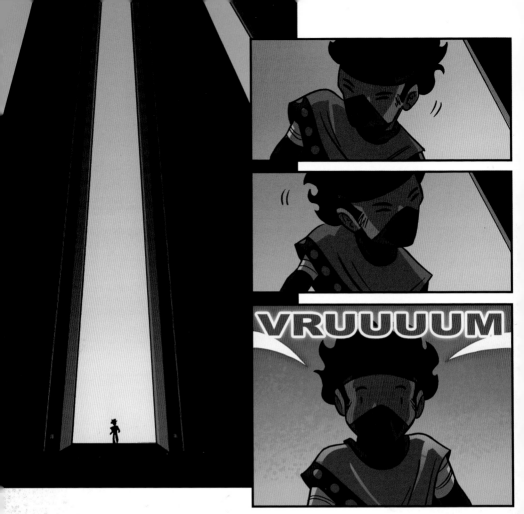

VRUUUUM

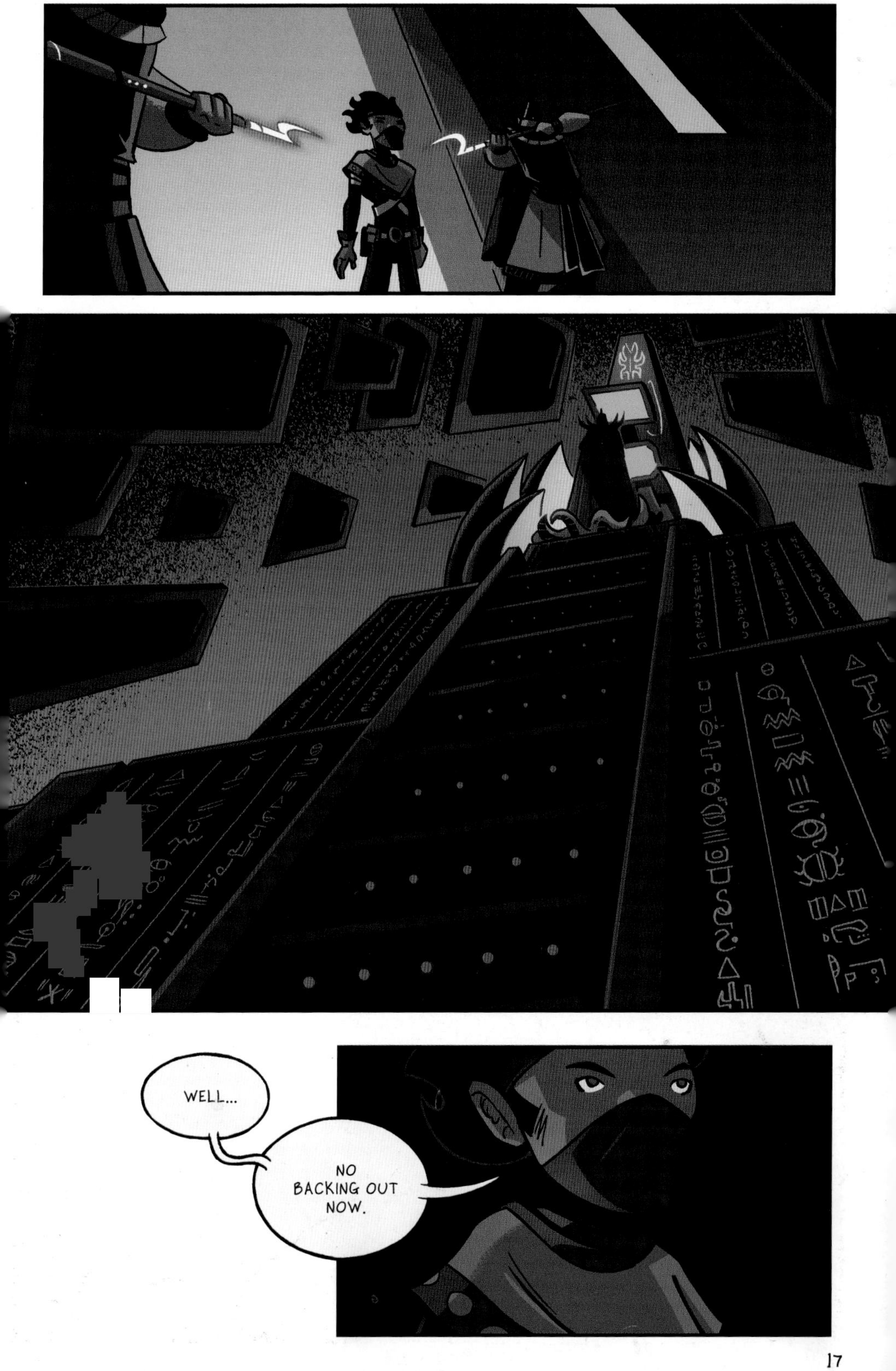
WELL...
NO BACKING OUT NOW.

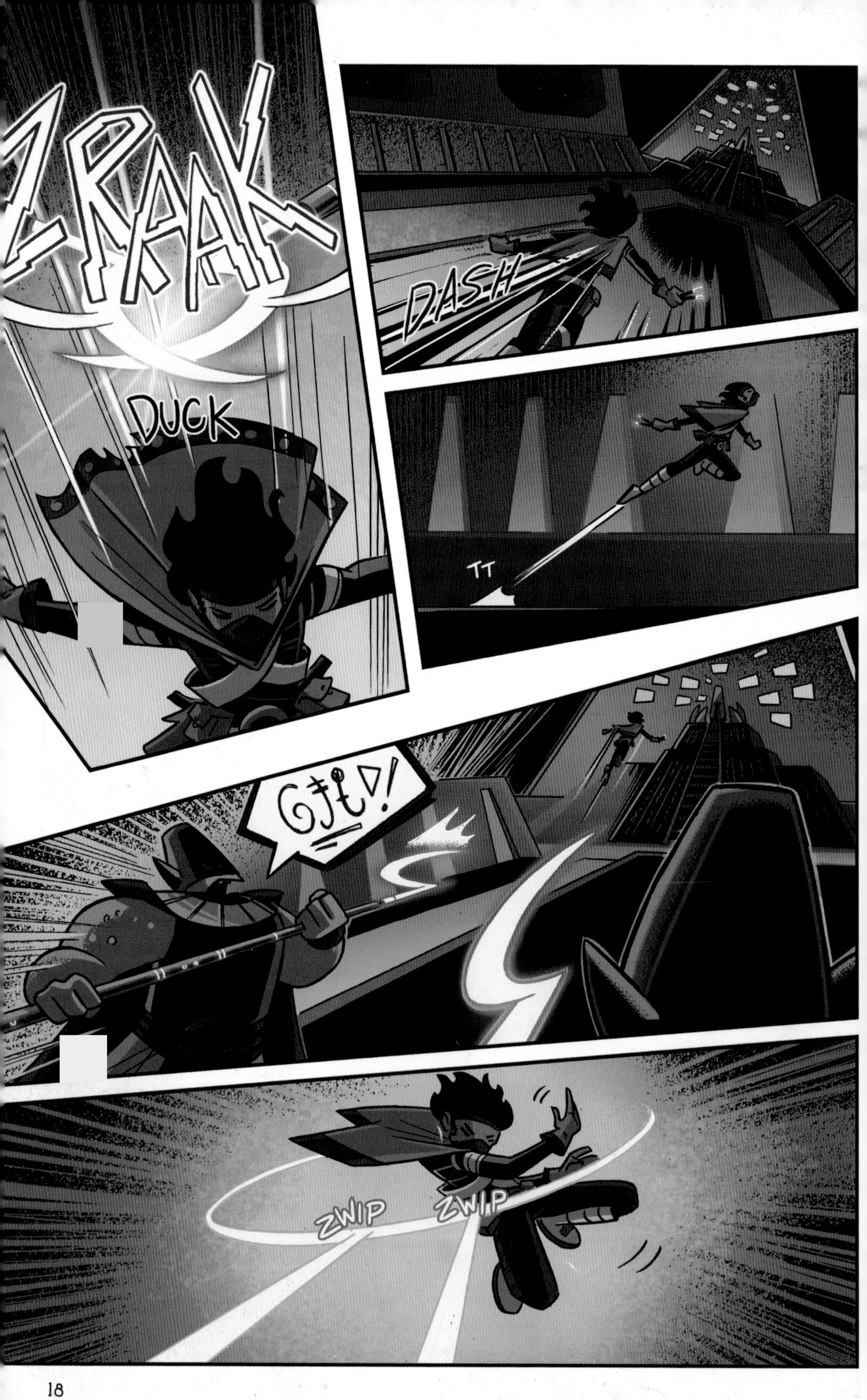
ZRAAK
DASH
DUCK
TT
ZWIP
ZWIP

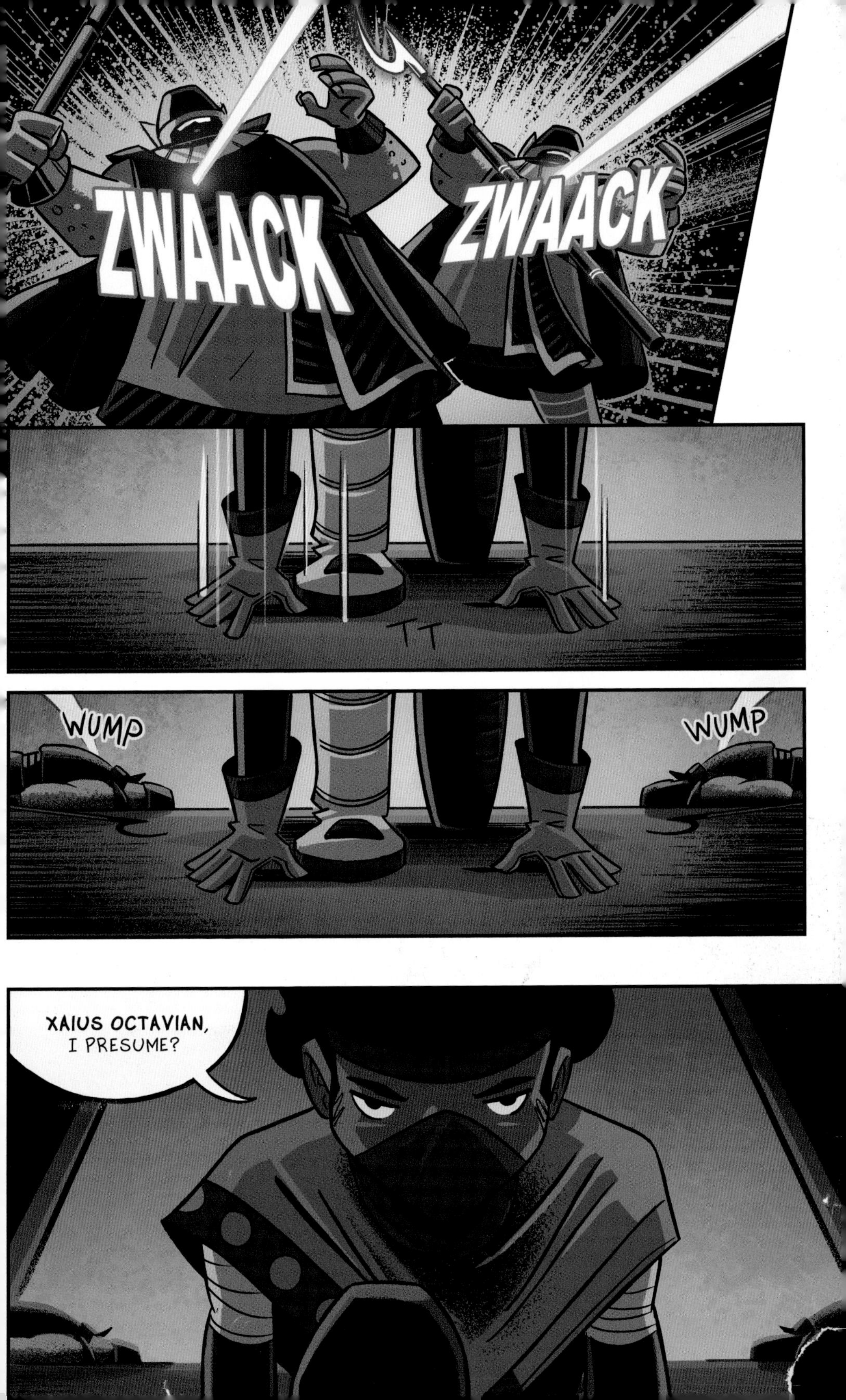
ZWAACK
ZWAACK
TT
WUMP
WUMP
XAIUS OCTAVIAN, I PRESUME?

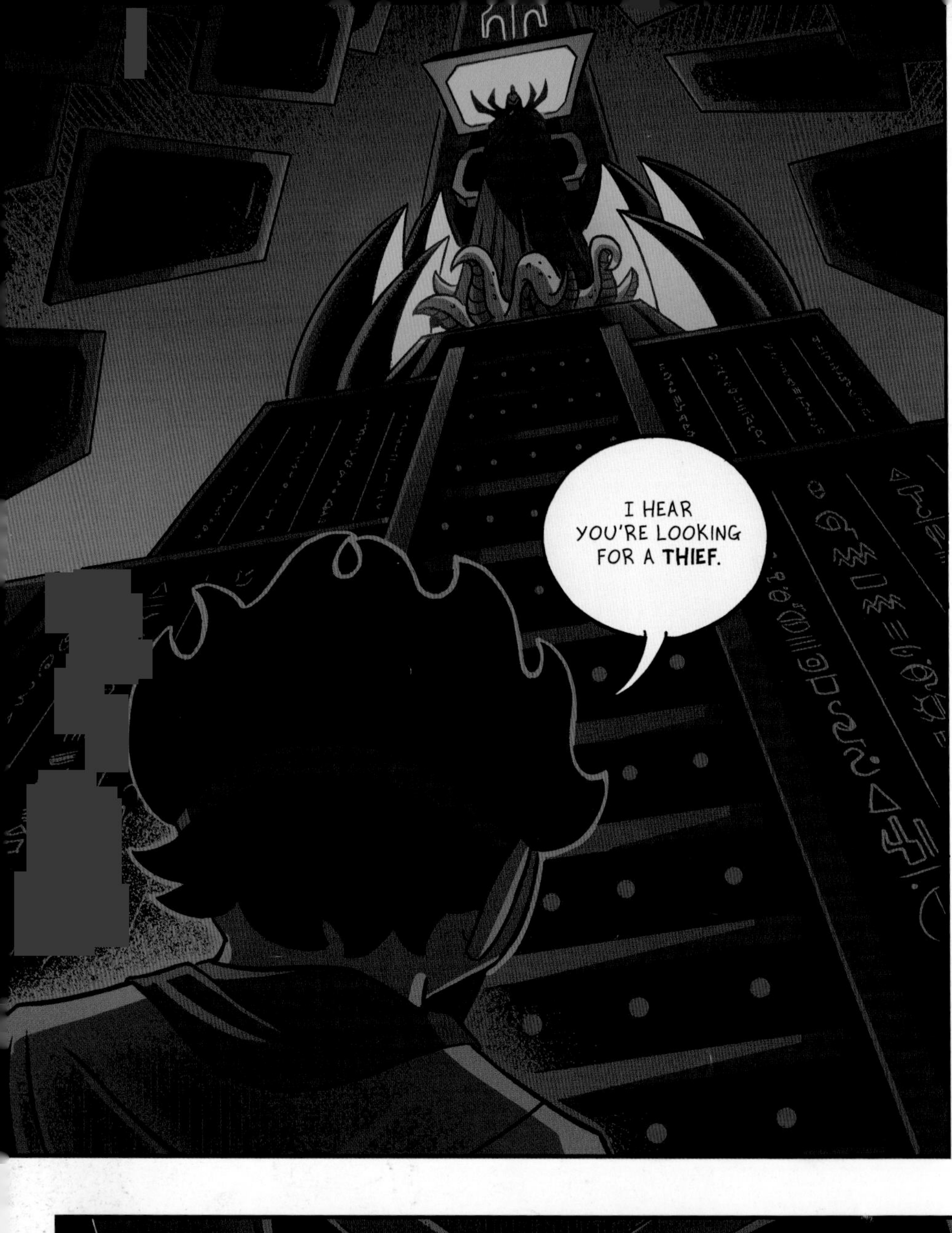
I HEAR YOU'RE LOOKING FOR A **THIEF**.

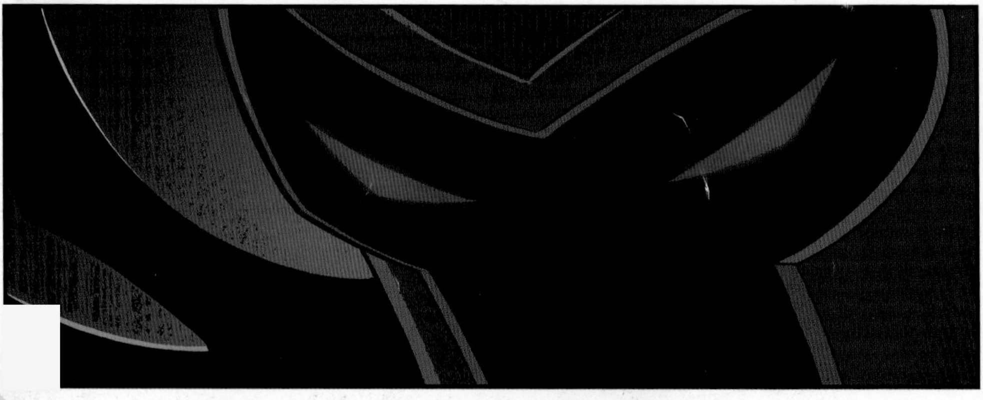

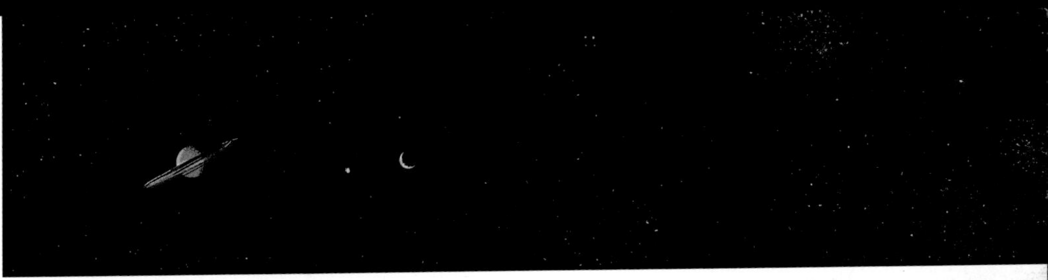

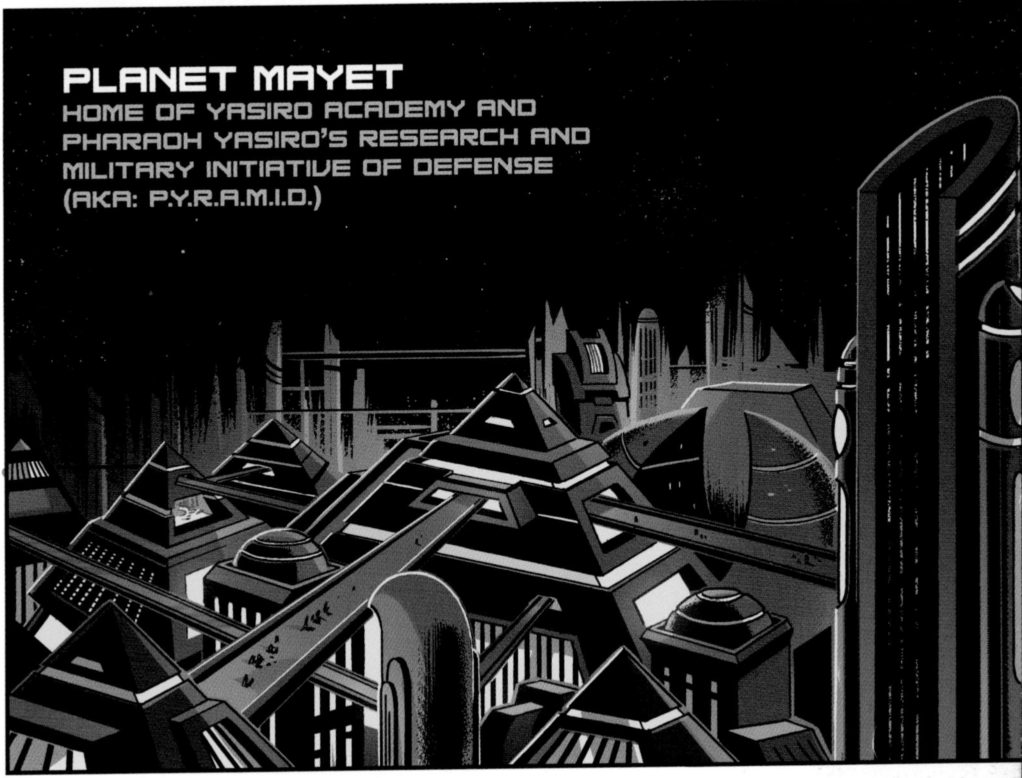
PLANET MAYET
HOME OF YASIRO ACADEMY AND PHARAOH YASIRO'S RESEARCH AND MILITARY INITIATIVE OF DEFENSE (AKA: P.Y.R.A.M.I.D.)

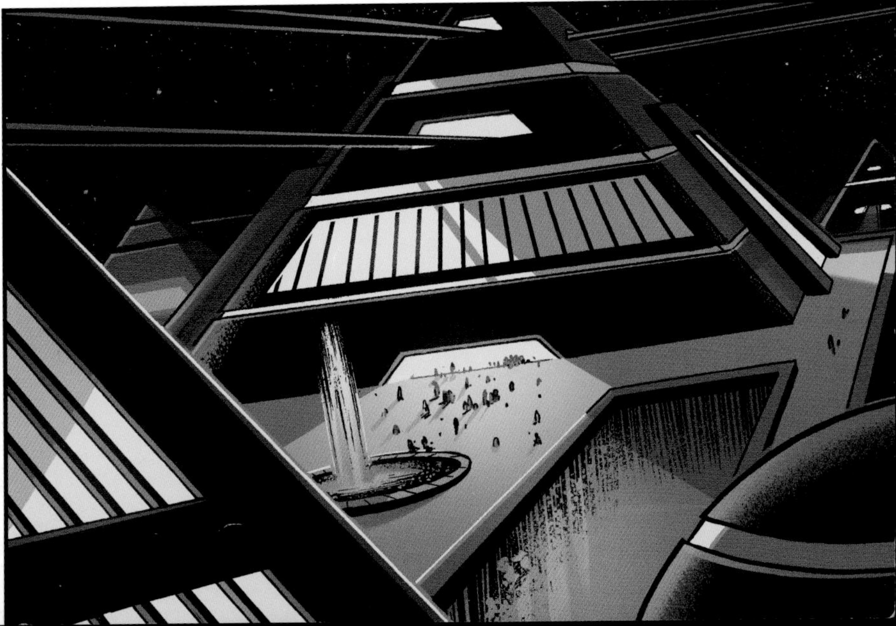

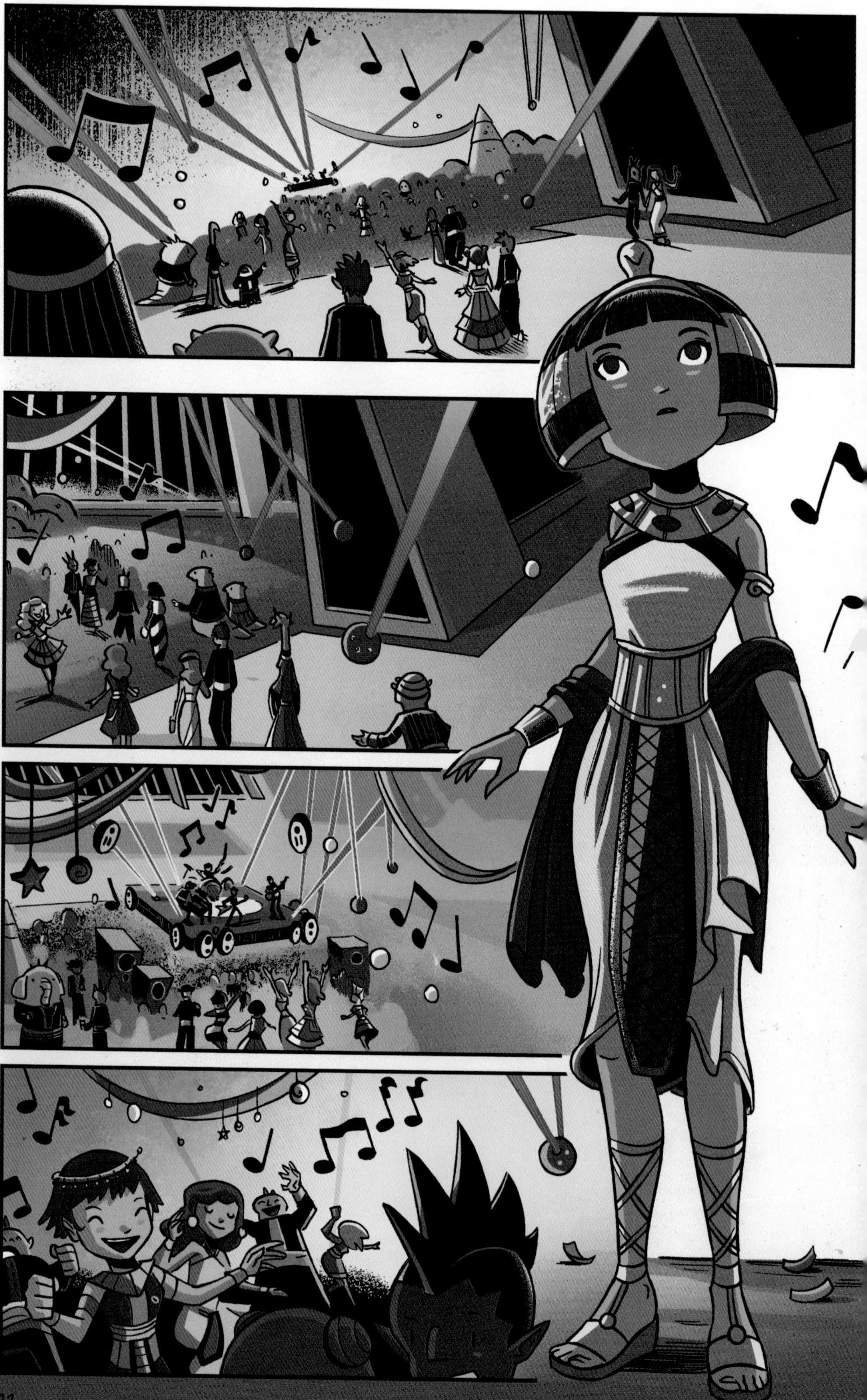

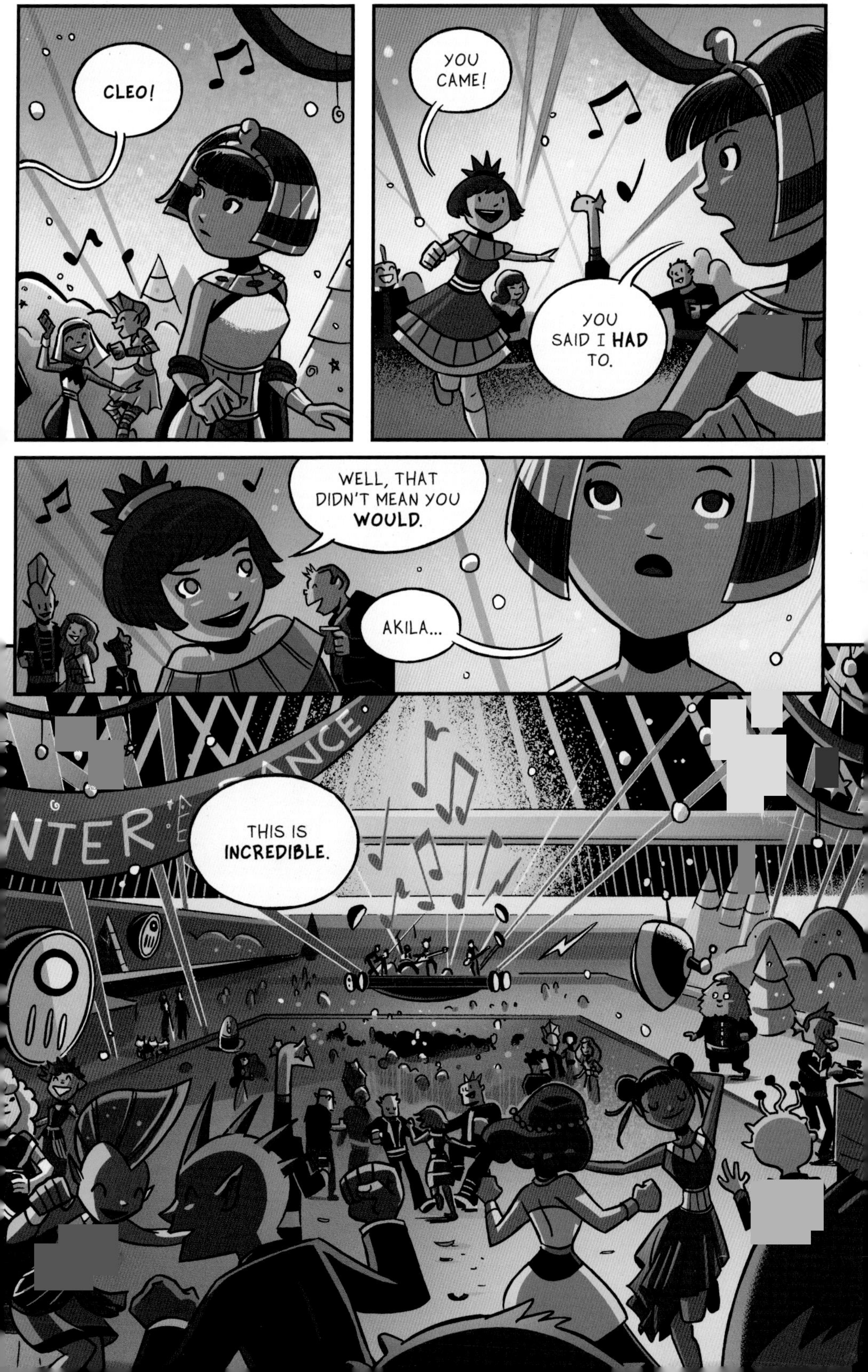
CLEO!
YOU CAME!
YOU SAID I HAD TO.
WELL, THAT DIDN'T MEAN YOU WOULD.
AKILA...
THIS IS INCREDIBLE.

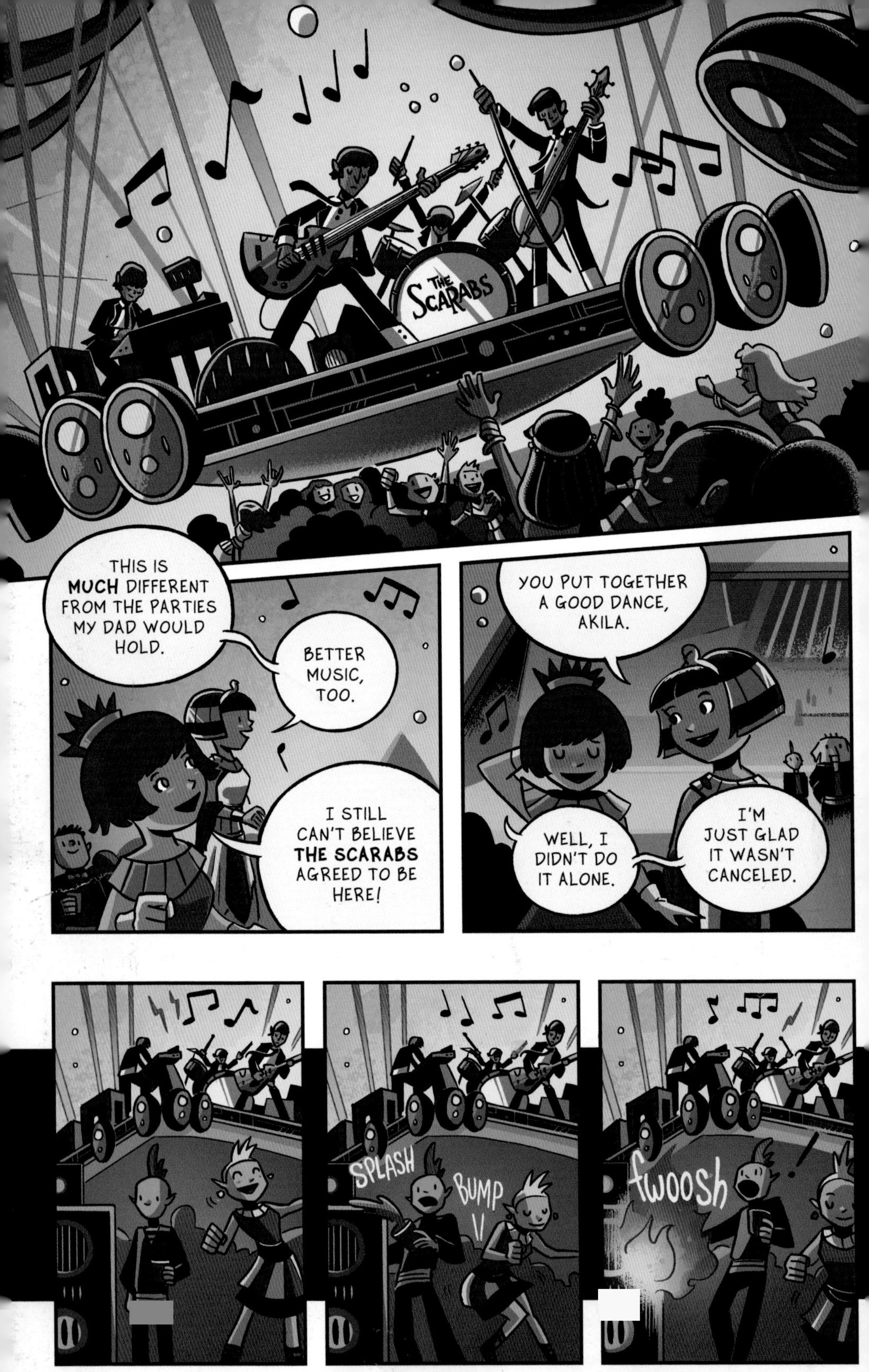
THE SCARABS
THIS IS MUCH DIFFERENT FROM THE PARTIES MY DAD WOULD HOLD.
BETTER MUSIC, TOO.
I STILL CAN'T BELIEVE THE SCARABS AGREED TO BE HERE!
YOU PUT TOGETHER A GOOD DANCE, AKILA.
WELL, I DIDN'T DO IT ALONE.
I'M JUST GLAD IT WASN'T CANCELED.
SPLASH
BUMP
fwoosh

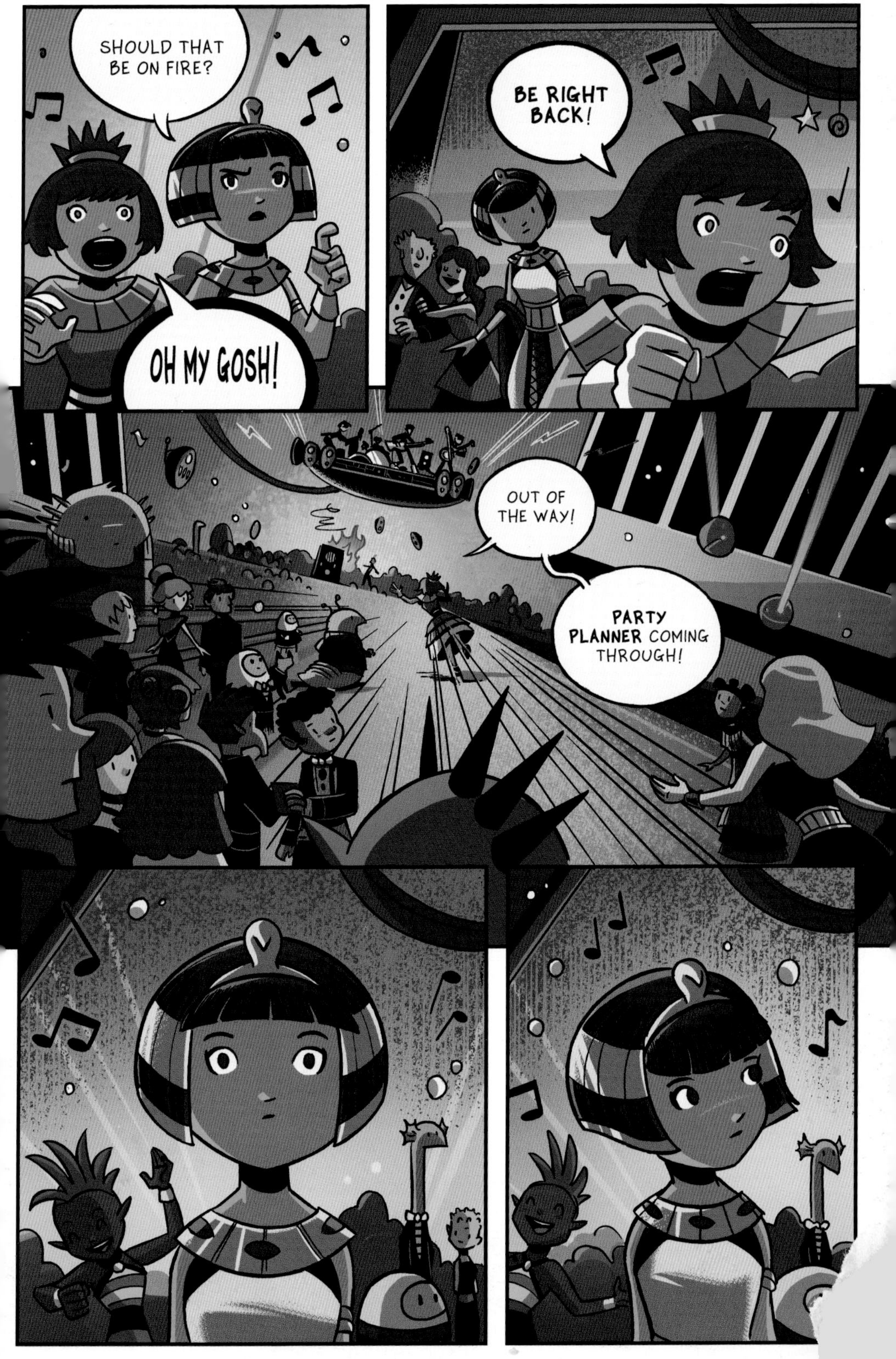
SHOULD THAT BE ON FIRE?
OH MY GOSH!
BE RIGHT BACK!
OUT OF THE WAY!
PARTY PLANNER COMING THROUGH!

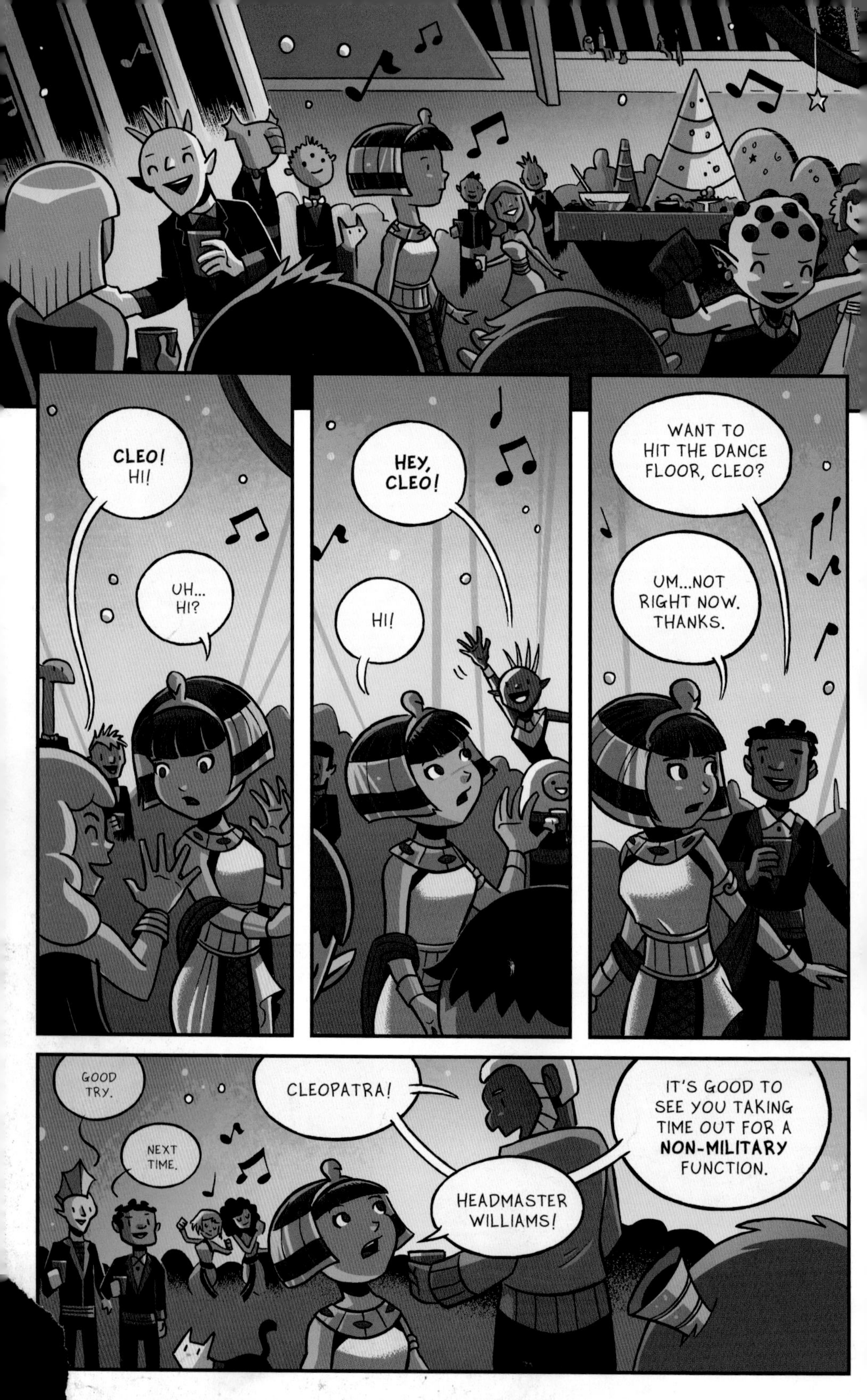
CLEO! HI!
UH... HI?
HEY, CLEO!
HI!
WANT TO HIT THE DANCE FLOOR, CLEO?
UM...NOT RIGHT NOW. THANKS.
GOOD TRY.
NEXT TIME.
CLEOPATRA!
HEADMASTER WILLIAMS!
IT'S GOOD TO SEE YOU TAKING TIME OUT FOR A NON-MILITARY FUNCTION.

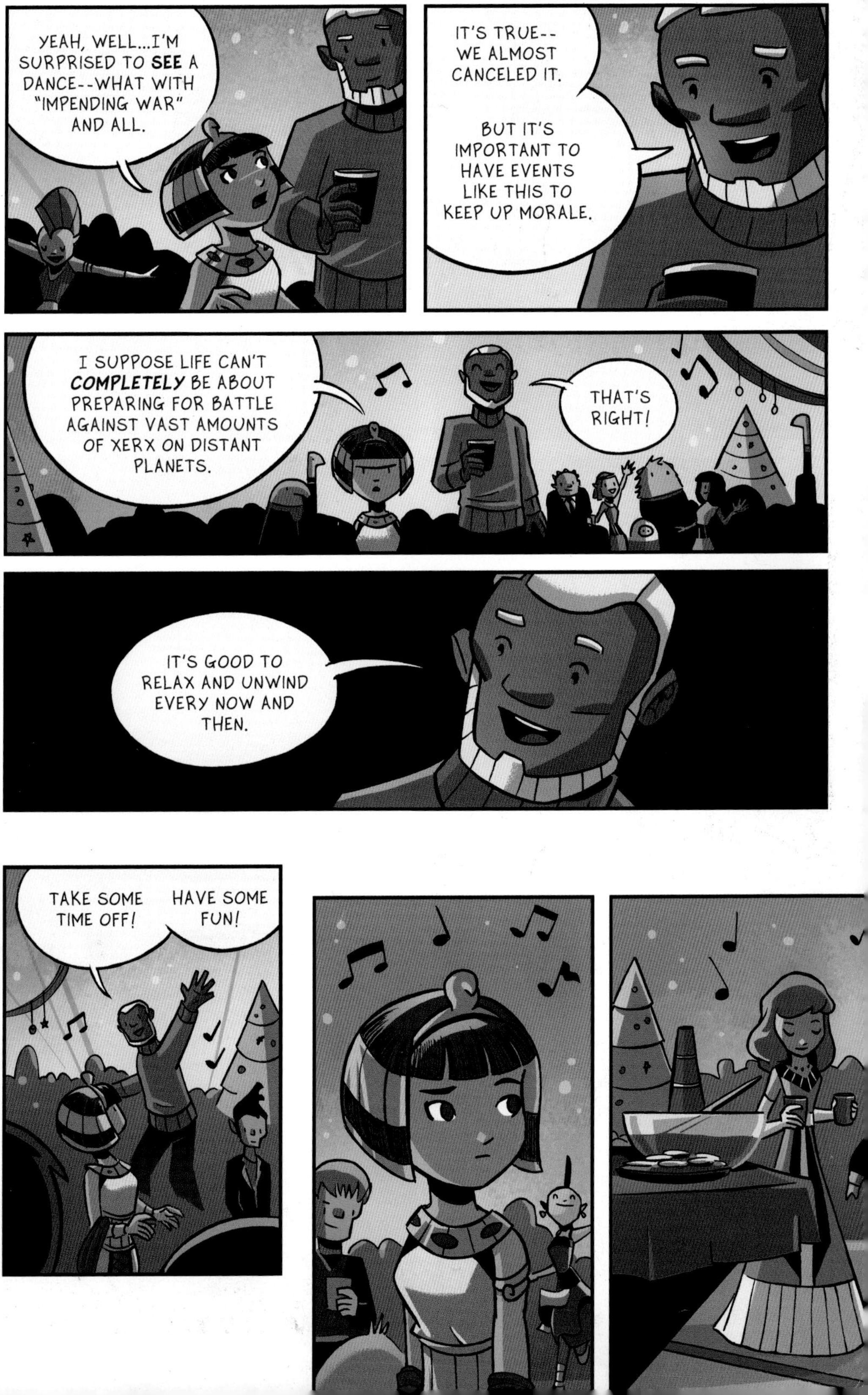
YEAH, WELL...I'M SURPRISED TO **SEE** A DANCE--WHAT WITH "IMPENDING WAR" AND ALL.
IT'S TRUE-- WE ALMOST CANCELED IT.
BUT IT'S IMPORTANT TO HAVE EVENTS LIKE THIS TO KEEP UP MORALE.
I SUPPOSE LIFE CAN'T ***COMPLETELY*** BE ABOUT PREPARING FOR BATTLE AGAINST VAST AMOUNTS OF XERX ON DISTANT PLANETS.
THAT'S RIGHT!
IT'S GOOD TO RELAX AND UNWIND EVERY NOW AND THEN.
TAKE SOME TIME OFF!
HAVE SOME FUN!

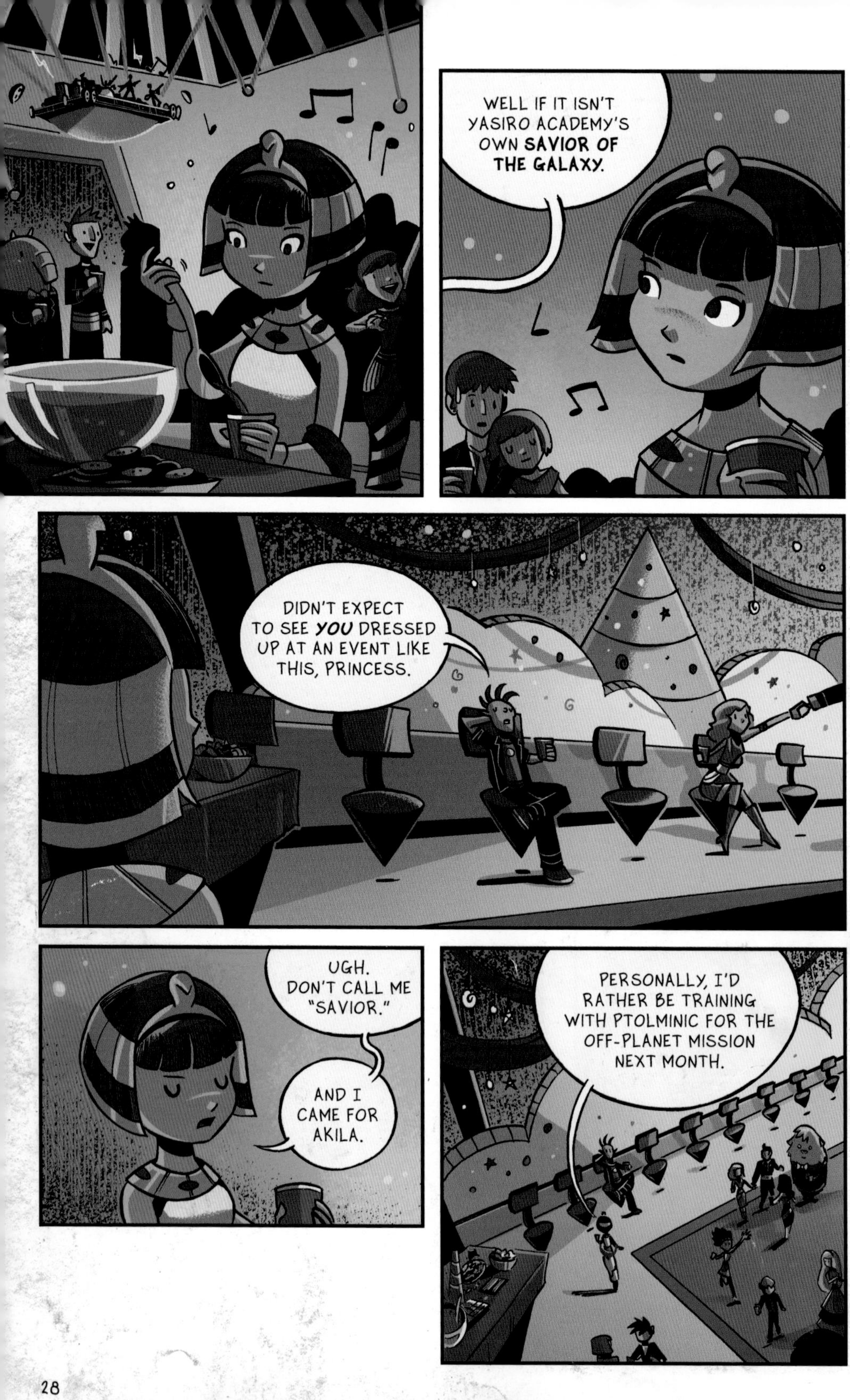
WELL IF IT ISN'T YASIRO ACADEMY'S OWN **SAVIOR OF THE GALAXY.**
DIDN'T EXPECT TO SEE ***YOU*** DRESSED UP AT AN EVENT LIKE THIS, PRINCESS.
UGH. DON'T CALL ME "SAVIOR."
AND I CAME FOR AKILA.
PERSONALLY, I'D RATHER BE TRAINING WITH PTOLMINIC FOR THE OFF-PLANET MISSION NEXT MONTH.

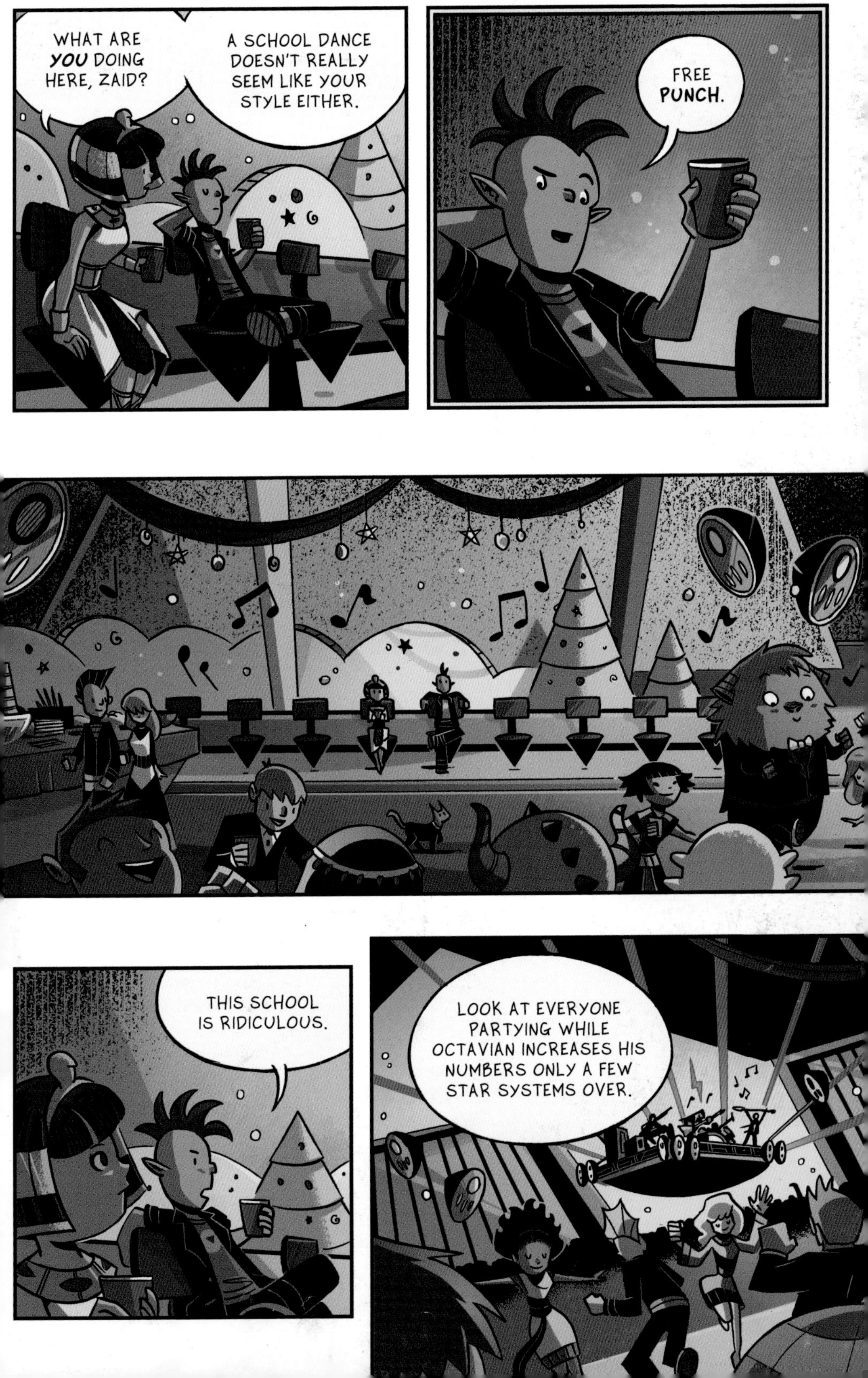
WHAT ARE *YOU* DOING HERE, ZAID?
A SCHOOL DANCE DOESN'T REALLY SEEM LIKE YOUR STYLE EITHER.
FREE **PUNCH.**
THIS SCHOOL IS RIDICULOUS.
LOOK AT EVERYONE PARTYING WHILE OCTAVIAN INCREASES HIS NUMBERS ONLY A FEW STAR SYSTEMS OVER.

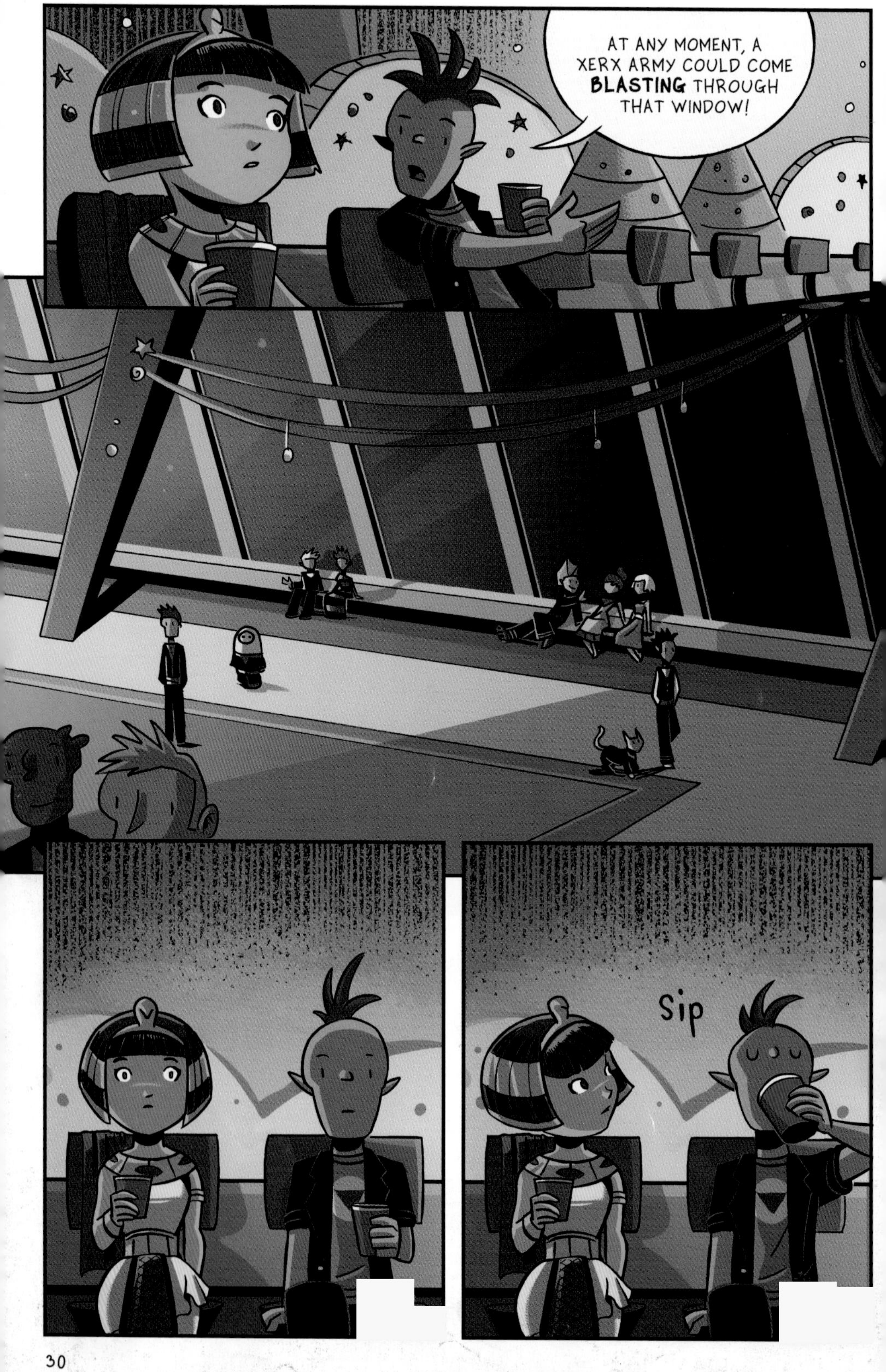
AT ANY MOMENT, A XERX ARMY COULD COME **BLASTING** THROUGH THAT WINDOW!
Sip

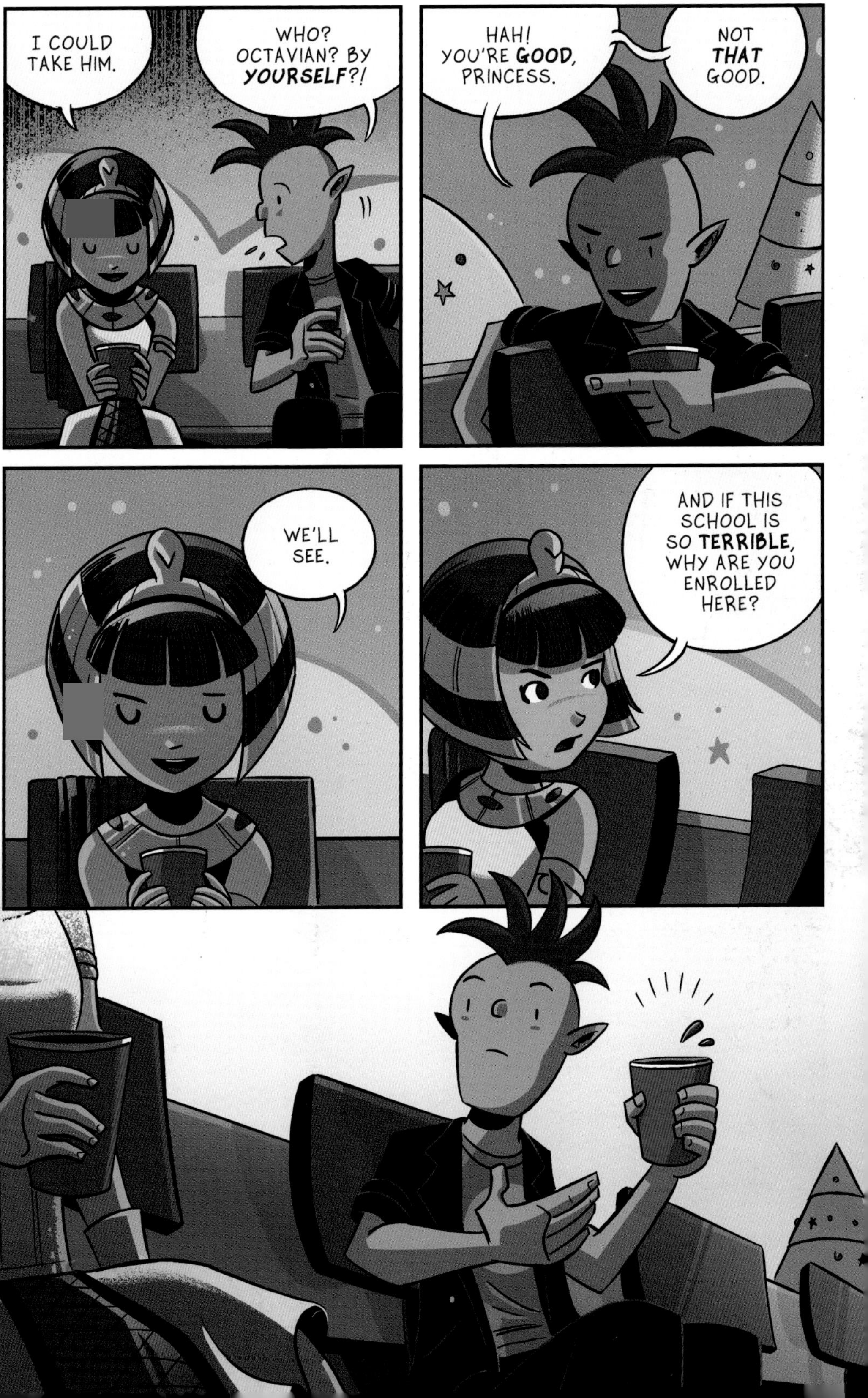
I COULD TAKE HIM.
WHO? OCTAVIAN? BY YOURSELF?!
HAH! YOU'RE GOOD, PRINCESS.
NOT THAT GOOD.
WE'LL SEE.
AND IF THIS SCHOOL IS SO TERRIBLE, WHY ARE YOU ENROLLED HERE?

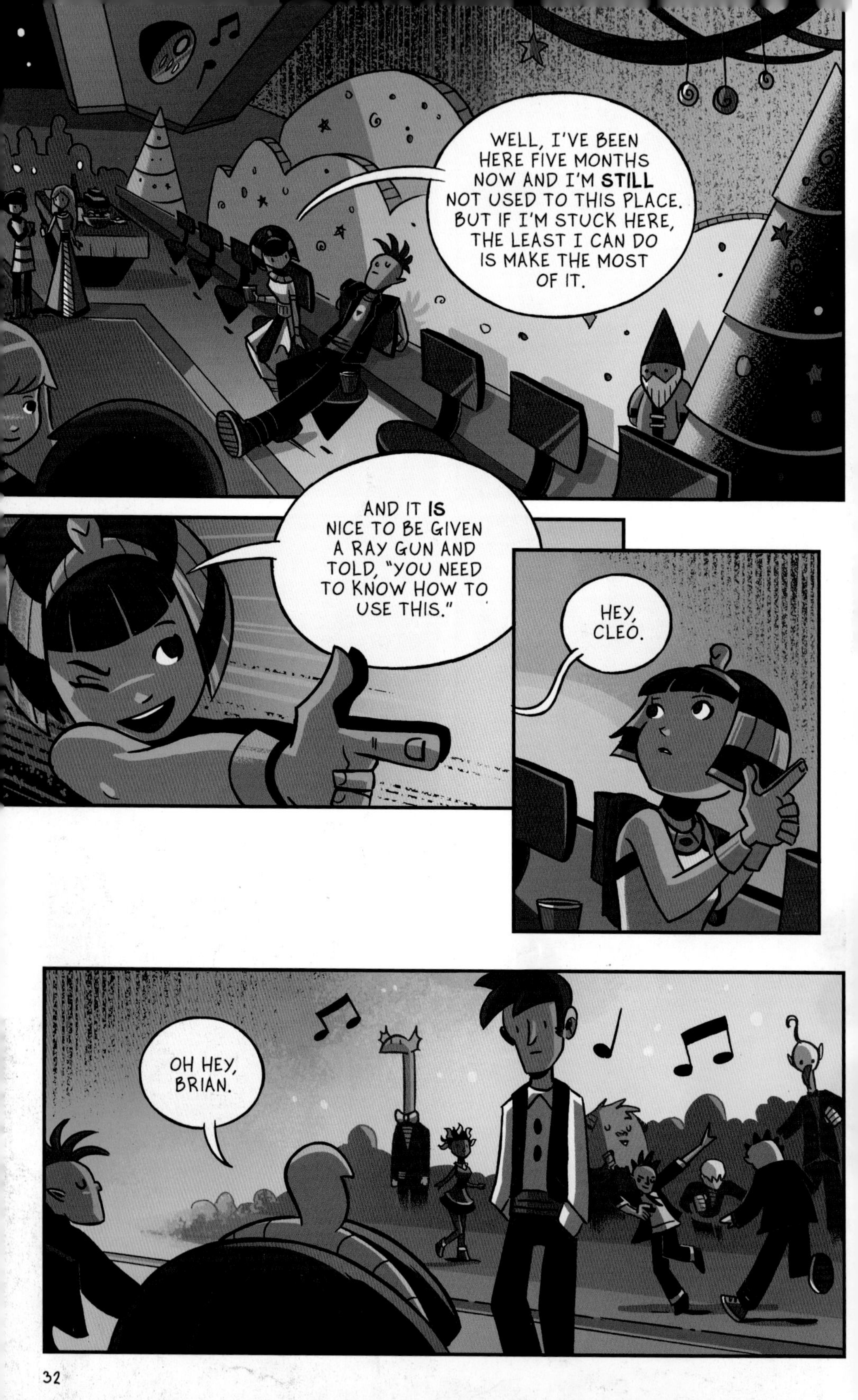
WELL, I'VE BEEN HERE FIVE MONTHS NOW AND I'M **STILL** NOT USED TO THIS PLACE. BUT IF I'M STUCK HERE, THE LEAST I CAN DO IS MAKE THE MOST OF IT.
AND IT **IS** NICE TO BE GIVEN A RAY GUN AND TOLD, "YOU NEED TO KNOW HOW TO USE THIS."
HEY, CLEO.
OH HEY, BRIAN.

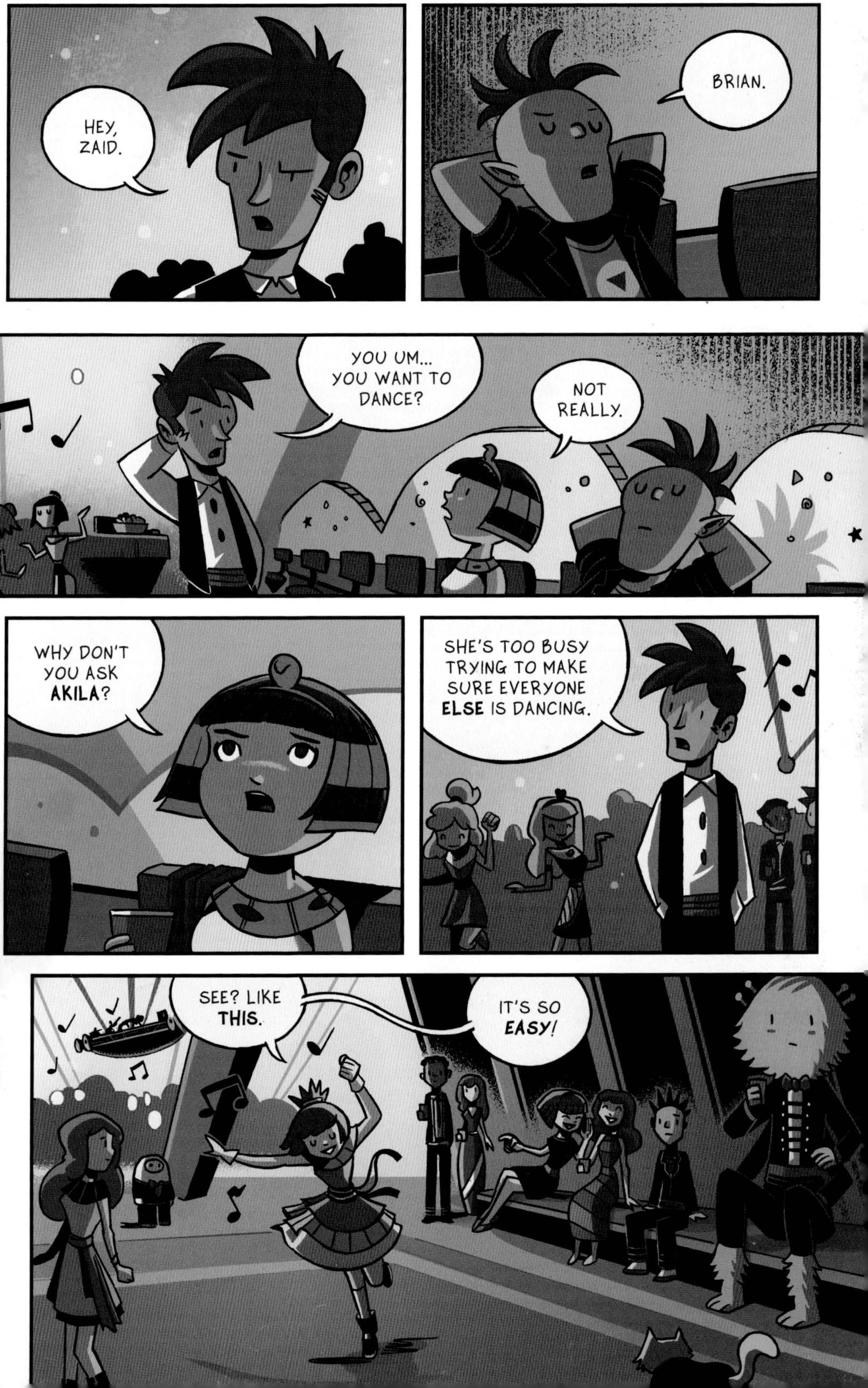
HEY, ZAID.
BRIAN.
YOU UM... YOU WANT TO DANCE?
NOT REALLY.
WHY DON'T YOU ASK **AKILA**?
SHE'S TOO BUSY TRYING TO MAKE SURE EVERYONE **ELSE** IS DANCING.
SEE? LIKE **THIS**.
IT'S SO ***EASY***!

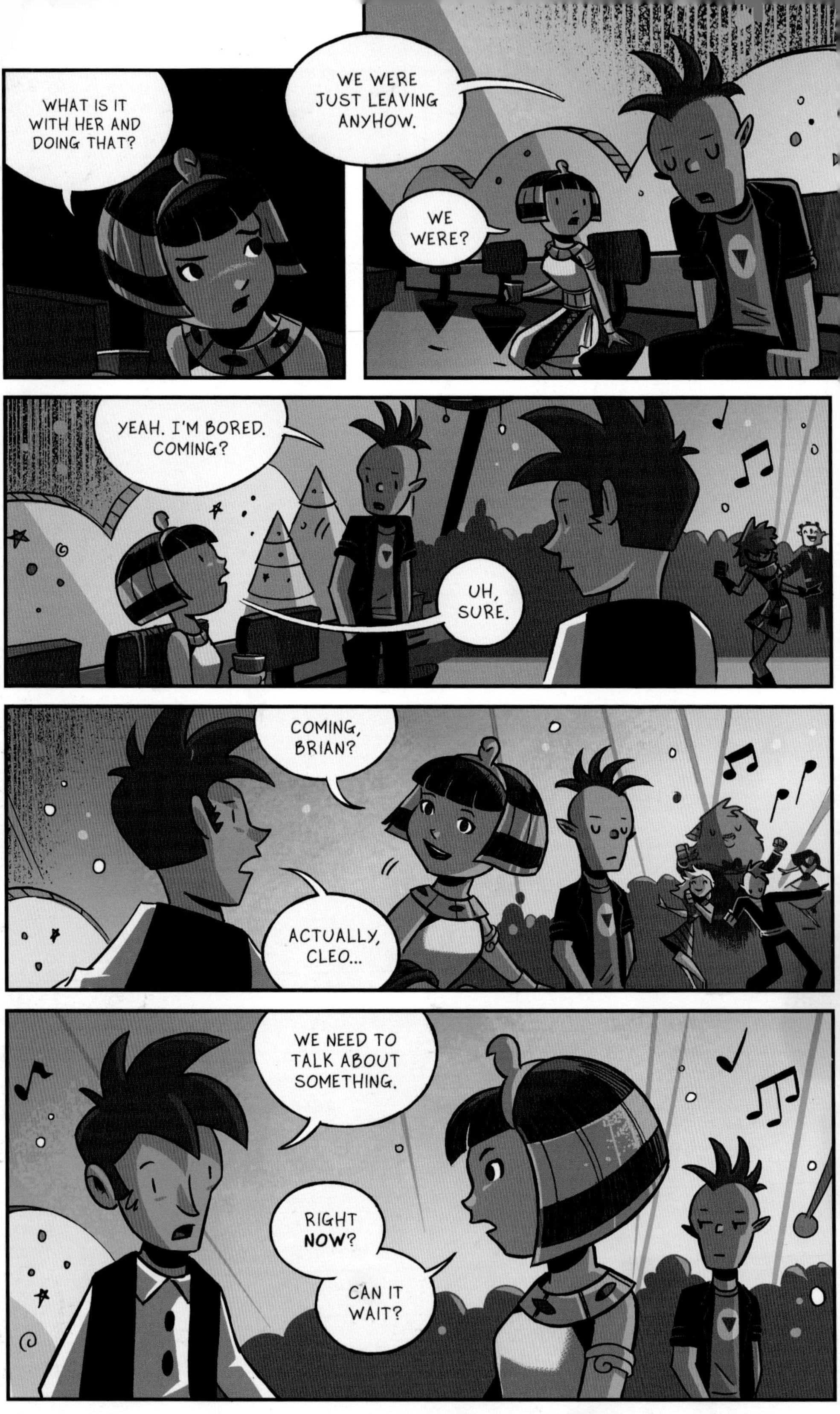
WHAT IS IT WITH HER AND DOING THAT?
WE WERE JUST LEAVING ANYHOW.
WE WERE?
YEAH. I'M BORED. COMING?
UH, SURE.
COMING, BRIAN?
ACTUALLY, CLEO...
WE NEED TO TALK ABOUT SOMETHING.
RIGHT **NOW**?
CAN IT WAIT?

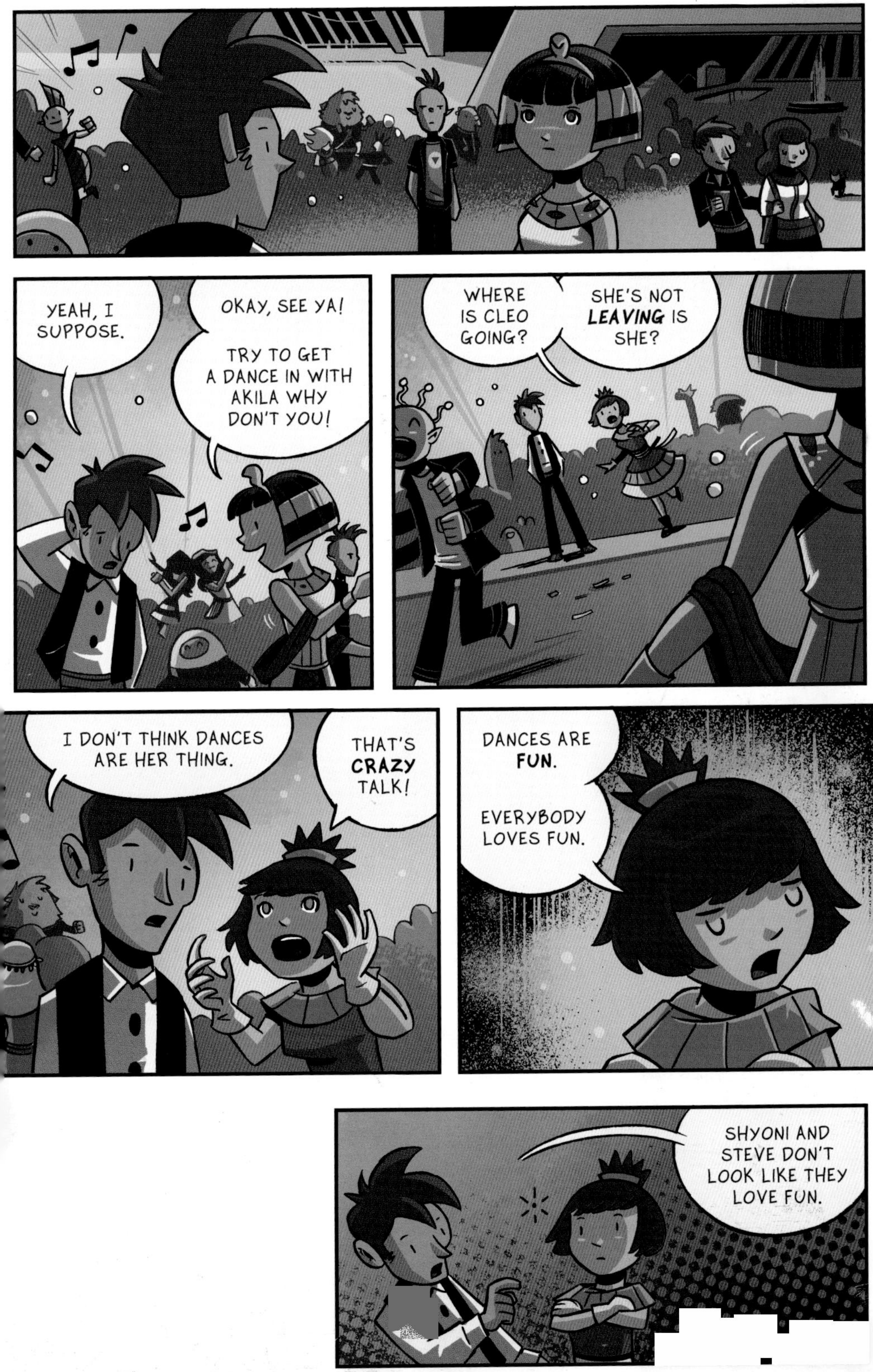

YEAH, I SUPPOSE.
OKAY, SEE YA!
TRY TO GET A DANCE IN WITH AKILA WHY DON'T YOU!
WHERE IS CLEO GOING?
SHE'S NOT **LEAVING** IS SHE?
I DON'T THINK DANCES ARE HER THING.
THAT'S **CRAZY** TALK!
DANCES ARE **FUN**.
EVERYBODY LOVES FUN.
SHYONI AND STEVE DON'T LOOK LIKE THEY LOVE FUN.

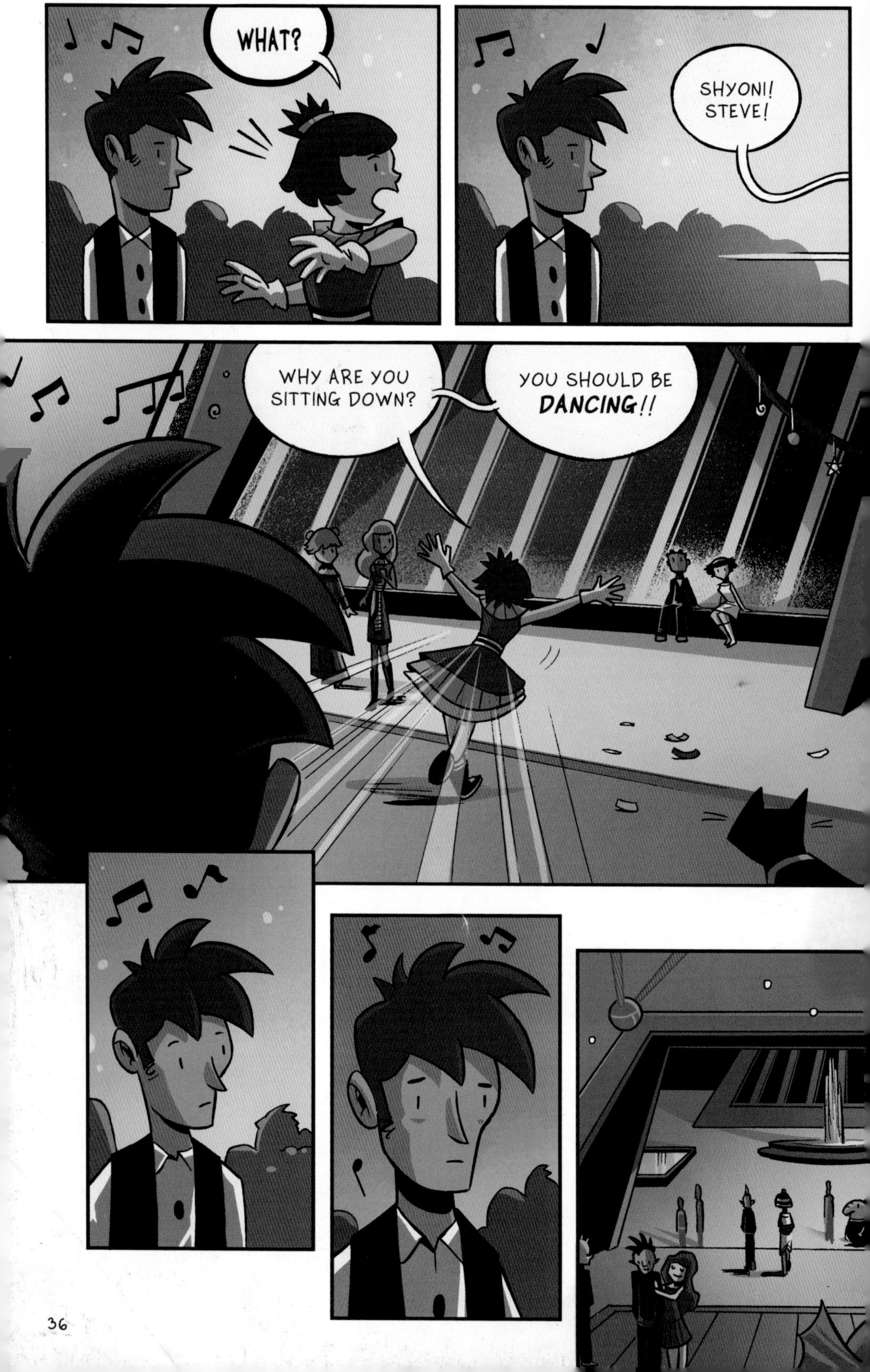
WHAT?
SHYONI! STEVE!
WHY ARE YOU SITTING DOWN?
YOU SHOULD BE DANCING!!

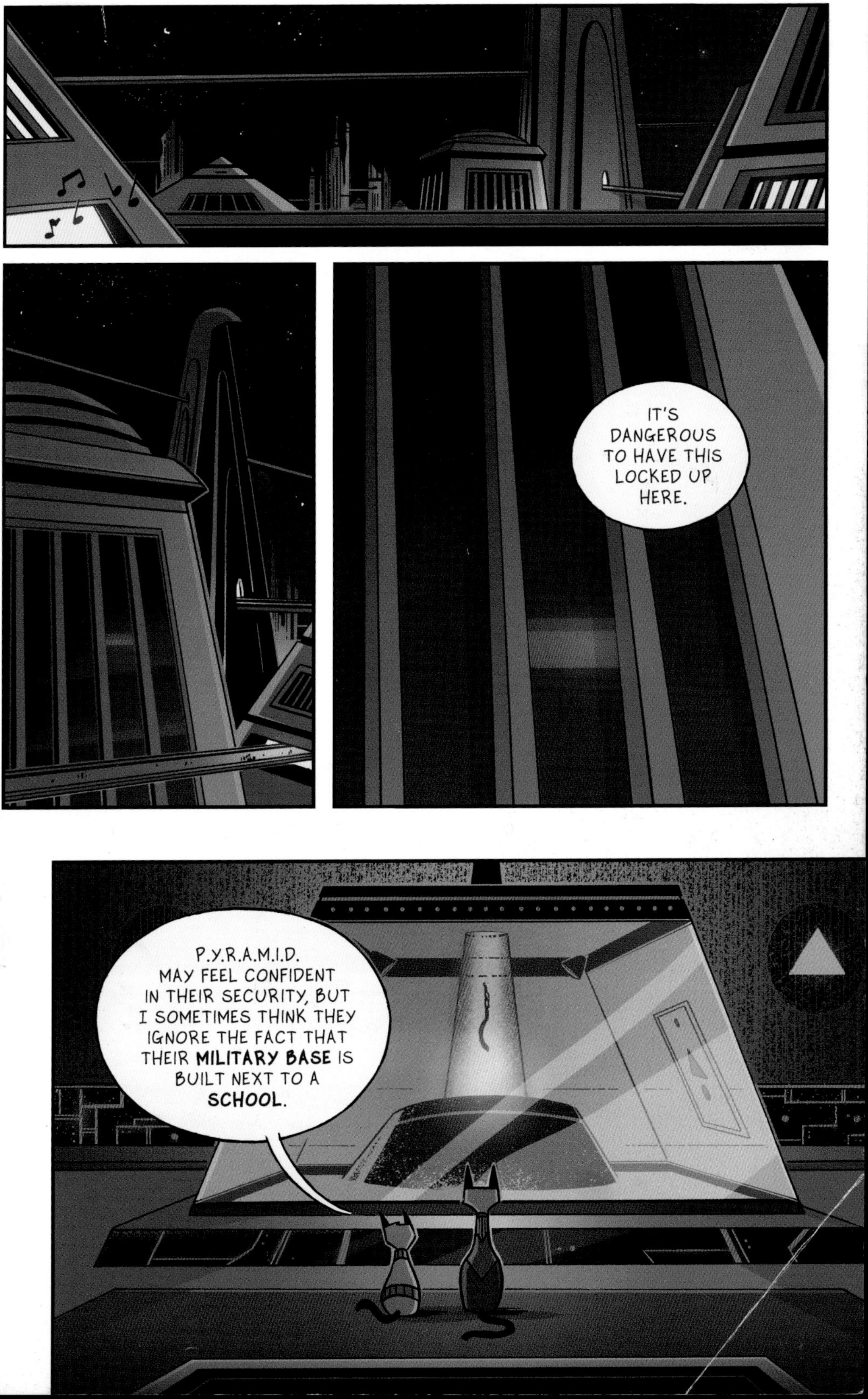
IT'S DANGEROUS TO HAVE THIS LOCKED UP HERE.
P.Y.R.A.M.I.D. MAY FEEL CONFIDENT IN THEIR SECURITY, BUT I SOMETIMES THINK THEY IGNORE THE FACT THAT THEIR **MILITARY BASE** IS BUILT NEXT TO A **SCHOOL**.

A SCHOOL FULL OF CADETS **TRAINED** TO RESIST ANY ATTACK, KHENSU.

RELAX. IT'S ONLY HERE UNTIL IT'S TRANSFERRED TO **KARNEK** FOR SCIENTIFIC EVALUATION TOMORROW. AFTER THAT WE'LL KNOW ITS TRUE NATURE.

SO YOU STILL DON'T BELIEVE--?

IN **MYSTICAL ARTIFACTS**?

NO, KHENSU.

THAT SAID, THE CURRENT SITUATION BEING WHAT IT IS...OUR SO-CALLED **SAVIOR**...

CLEO.

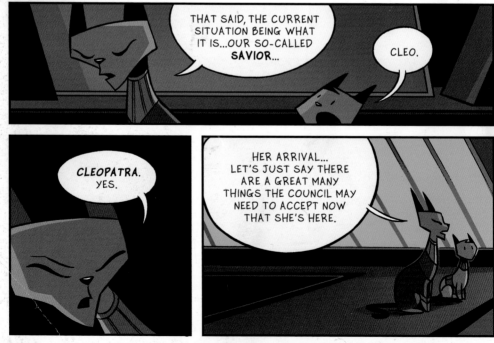

CLEOPATRA. YES.

HER ARRIVAL... LET'S JUST SAY THERE ARE A GREAT MANY THINGS THE COUNCIL MAY NEED TO ACCEPT NOW THAT SHE'S HERE.

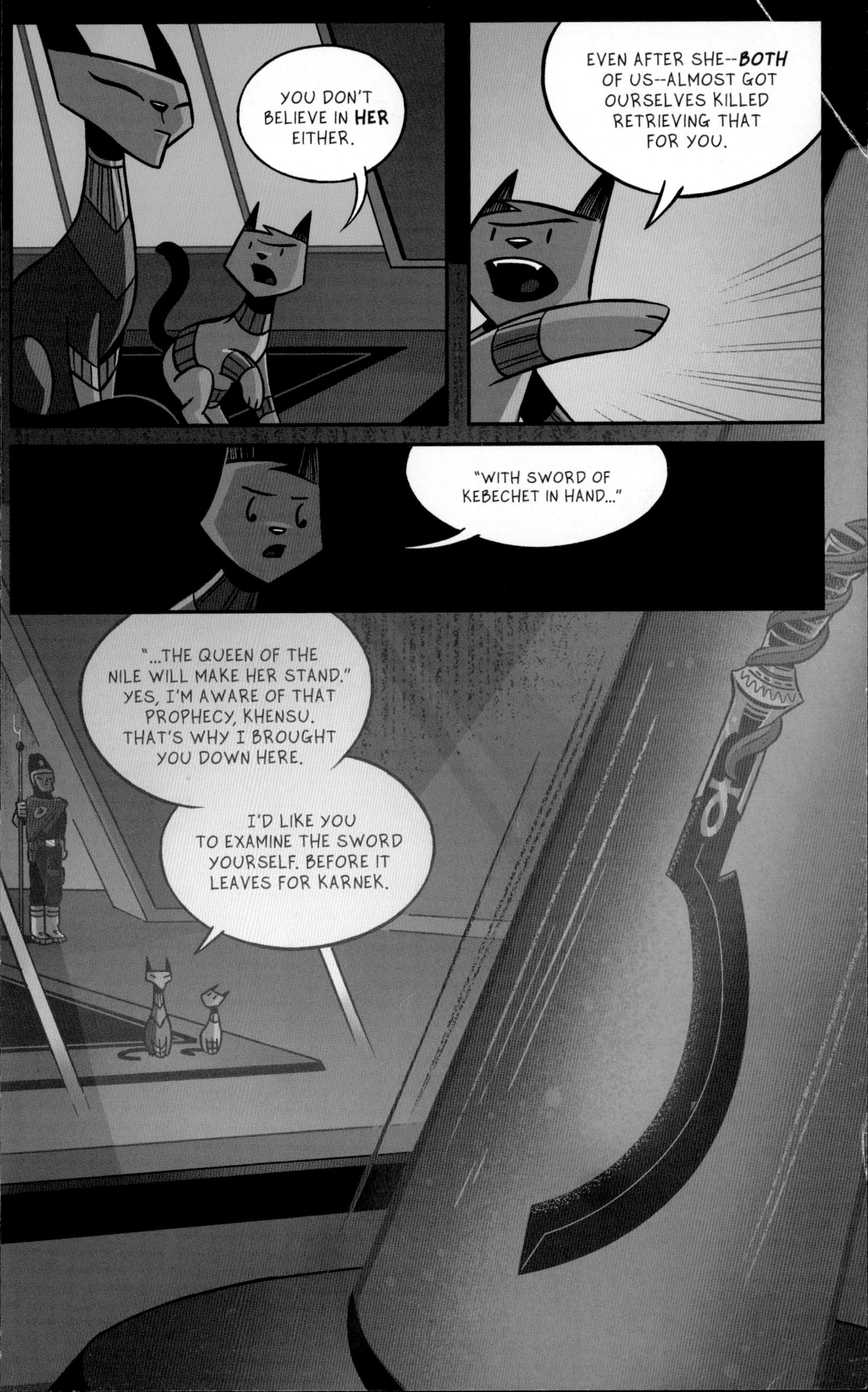
YOU DON'T BELIEVE IN **HER** EITHER.
EVEN AFTER SHE--**BOTH** OF US--ALMOST GOT OURSELVES KILLED RETRIEVING THAT FOR YOU.
"WITH SWORD OF KEBECHET IN HAND..."
"...THE QUEEN OF THE NILE WILL MAKE HER STAND." YES, I'M AWARE OF THAT PROPHECY, KHENSU. THAT'S WHY I BROUGHT YOU DOWN HERE.
I'D LIKE YOU TO EXAMINE THE SWORD YOURSELF. BEFORE IT LEAVES FOR KARNEK.

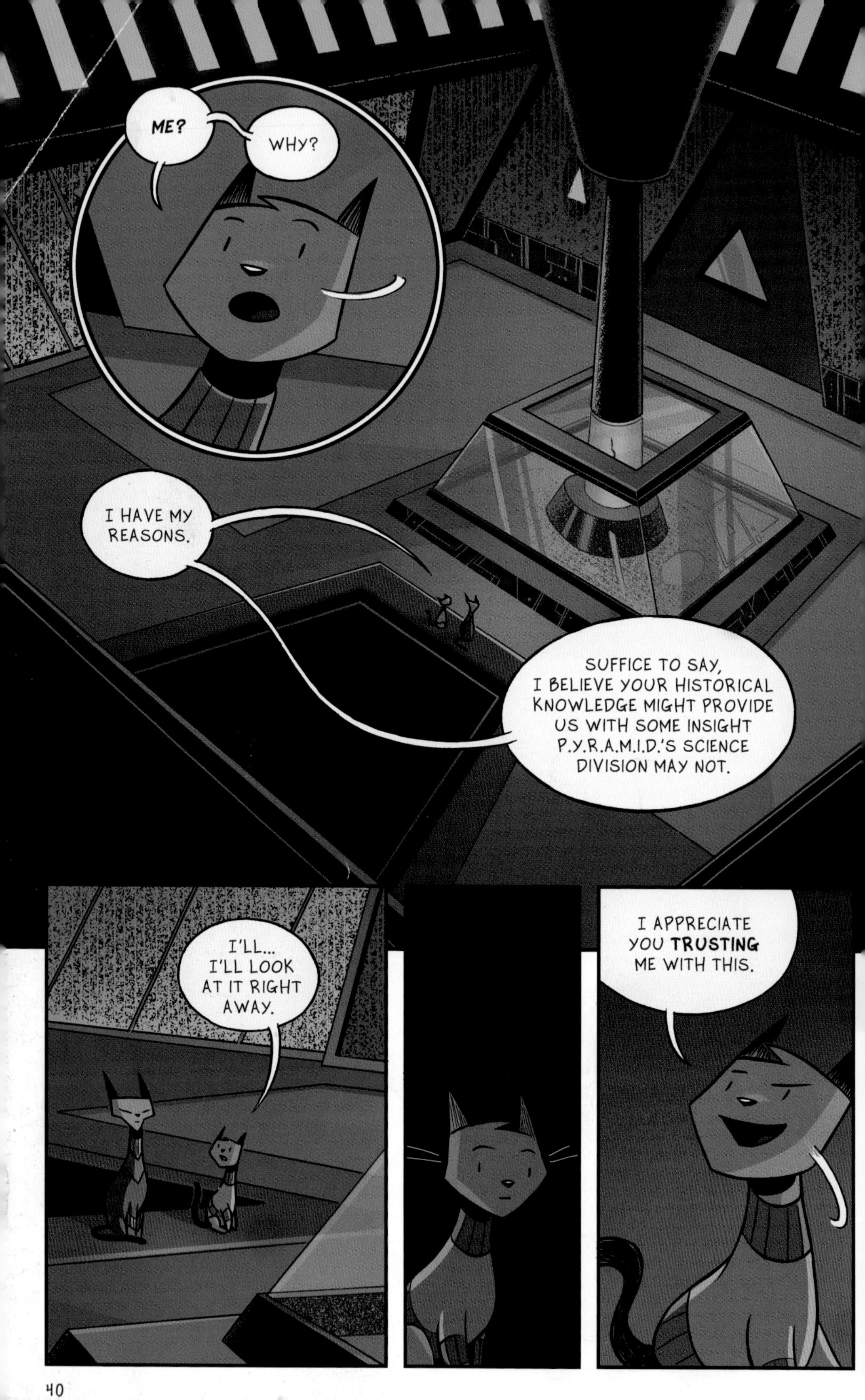
ME?
WHY?
I HAVE MY REASONS.
SUFFICE TO SAY, I BELIEVE YOUR HISTORICAL KNOWLEDGE MIGHT PROVIDE US WITH SOME INSIGHT P.Y.R.A.M.I.D.'S SCIENCE DIVISION MAY NOT.
I'LL... I'LL LOOK AT IT RIGHT AWAY.
I APPRECIATE YOU **TRUSTING** ME WITH THIS.

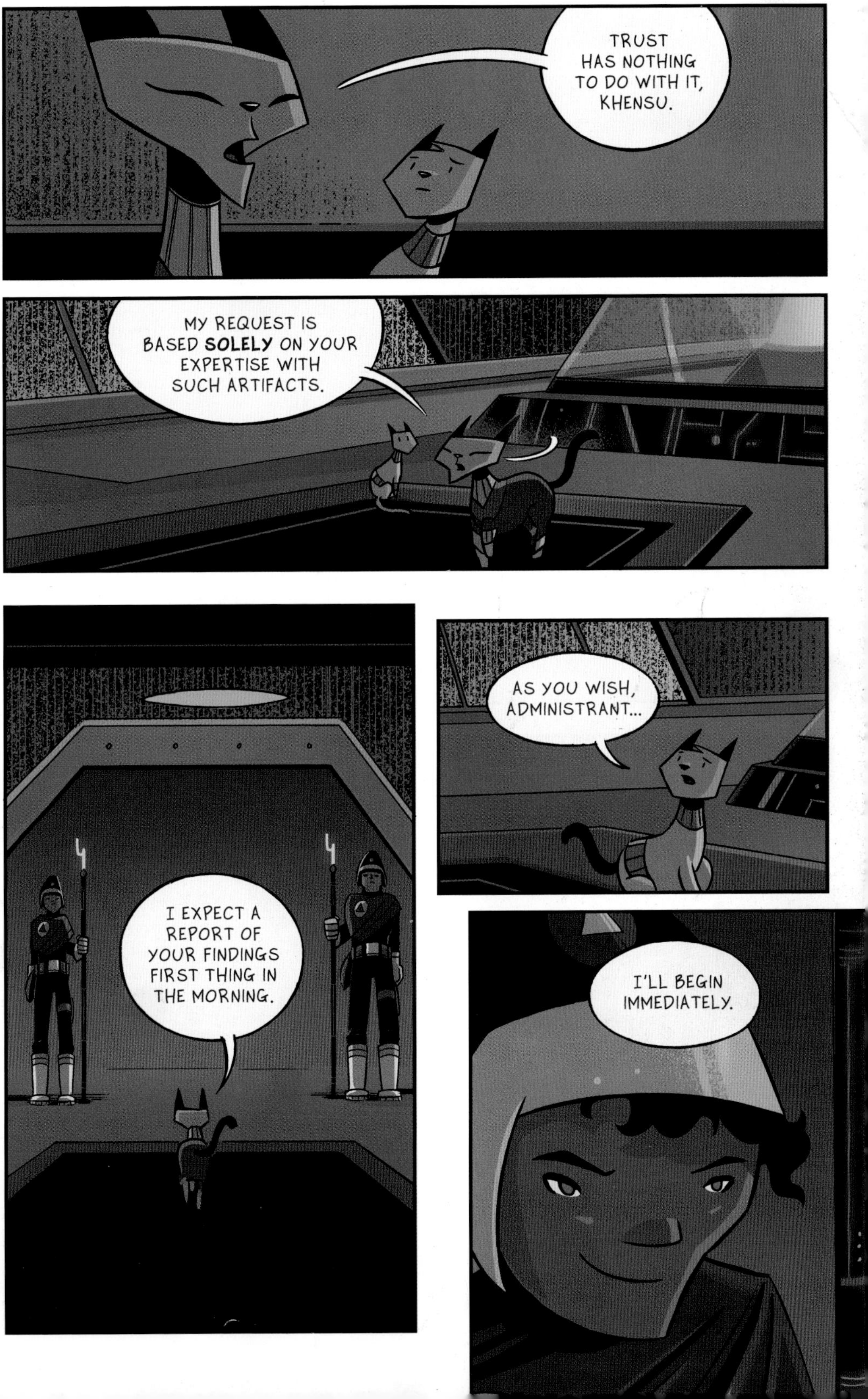
TRUST HAS NOTHING TO DO WITH IT, KHENSU.
MY REQUEST IS BASED SOLELY ON YOUR EXPERTISE WITH SUCH ARTIFACTS.
AS YOU WISH, ADMINISTRANT...
I EXPECT A REPORT OF YOUR FINDINGS FIRST THING IN THE MORNING.
I'LL BEGIN IMMEDIATELY.

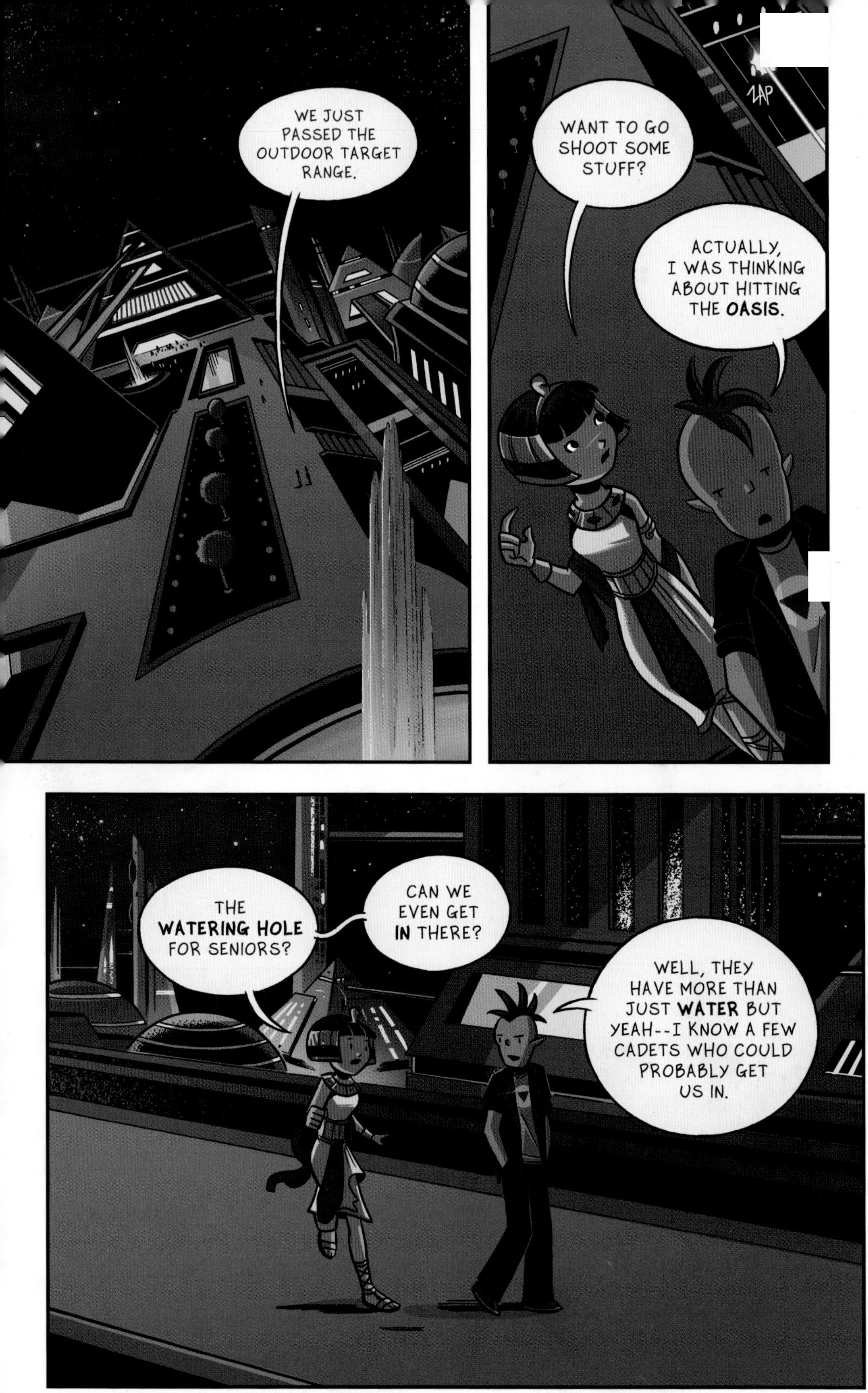
WE JUST PASSED THE OUTDOOR TARGET RANGE.
ZAP
WANT TO GO SHOOT SOME STUFF?
ACTUALLY, I WAS THINKING ABOUT HITTING THE **OASIS.**
THE **WATERING HOLE** FOR SENIORS?
CAN WE EVEN GET **IN** THERE?
WELL, THEY HAVE MORE THAN JUST **WATER** BUT YEAH--I KNOW A FEW CADETS WHO COULD PROBABLY GET US IN.

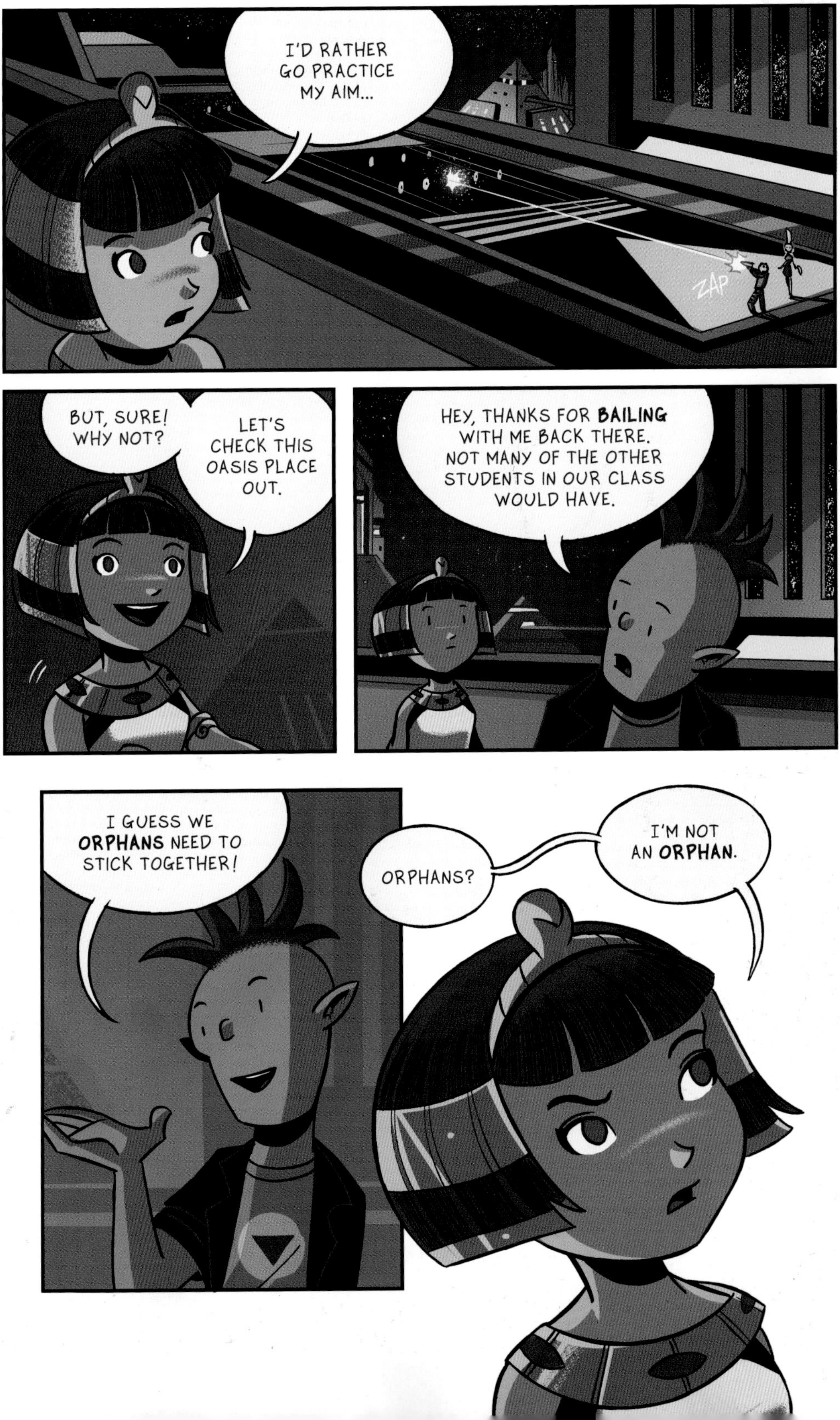

I'D RATHER GO PRACTICE MY AIM...
ZAP
BUT, SURE! WHY NOT?
LET'S CHECK THIS OASIS PLACE OUT.
HEY, THANKS FOR **BAILING** WITH ME BACK THERE. NOT MANY OF THE OTHER STUDENTS IN OUR CLASS WOULD HAVE.
I GUESS WE **ORPHANS** NEED TO STICK TOGETHER!
ORPHANS?
I'M NOT AN **ORPHAN.**

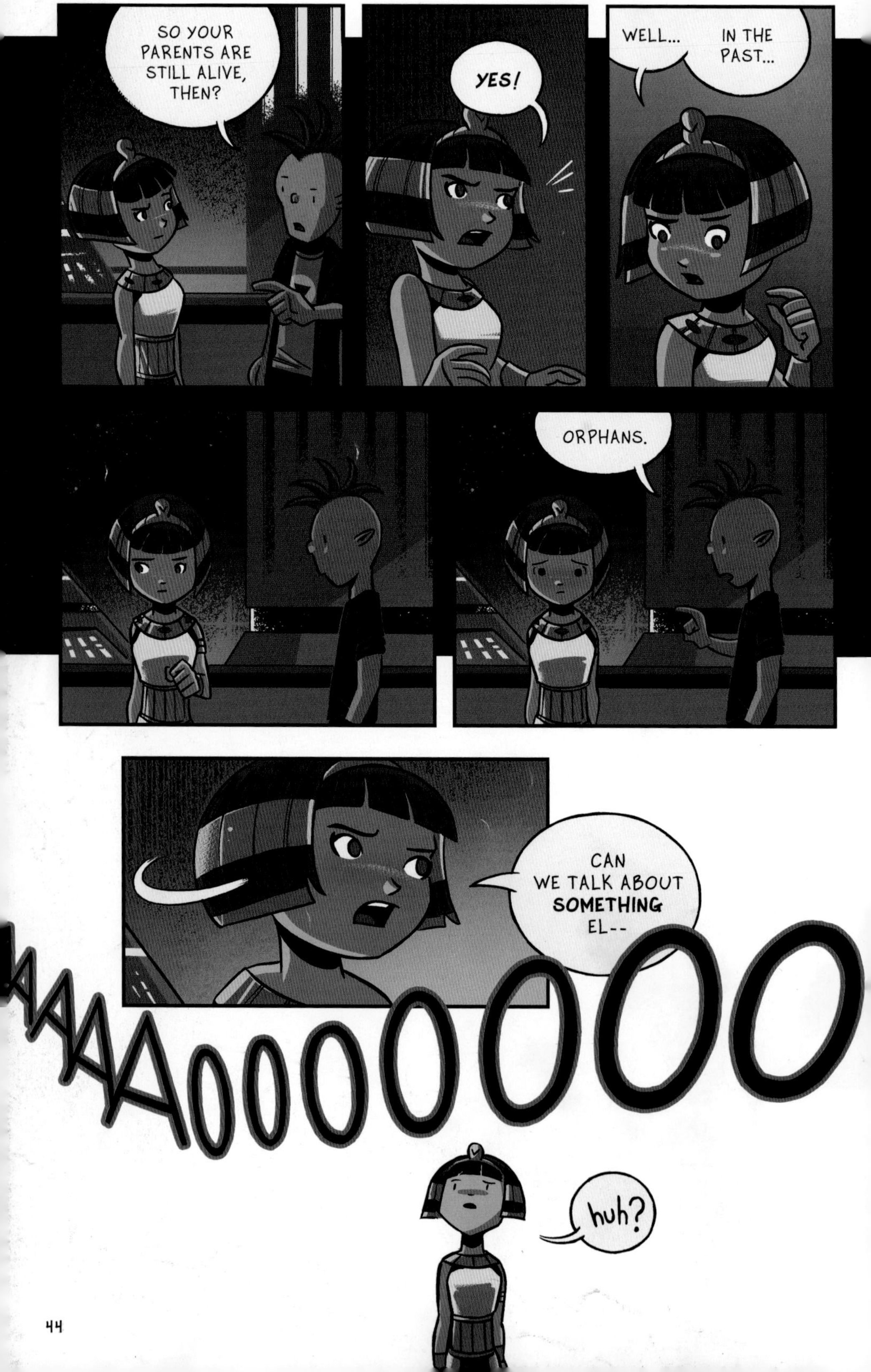
SO YOUR PARENTS ARE STILL ALIVE, THEN?
YES!
WELL...
IN THE PAST...
ORPHANS.
CAN WE TALK ABOUT **SOMETHING** EL--
AAAAOOOOOOOOO
huh?

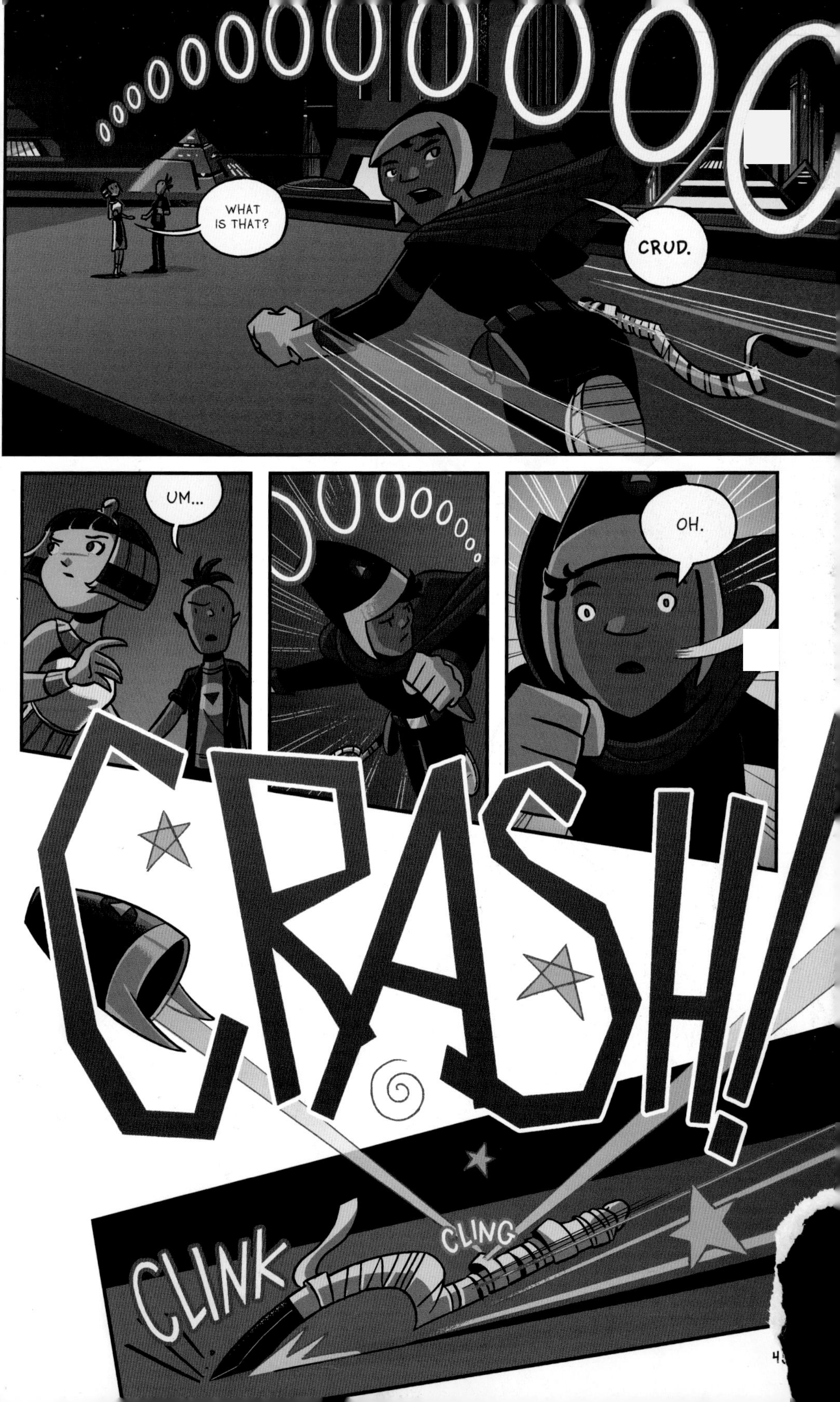

OOOOOOOOOOOOO
WHAT IS THAT?
CRUD.
UM...
OOOOOOOOO
OH.
CRASH!!
CLINK
CLING

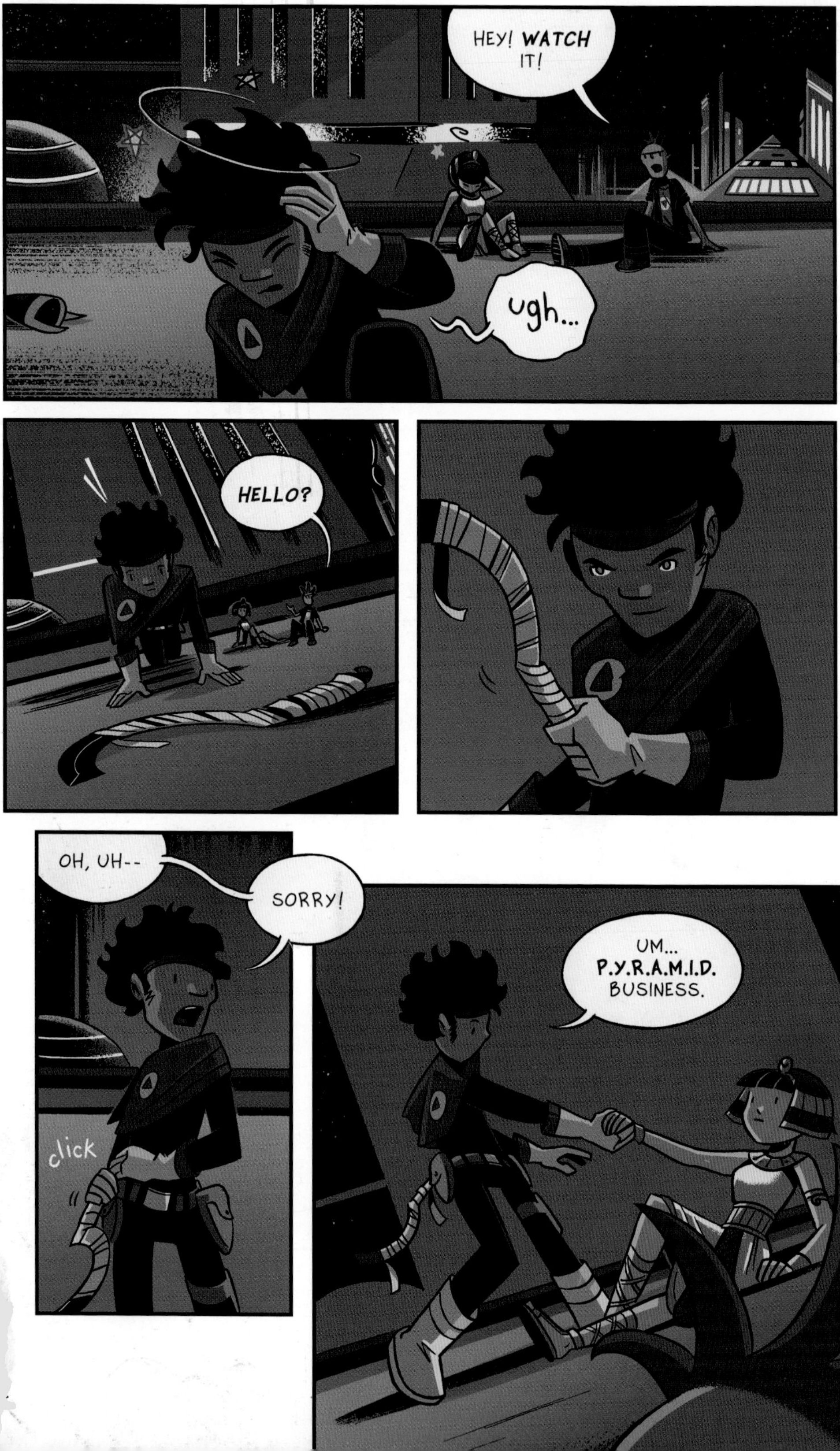
HEY! WATCH IT!
ugh...
HELLO?
OH, UH--
SORRY!
click
UM... P.Y.R.A.M.I.D. BUSINESS.

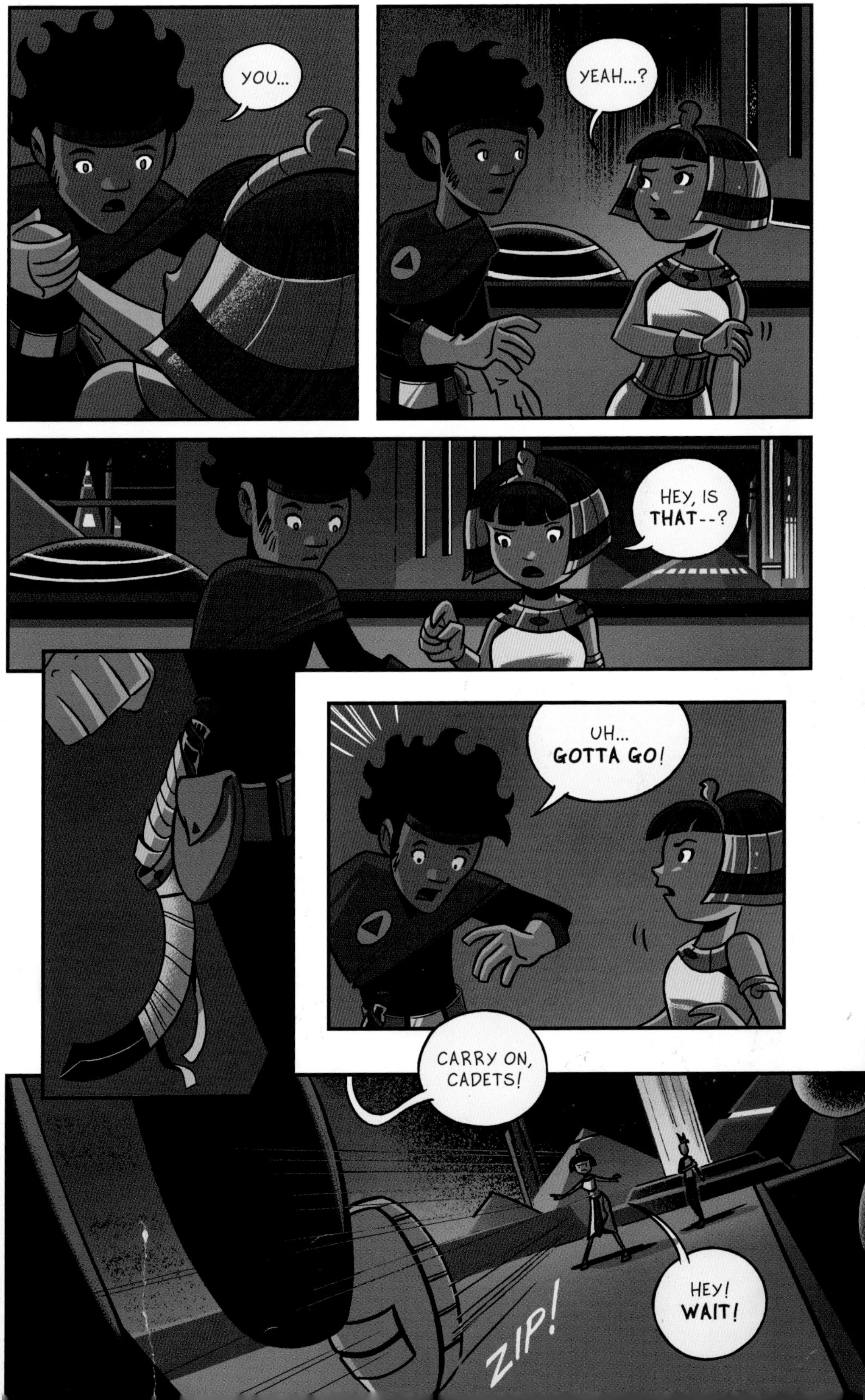
YOU...
YEAH...?
HEY, IS THAT--?
UH... GOTTA GO!
CARRY ON, CADETS!
HEY! WAIT!
ZIP!

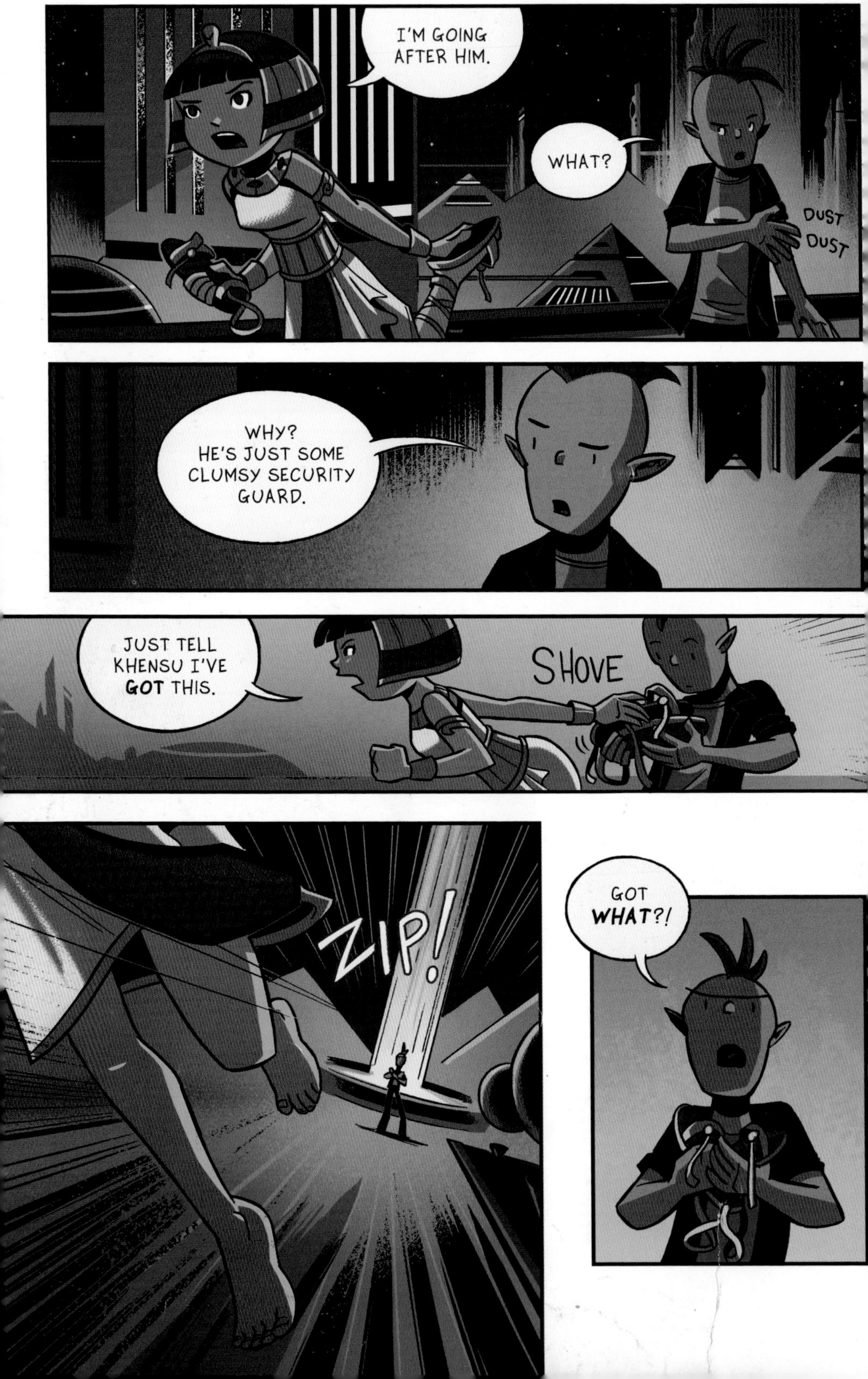
I'M GOING AFTER HIM.
WHAT?
DUST DUST
WHY? HE'S JUST SOME CLUMSY SECURITY GUARD.
JUST TELL KHENSU I'VE **GOT** THIS.
SHOVE
ZIP!
GOT **WHAT?!**

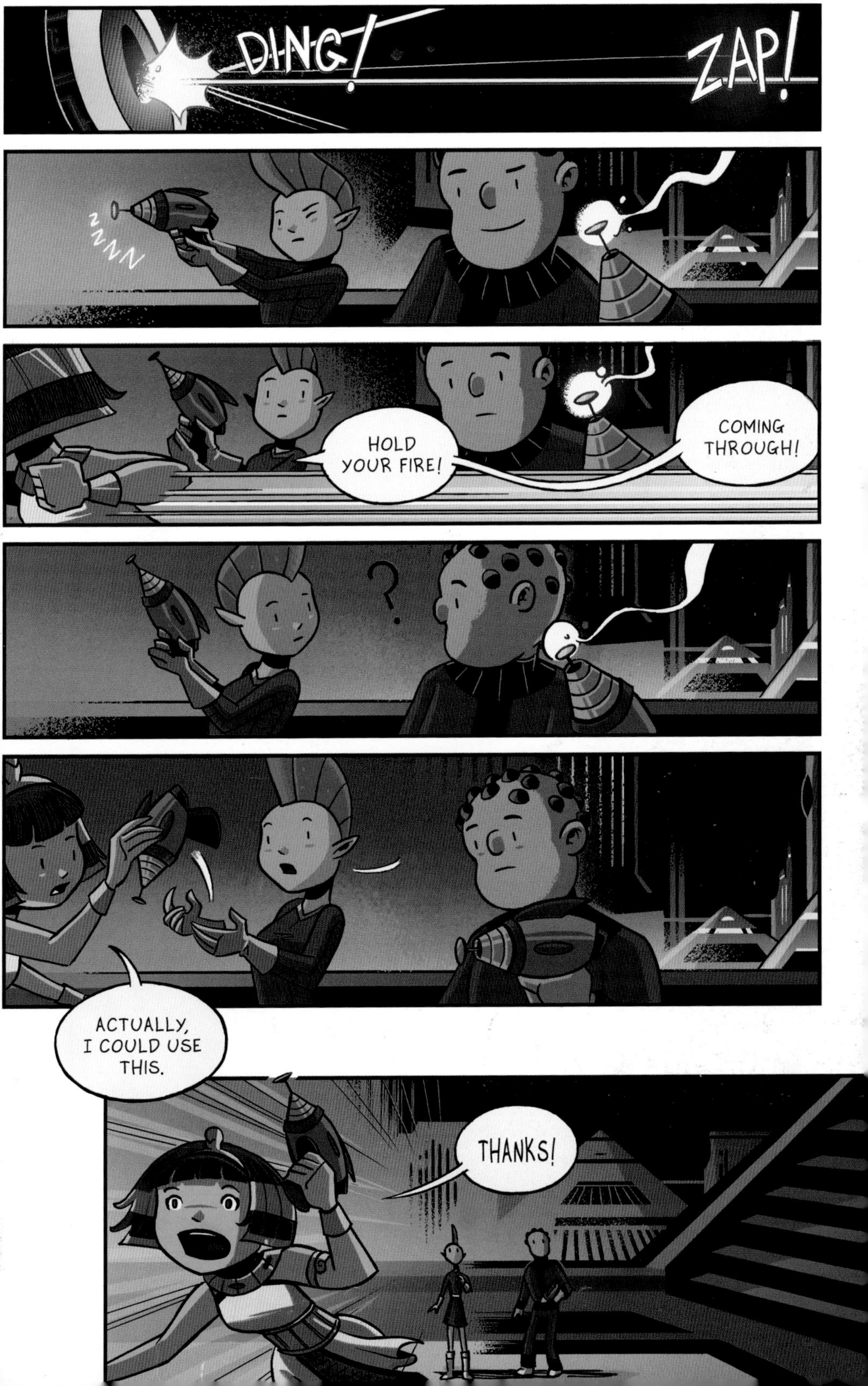
DING!
ZAP!
ZZZZ
HOLD YOUR FIRE!
COMING THROUGH!
?
ACTUALLY, I COULD USE THIS.
THANKS!

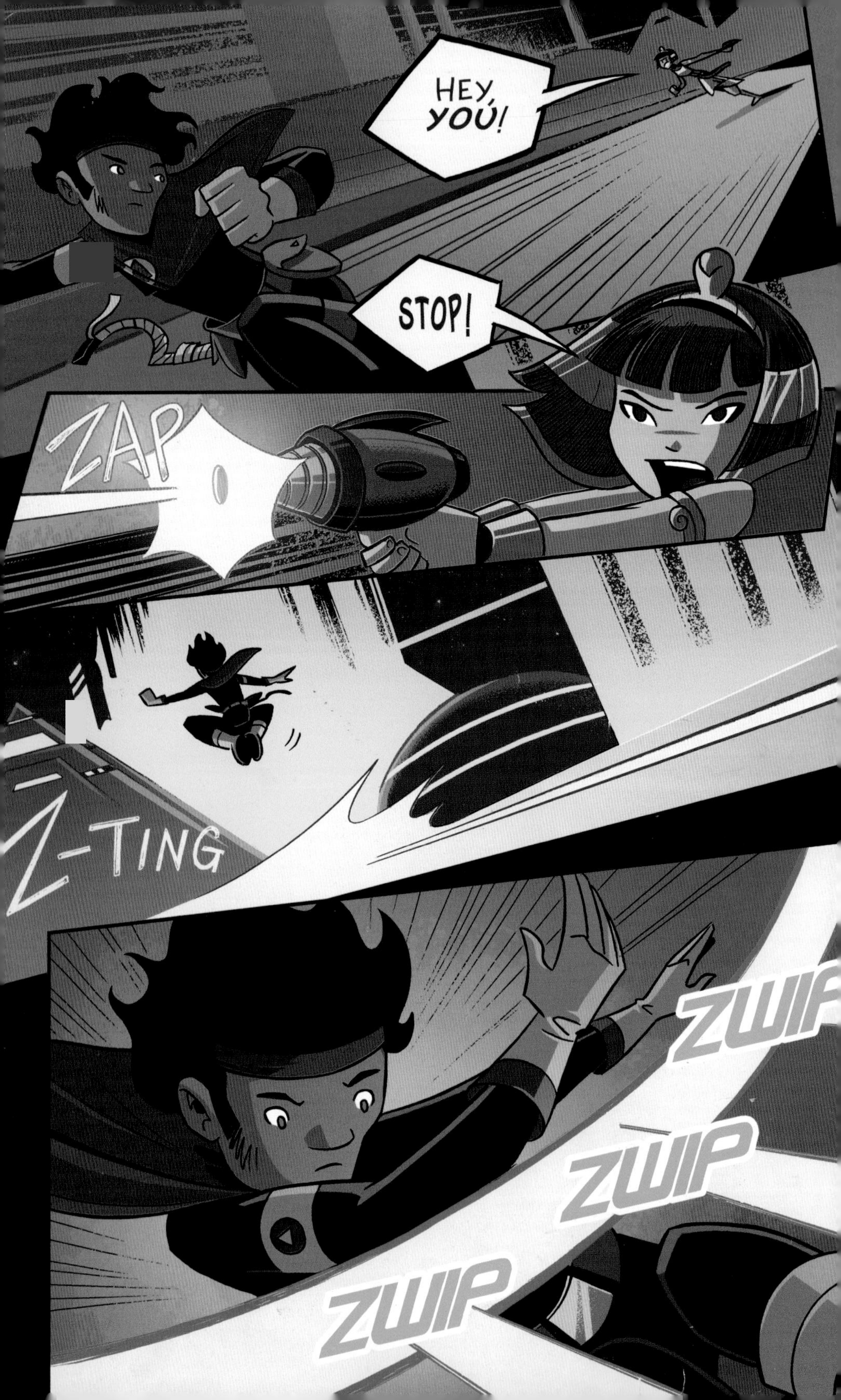
HEY, YOU!
STOP!
ZAP
Z-TING
ZWIP
ZWIP
ZWIP

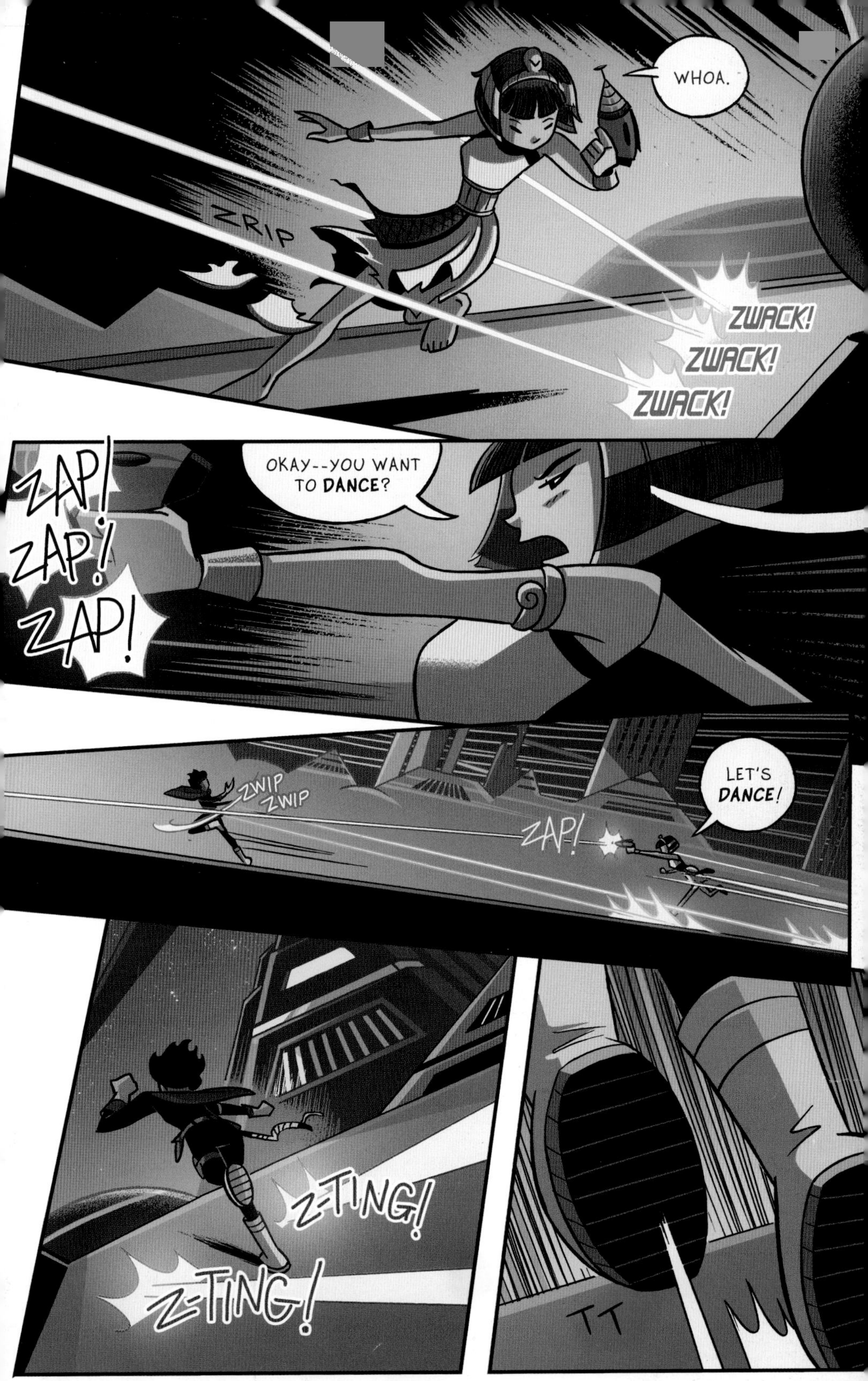
WHOA.
ZRIP
ZWACK!
ZWACK!
ZWACK!
OKAY--YOU WANT TO DANCE?
ZAP!
ZAP!
ZAP!
ZWIP
ZWIP
LET'S DANCE!
ZAP!
Z-TING!
Z-TING!
TT

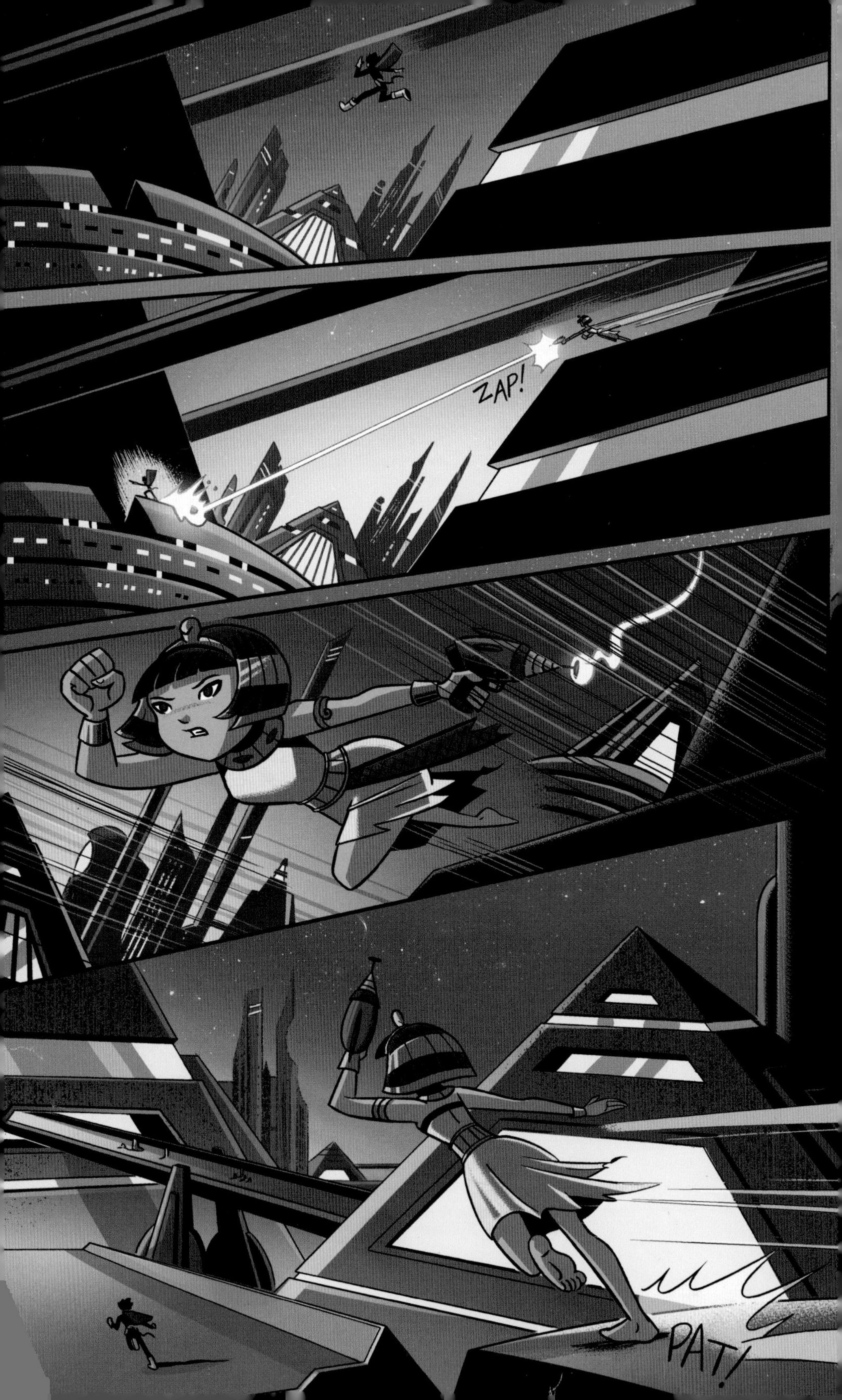
ZAP!
PAT!

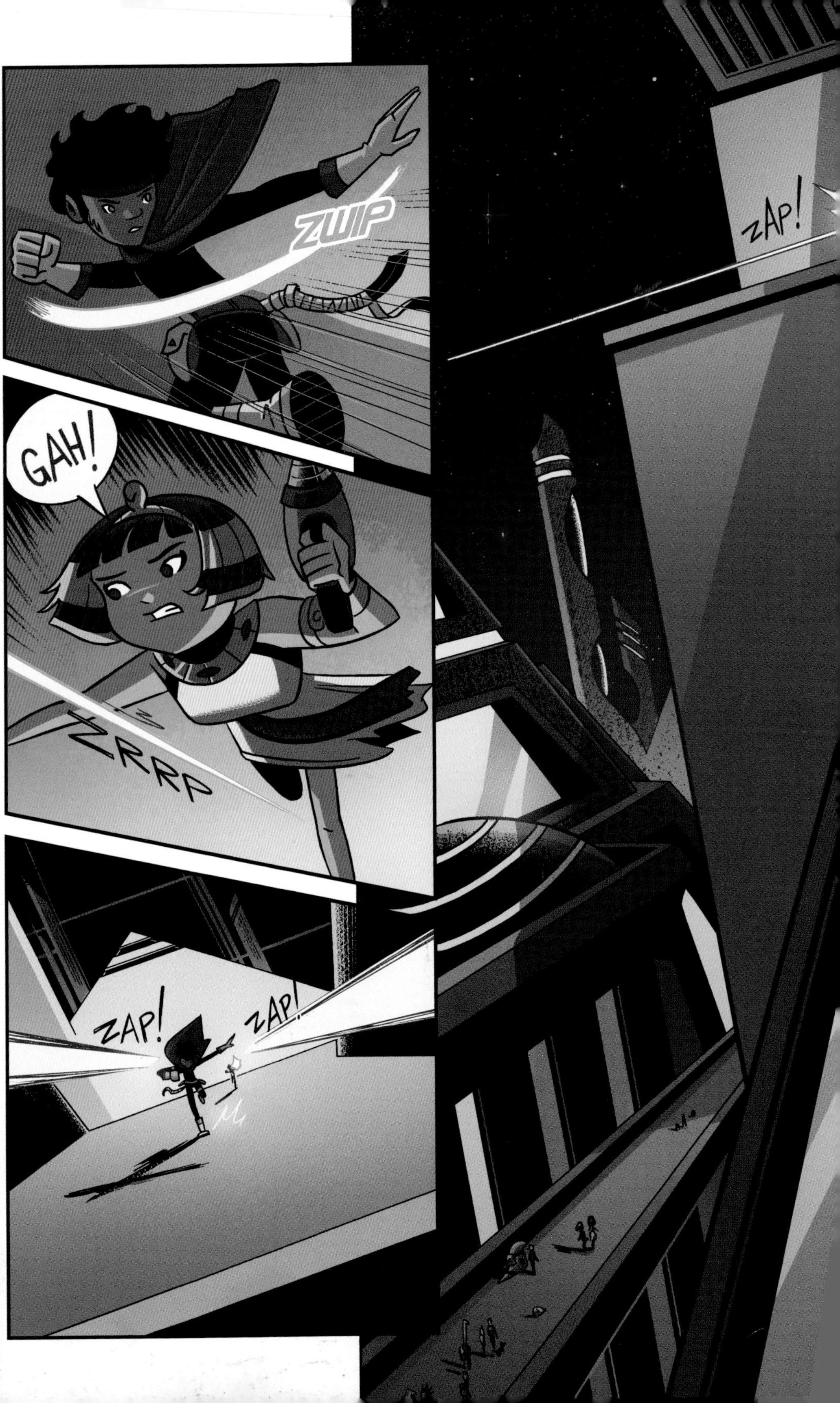
ZWIP
ZAP!
GAH!
ZRRRP
ZAP!
ZAP!

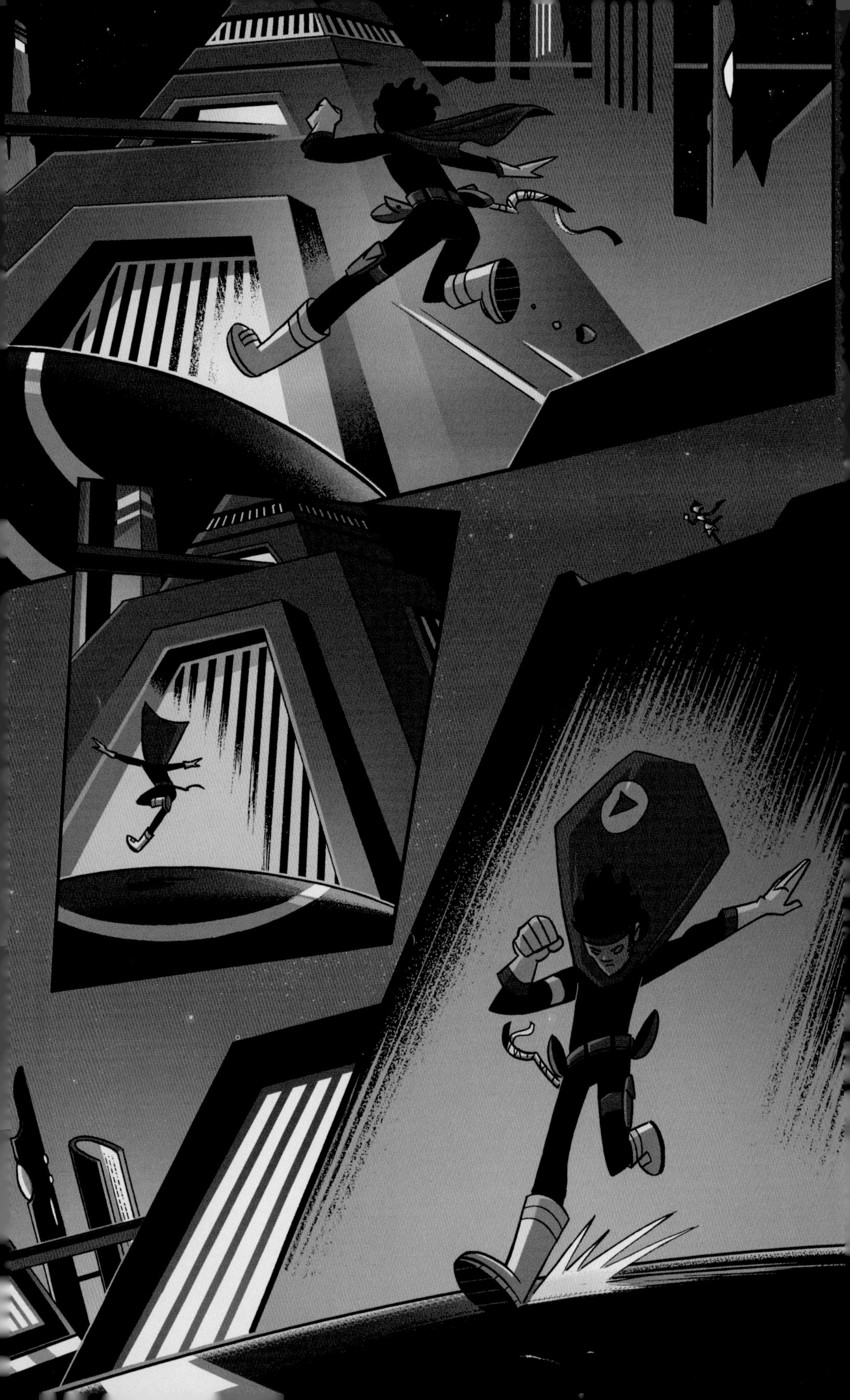

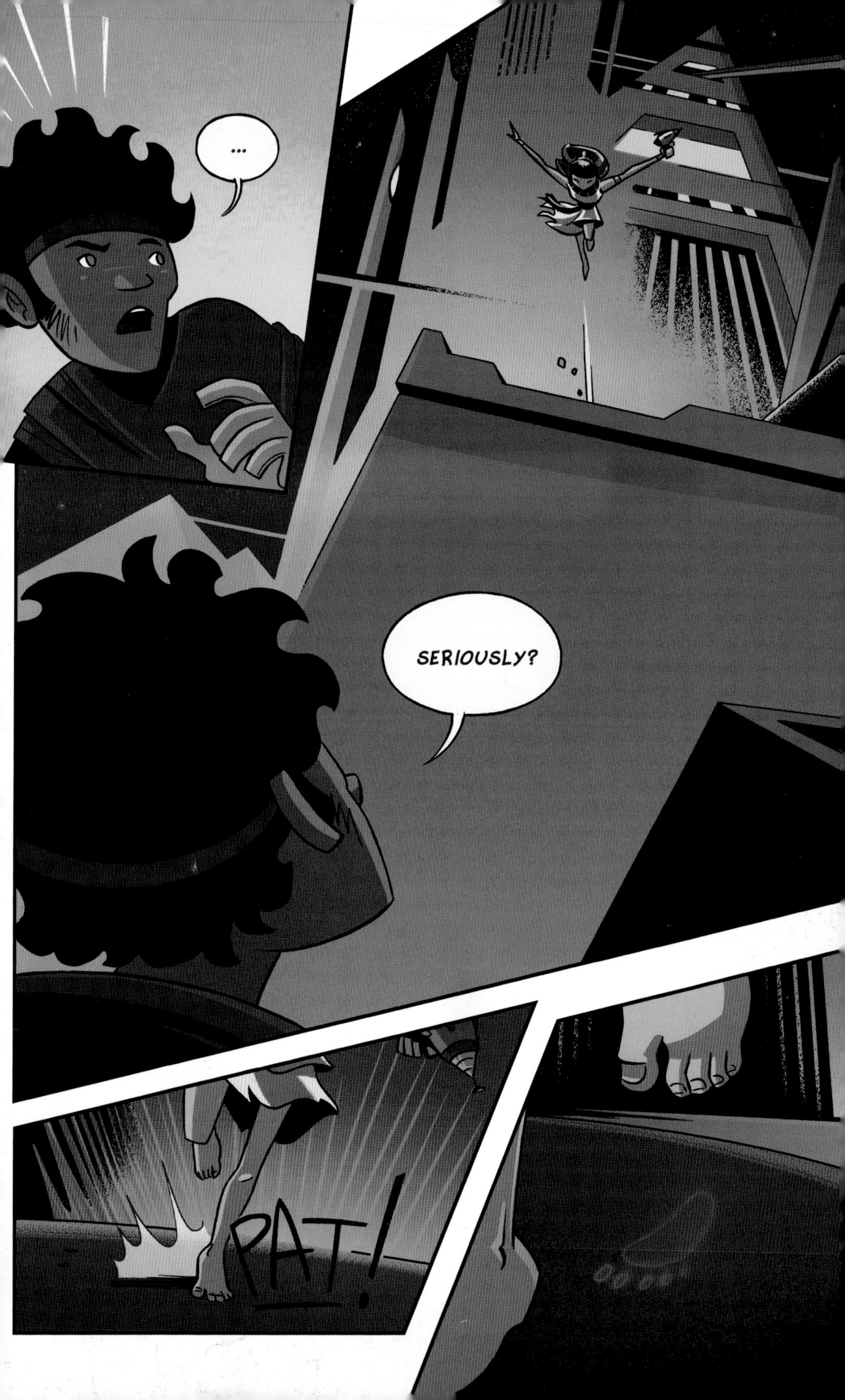
...
SERIOUSLY?
PAT!

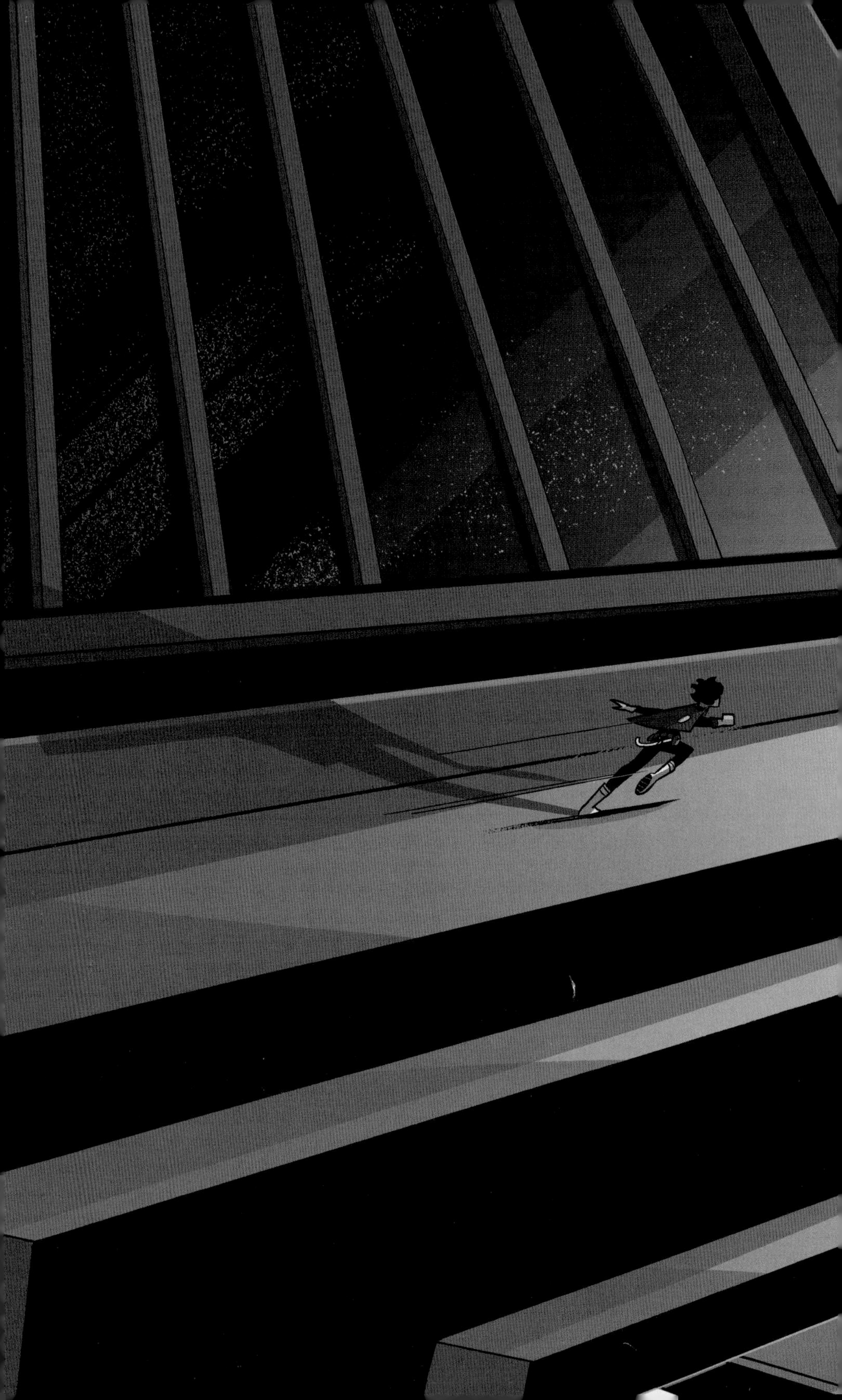

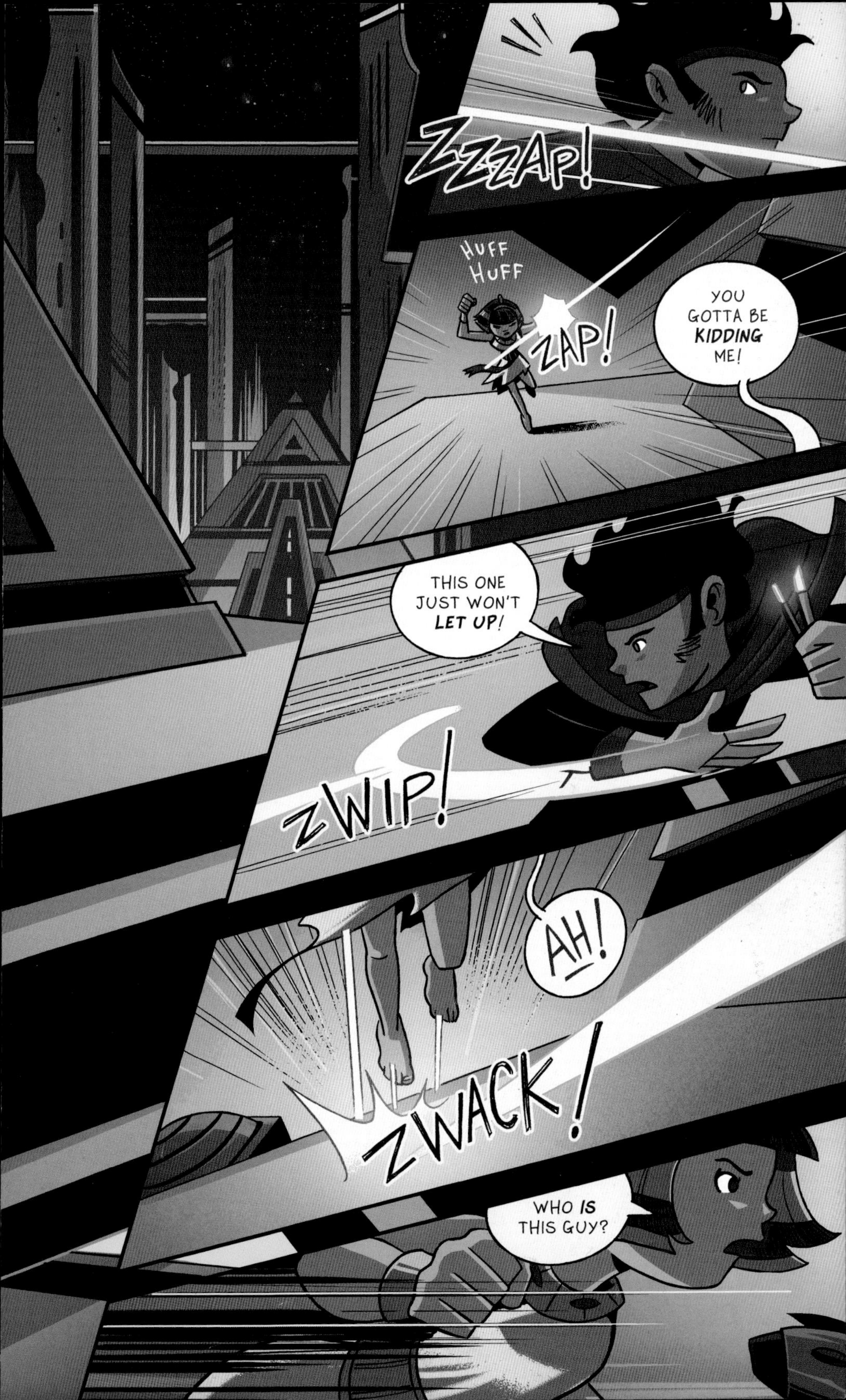
ZZZAP!
HUFF
HUFF
ZAP!
YOU GOTTA BE KIDDING ME!
THIS ONE JUST WON'T LET UP!
ZWIP!
AH!
ZWACK!
WHO IS THIS GUY?

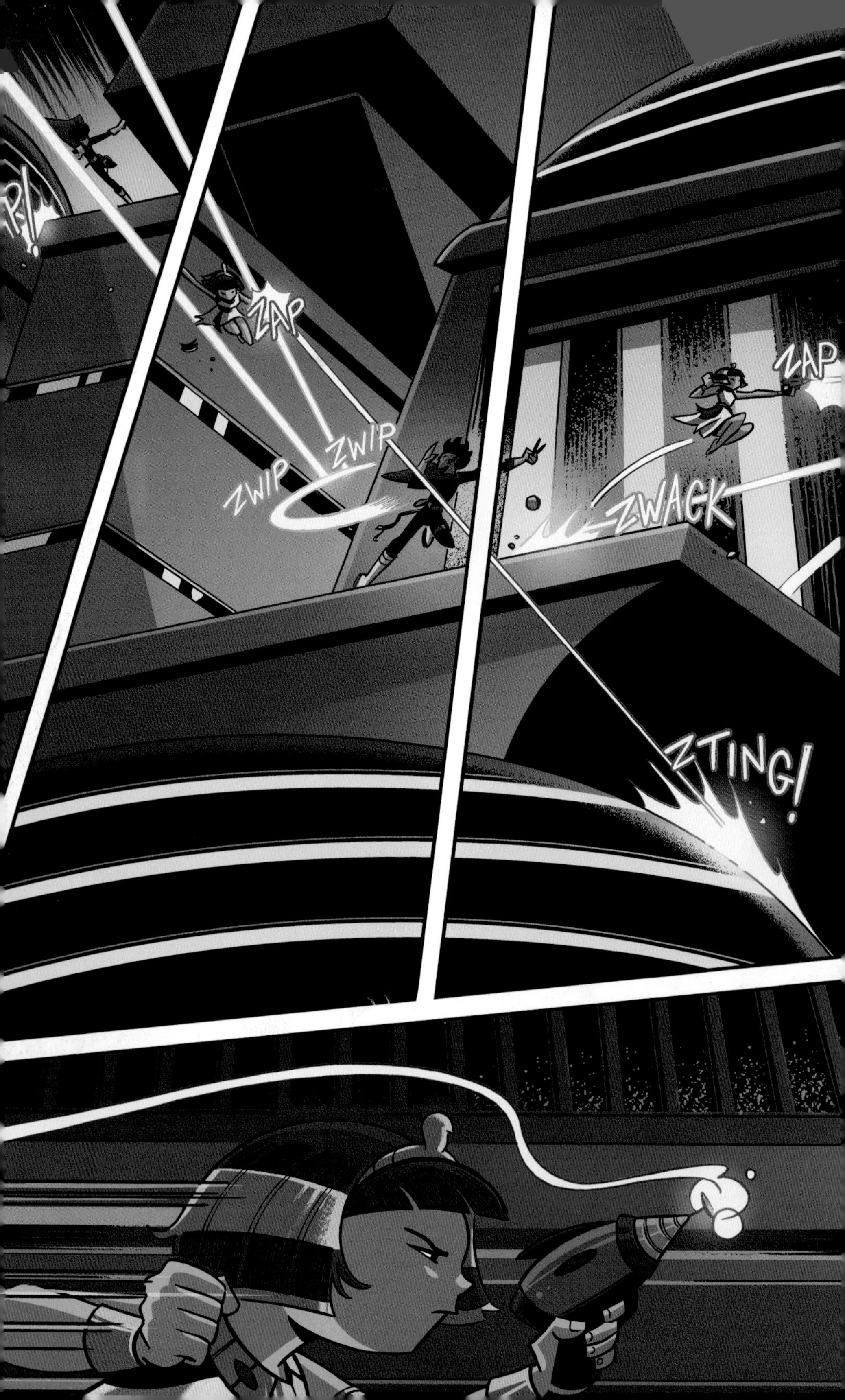
ZAP
ZWIP
ZWIP
ZAP
ZWACK
ZTING!

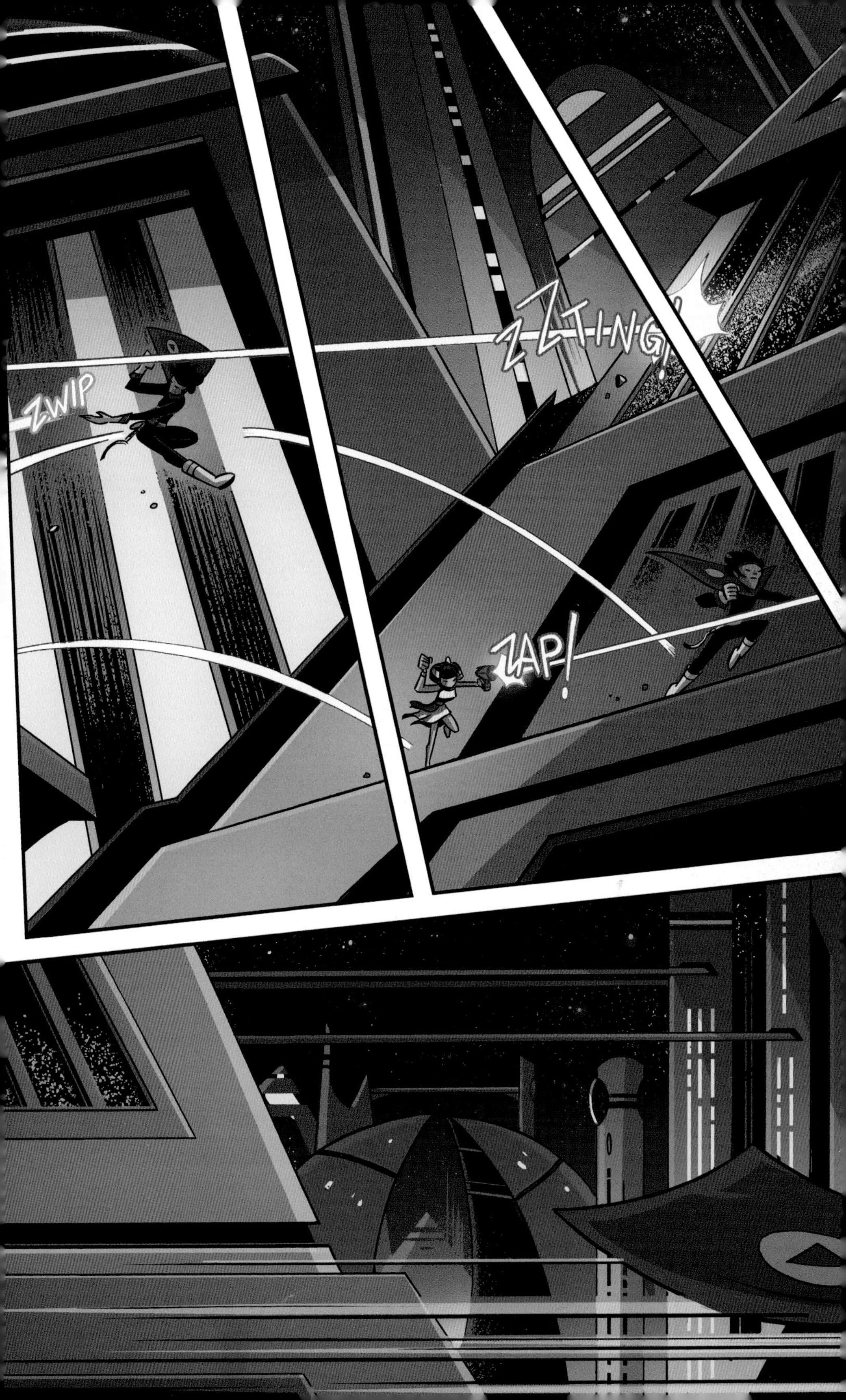
ZWIP
ZZTING!
ZAP!

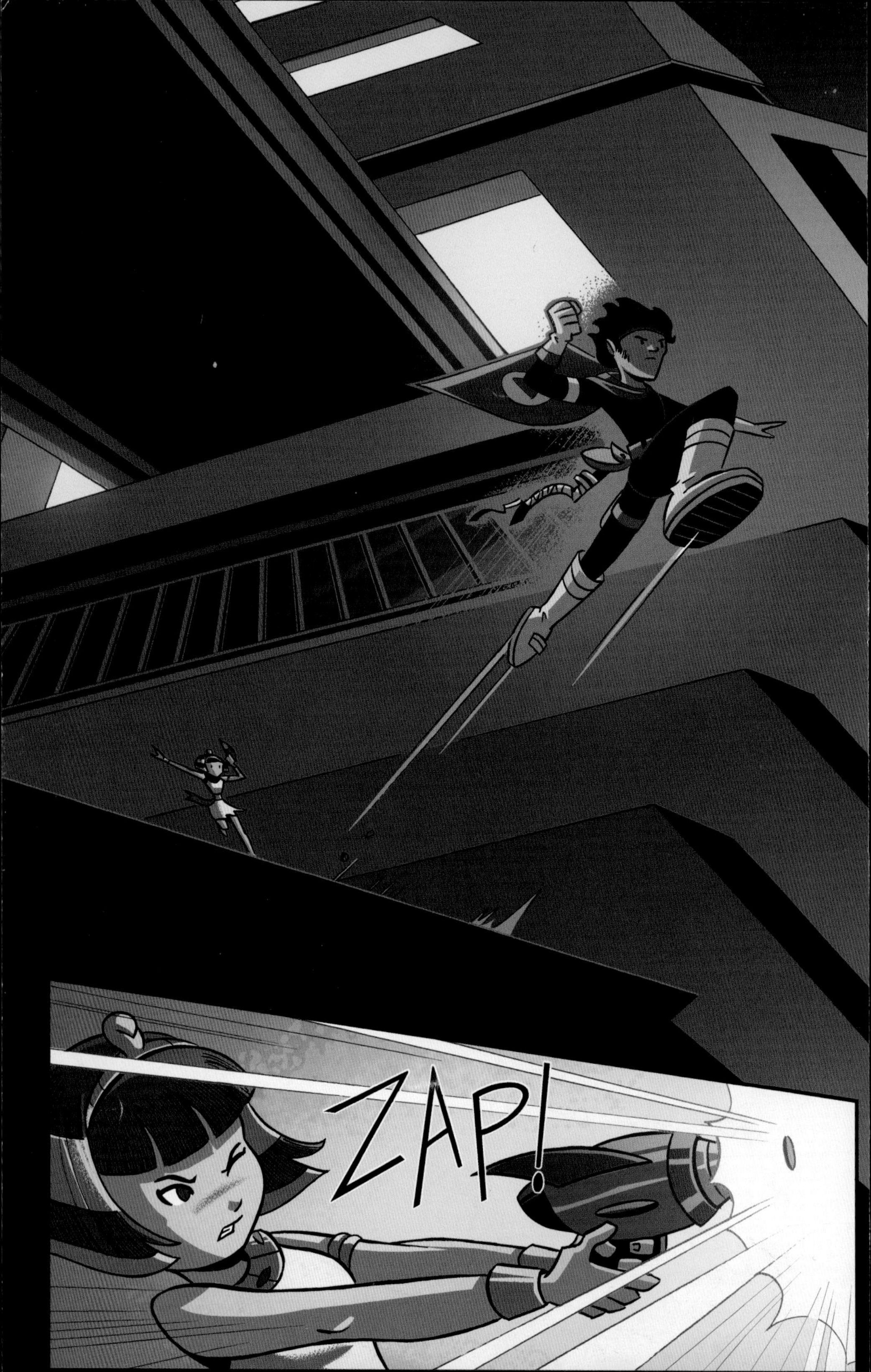
ZAP!

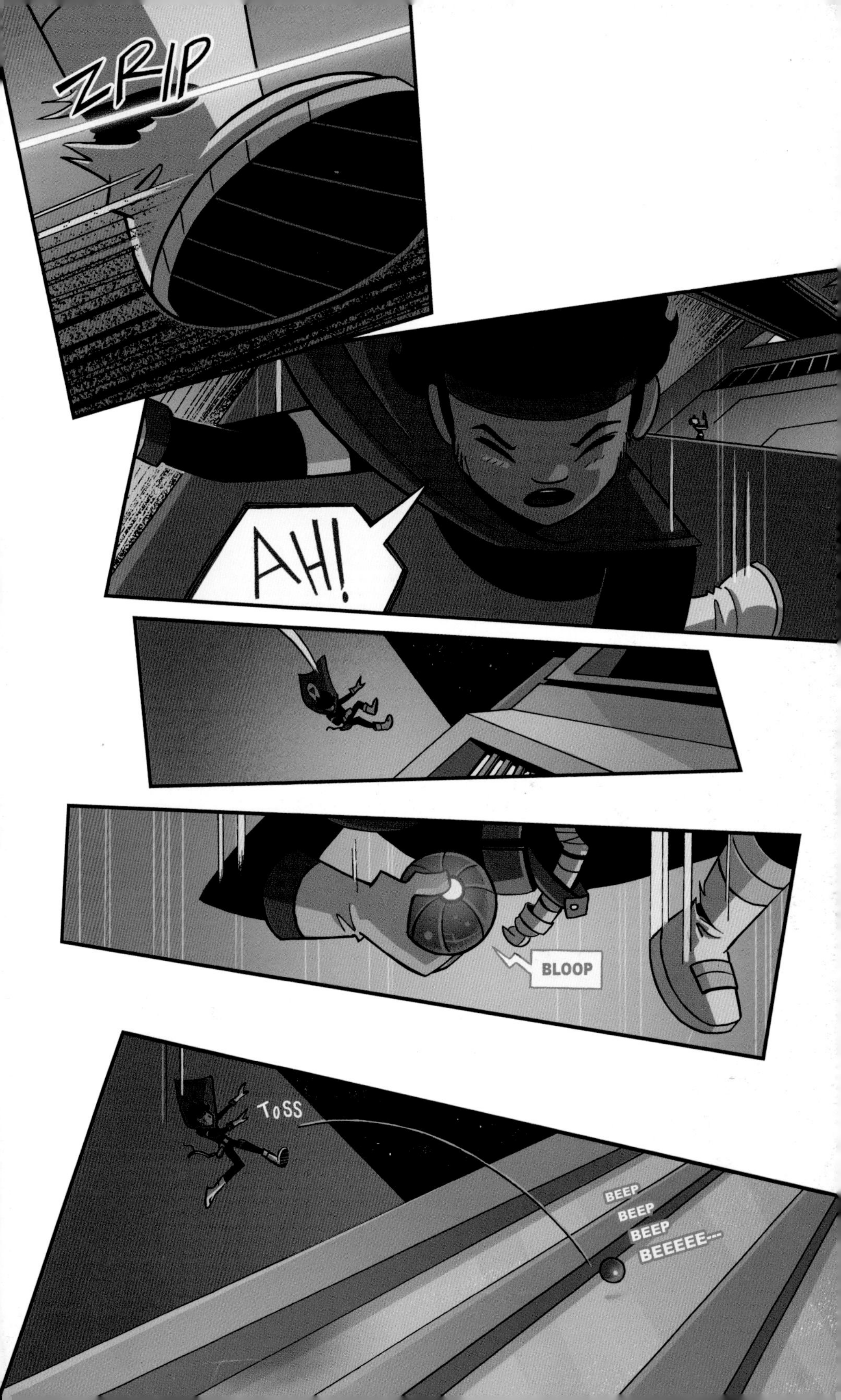
ZRIP
AH!
BLOOP
TOSS
BEEP
BEEP
BEEP
BEEEEE---

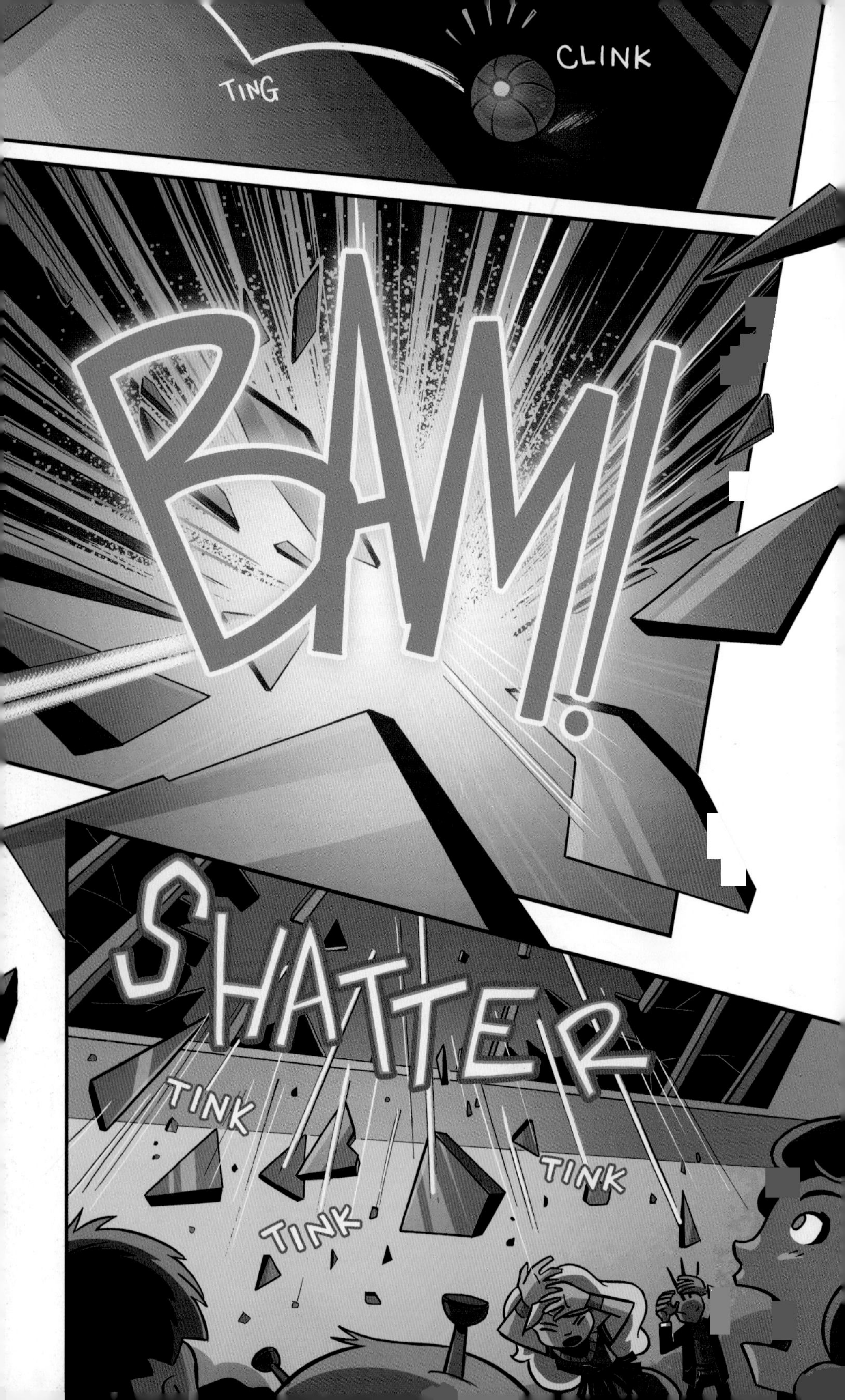
TING
CLINK
BAM!
SHATTER
TINK
TINK
TINK

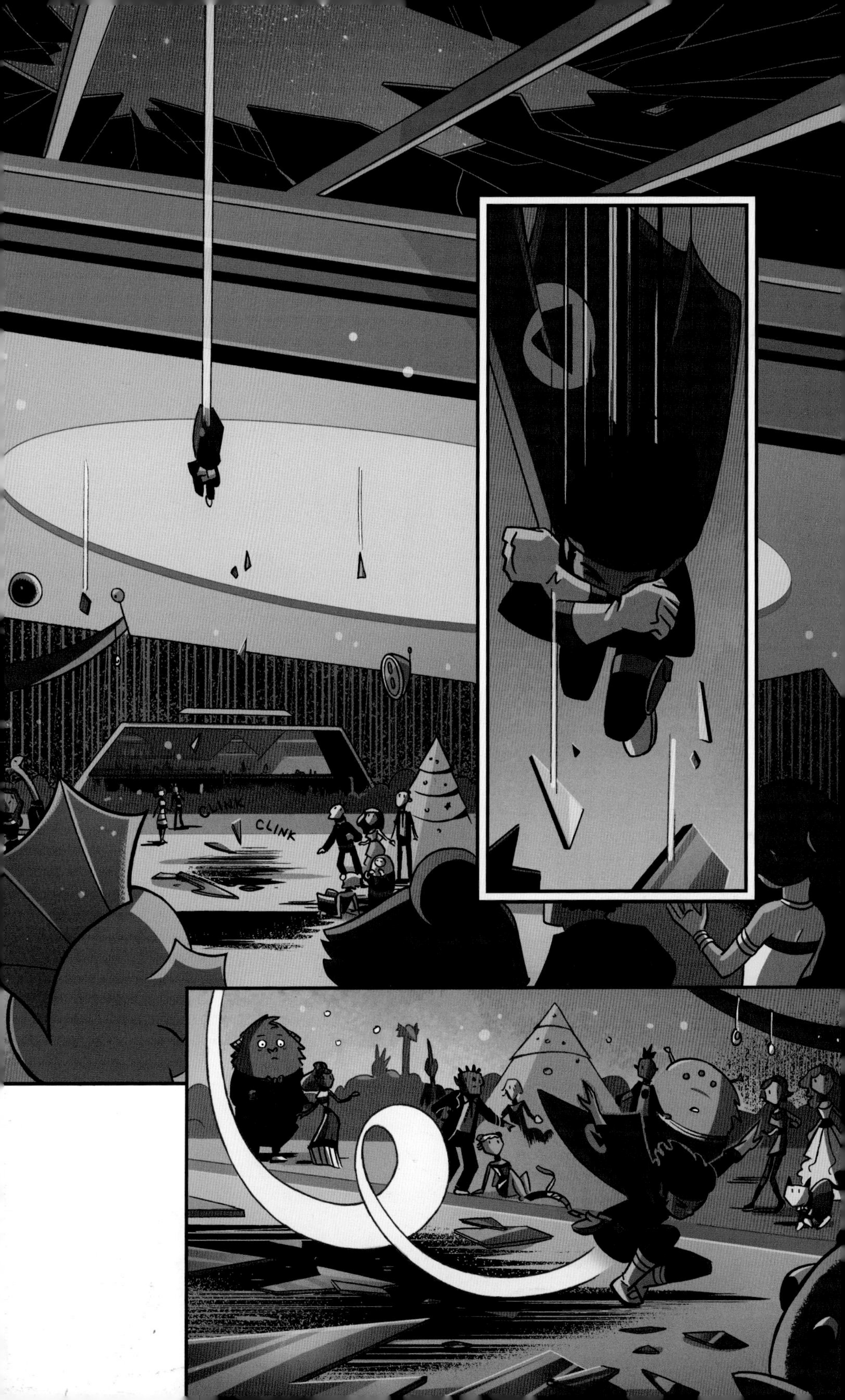
CLINK
CLINK

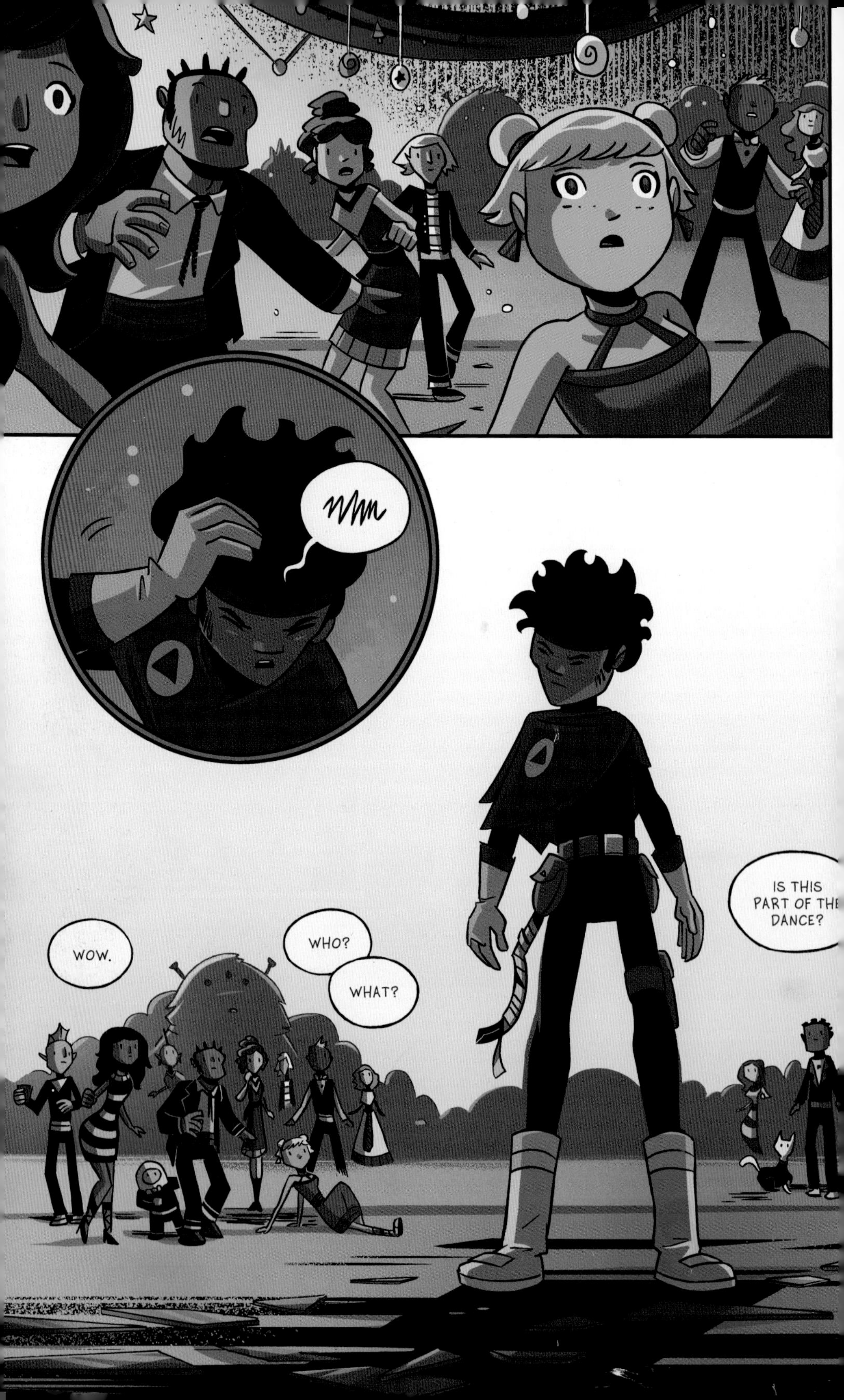
WOW.
WHO?
WHAT?
IS THIS PART OF THE DANCE?

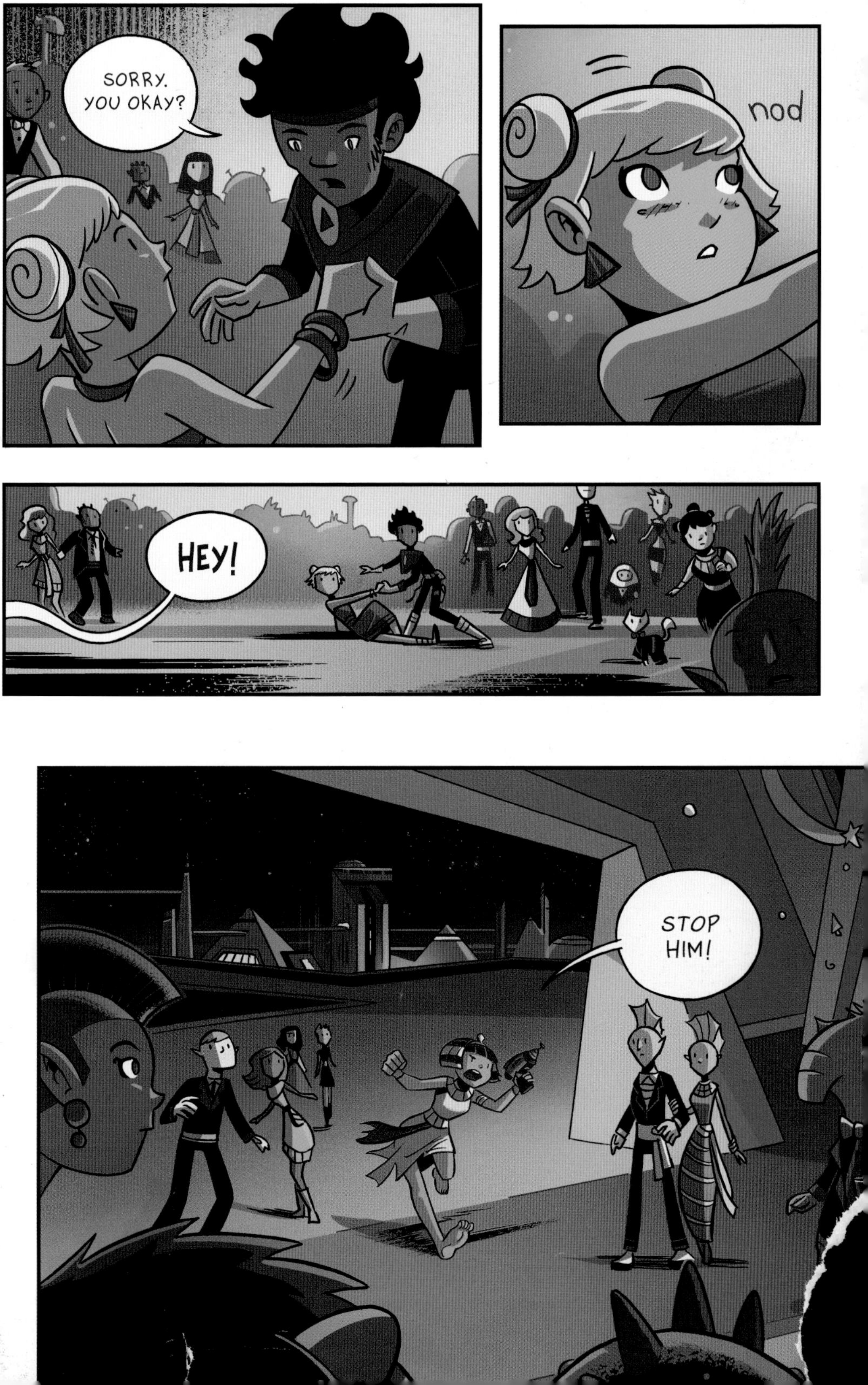
SORRY. YOU OKAY?
nod
HEY!
STOP HIM!

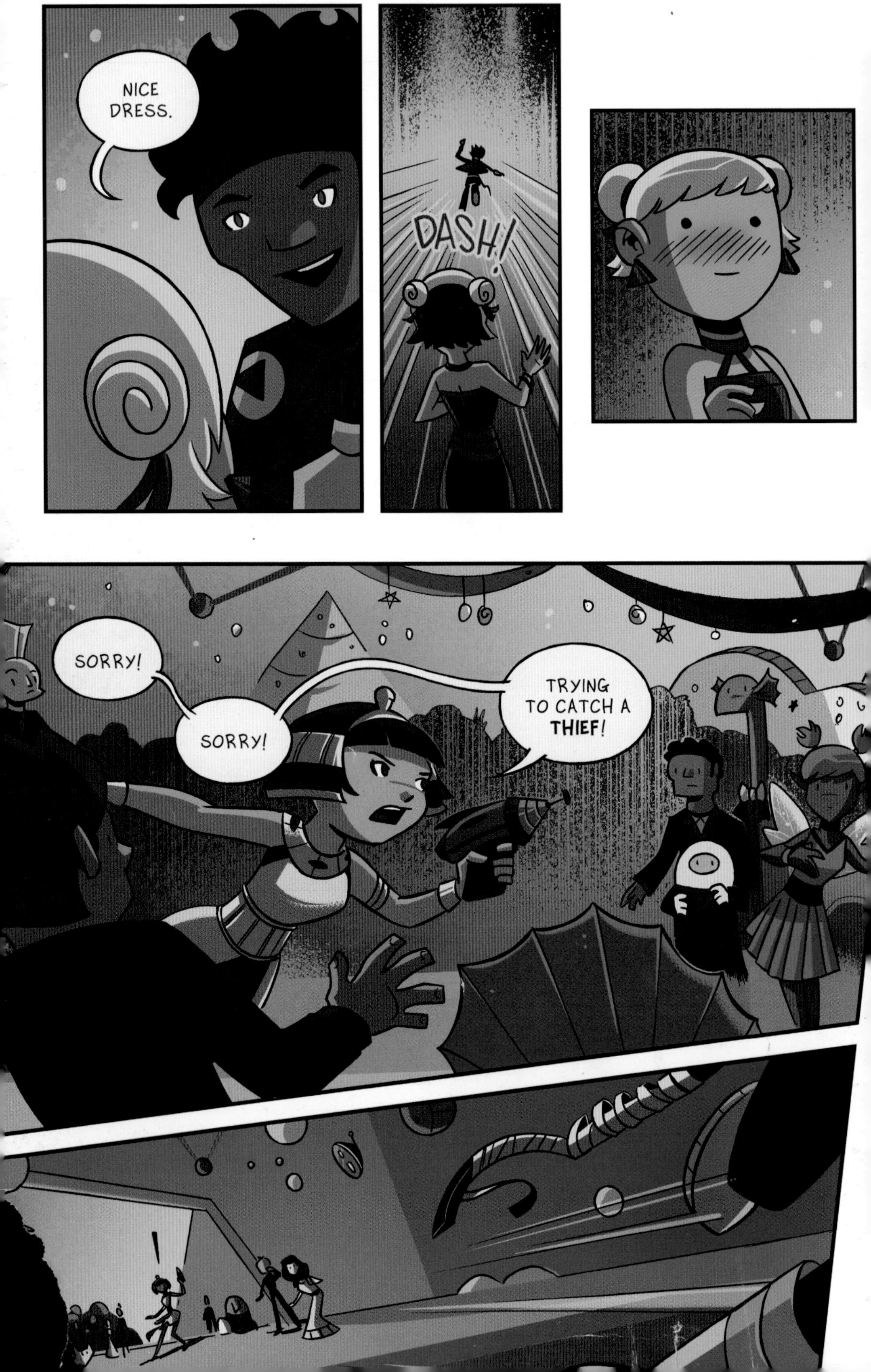
NICE DRESS.
DASH!
SORRY!
SORRY!
TRYING TO CATCH A THIEF!
!

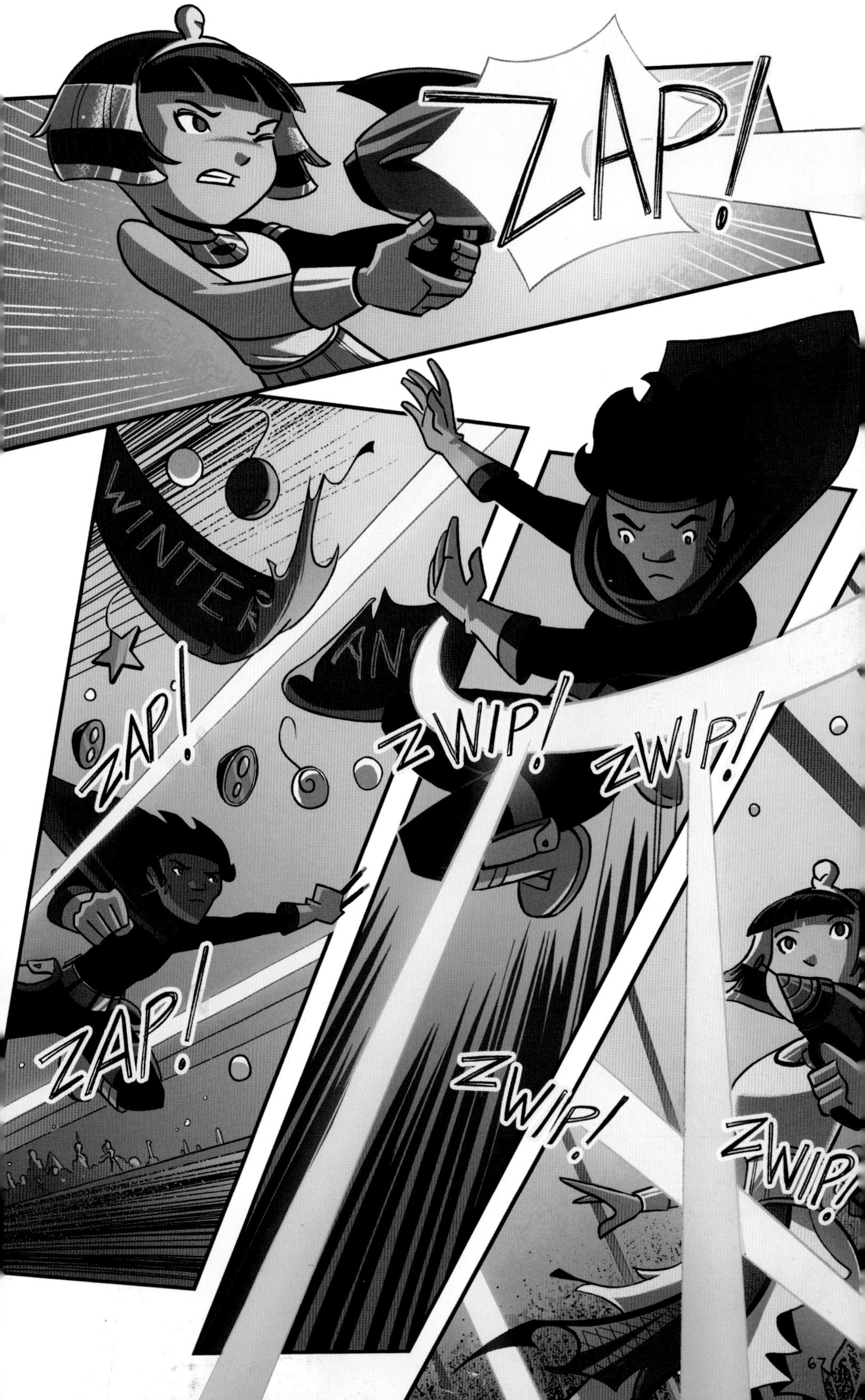
ZAP!
WINTER
ZAP!
ZWIP!
ZWIP!
ZAP!
ZWIP!
ZWIP!

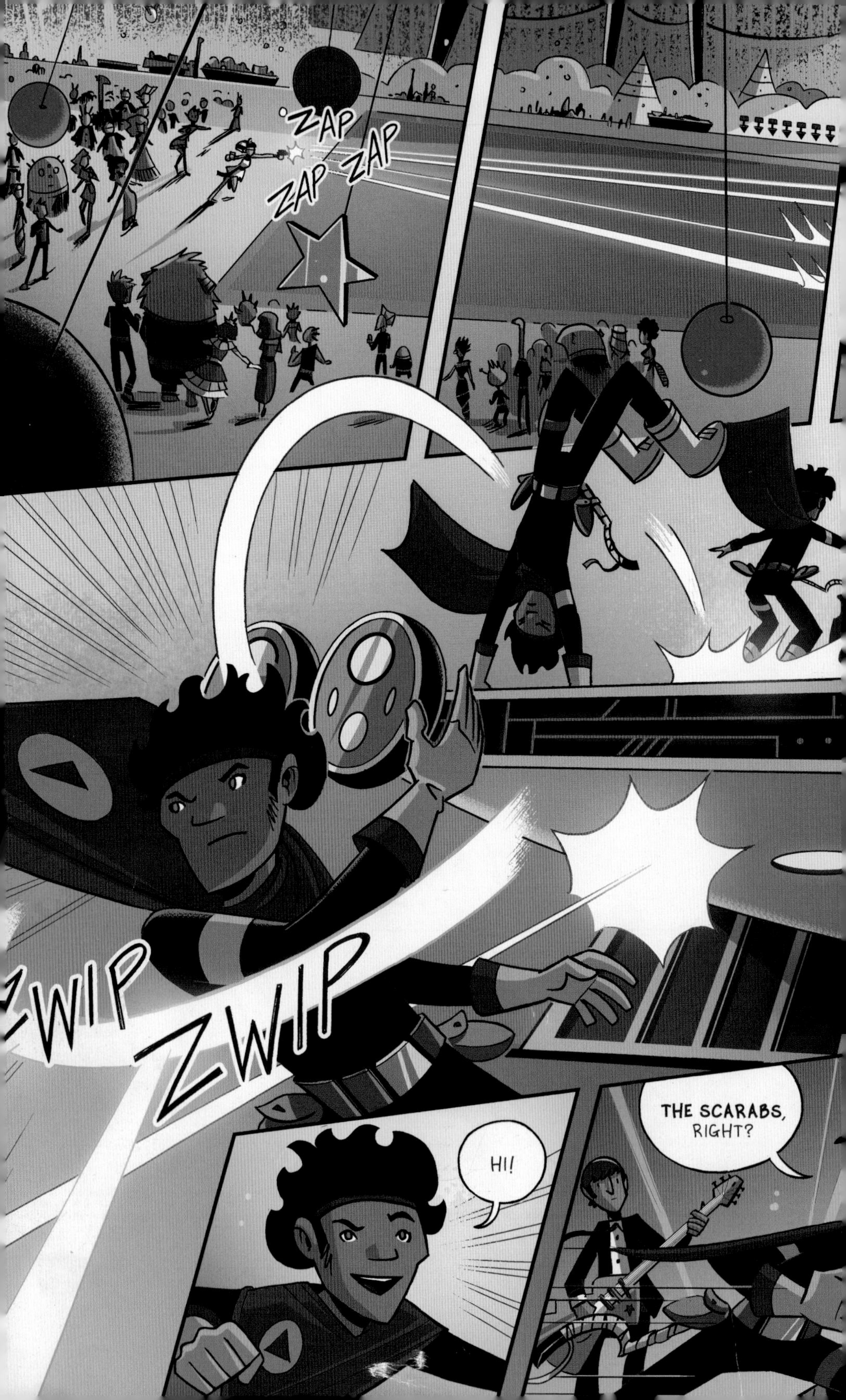
ZAP
ZAP ZAP
ZWIP ZWIP
HI!
THE SCARABS, RIGHT?

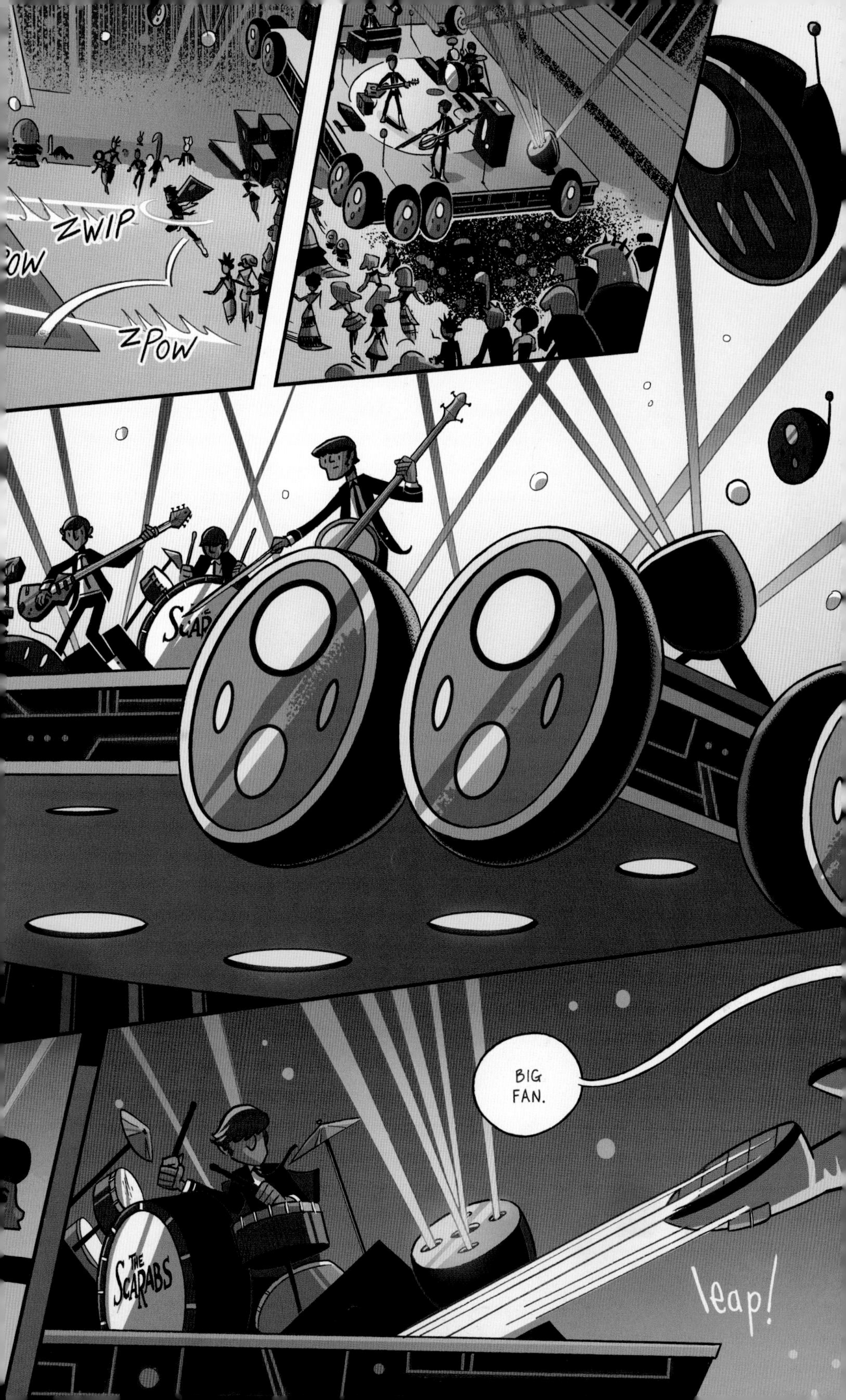
ZWIP
POW
ZPOW
THE SCARABS
BIG FAN.
THE SCARABS
leap!

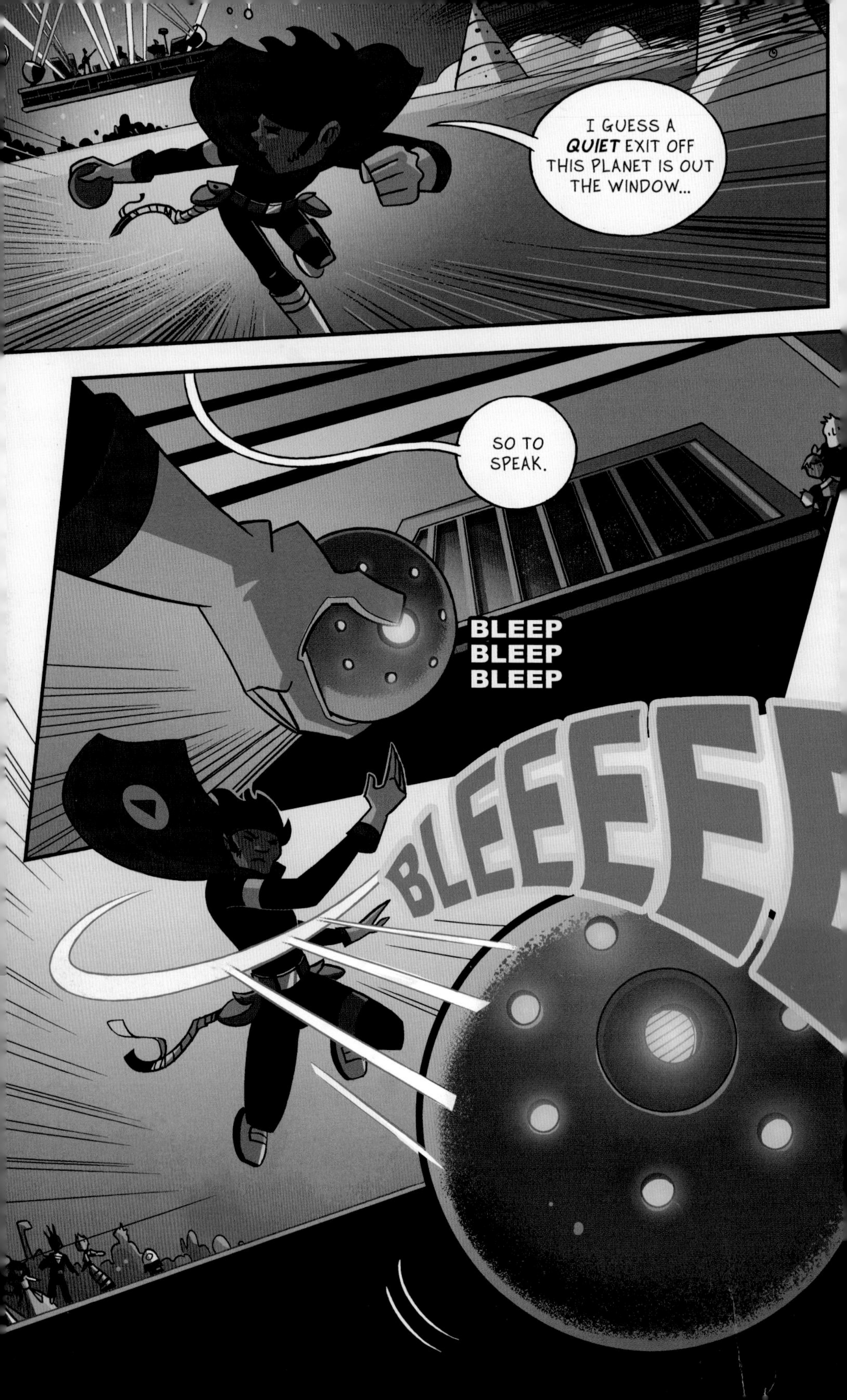
I GUESS A **QUIET** EXIT OFF THIS PLANET IS OUT THE WINDOW...
SO TO SPEAK.
BLEEP
BLEEP
BLEEP
BLEEEEE

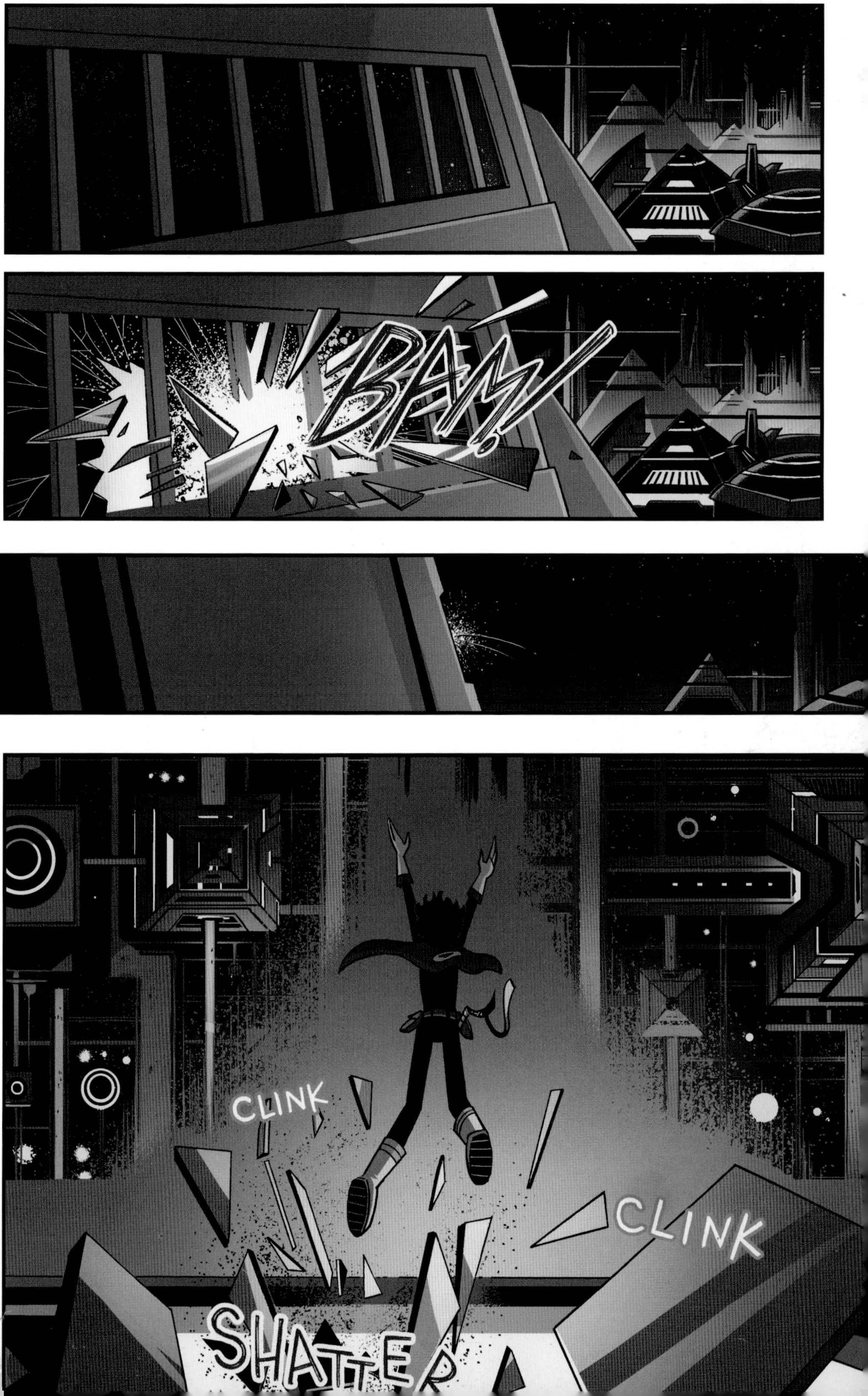
BAM!
CLINK
CLINK
SHATTER

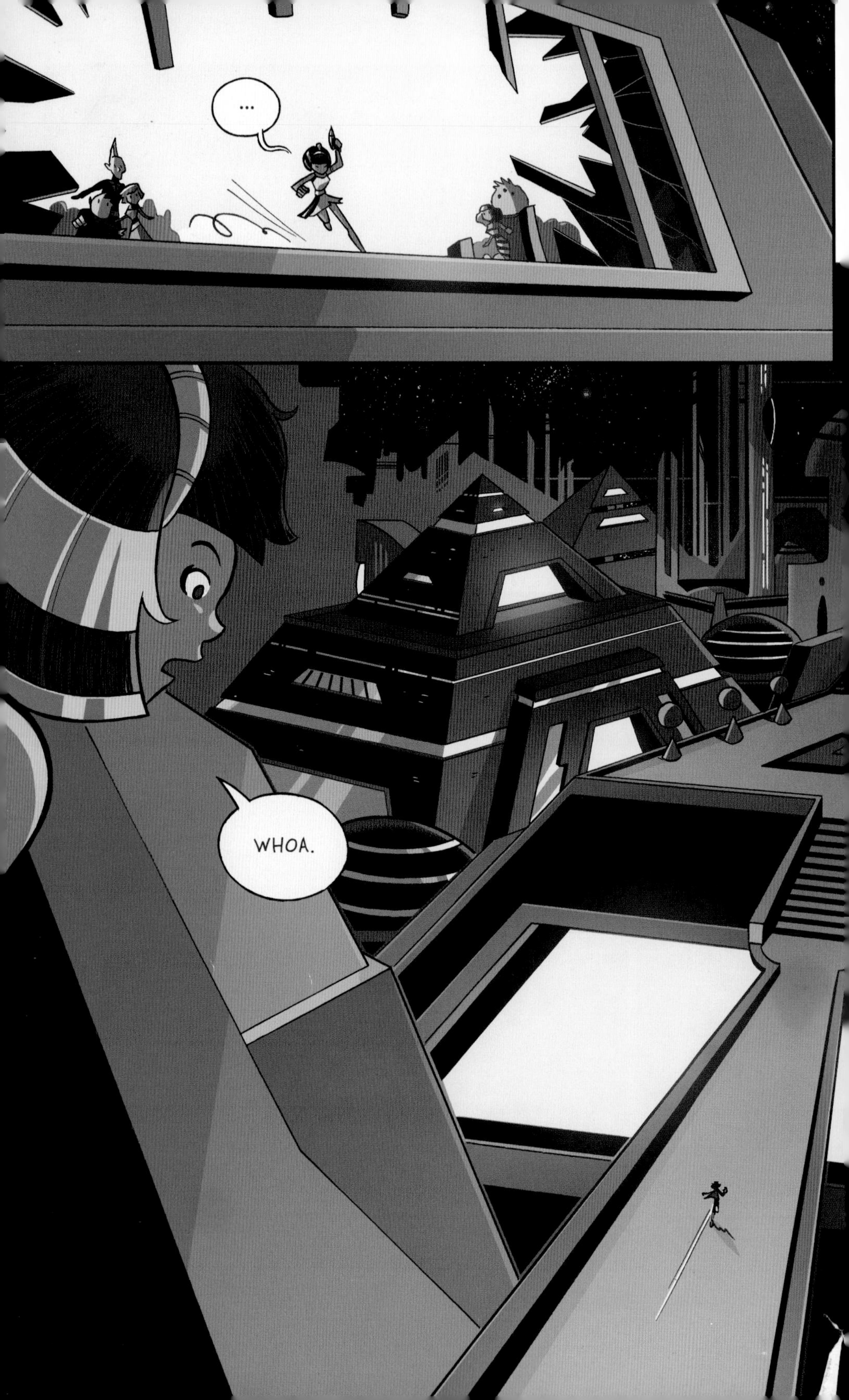
...
WHOA.

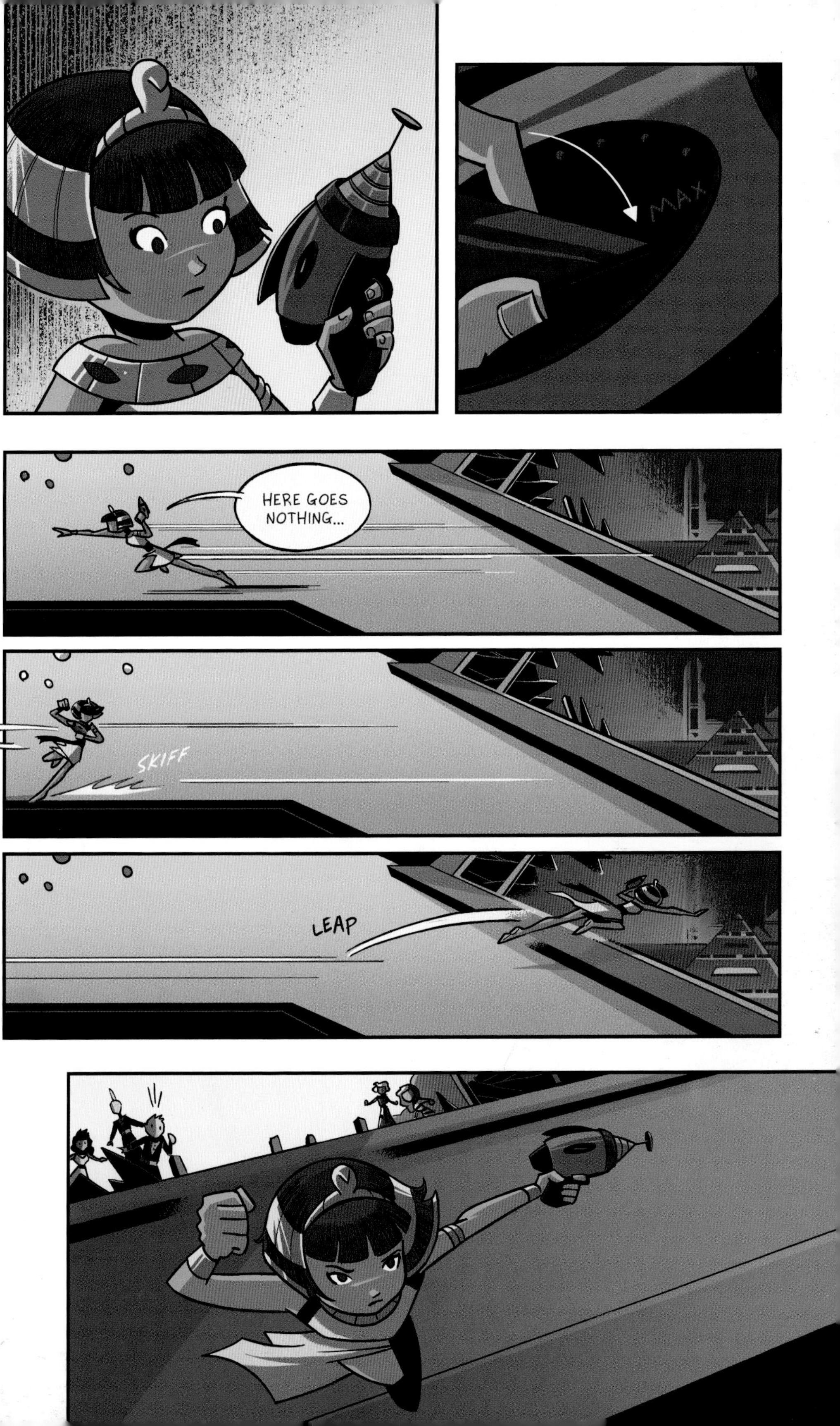
MAX
HERE GOES NOTHING...
SKIFF
LEAP

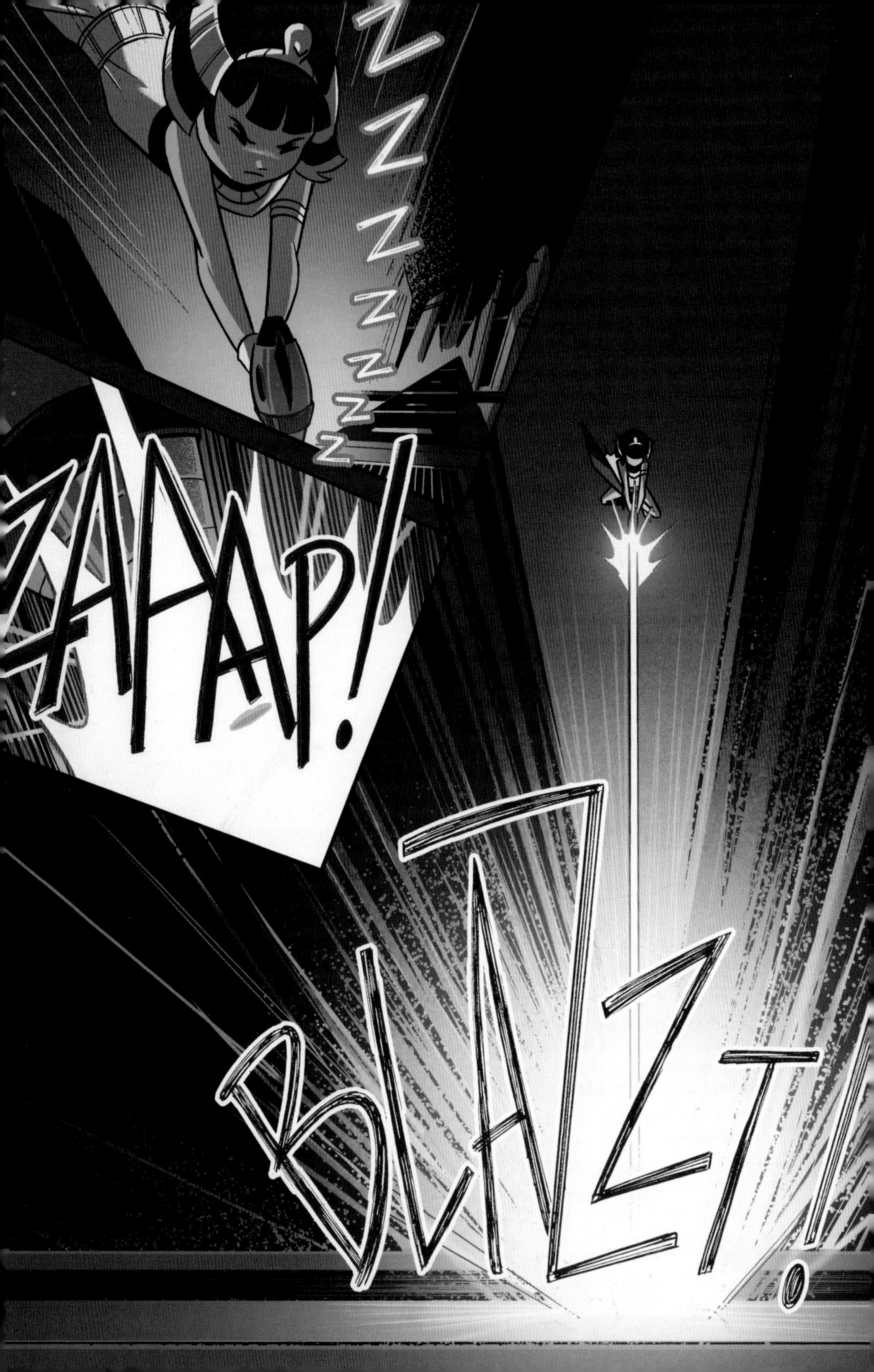
ZZZZZZZZ
ZAAAP!
BLLAZZT!

SSSS
TT
CADETS!
STAY AWAY FROM THE WINDOW!
WOW.
DID YOU **SEE** THAT?
I THINK I'M IN LOVE.
HUH.
WAIT TILL I TELL PTOLMINIC ABOUT **THAT**!

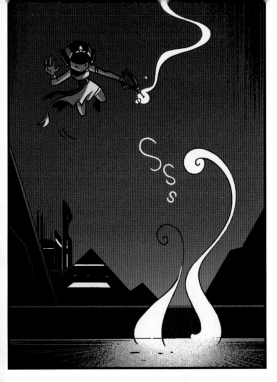

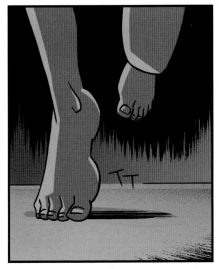

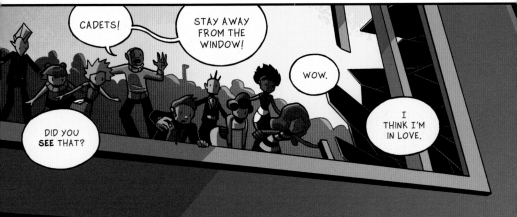

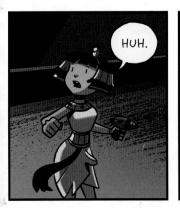

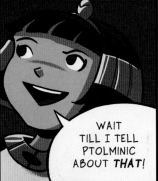

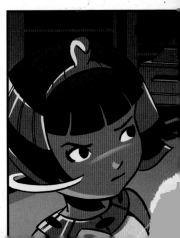

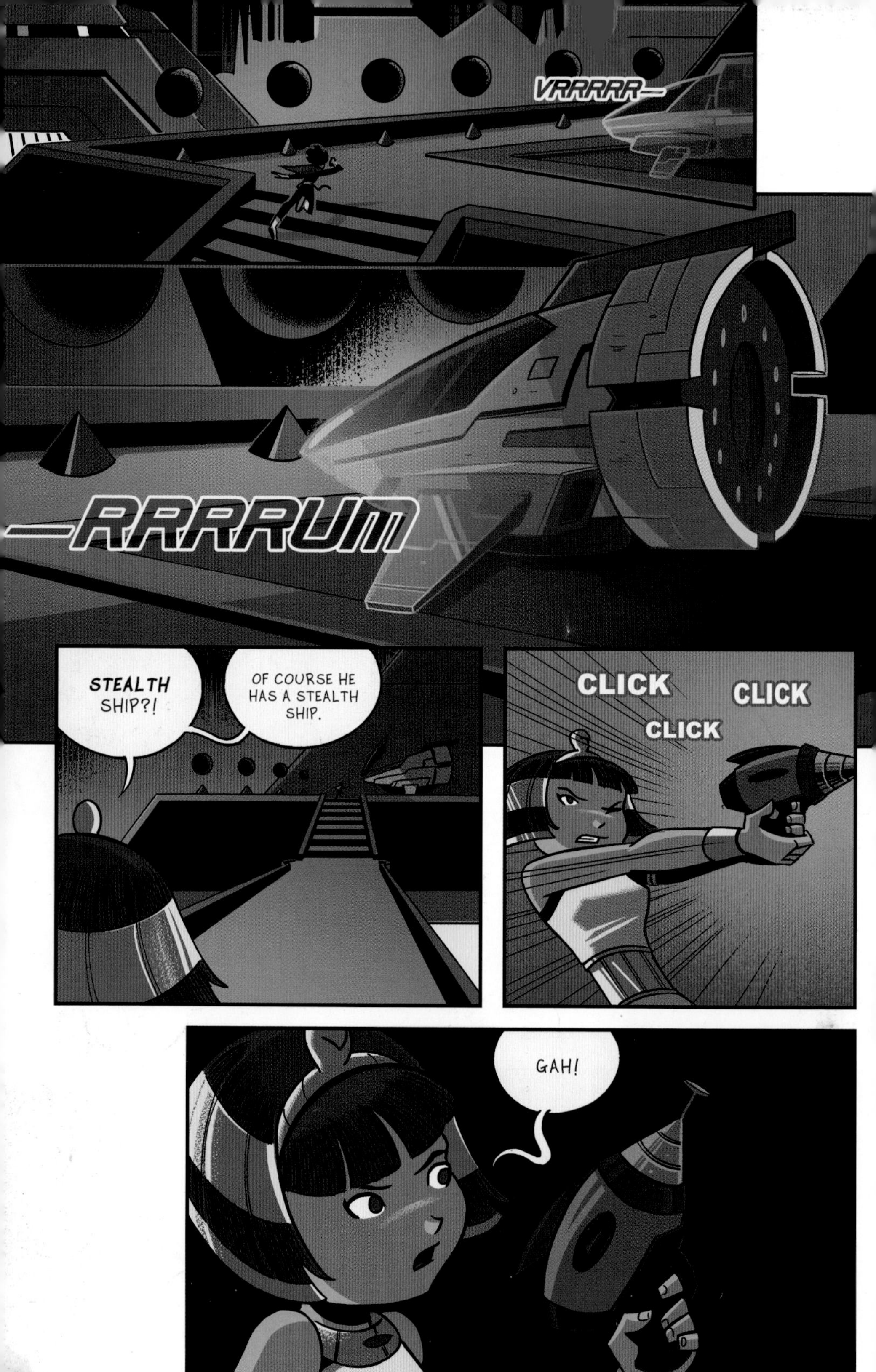
VRRRRR—
—RRRRUM
STEALTH SHIP?!
OF COURSE HE HAS A STEALTH SHIP.
CLICK
CLICK
CLICK
GAH!

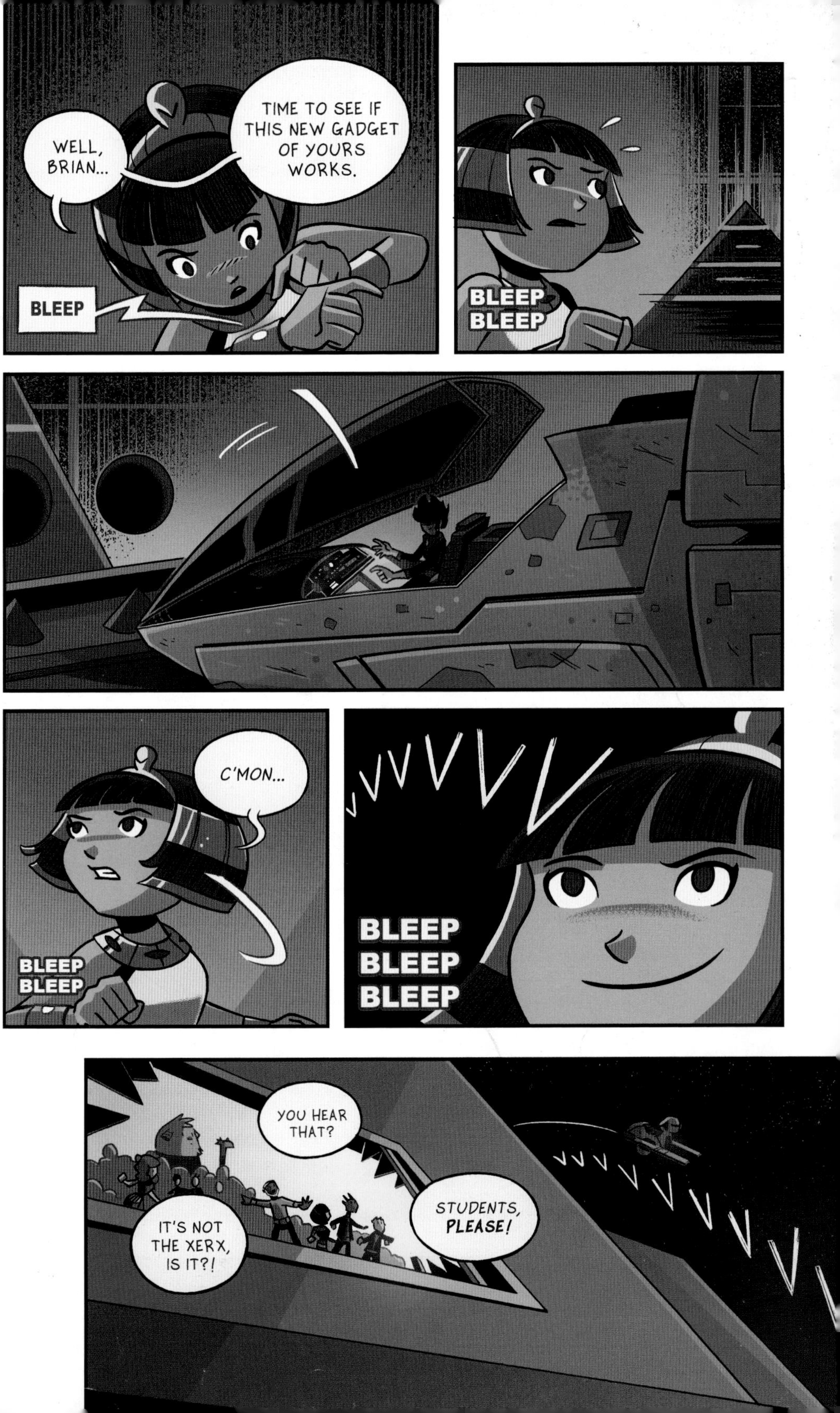
WELL, BRIAN...
TIME TO SEE IF THIS NEW GADGET OF YOURS WORKS.
BLEEP
BLEEP BLEEP
C'MON...
BLEEP BLEEP
BLEEP BLEEP BLEEP
YOU HEAR THAT?
IT'S NOT THE XERX, IS IT?!
STUDENTS, PLEASE!

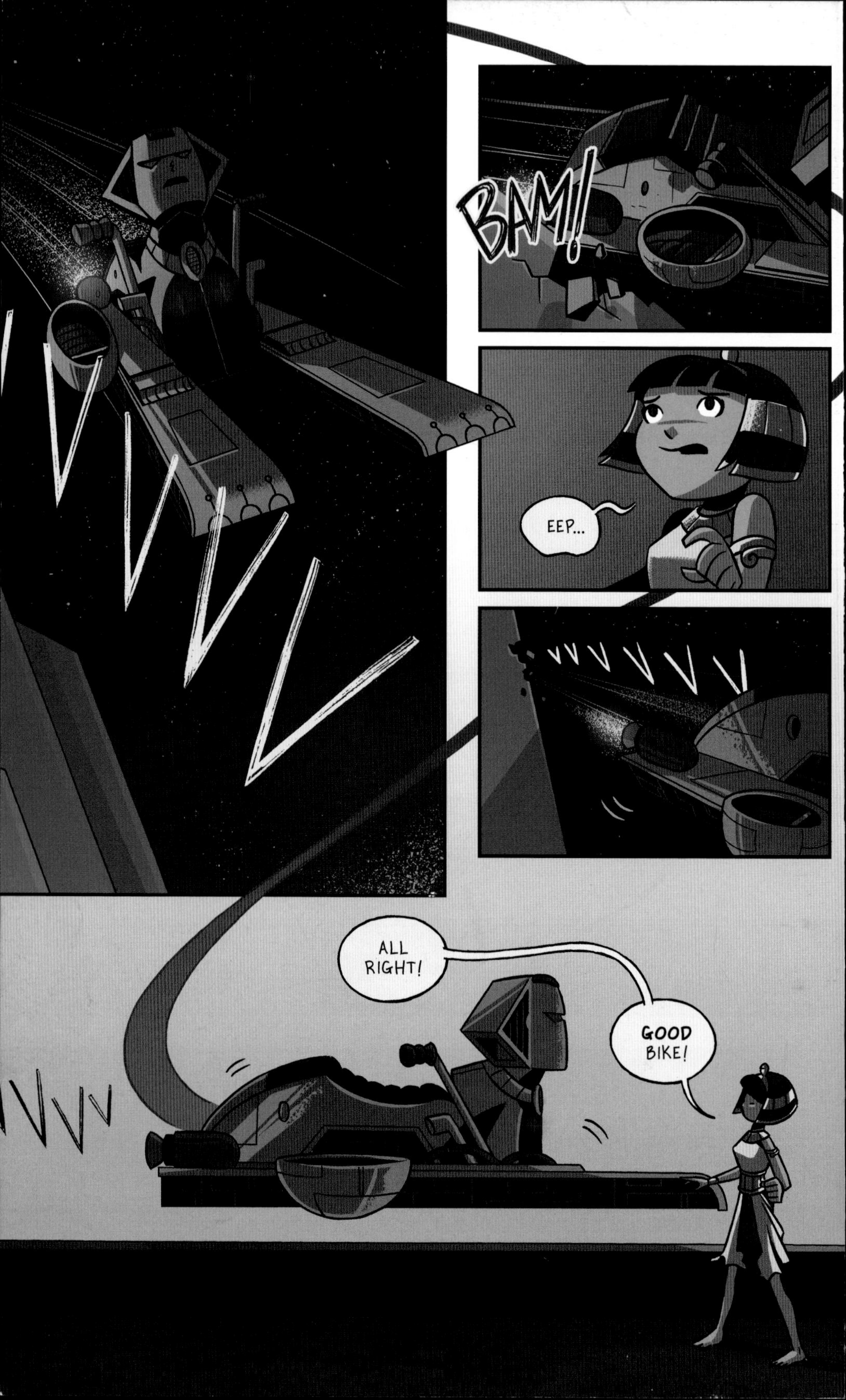
BAM!
EEP...
ALL RIGHT!
GOOD BIKE!

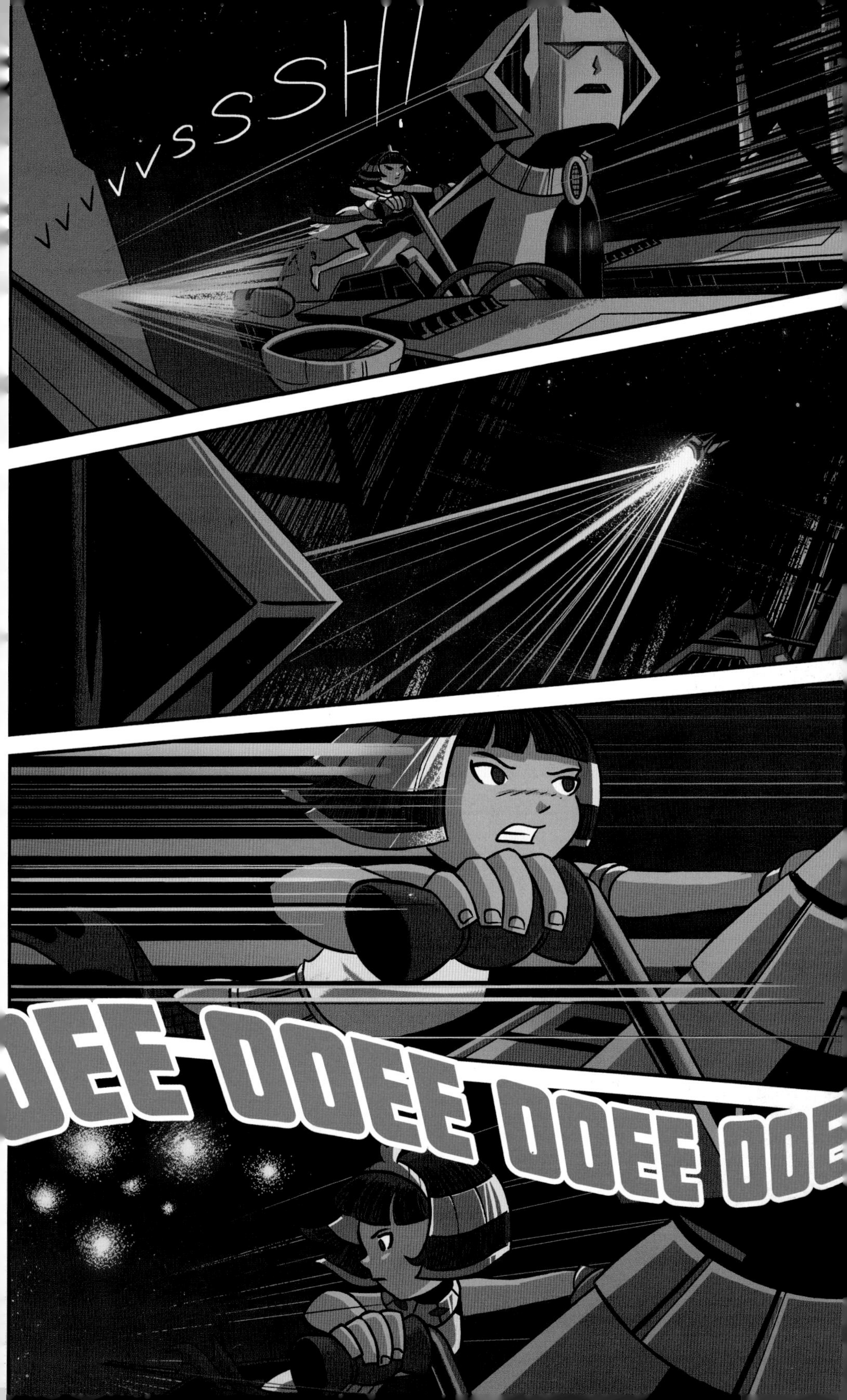
VVVVVVSSSSH!
OOEE OOEE OOEE OOE

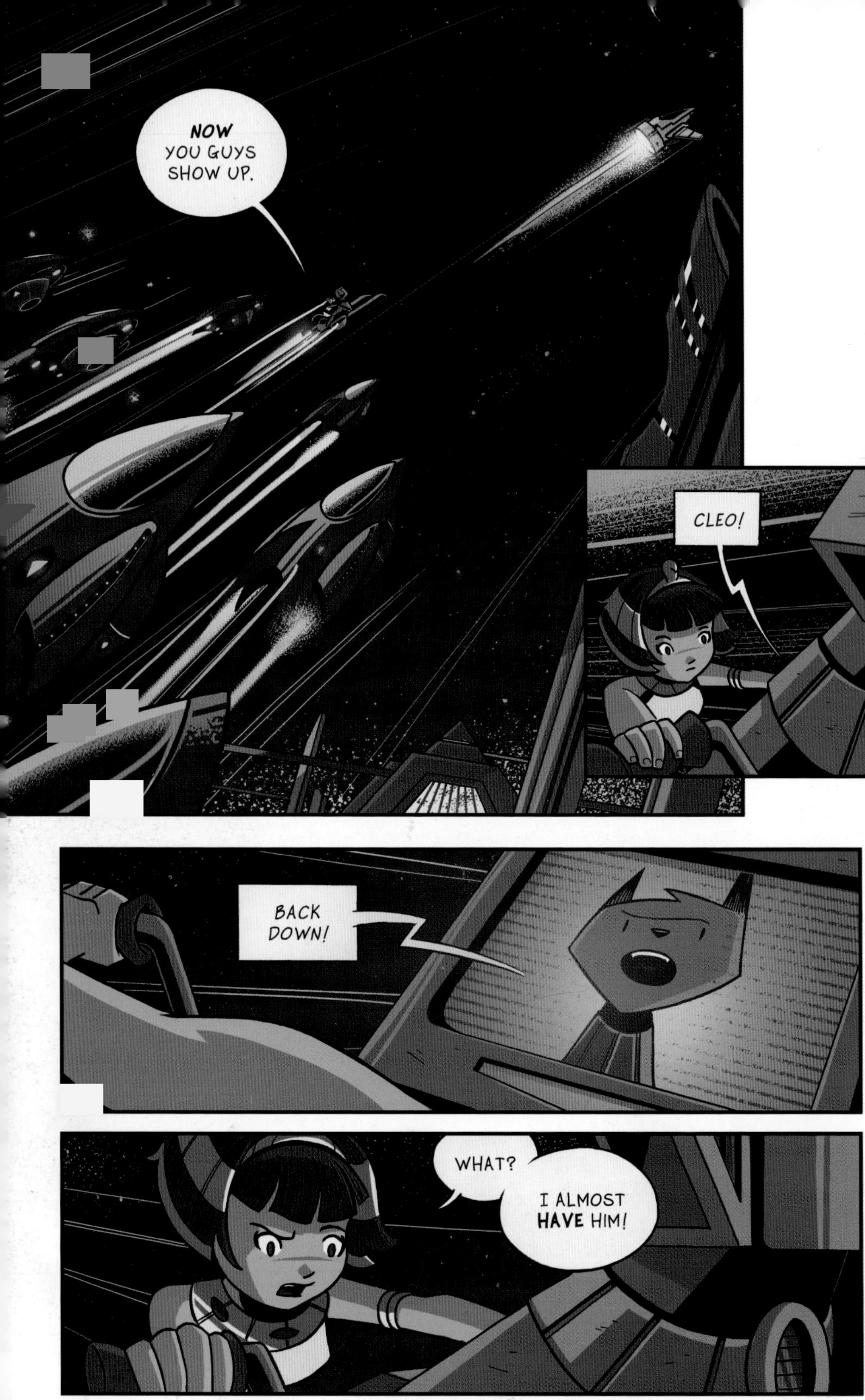
NOW YOU GUYS SHOW UP.
CLEO!
BACK DOWN!
WHAT?
I ALMOST HAVE HIM!

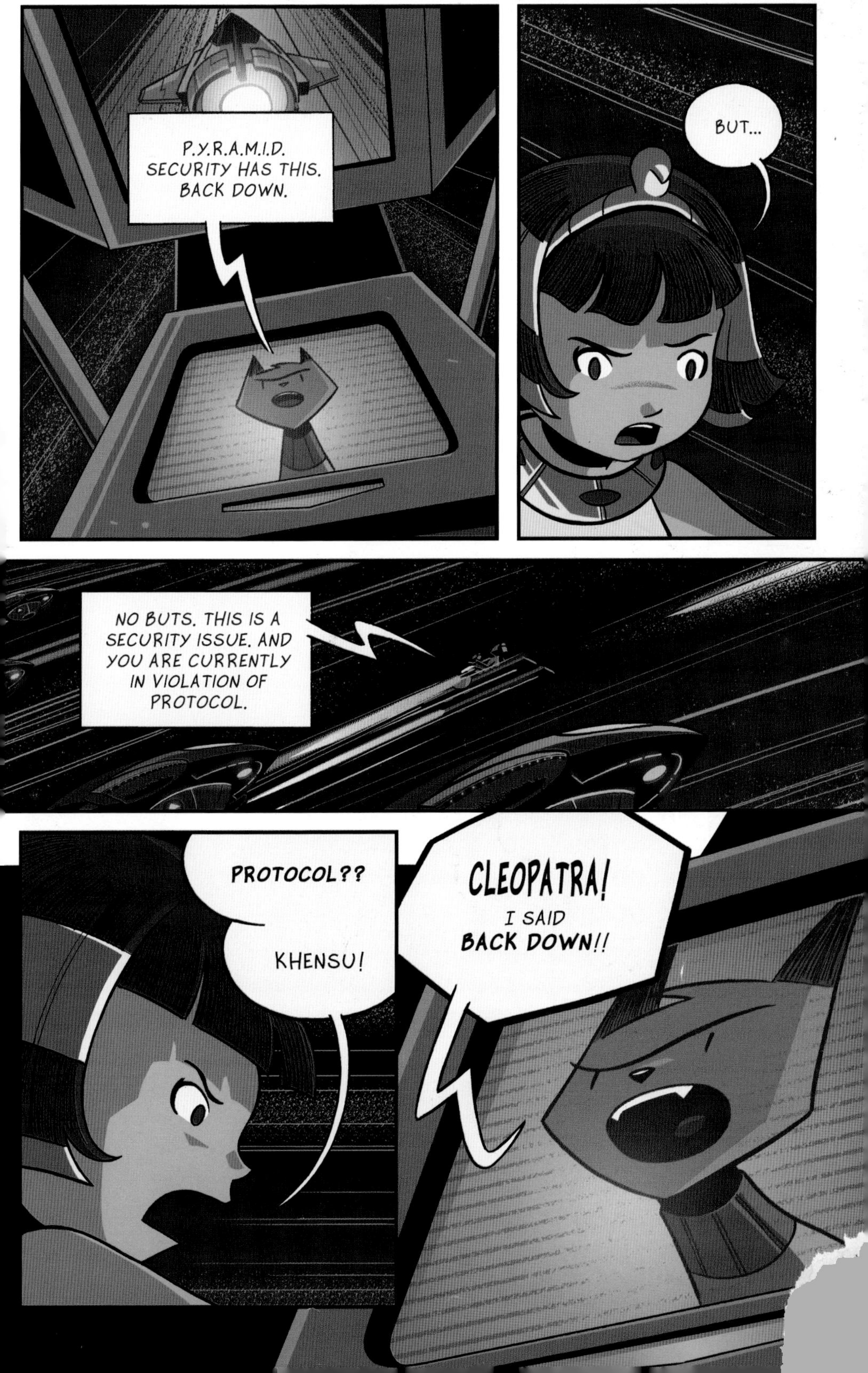
P.Y.R.A.M.I.D. SECURITY HAS THIS. BACK DOWN.
BUT...
NO BUTS. THIS IS A SECURITY ISSUE. AND YOU ARE CURRENTLY IN VIOLATION OF PROTOCOL.
PROTOCOL??
KHENSU!
CLEOPATRA! I SAID BACK DOWN!!

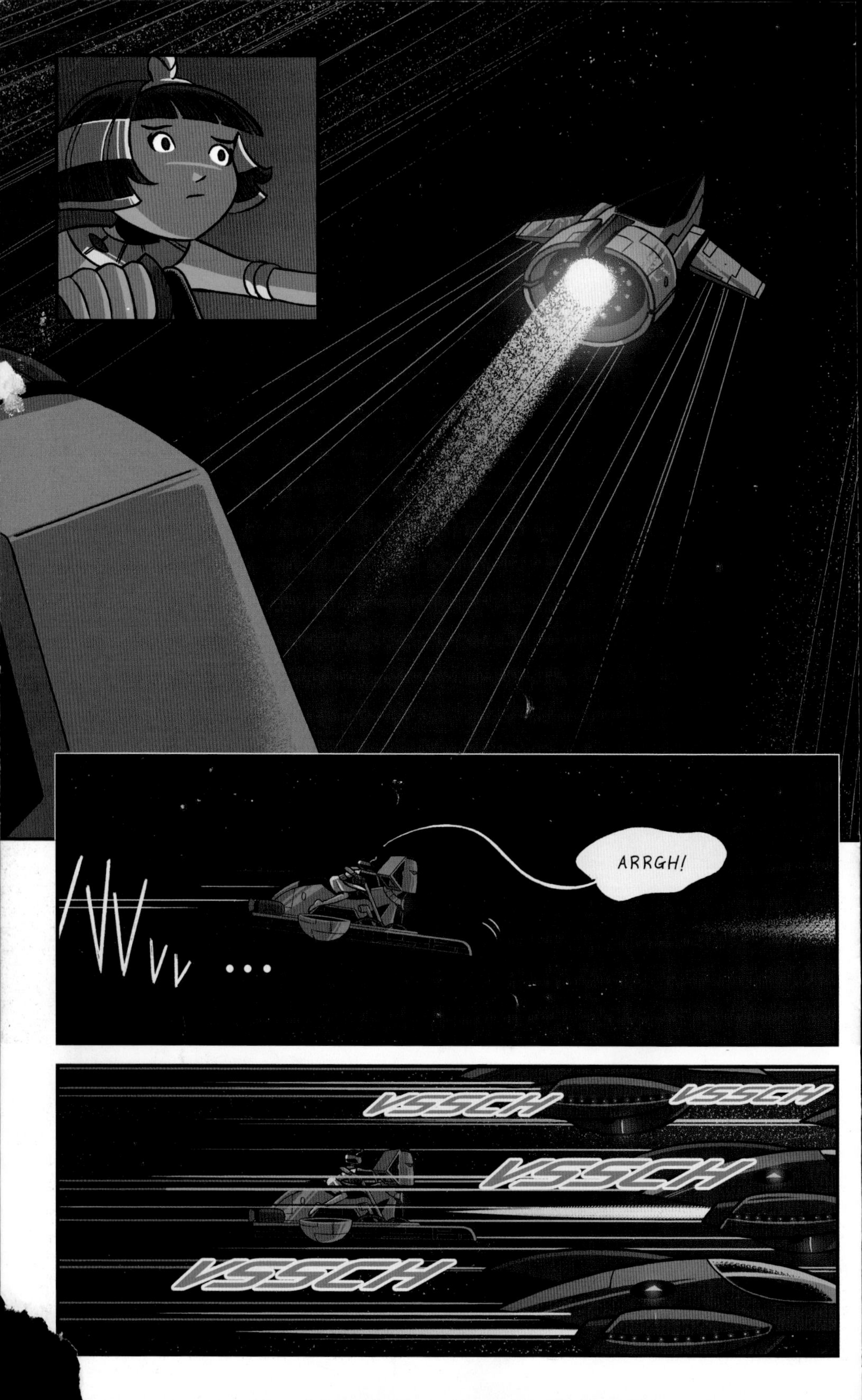
ARRGH!
VSSCH
VSSCH
VSSCH
VSSCH

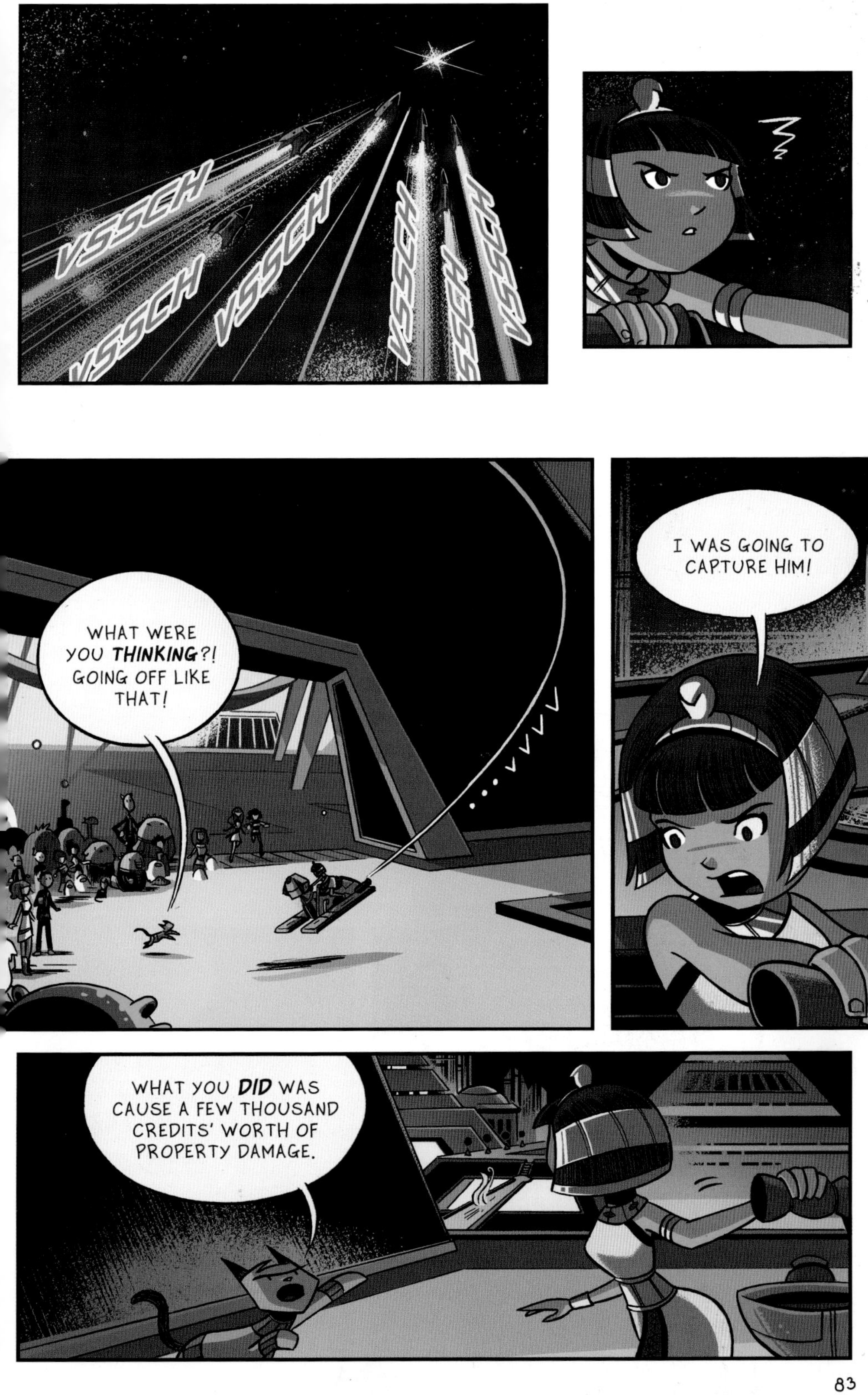
VSSCH
VSSCH
VSSCH
VSSCH
VSSCH
VSSCH
WHAT WERE YOU **THINKING**?! GOING OFF LIKE THAT!
I WAS GOING TO CAPTURE HIM!
WHAT YOU **DID** WAS CAUSE A FEW THOUSAND CREDITS' WORTH OF PROPERTY DAMAGE.

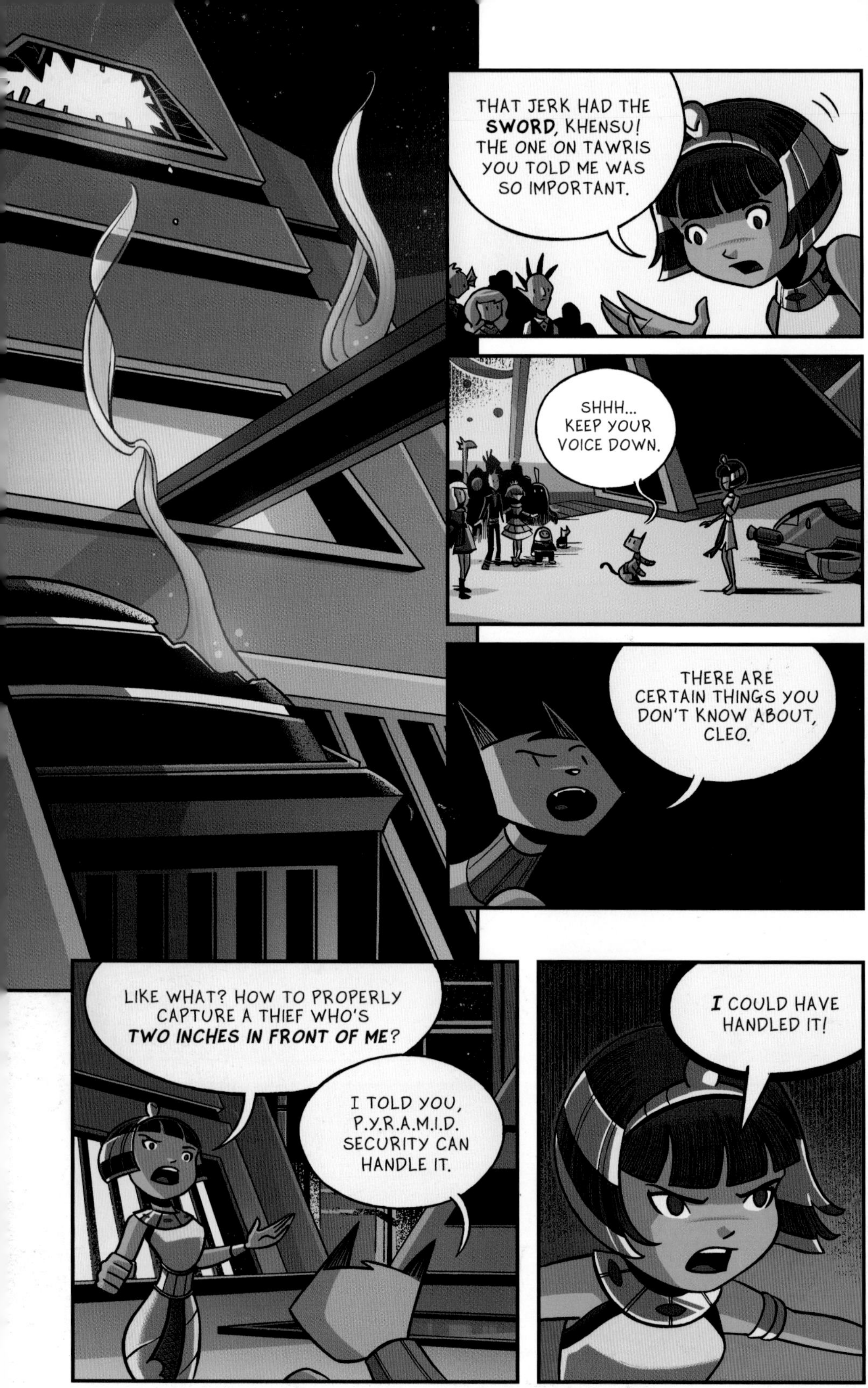
THAT JERK HAD THE **SWORD,** KHENSU! THE ONE ON TAWRIS YOU TOLD ME WAS SO IMPORTANT.
SHHH... KEEP YOUR VOICE DOWN.
THERE ARE CERTAIN THINGS YOU DON'T KNOW ABOUT, CLEO.
LIKE WHAT? HOW TO PROPERLY CAPTURE A THIEF WHO'S ***TWO INCHES IN FRONT OF ME***?
I TOLD YOU, P.Y.R.A.M.I.D. SECURITY CAN HANDLE IT.
I COULD HAVE HANDLED IT!

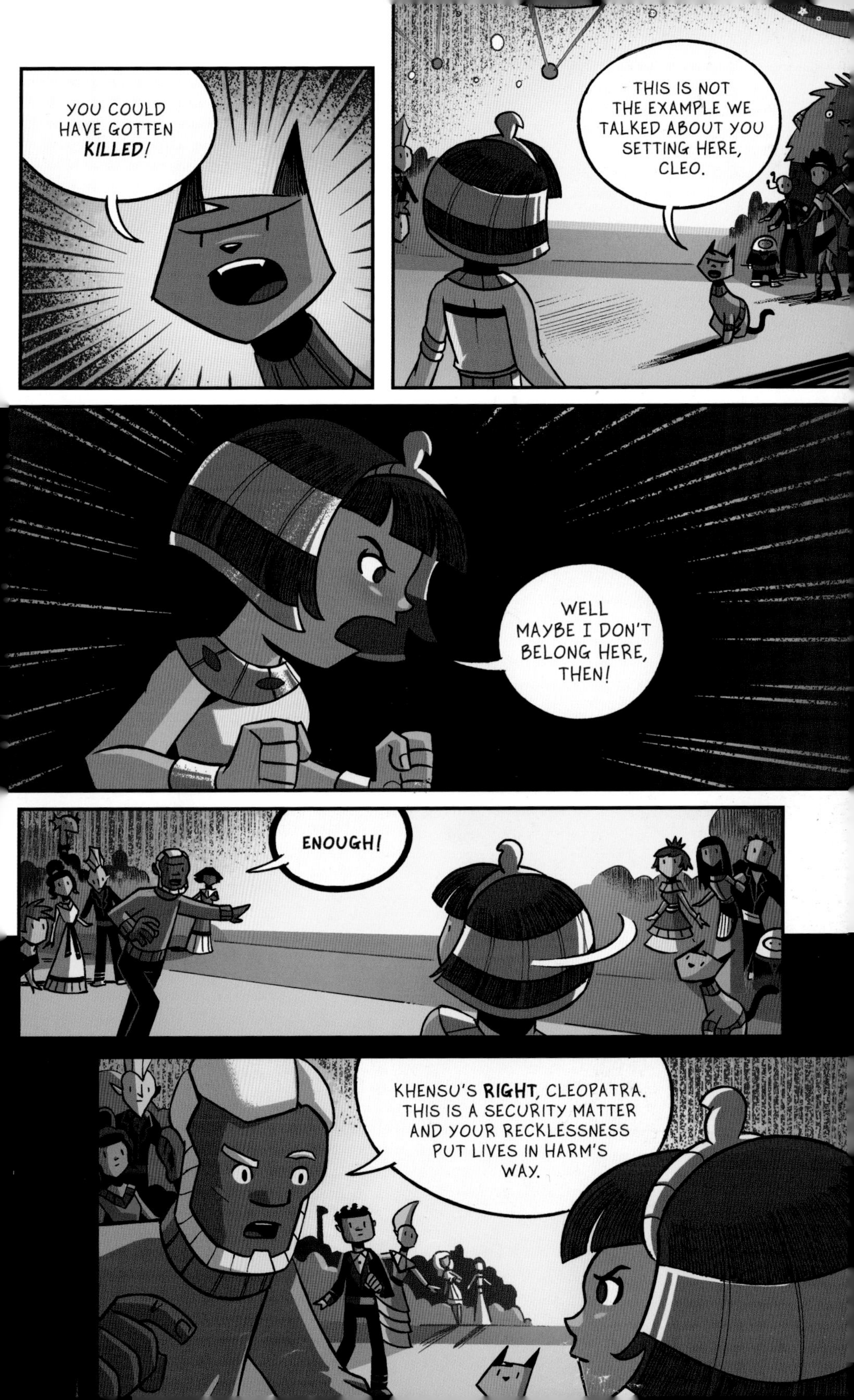
YOU COULD HAVE GOTTEN KILLED!
THIS IS NOT THE EXAMPLE WE TALKED ABOUT YOU SETTING HERE, CLEO.
WELL MAYBE I DON'T BELONG HERE, THEN!
ENOUGH!
KHENSU'S RIGHT, CLEOPATRA. THIS IS A SECURITY MATTER AND YOUR RECKLESSNESS PUT LIVES IN HARM'S WAY.

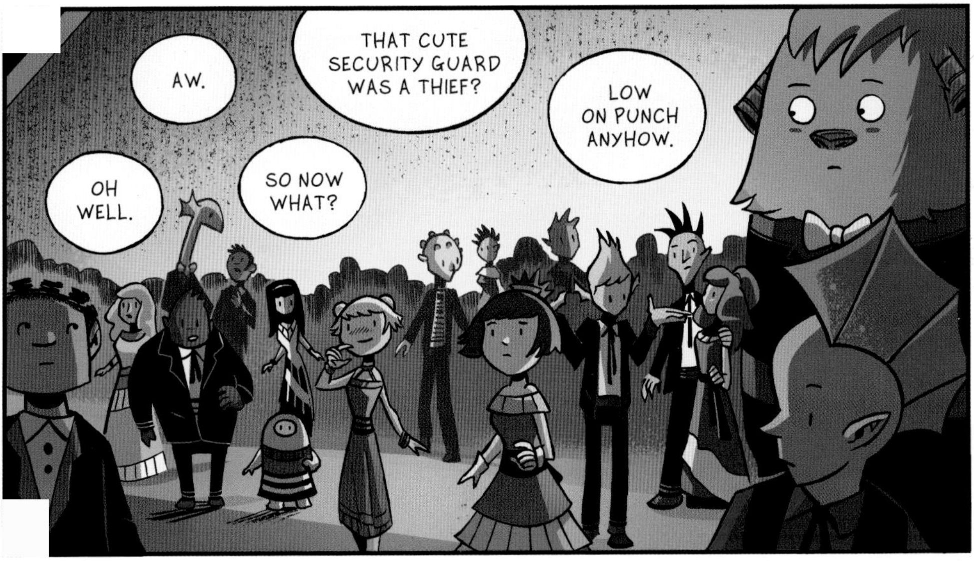
OH WELL.
AW.
SO NOW WHAT?
THAT CUTE SECURITY GUARD WAS A THIEF?
LOW ON PUNCH ANYHOW.

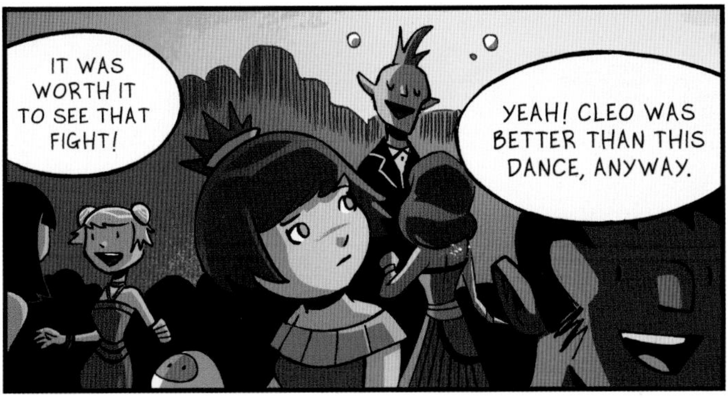
IT WAS WORTH IT TO SEE THAT FIGHT!
YEAH! CLEO WAS BETTER THAN THIS DANCE, ANYWAY.

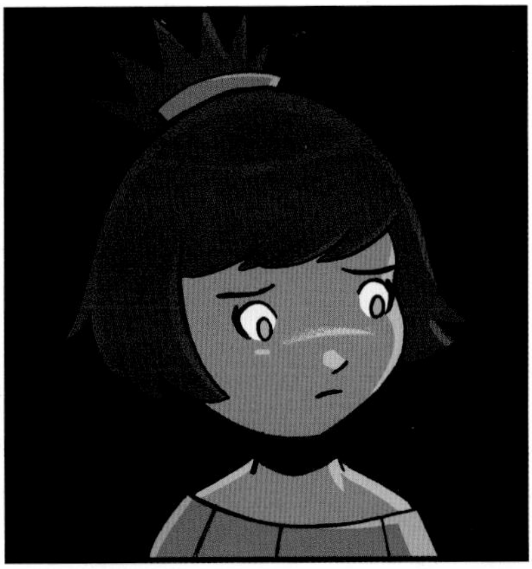

CHAPTER TWO

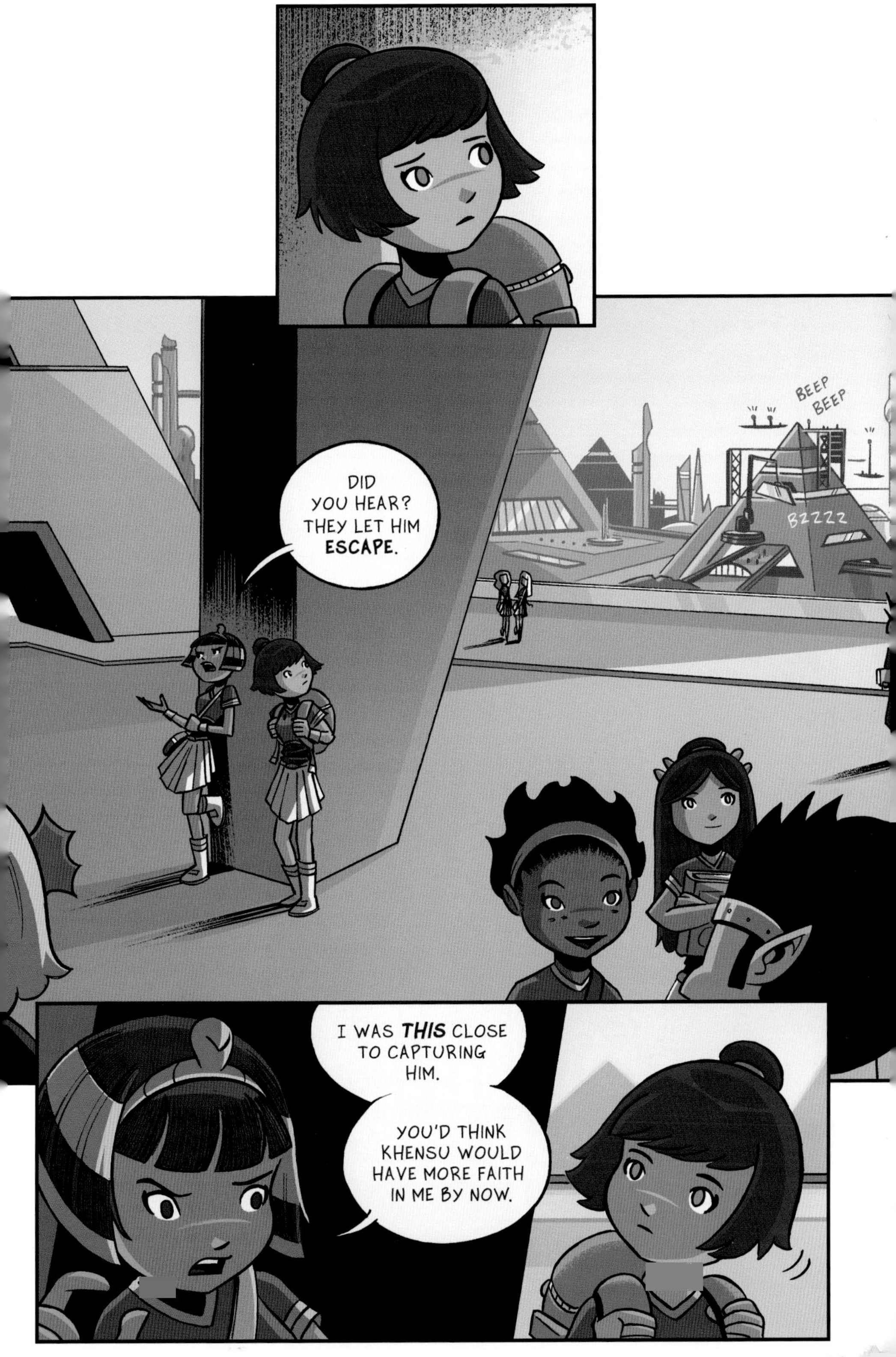
BEEP BEEP
BZZZZ
DID YOU HEAR? THEY LET HIM ESCAPE.
I WAS THIS CLOSE TO CAPTURING HIM.
YOU'D THINK KHENSU WOULD HAVE MORE FAITH IN ME BY NOW.

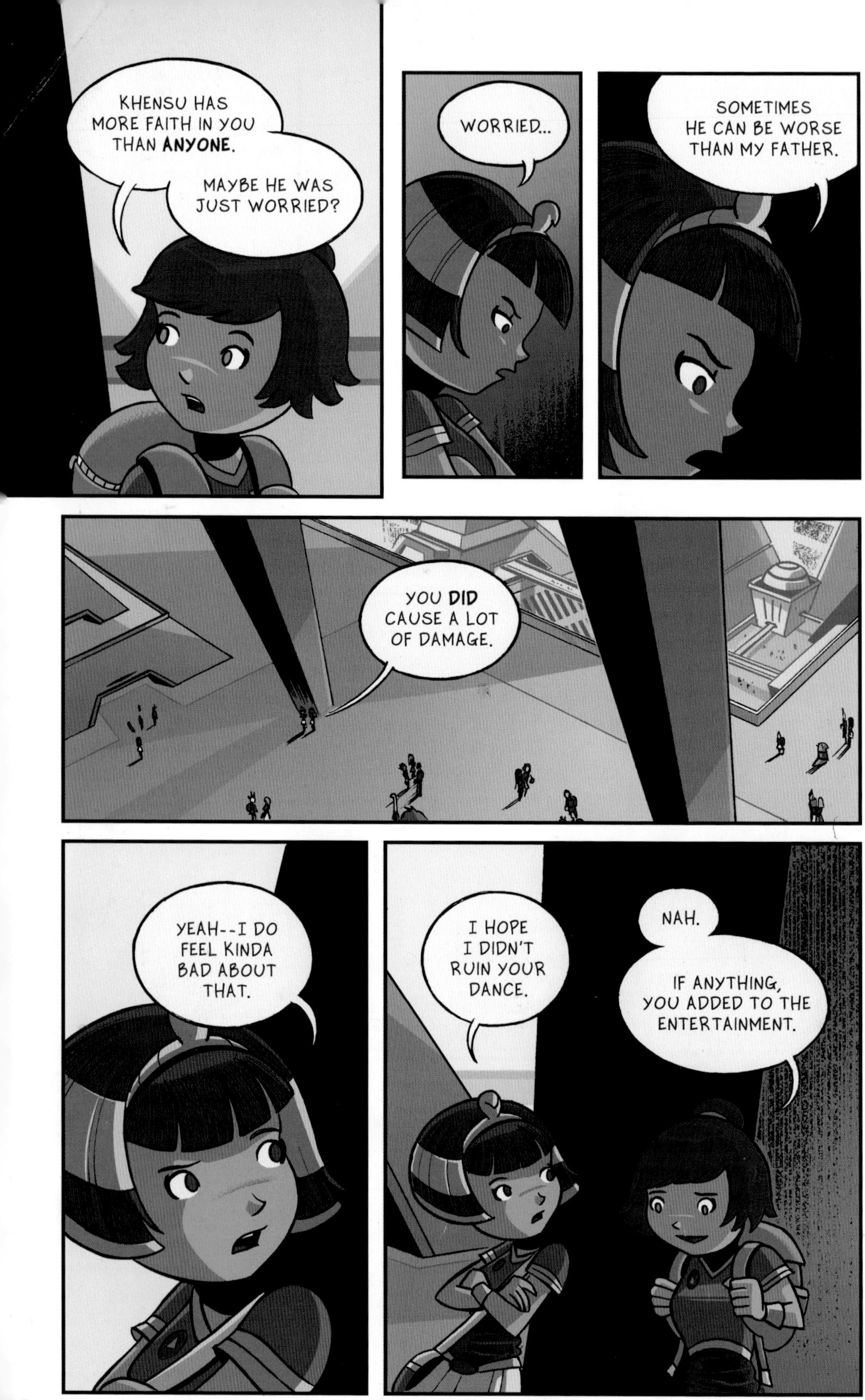
KHENSU HAS MORE FAITH IN YOU THAN **ANYONE**.
MAYBE HE WAS JUST WORRIED?
WORRIED...
SOMETIMES HE CAN BE WORSE THAN MY FATHER.
YOU **DID** CAUSE A LOT OF DAMAGE.
YEAH--I DO FEEL KINDA BAD ABOUT THAT.
I HOPE I DIDN'T RUIN YOUR DANCE.
NAH.
IF ANYTHING, YOU ADDED TO THE ENTERTAINMENT.

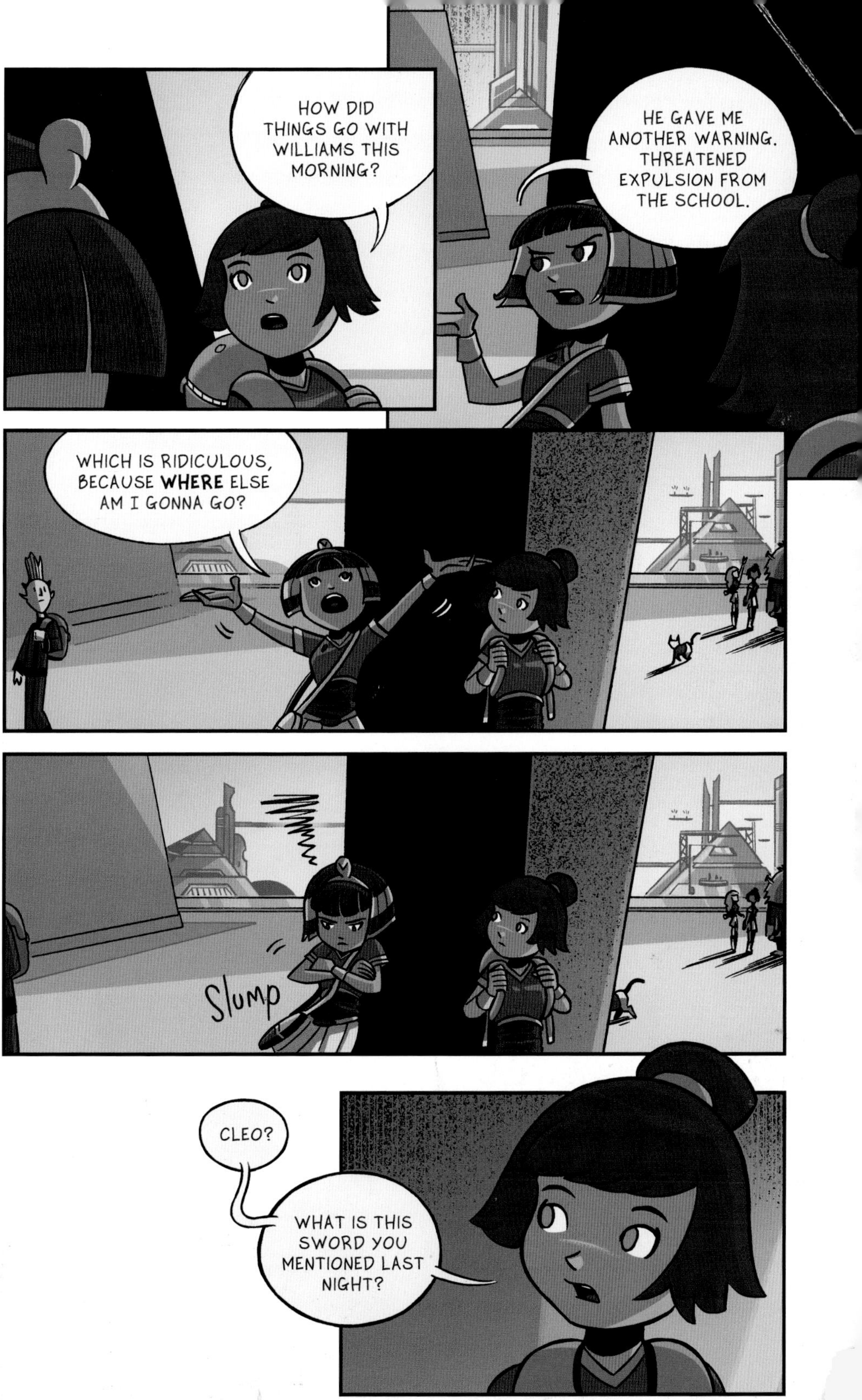
HOW DID THINGS GO WITH WILLIAMS THIS MORNING?
HE GAVE ME ANOTHER WARNING. THREATENED EXPULSION FROM THE SCHOOL.
WHICH IS RIDICULOUS, BECAUSE **WHERE** ELSE AM I GONNA GO?
Slump
CLEO?
WHAT IS THIS SWORD YOU MENTIONED LAST NIGHT?

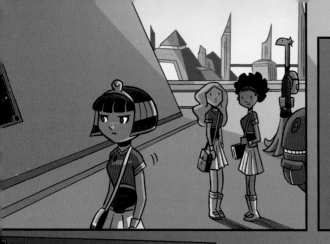

CLEOPATRA HAS ARRIVED!

REMEMBER THE WORDS
OF THE SCROLL
(PHARAOH YASIRO TRANSLATION)

A HERO WILL ARRIVE FROM EARTH.
DAUGHTER OF AULETES, DESCENDANT OF SOTER.
WHEN THE MOON OF DUAT HAS TOUCHED ITS PEAK
ON THE EVE OF THE GOLDEN LION.

SHE WILL WEAR THE CROWN OF THE IBIS.
SHE WILL JOIN IN YOUR FIGHT.
SHE WILL CONTAIN LOST KNOWLEDGE.
SHE WILL OFFER HOPE FROM YOUR BLIGHT.
THE SERPENT WILL FALL BY HER SWORD.
THE APE WILL COWER BY HER MIGHT.
THE SPIDER WILL GROW DEAF BY HER WORD.
THE JACKAL WILL COLLAPSE BY HER SIGHT.

SHE WILL COMMAND THE ARMIES OF FIRE.
SHE WILL COMMAND THE NIGHT.
SHE WILL EXTINGUISH AN EMPIRE.
SHE WILL PUT AN END TO THEIR PLIGHT.
FEAR HAS BEEN BANISHED.
BLACKNESS BURNS WHITE.
SING PRAISES TO THE QUEEN OF THE NILE!
FOR SHE HAS TURNED DARKNESS TO LIGHT.

CLEO!

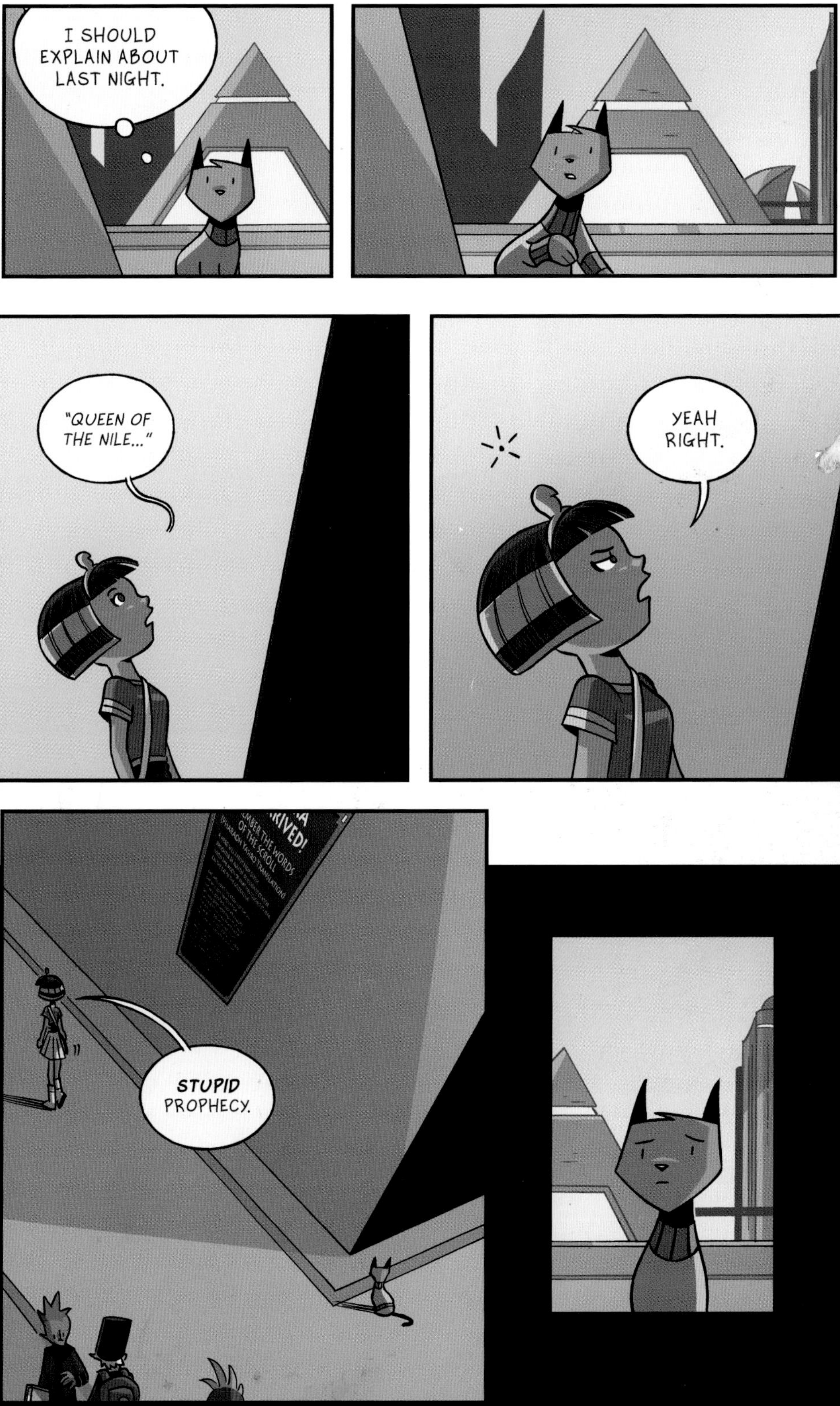
I SHOULD EXPLAIN ABOUT LAST NIGHT.
"QUEEN OF THE NILE..."
YEAH RIGHT.
STUPID PROPHECY.

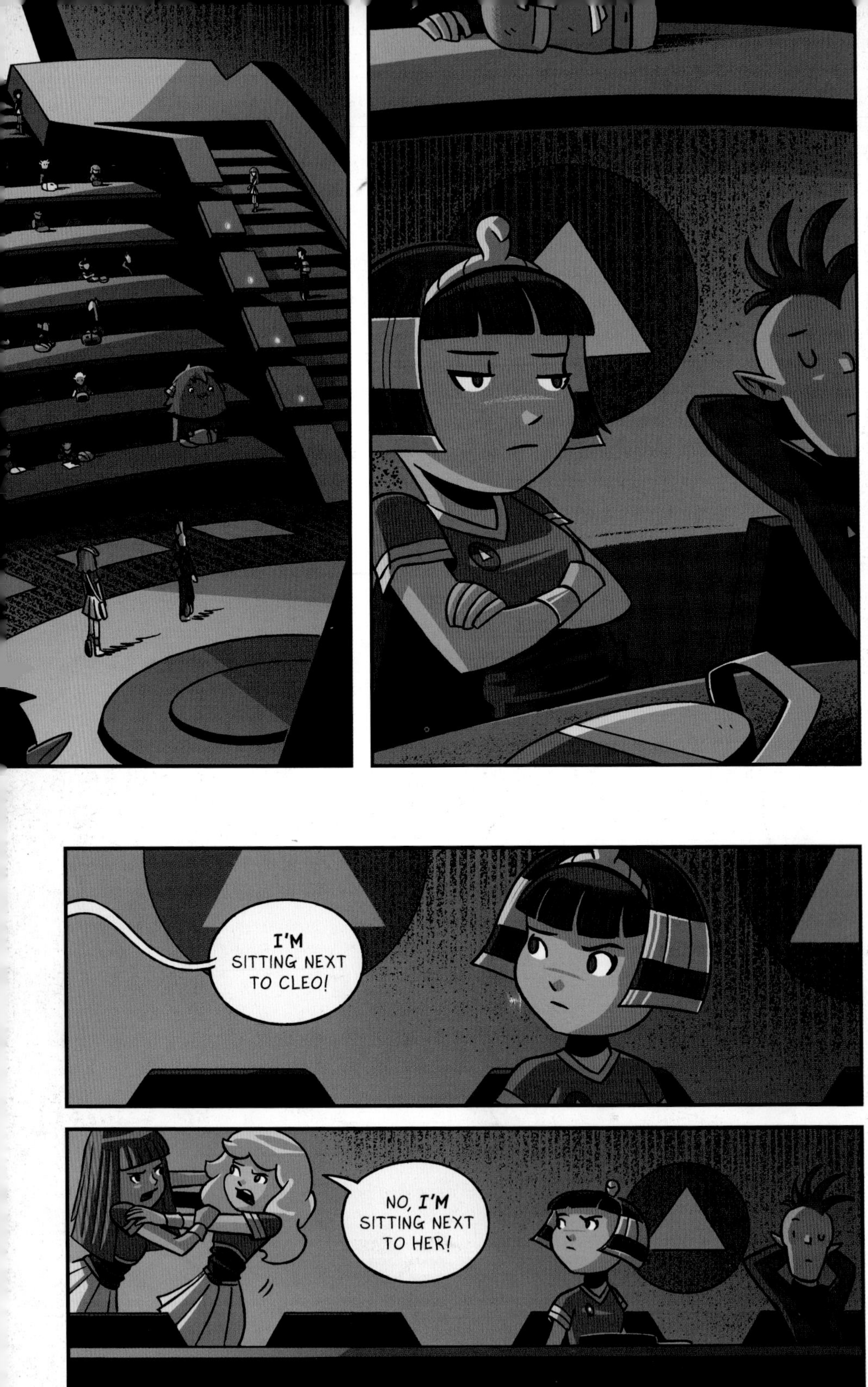
I'M SITTING NEXT TO CLEO!
NO, I'M SITTING NEXT TO HER!

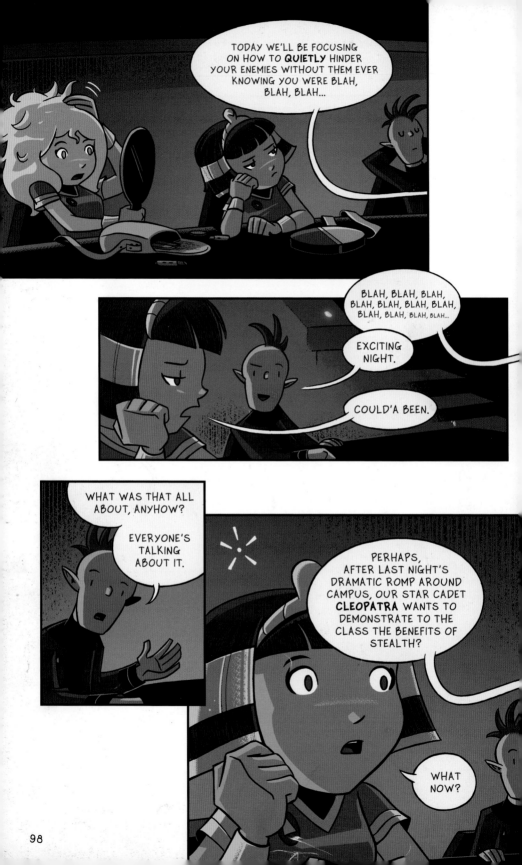

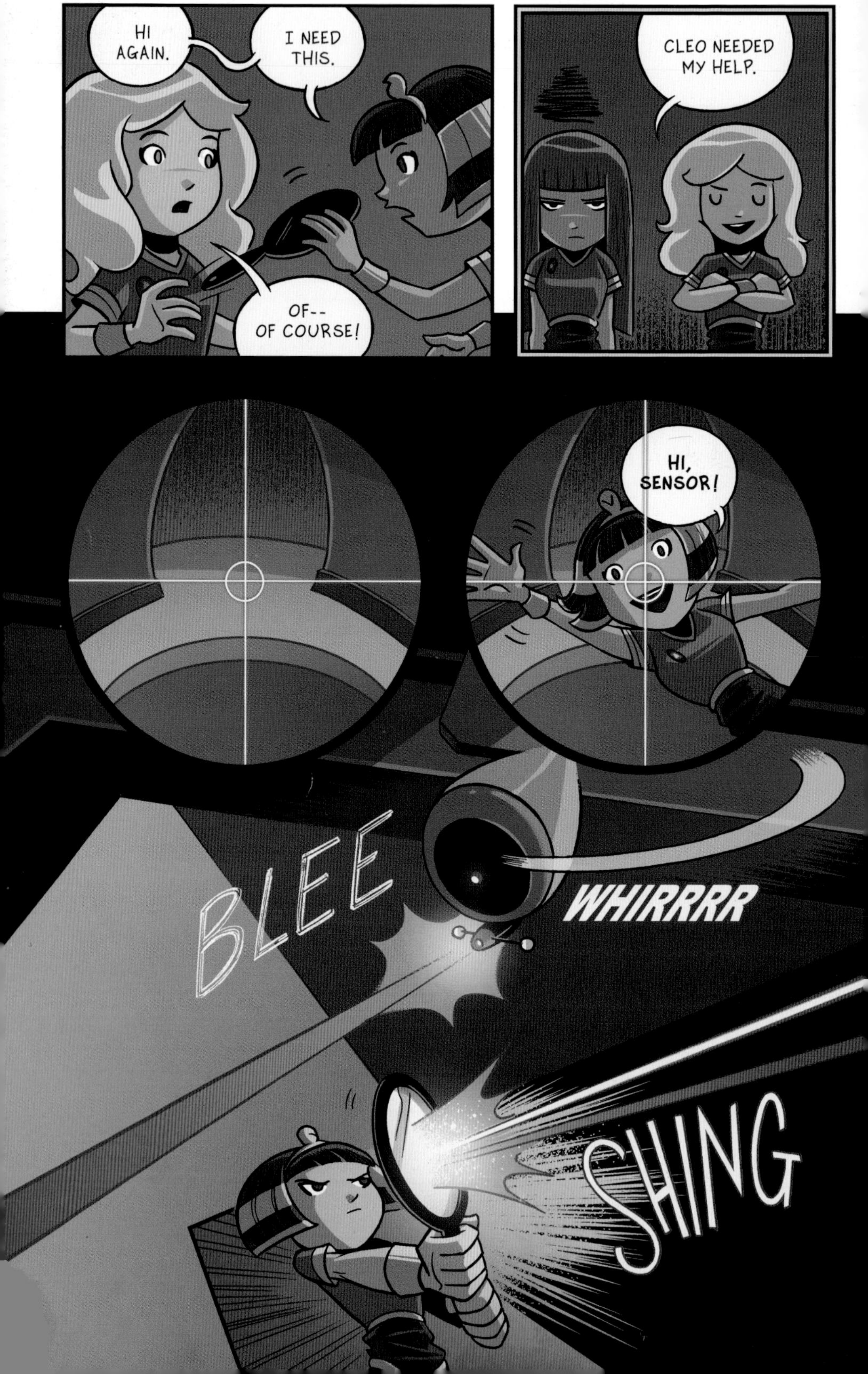
HI AGAIN.
I NEED THIS.
OF-- OF COURSE!
CLEO NEEDED MY HELP.
HI, SENSOR!
BLEE
WHIRRRR
SHING

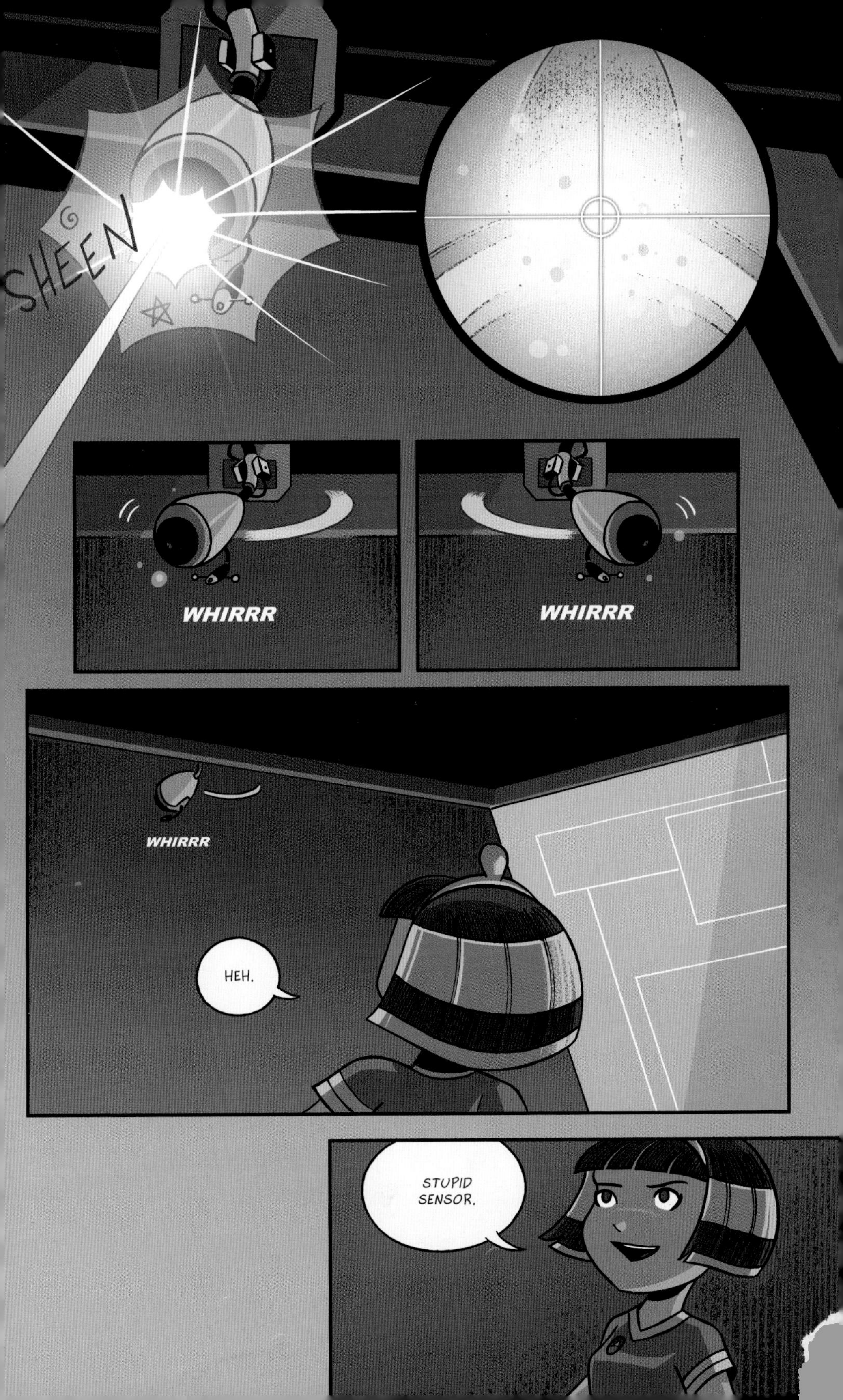
SHEEN
WHIRRR
WHIRRR
WHIRRR
HEH.
STUPID SENSOR.

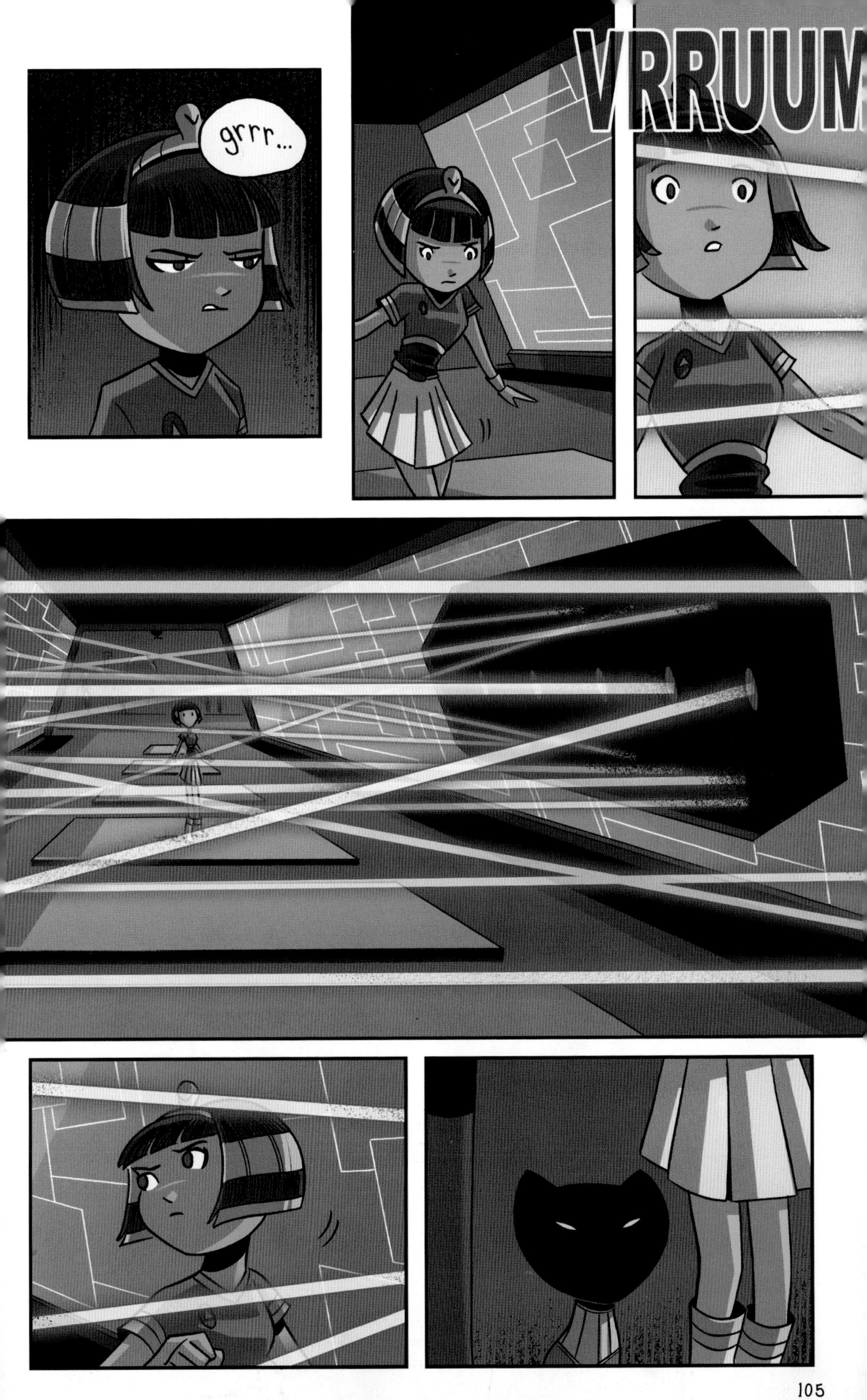
grrr...
VRRUUM

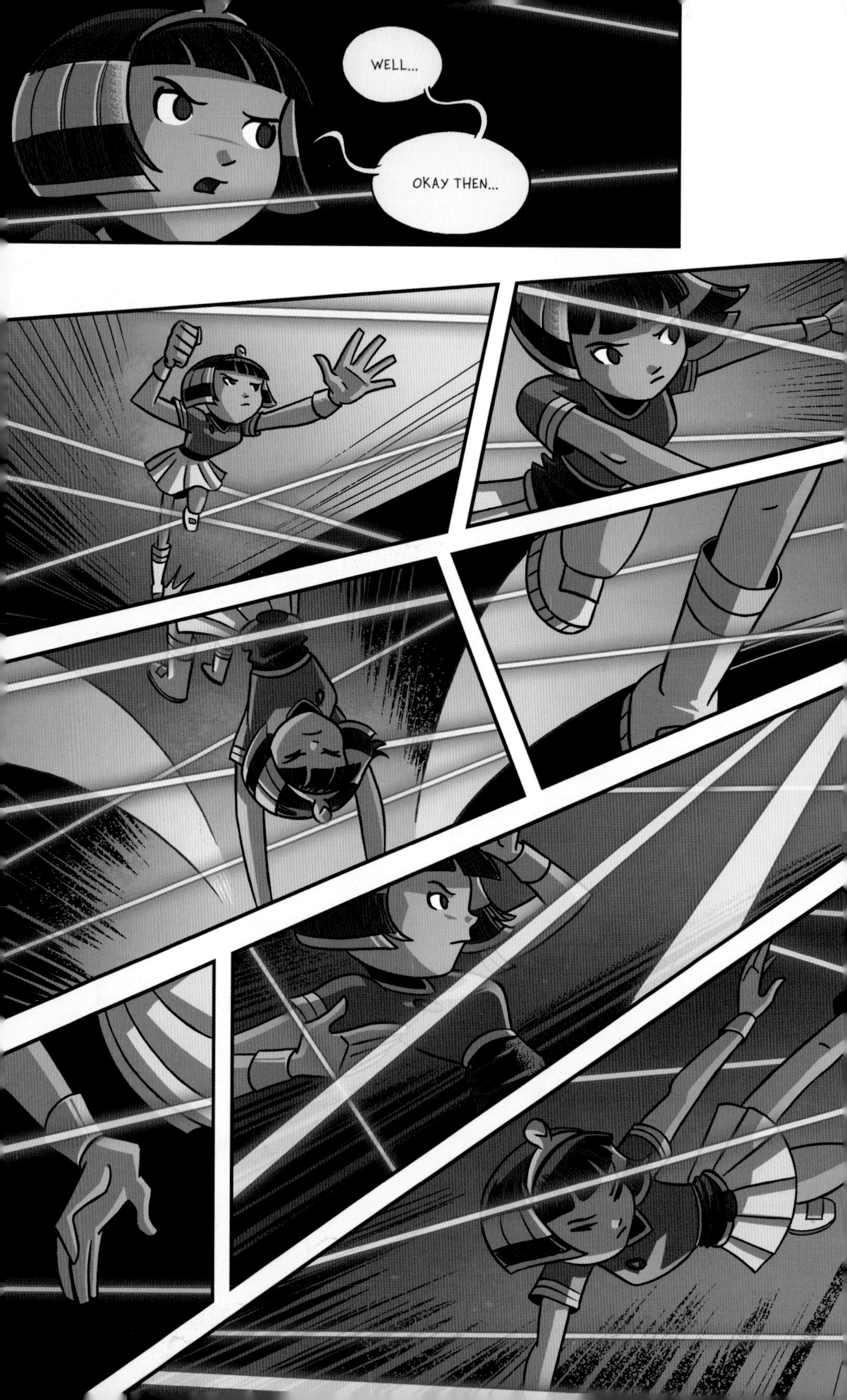
WELL...
OKAY THEN...

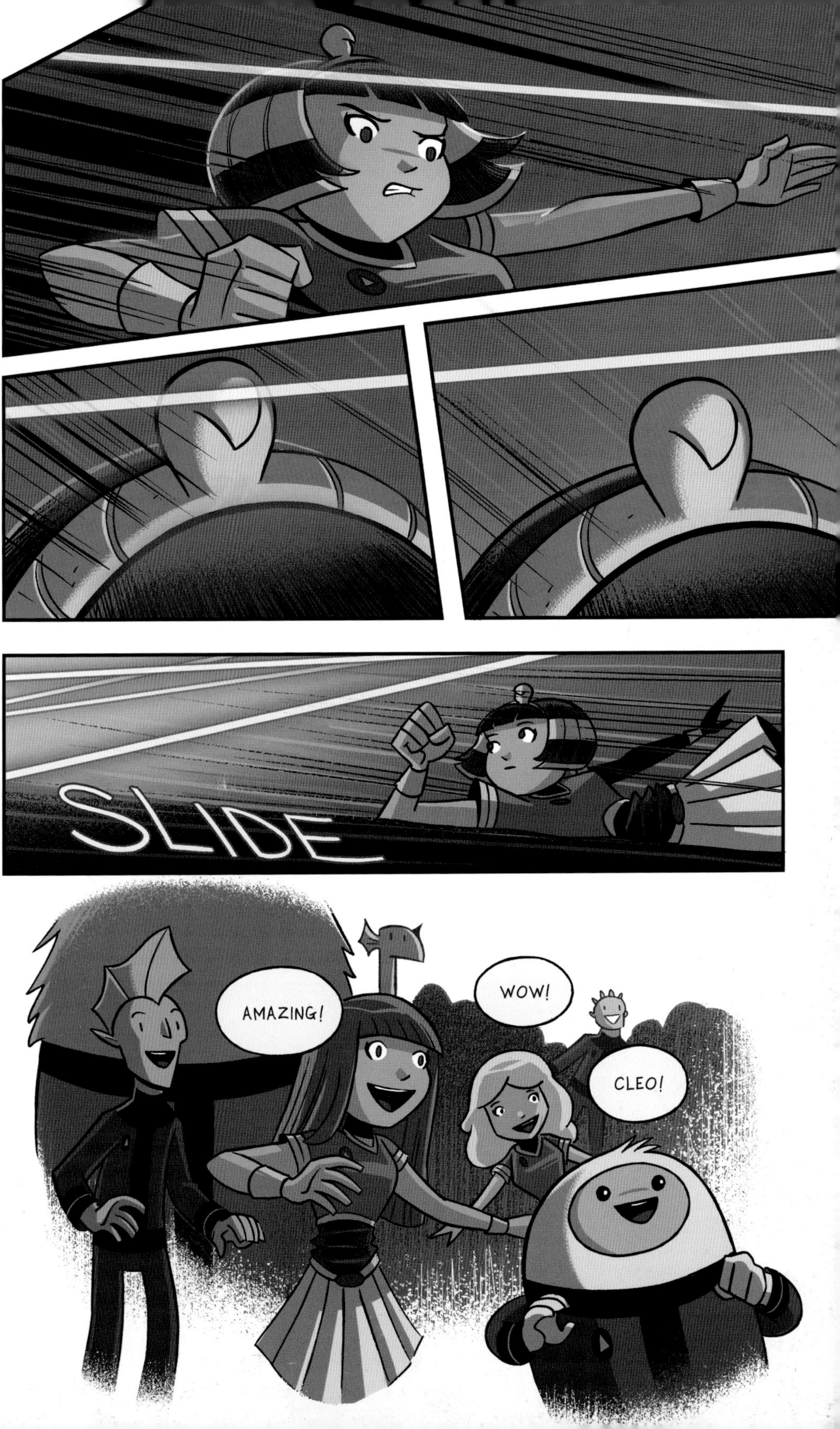
SLIDE
AMAZING!
WOW!
CLEO!

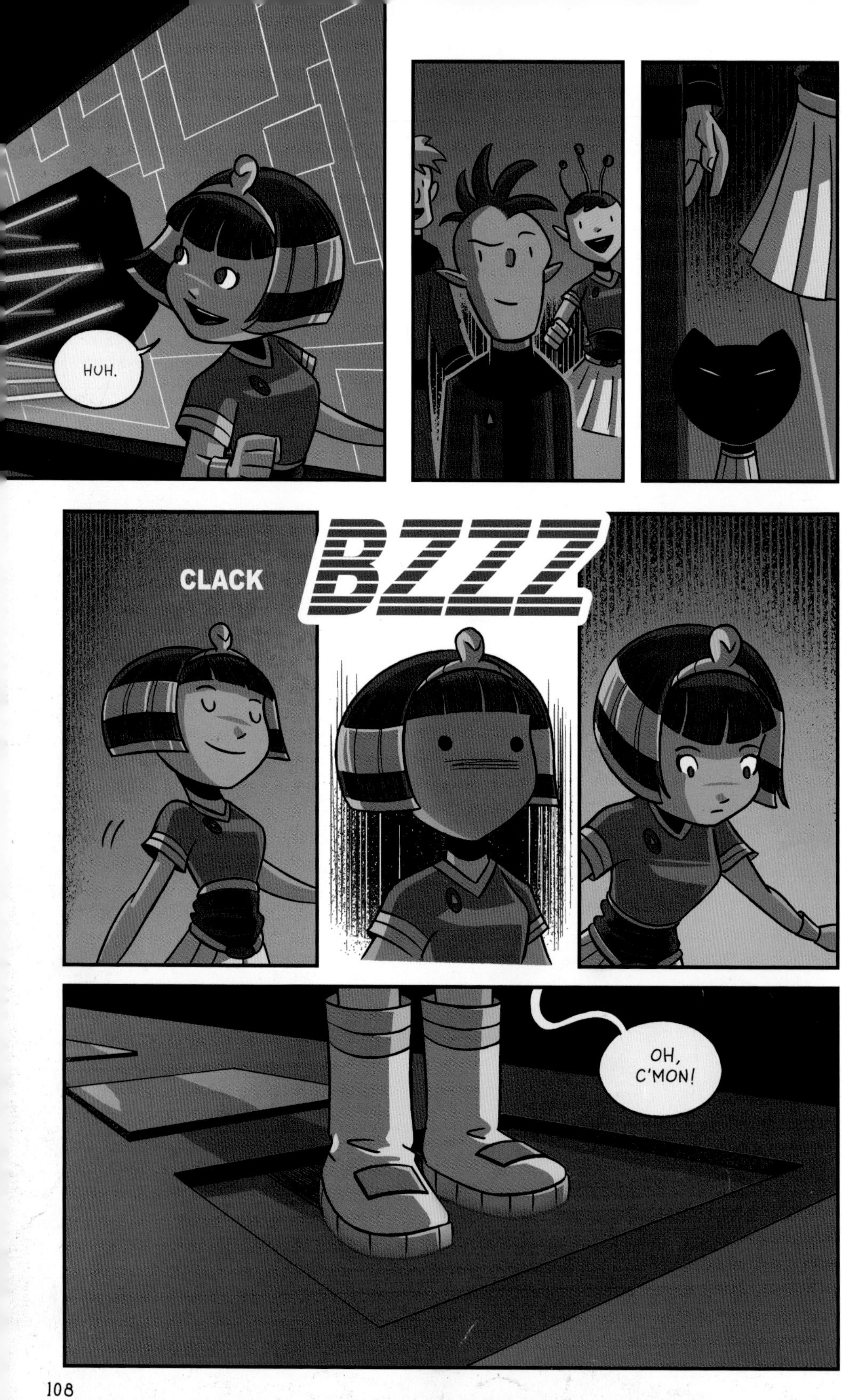
HUH.
CLACK
BZZZ
OH, C'MON!

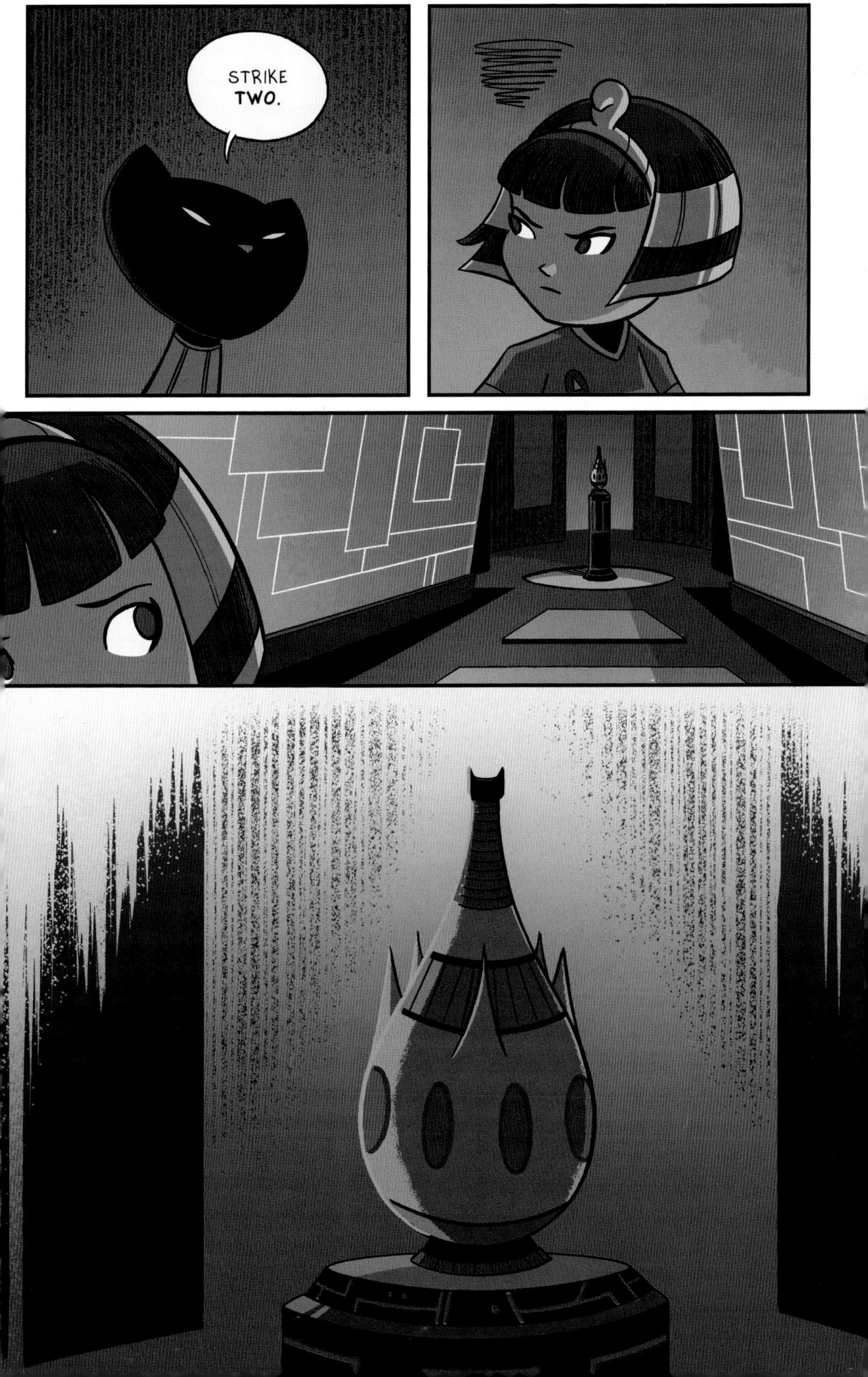
STRIKE
TWO.

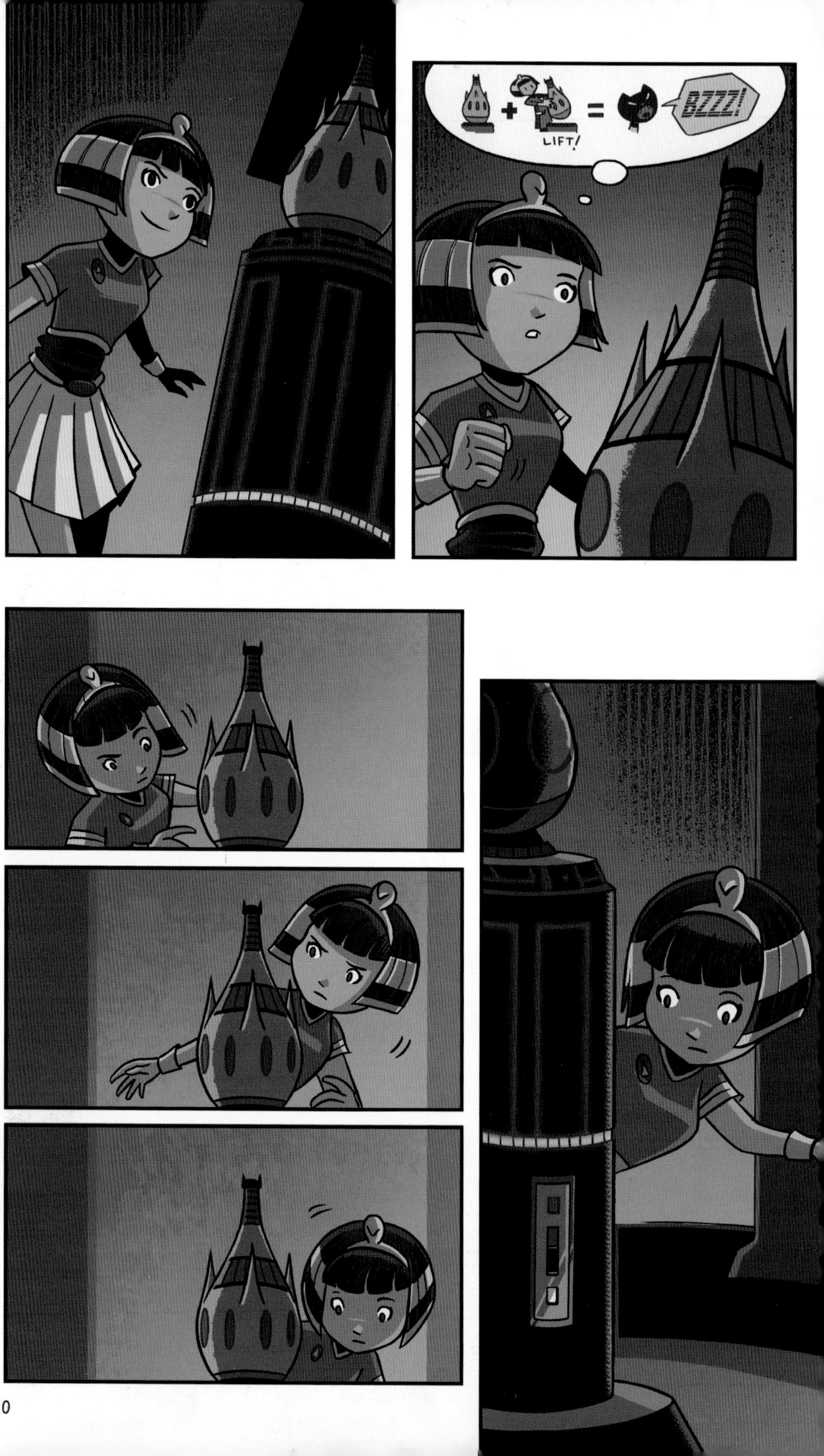
LIFT!
BZZZ!

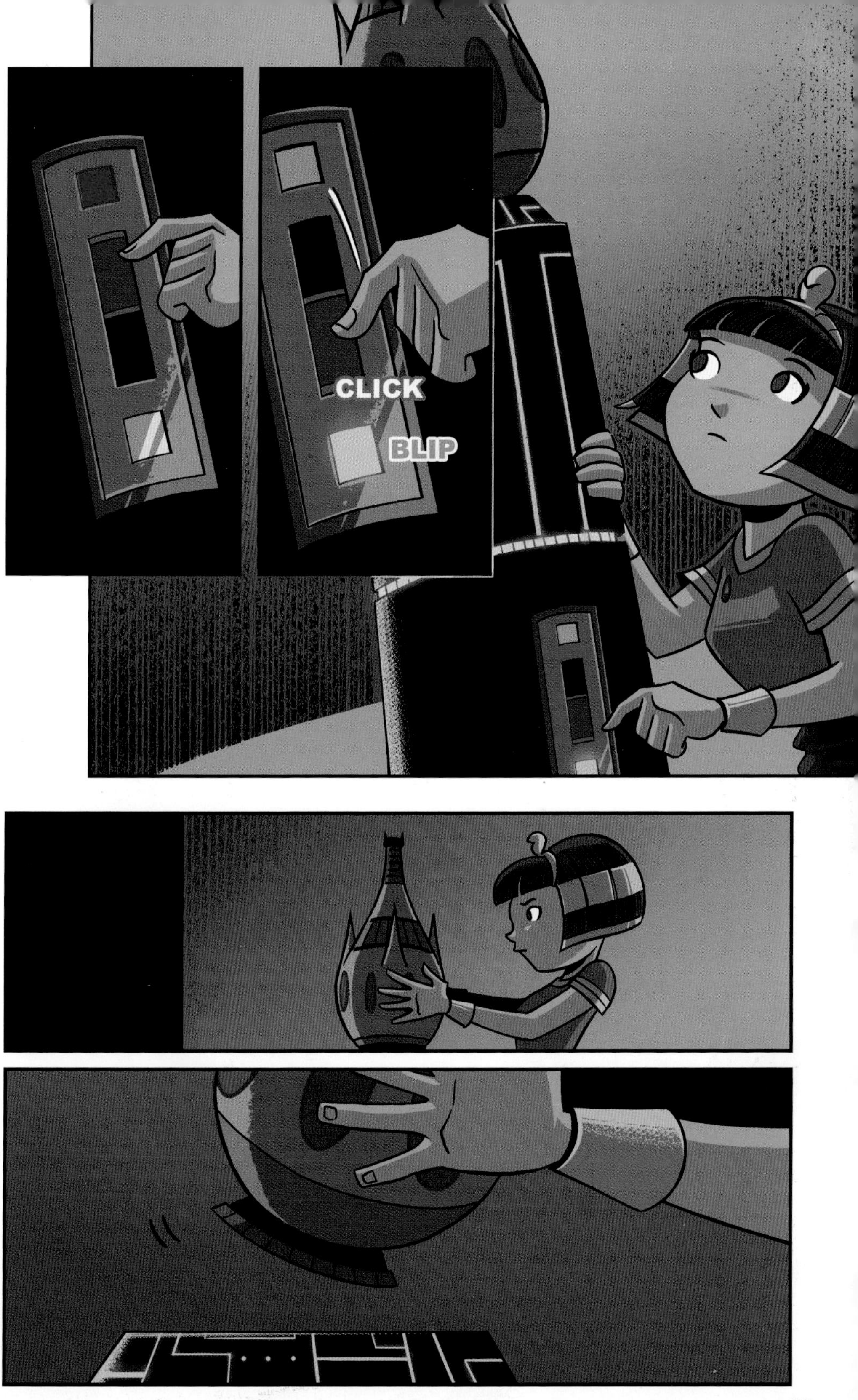
CLICK
BLIP

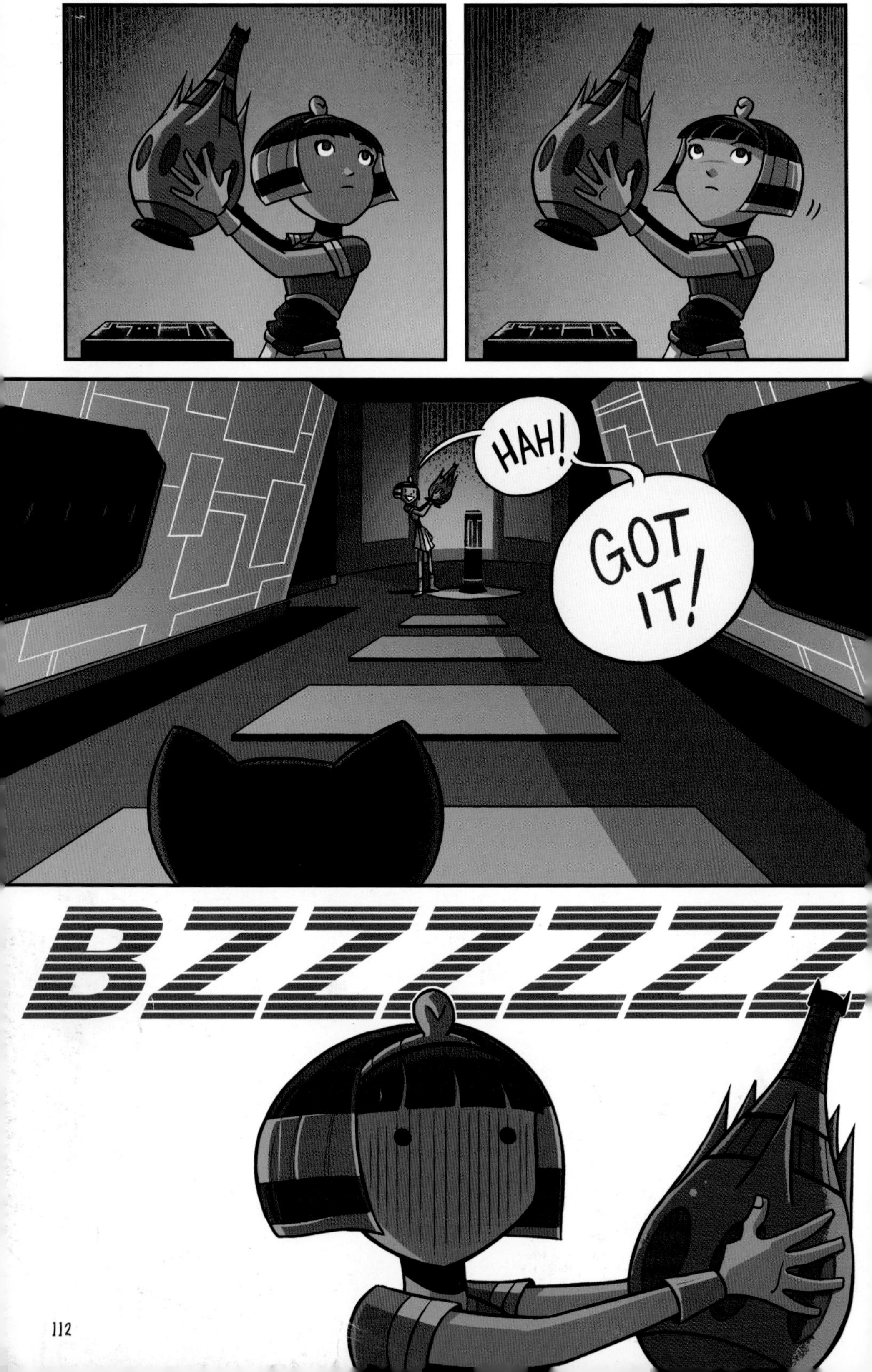
HAH!
GOT IT!
BZZZZZ

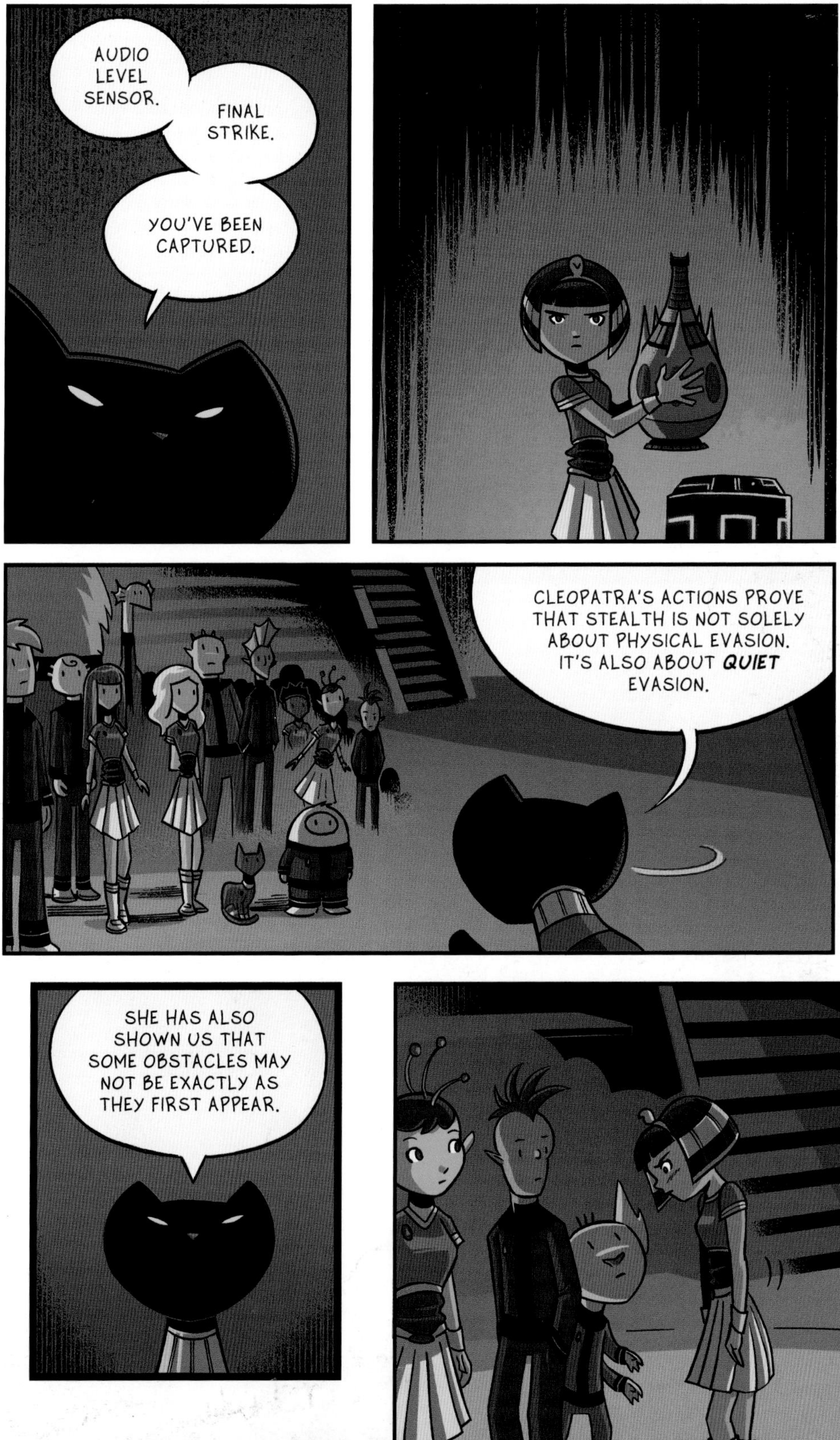
AUDIO LEVEL SENSOR.
FINAL STRIKE.
YOU'VE BEEN CAPTURED.
CLEOPATRA'S ACTIONS PROVE THAT STEALTH IS NOT SOLELY ABOUT PHYSICAL EVASION. IT'S ALSO ABOUT **QUIET** EVASION.
SHE HAS ALSO SHOWN US THAT SOME OBSTACLES MAY NOT BE EXACTLY AS THEY FIRST APPEAR.

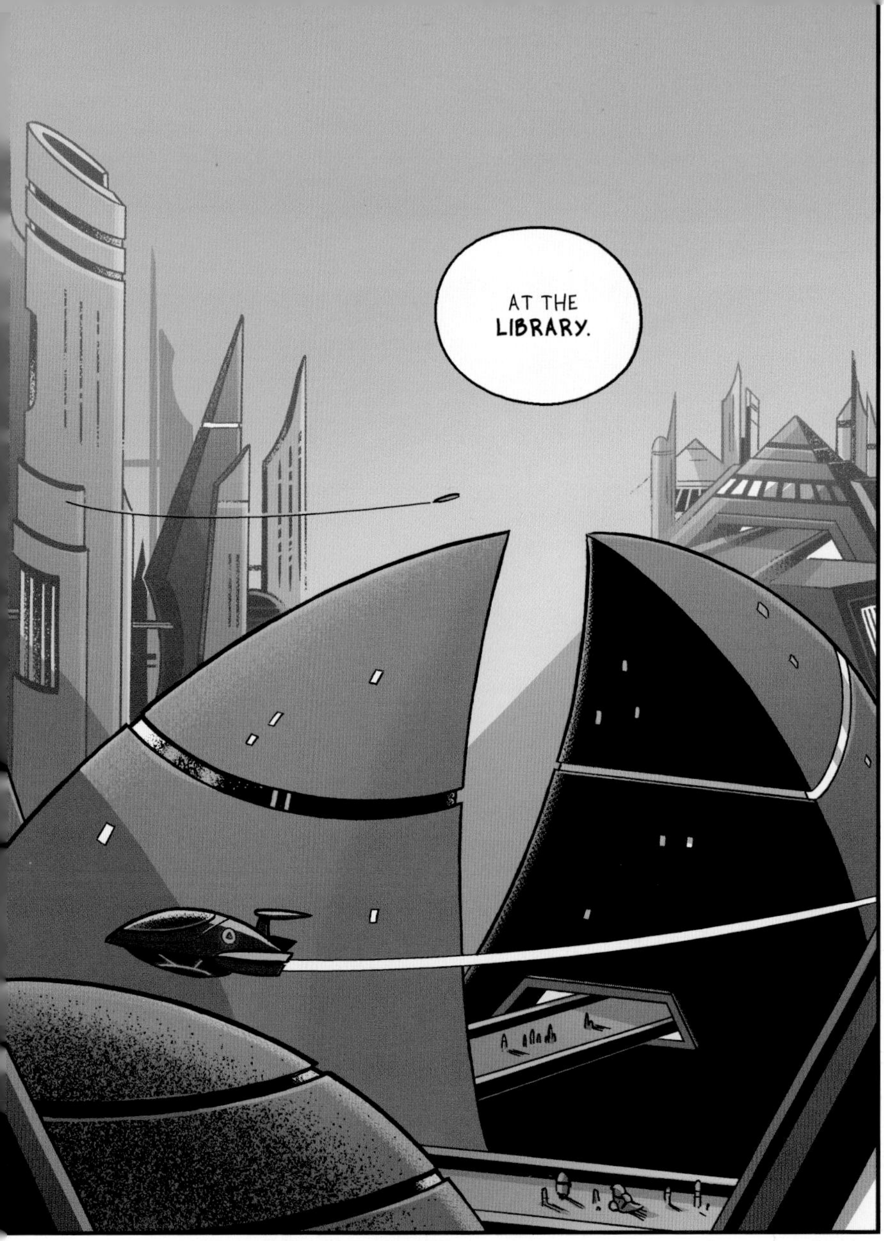
AT THE LIBRARY.

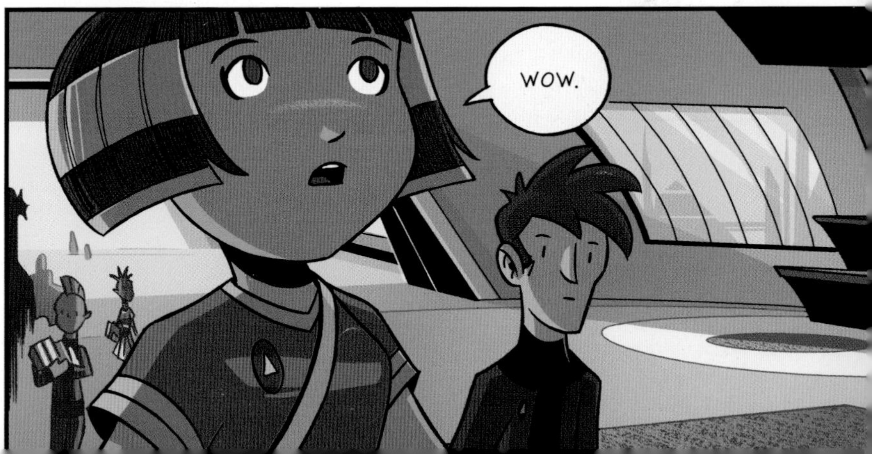
WOW.

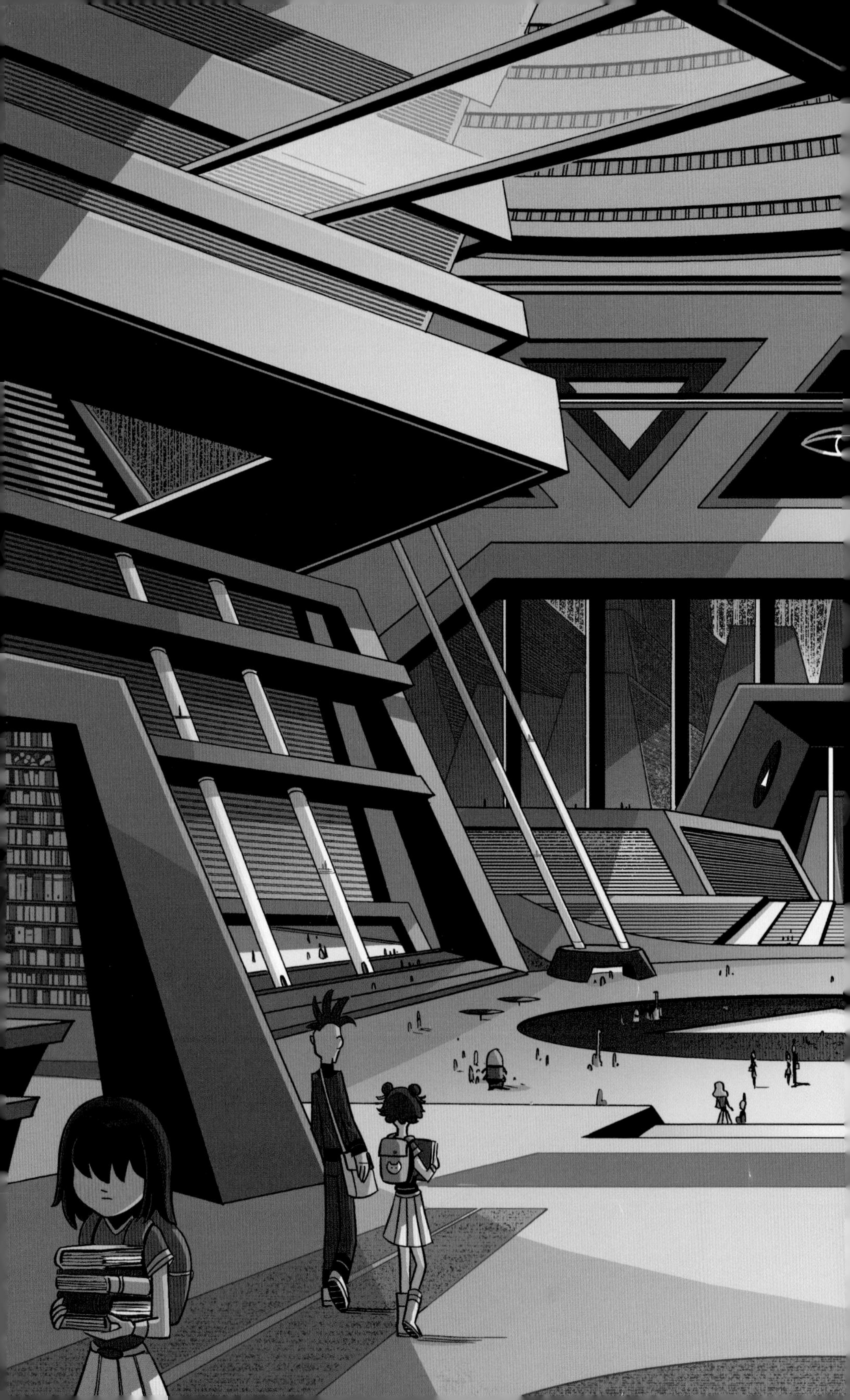

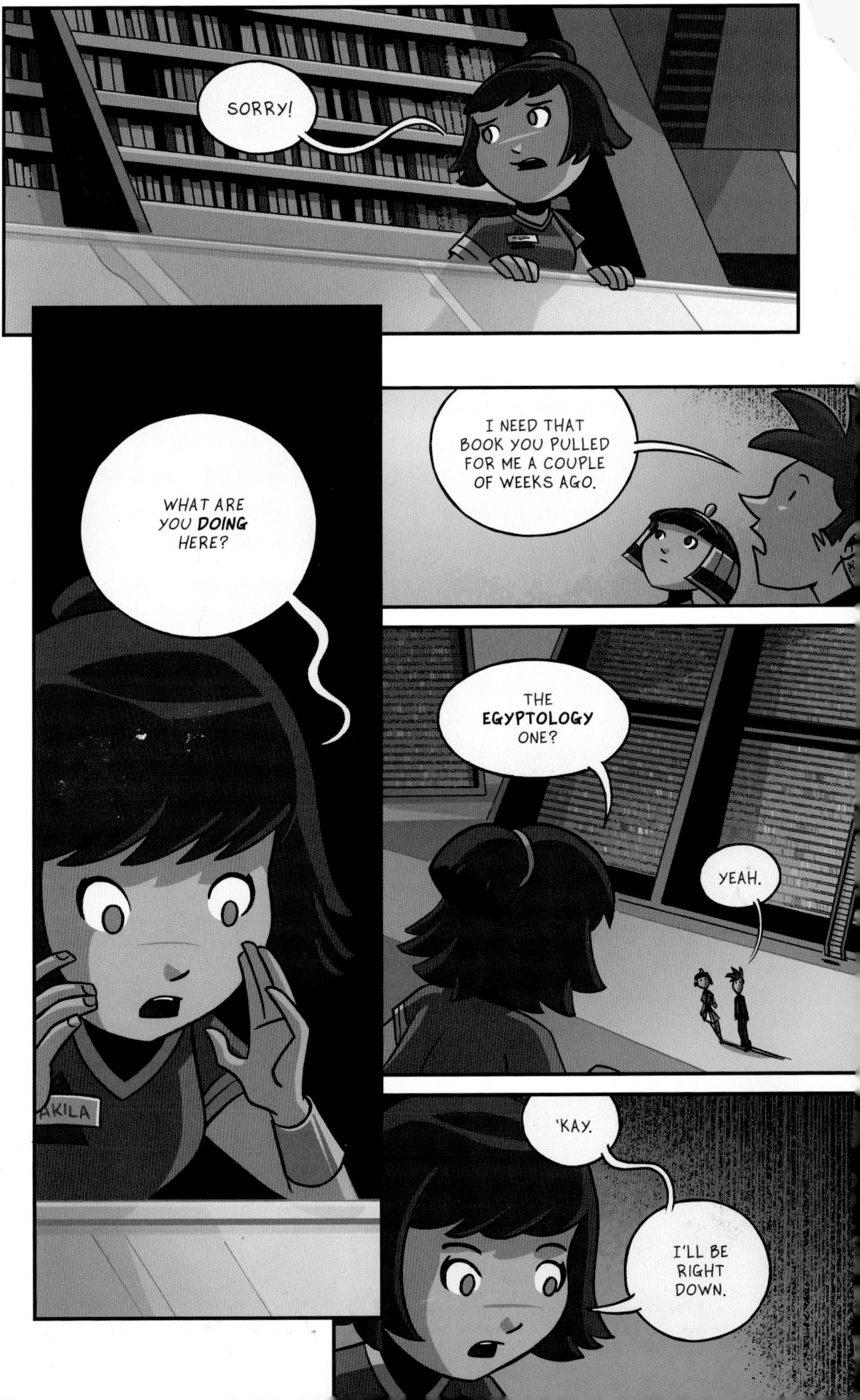
SORRY!
WHAT ARE YOU **DOING** HERE?
I NEED THAT BOOK YOU PULLED FOR ME A COUPLE OF WEEKS AGO.
THE **EGYPTOLOGY** ONE?
YEAH.
'KAY.
I'LL BE RIGHT DOWN.
AKILA

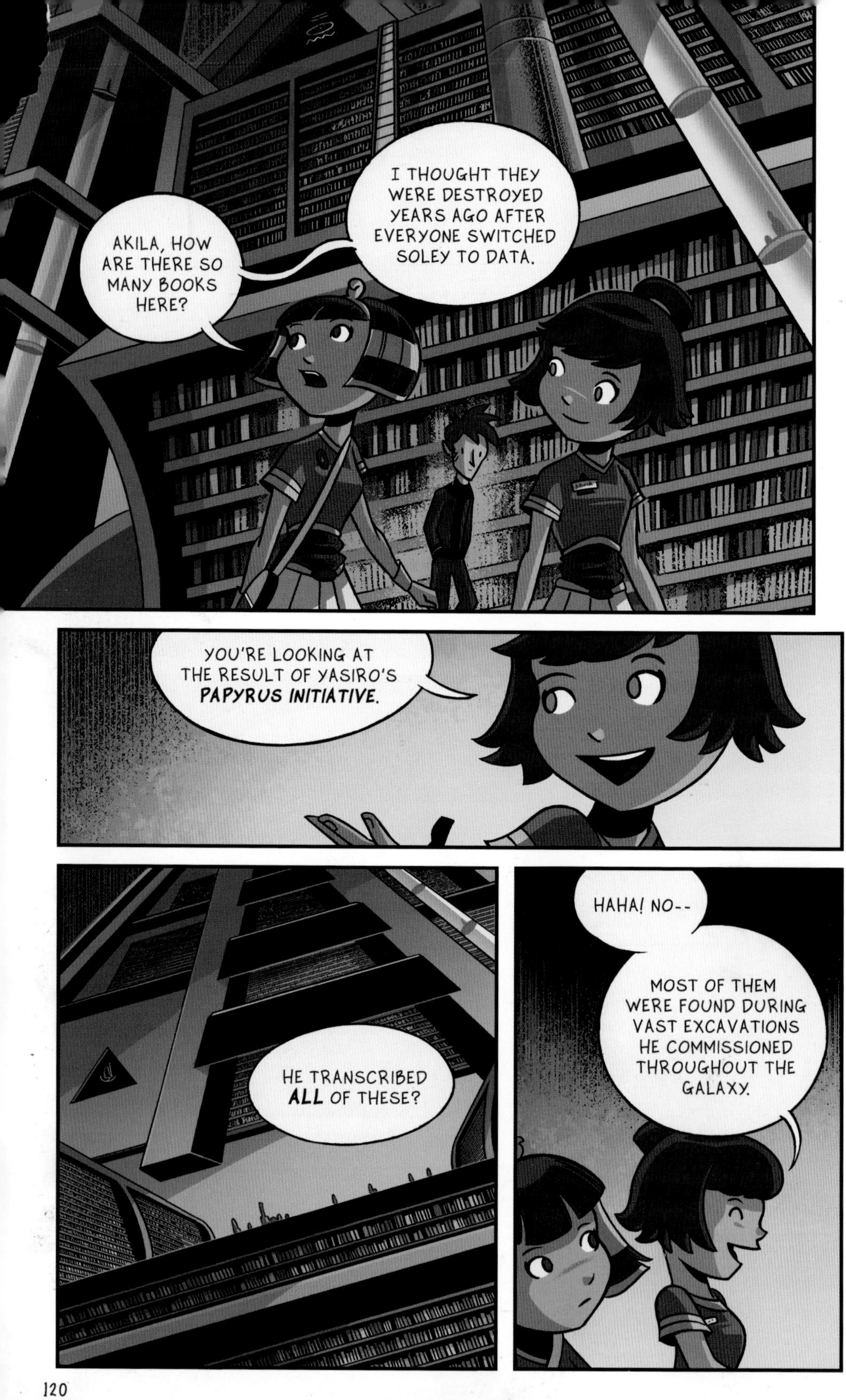
AKILA, HOW ARE THERE SO MANY BOOKS HERE?
I THOUGHT THEY WERE DESTROYED YEARS AGO AFTER EVERYONE SWITCHED SOLEY TO DATA.
YOU'RE LOOKING AT THE RESULT OF YASIRO'S **PAPYRUS INITIATIVE**.
HE TRANSCRIBED **ALL** OF THESE?
HAHA! NO--
MOST OF THEM WERE FOUND DURING VAST EXCAVATIONS HE COMMISSIONED THROUGHOUT THE GALAXY.

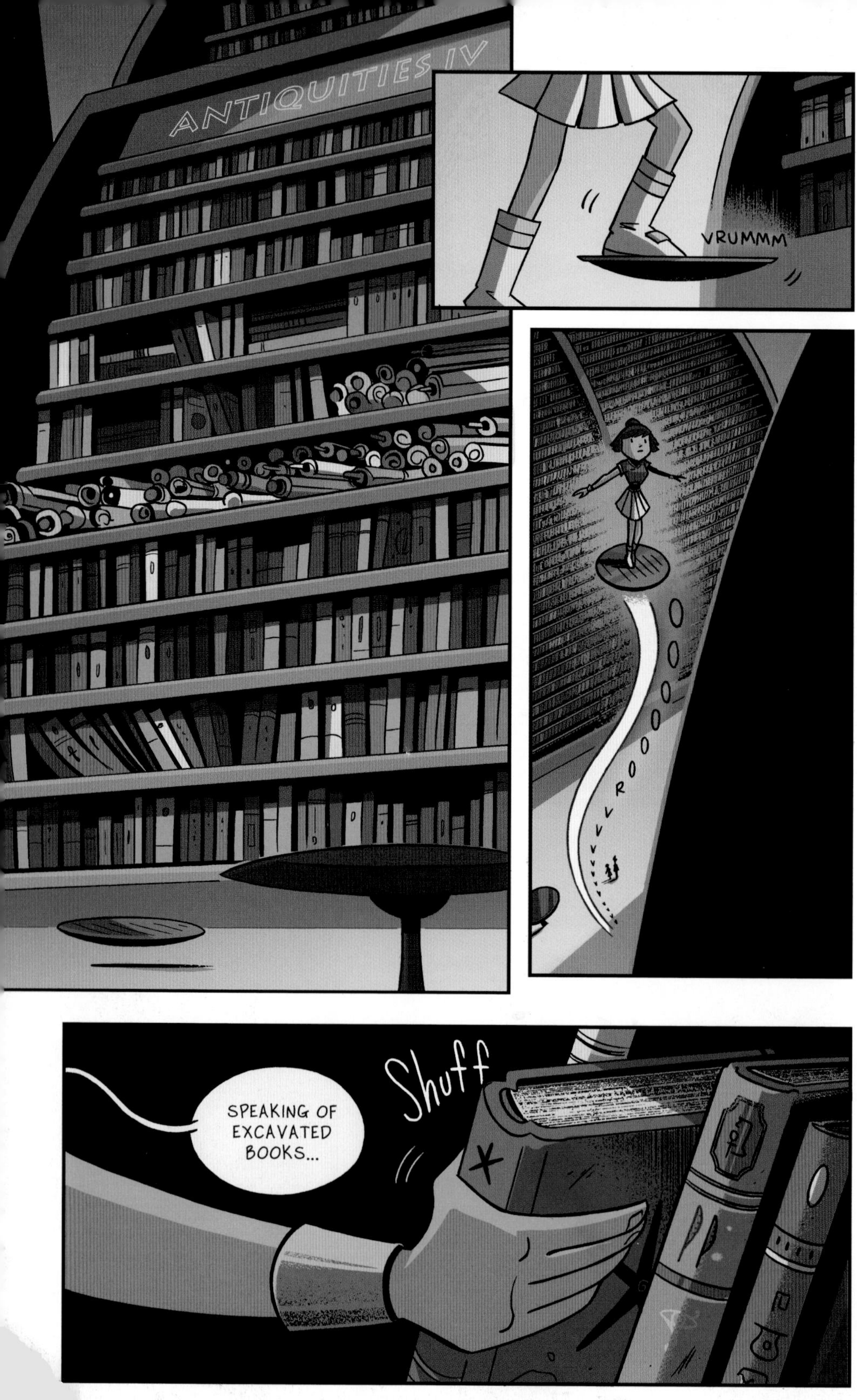
ANTIQUITIES IV
VRUMMM
VVVLROOOOOOO
Shuff
SPEAKING OF EXCAVATED BOOKS...

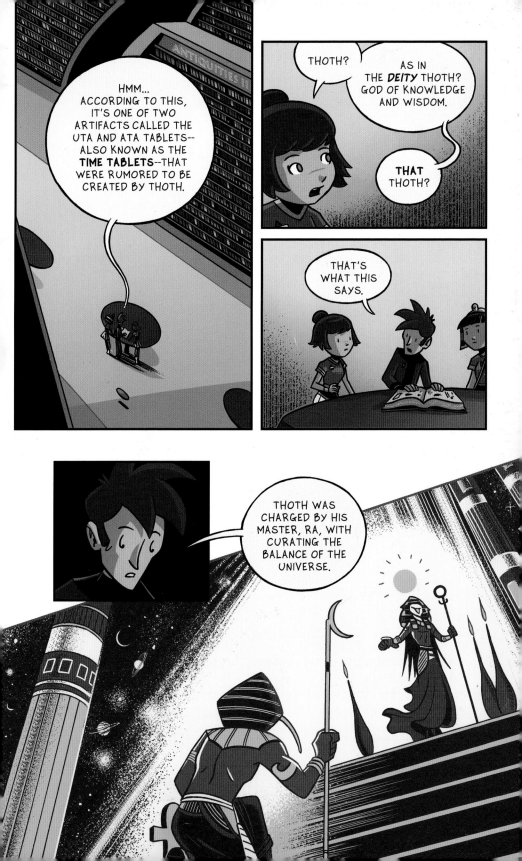

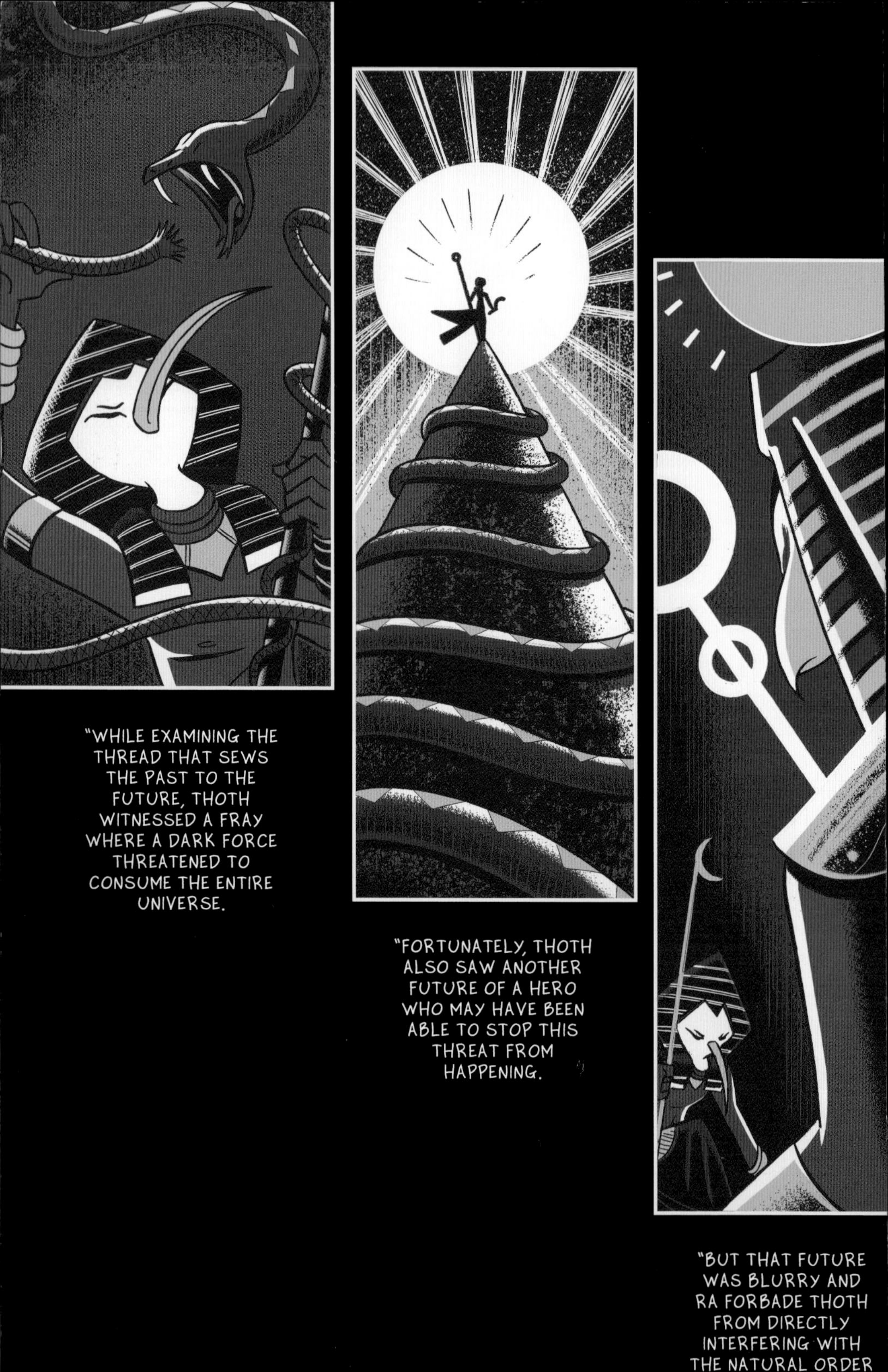
"WHILE EXAMINING THE THREAD THAT SEWS THE PAST TO THE FUTURE, THOTH WITNESSED A FRAY WHERE A DARK FORCE THREATENED TO CONSUME THE ENTIRE UNIVERSE.
"FORTUNATELY, THOTH ALSO SAW ANOTHER FUTURE OF A HERO WHO MAY HAVE BEEN ABLE TO STOP THIS THREAT FROM HAPPENING.
"BUT THAT FUTURE WAS BLURRY AND RA FORBADE THOTH FROM DIRECTLY INTERFERING WITH THE NATURAL ORDER

"HE THEN RETREATED TO THE MOON OF DUAT TO REGAIN HIS POWERS AND AWAIT THE HERO'S ARRIVAL."

"AT THE COST OF MOST OF HIS STRENGTH, THOTH EMBEDDED EACH TABLET WITH A PHYSICAL CONNECTION TO HIMSELF AND PLACED THEM AT THE BEGINNING OF CREATION--ONLY TO BE ACTIVATED IF THE RIGHT HERO CAME INTO CONTACT WITH THEM.

"INSTEAD, THOTH CREATED TWO TABLETS, EACH WITH THEIR OWN SPECIFIC FUNCTION. THE **UTA** TABLET PULLED FROM THE FUTURE AND THE **ATA** TABLET FROM THE PAST.

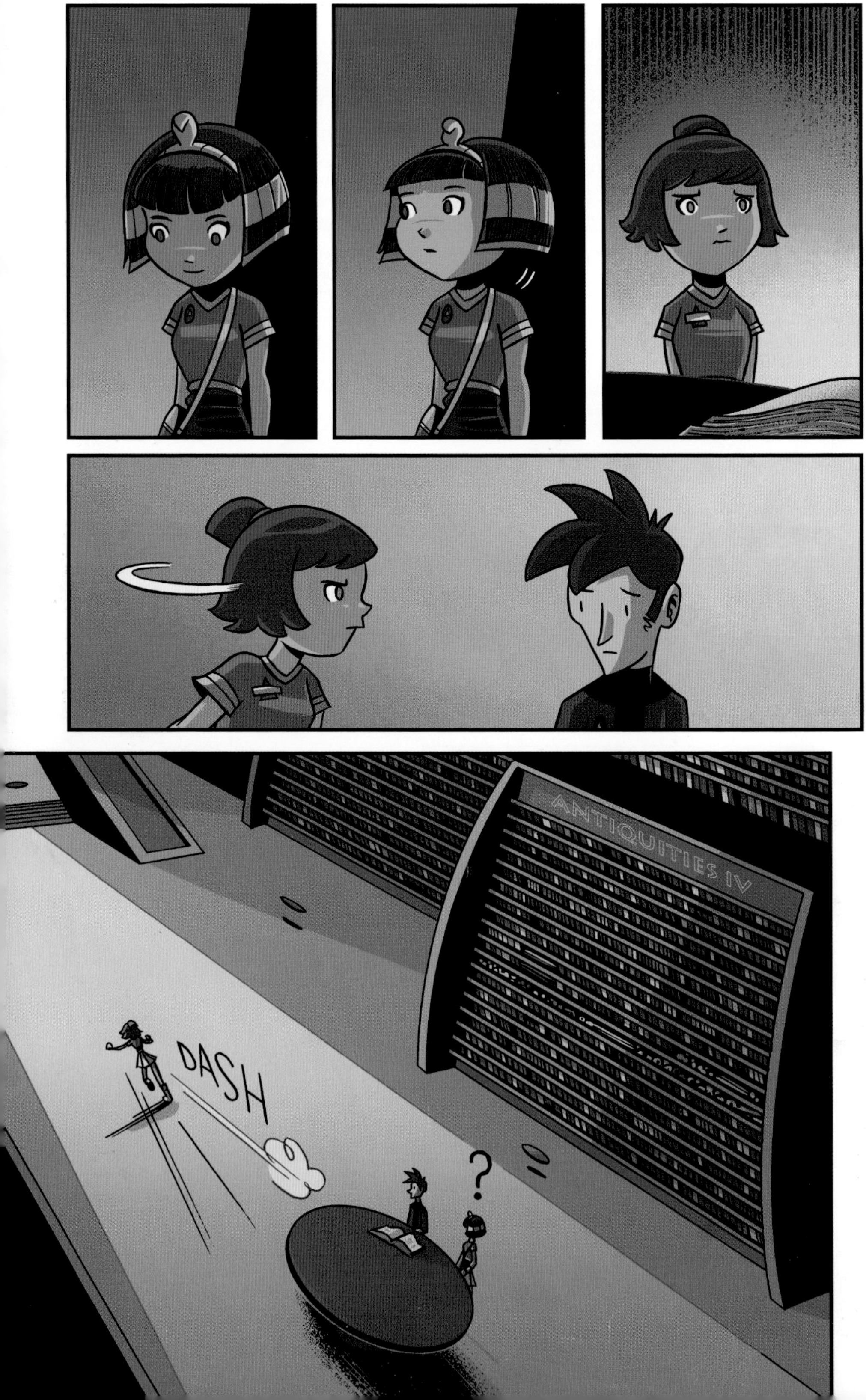
ANTIQUITIES IV
DASH
?

THE ENTIRE WORLD WAS LEFT UNINHABITABLE. WHAT REMAINS OF HER COLONY IS SCATTERED IN RESERVATIONS ACROSS THE GALAXY.

SHE ONLY MENTIONED HOW STRICT HER PARENTS WERE.

SHE...NEVER SAID ANYTHING ABOUT THAT.

HER PARENTS HAVE BEEN OFF ON A DEEP RECOVERY EXPEDITION FOR THREE YEARS.

SHE HASN'T SEEN OR TALKED TO THEM IN OVER TWO.

I DIDN'T KNOW THAT.

DO *YOU* BELIEVE IN THE PROPHECY, BRIAN?

HEH. I DON'T TEND TO BELIEVE IN PROPHETS AND VISIONS. THERE'S USUALLY A SCIENTIFIC EXPLANATION AT THE ROOT OF THESE THINGS.

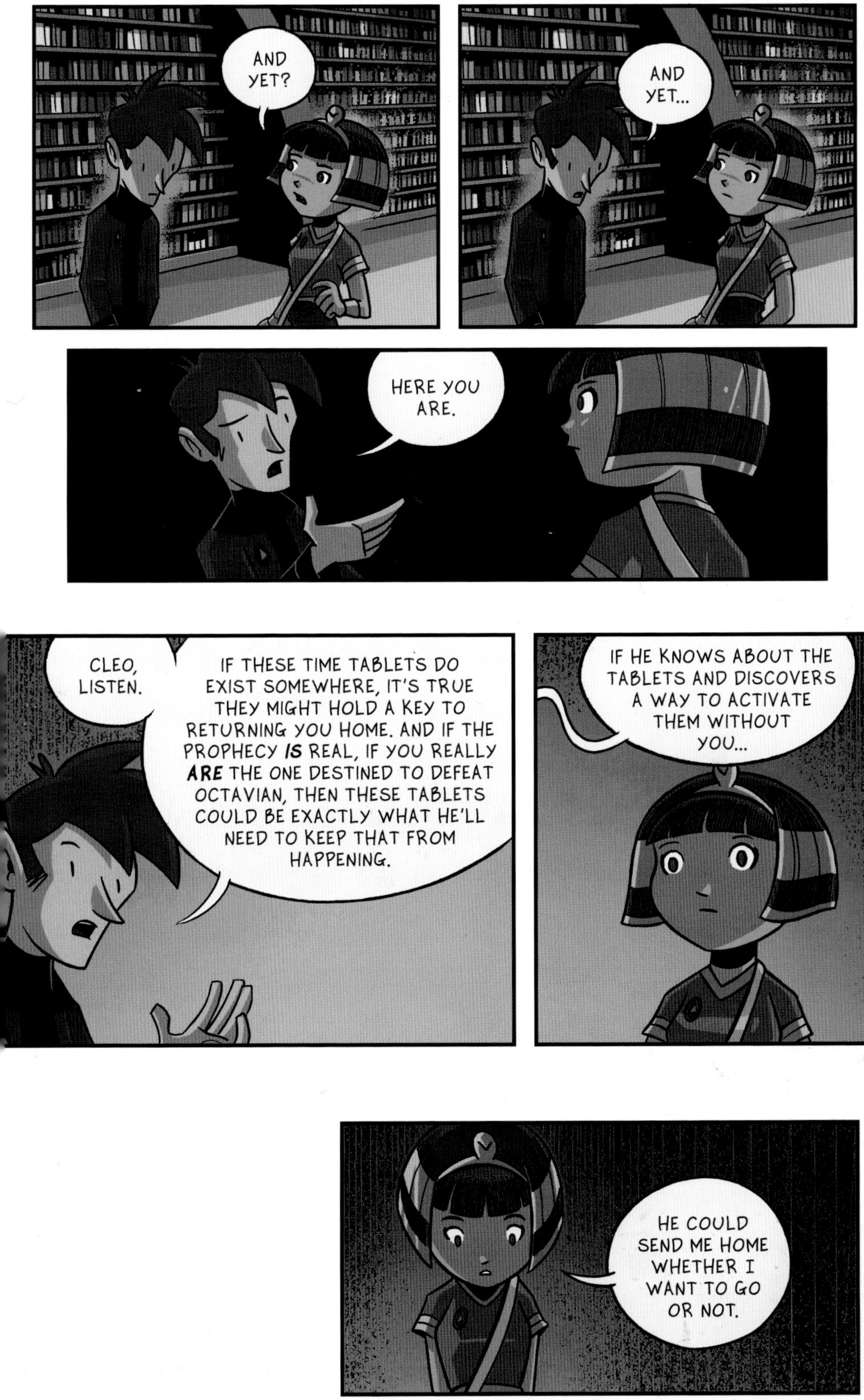
AND YET?
AND YET...
HERE YOU ARE.
CLEO, LISTEN.
IF THESE TIME TABLETS DO EXIST SOMEWHERE, IT'S TRUE THEY MIGHT HOLD A KEY TO RETURNING YOU HOME. AND IF THE PROPHECY **IS** REAL, IF YOU REALLY **ARE** THE ONE DESTINED TO DEFEAT OCTAVIAN, THEN THESE TABLETS COULD BE EXACTLY WHAT HE'LL NEED TO KEEP THAT FROM HAPPENING.
IF HE KNOWS ABOUT THE TABLETS AND DISCOVERS A WAY TO ACTIVATE THEM WITHOUT YOU...
HE COULD SEND ME HOME WHETHER I WANT TO GO OR NOT.

CHAPTER THREE

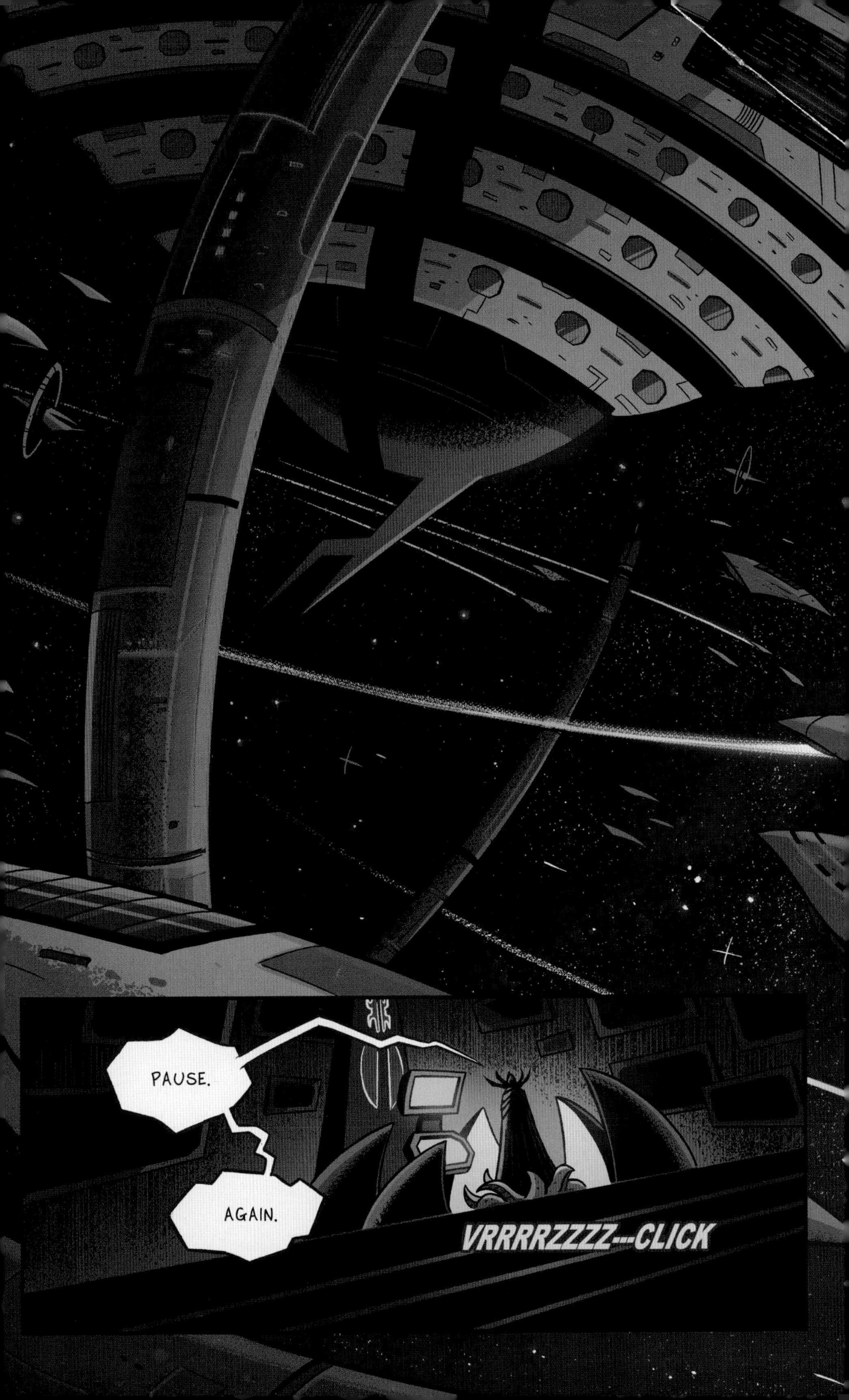
PAUSE.
AGAIN.
VRRRRZZZZ---CLICK

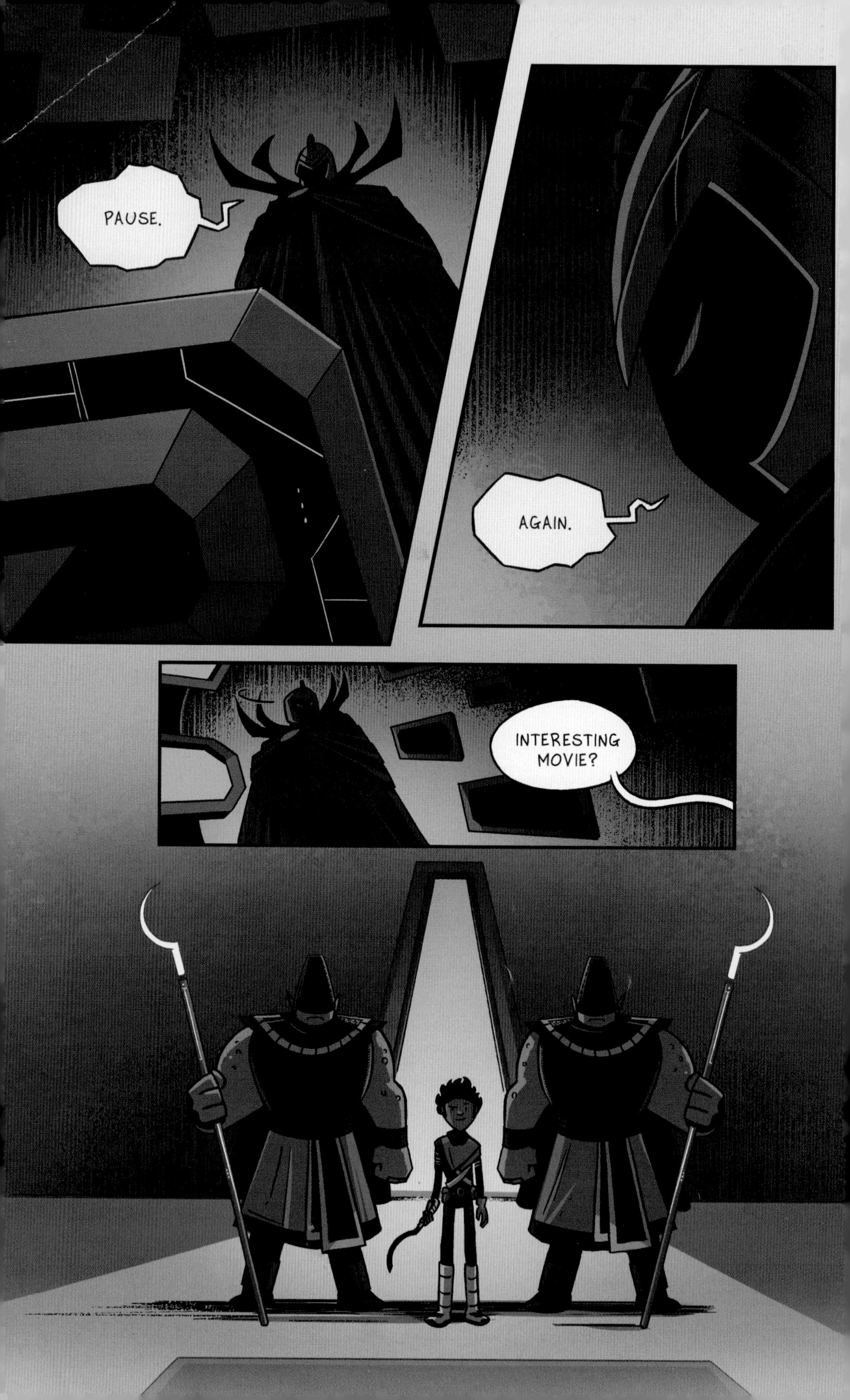
PAUSE.
AGAIN.
INTERESTING MOVIE?

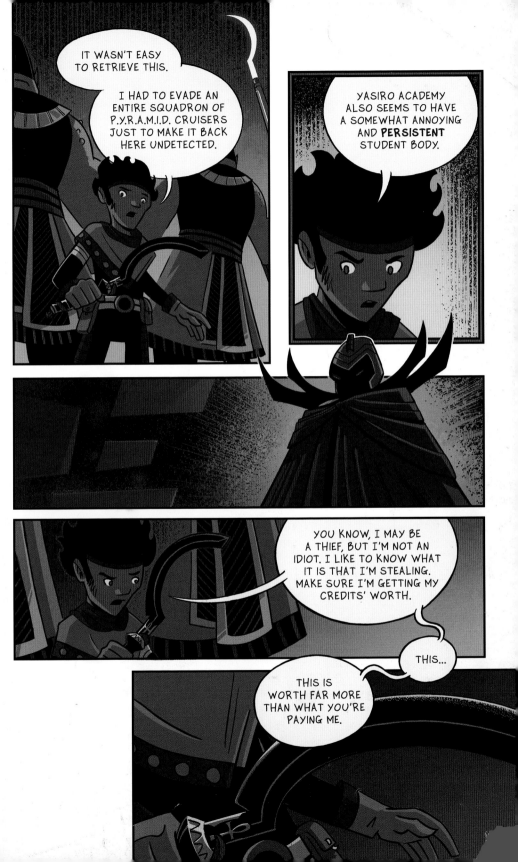

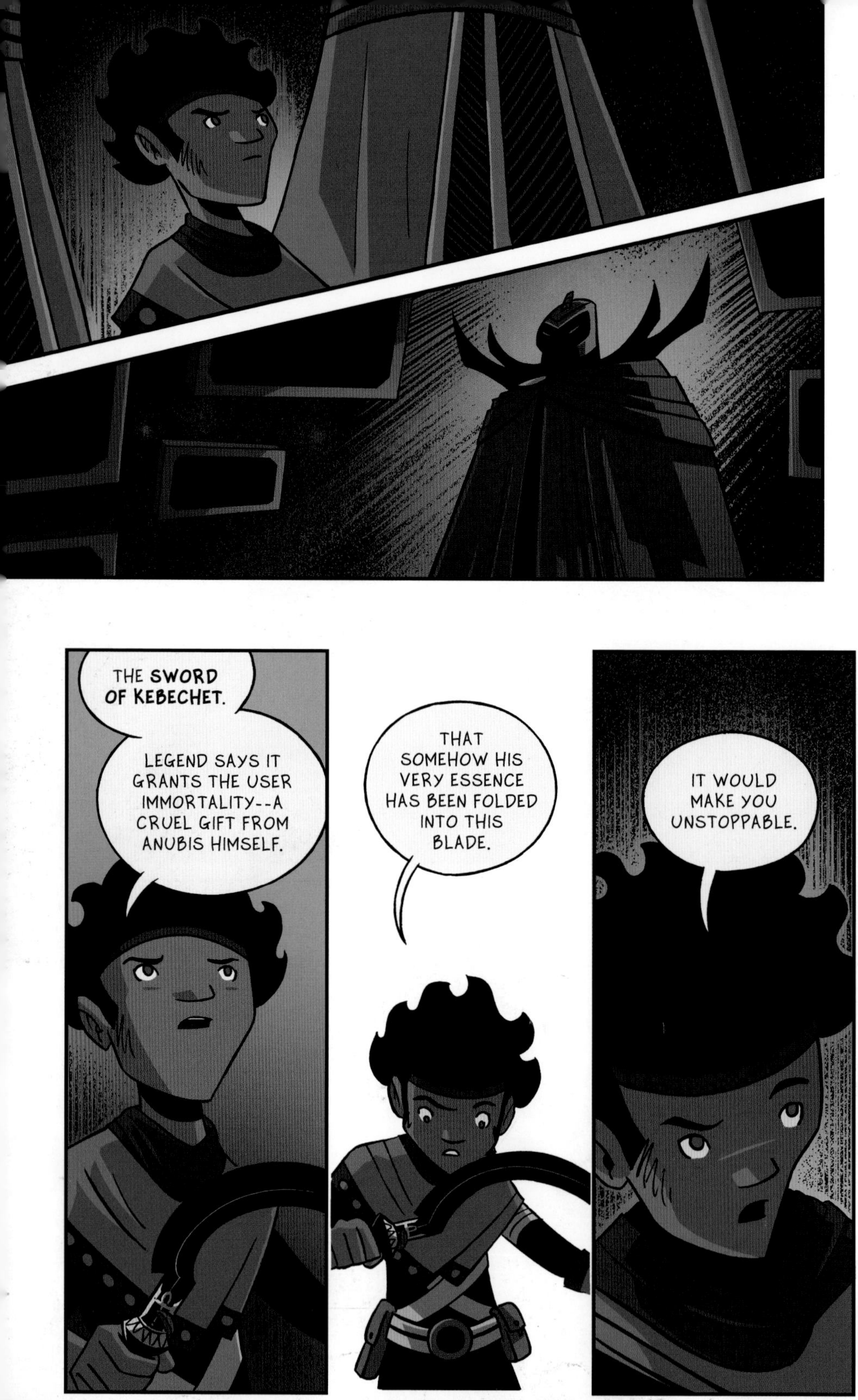
THE SWORD OF KEBECHET.
LEGEND SAYS IT GRANTS THE USER IMMORTALITY--A CRUEL GIFT FROM ANUBIS HIMSELF.
THAT SOMEHOW HIS VERY ESSENCE HAS BEEN FOLDED INTO THIS BLADE.
IT WOULD MAKE YOU UNSTOPPABLE.

139

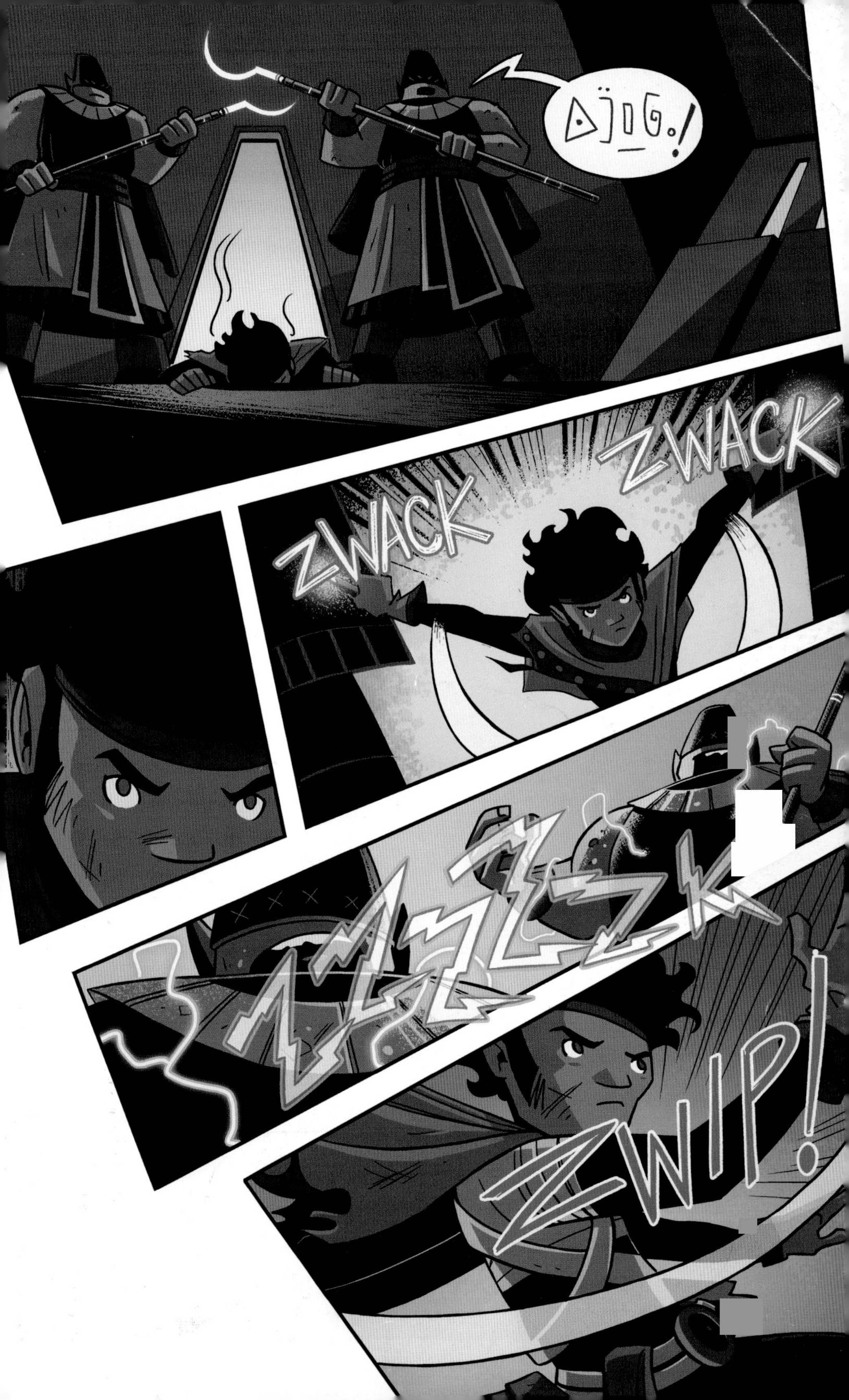
ZWACK
ZWACK
ZZZZK
ZWIP!

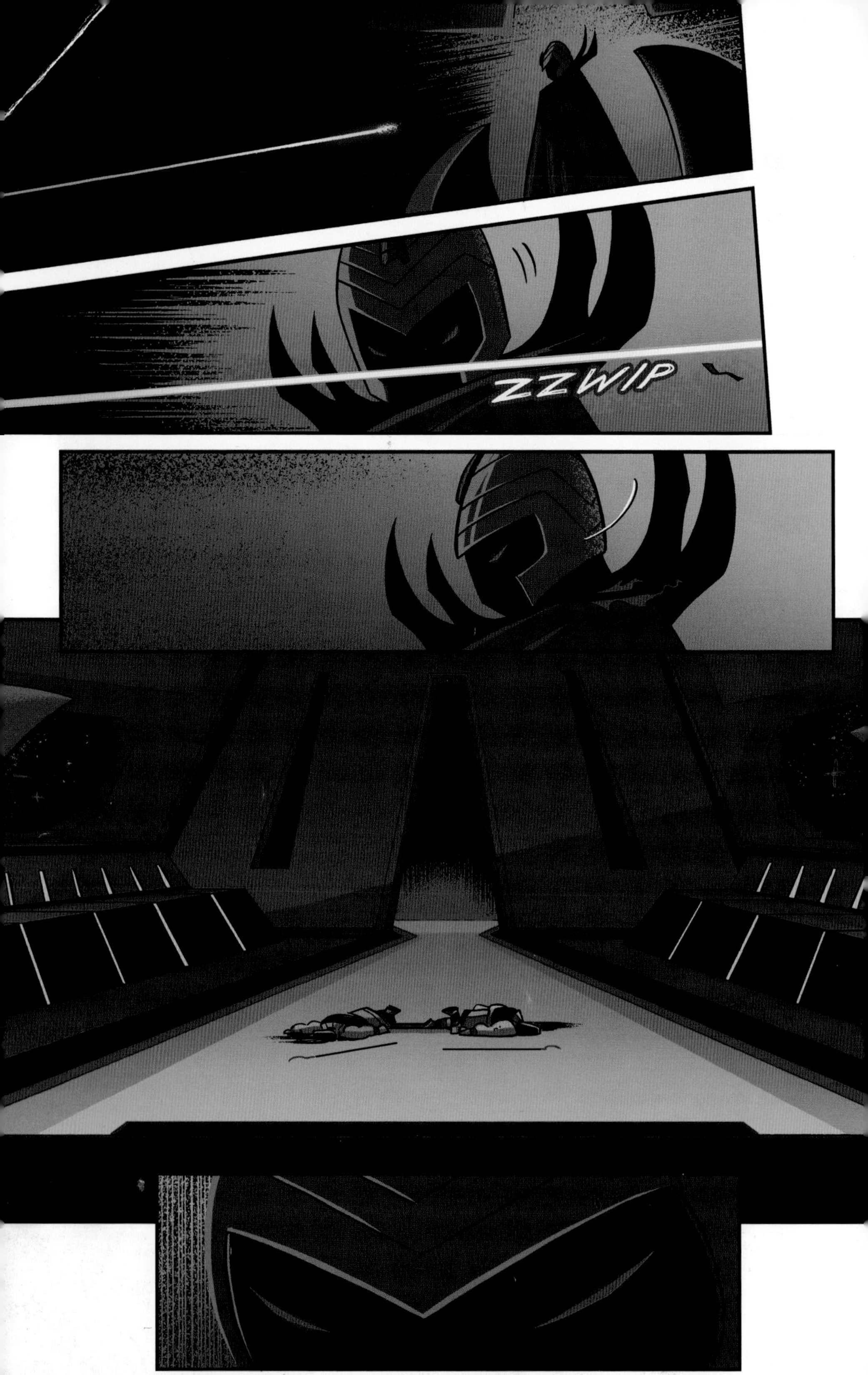
ZZWIP

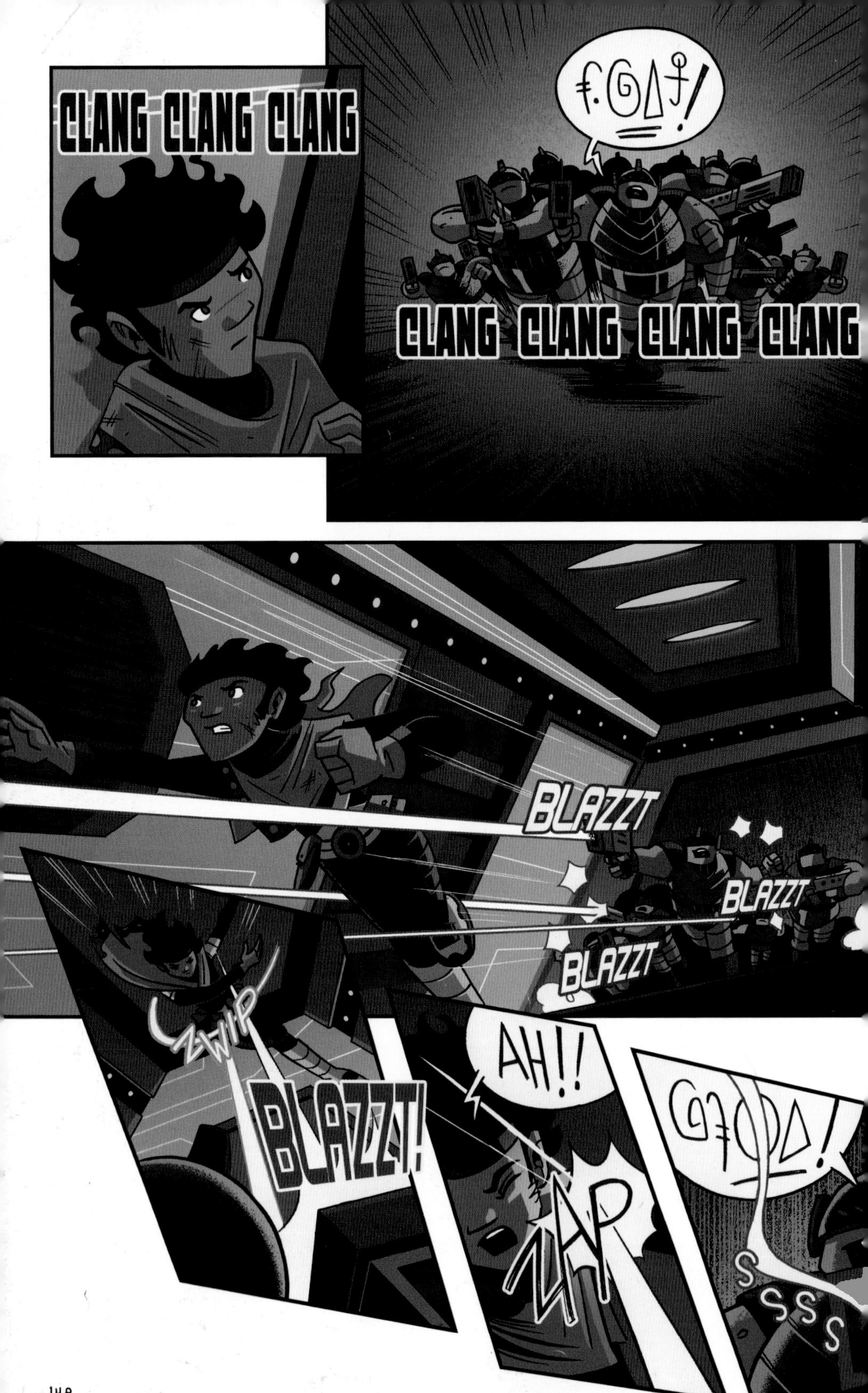
CLANG CLANG CLANG
CLANG CLANG CLANG CLANG
BLAZZT
BLAZZT
BLAZZT
ZWIP
BLAZZZT!
AH!!
ZAP
SSSSS

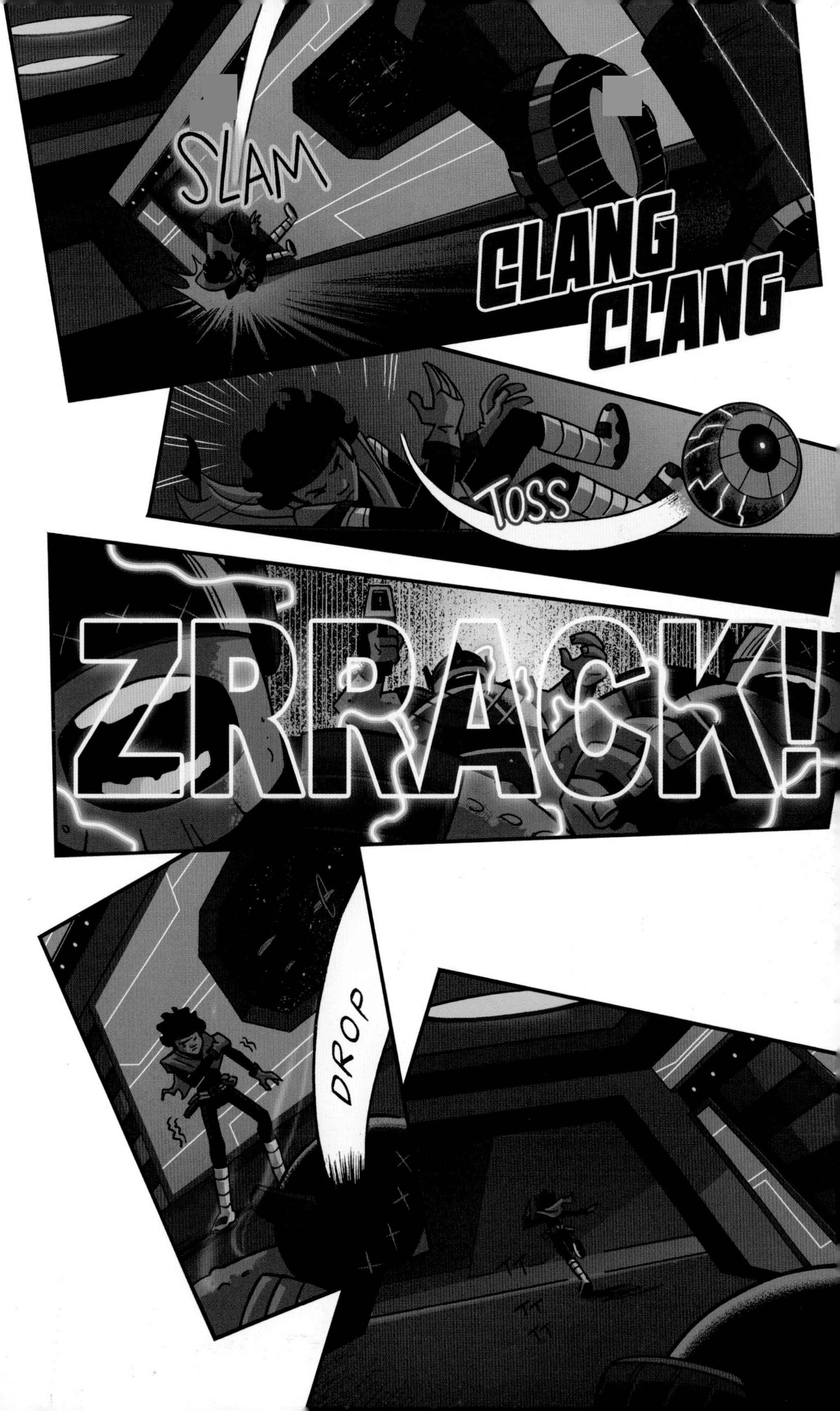
SLAM
CLANG
CLANG
TOSS
ZRRACK!
DROP

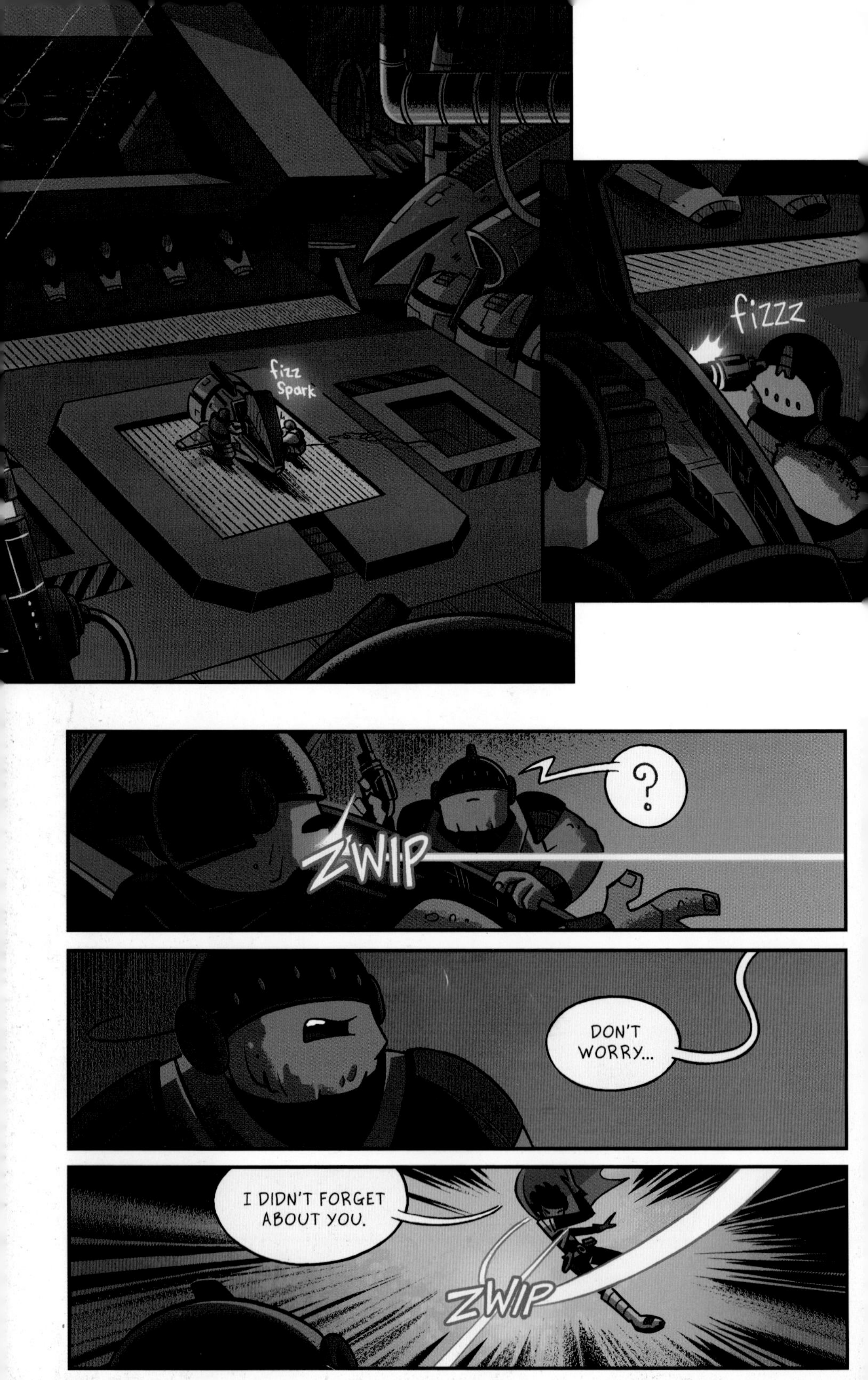
fizz
Spark
fizzz
?
ZWIP
DON'T WORRY...
I DIDN'T FORGET ABOUT YOU.
ZWIP

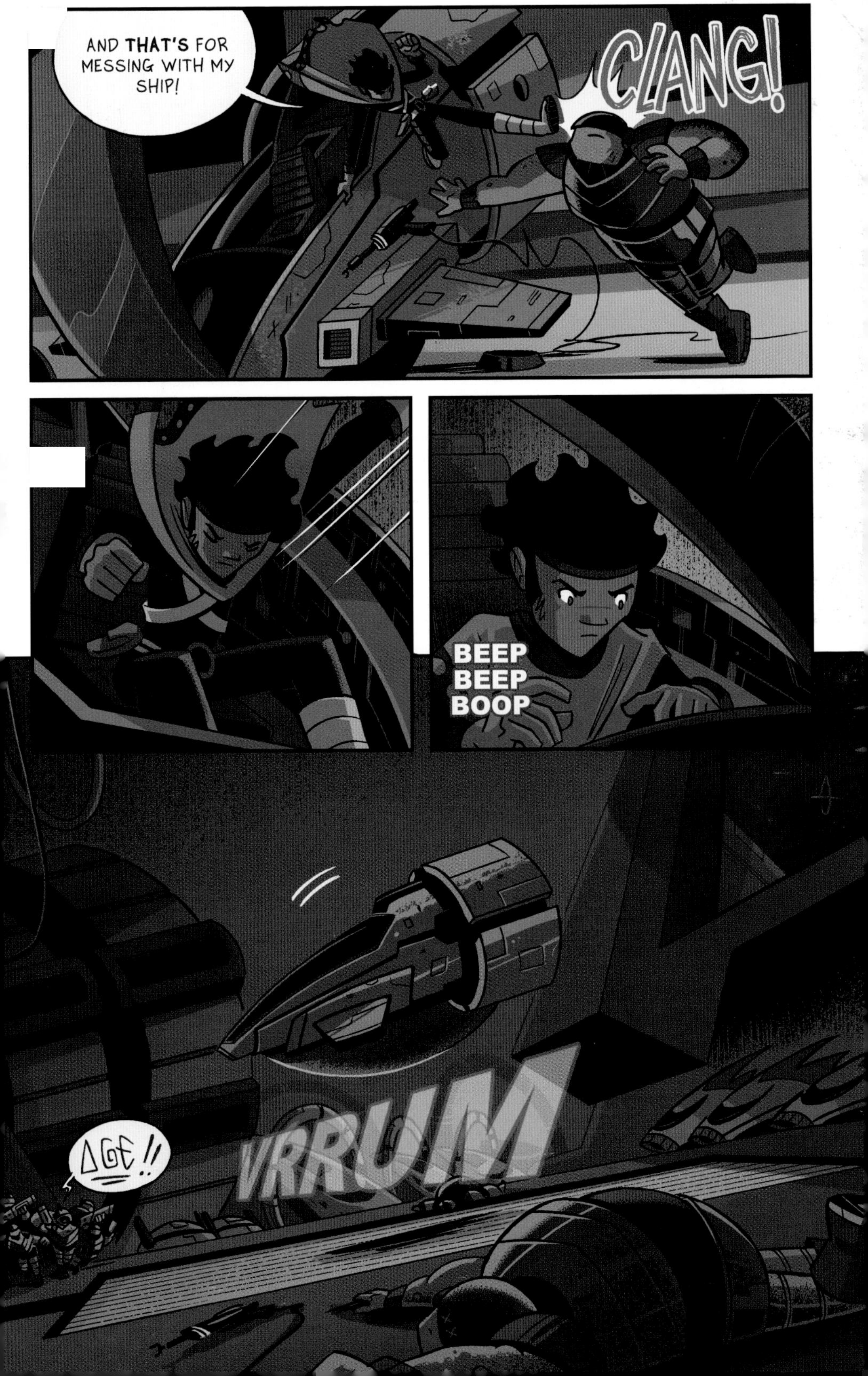

AND **THAT'S** FOR MESSING WITH MY SHIP!
CLANG!
BEEP BEEP BOOP
VRRUM

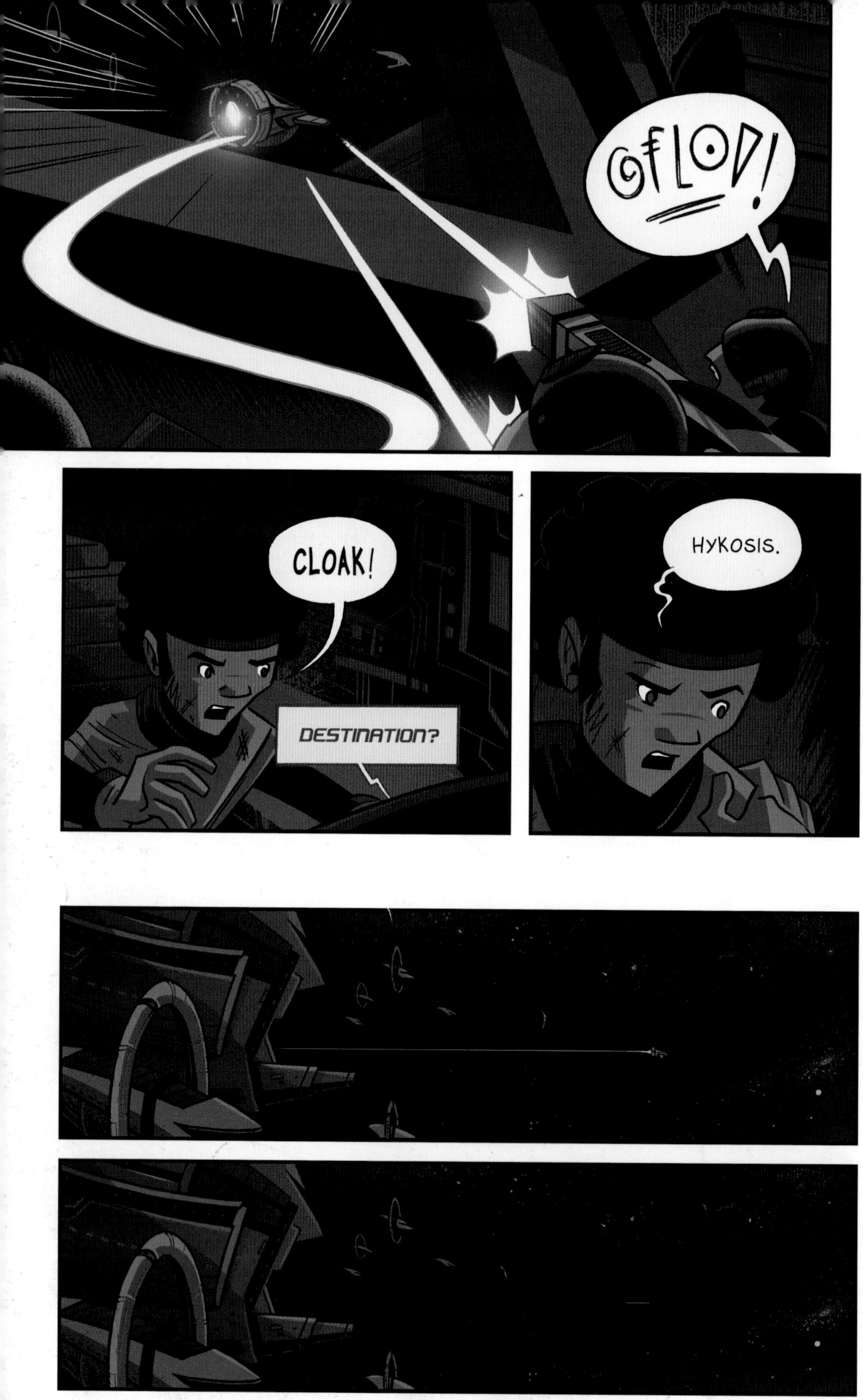
CLOAK!
DESTINATION?
HYKOSIS.

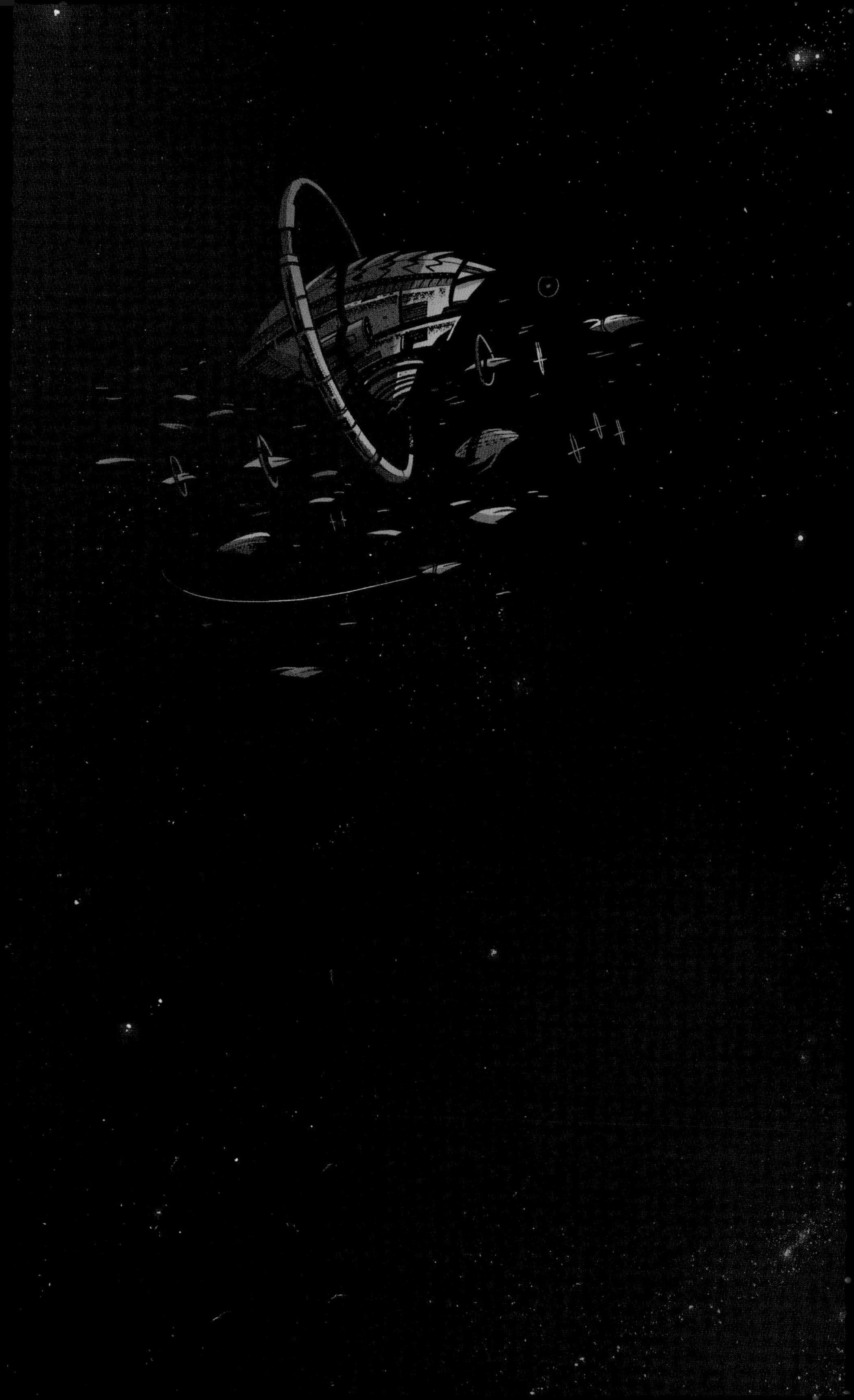

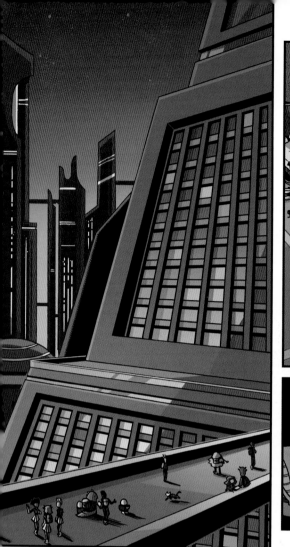

SHUF

UH, HEY.

OH. HEY.

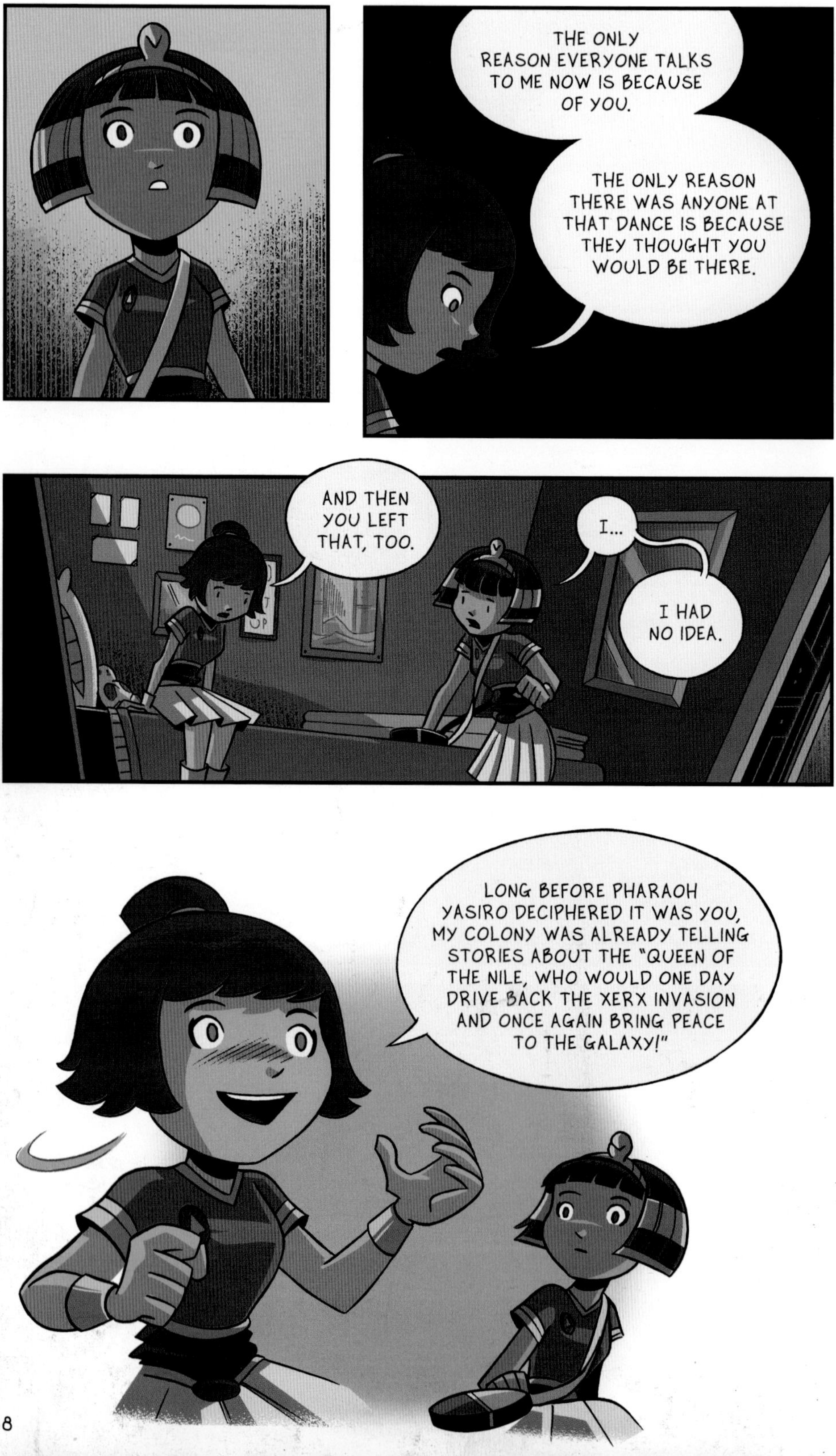
THE ONLY REASON EVERYONE TALKS TO ME NOW IS BECAUSE OF YOU.
THE ONLY REASON THERE WAS ANYONE AT THAT DANCE IS BECAUSE THEY THOUGHT YOU WOULD BE THERE.
AND THEN YOU LEFT THAT, TOO.
I...
I HAD NO IDEA.
LONG BEFORE PHARAOH YASIRO DECIPHERED IT WAS YOU, MY COLONY WAS ALREADY TELLING STORIES ABOUT THE "QUEEN OF THE NILE, WHO WOULD ONE DAY DRIVE BACK THE XERX INVASION AND ONCE AGAIN BRING PEACE TO THE GALAXY!"

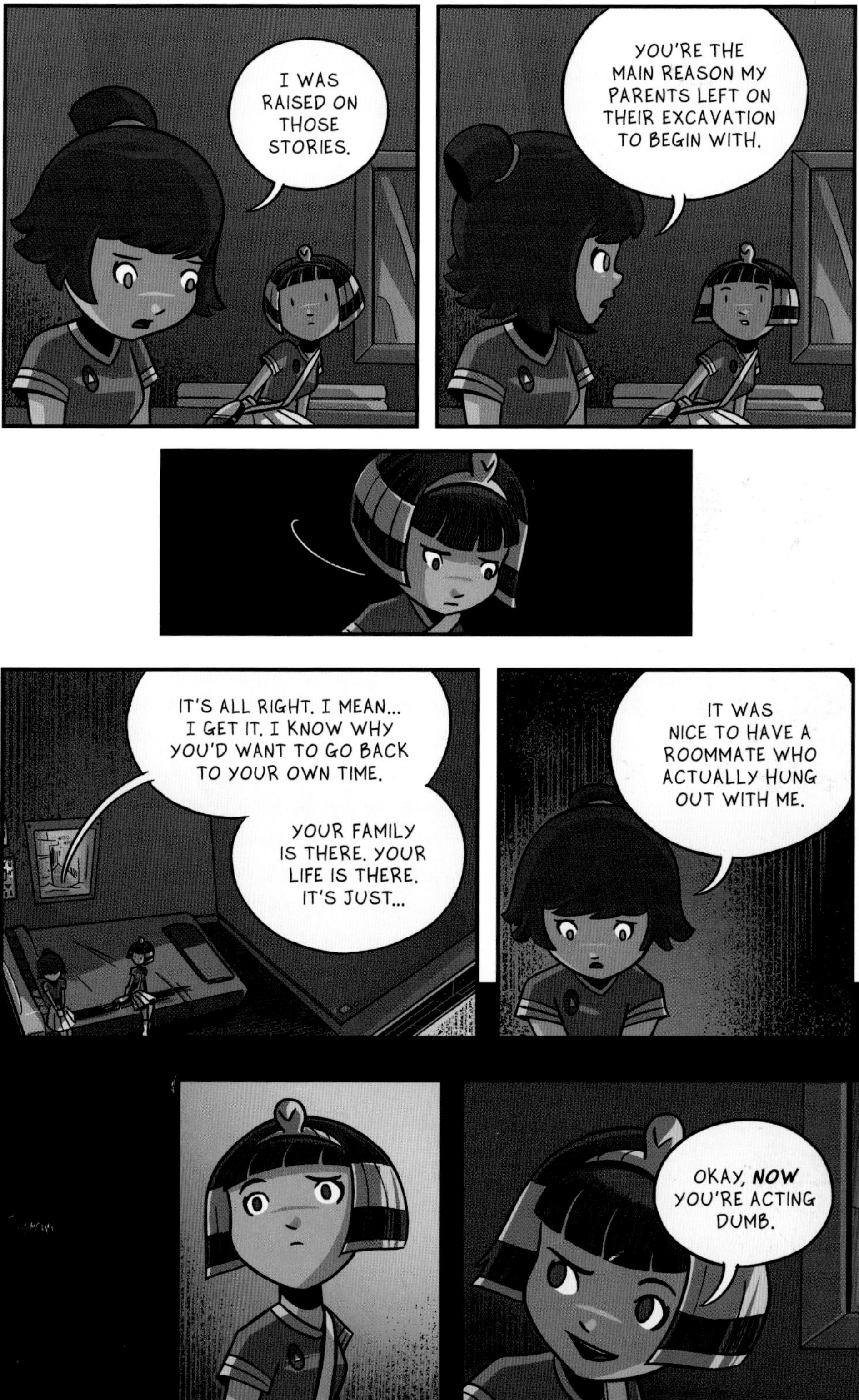
I WAS RAISED ON THOSE STORIES.
YOU'RE THE MAIN REASON MY PARENTS LEFT ON THEIR EXCAVATION TO BEGIN WITH.
IT'S ALL RIGHT. I MEAN... I GET IT. I KNOW WHY YOU'D WANT TO GO BACK TO YOUR OWN TIME.
YOUR FAMILY IS THERE. YOUR LIFE IS THERE. IT'S JUST...
IT WAS NICE TO HAVE A ROOMMATE WHO ACTUALLY HUNG OUT WITH ME.
OKAY, **NOW** YOU'RE ACTING DUMB.

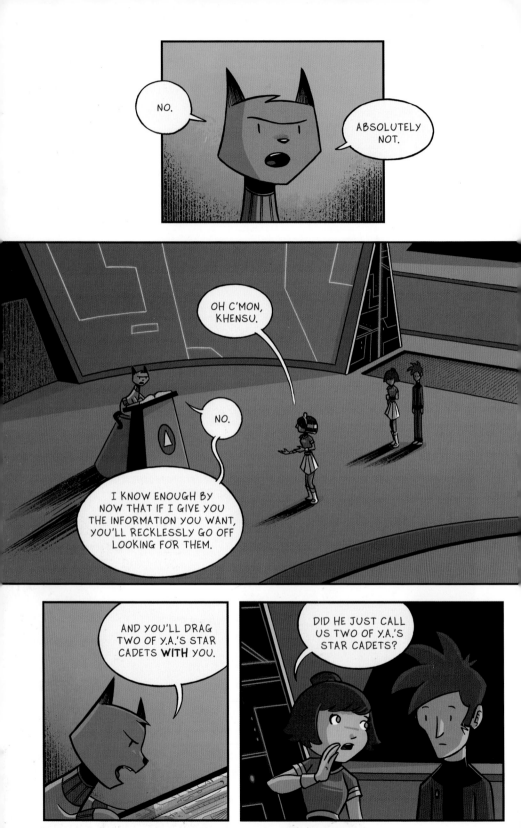

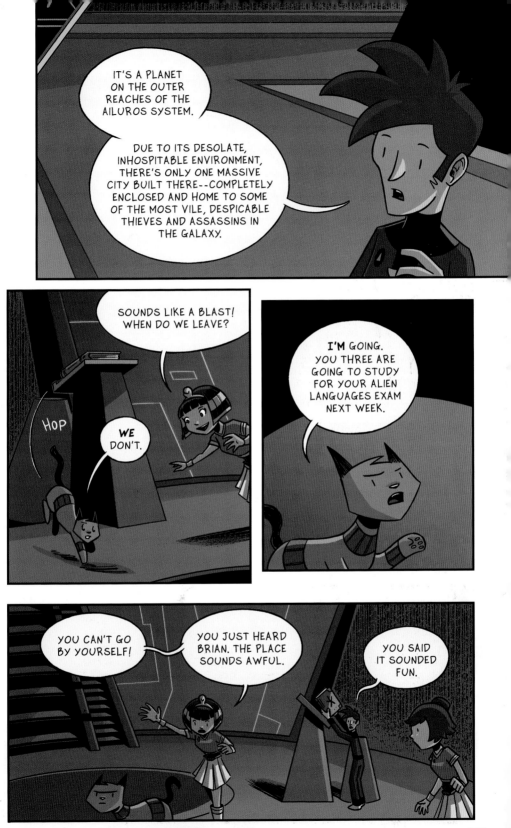

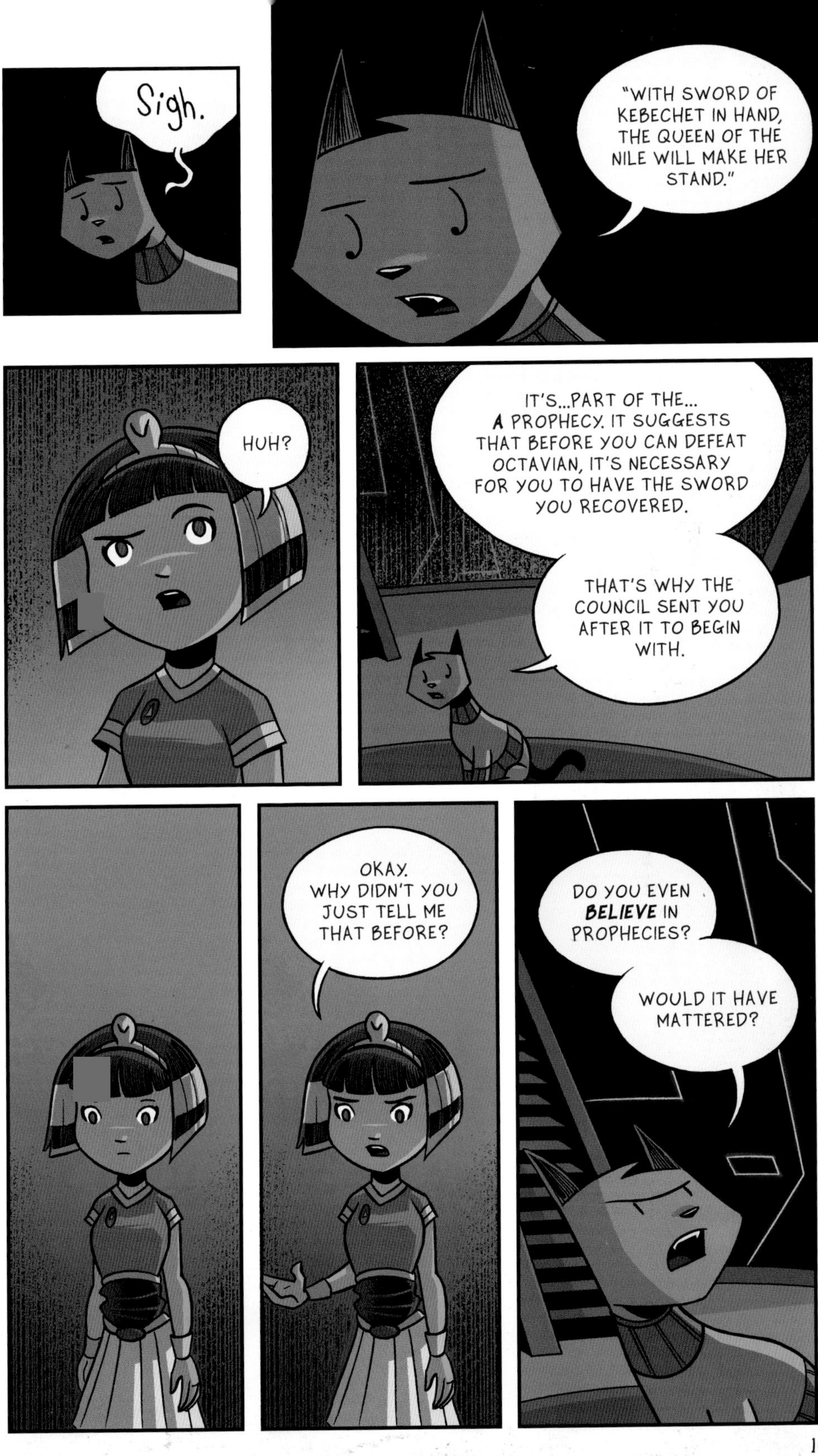
Sigh.
"WITH SWORD OF KEBECHET IN HAND, THE QUEEN OF THE NILE WILL MAKE HER STAND."
HUH?
IT'S...PART OF THE... A PROPHECY. IT SUGGESTS THAT BEFORE YOU CAN DEFEAT OCTAVIAN, IT'S NECESSARY FOR YOU TO HAVE THE SWORD YOU RECOVERED.
THAT'S WHY THE COUNCIL SENT YOU AFTER IT TO BEGIN WITH.
OKAY. WHY DIDN'T YOU JUST TELL ME THAT BEFORE?
DO YOU EVEN BELIEVE IN PROPHECIES?
WOULD IT HAVE MATTERED?

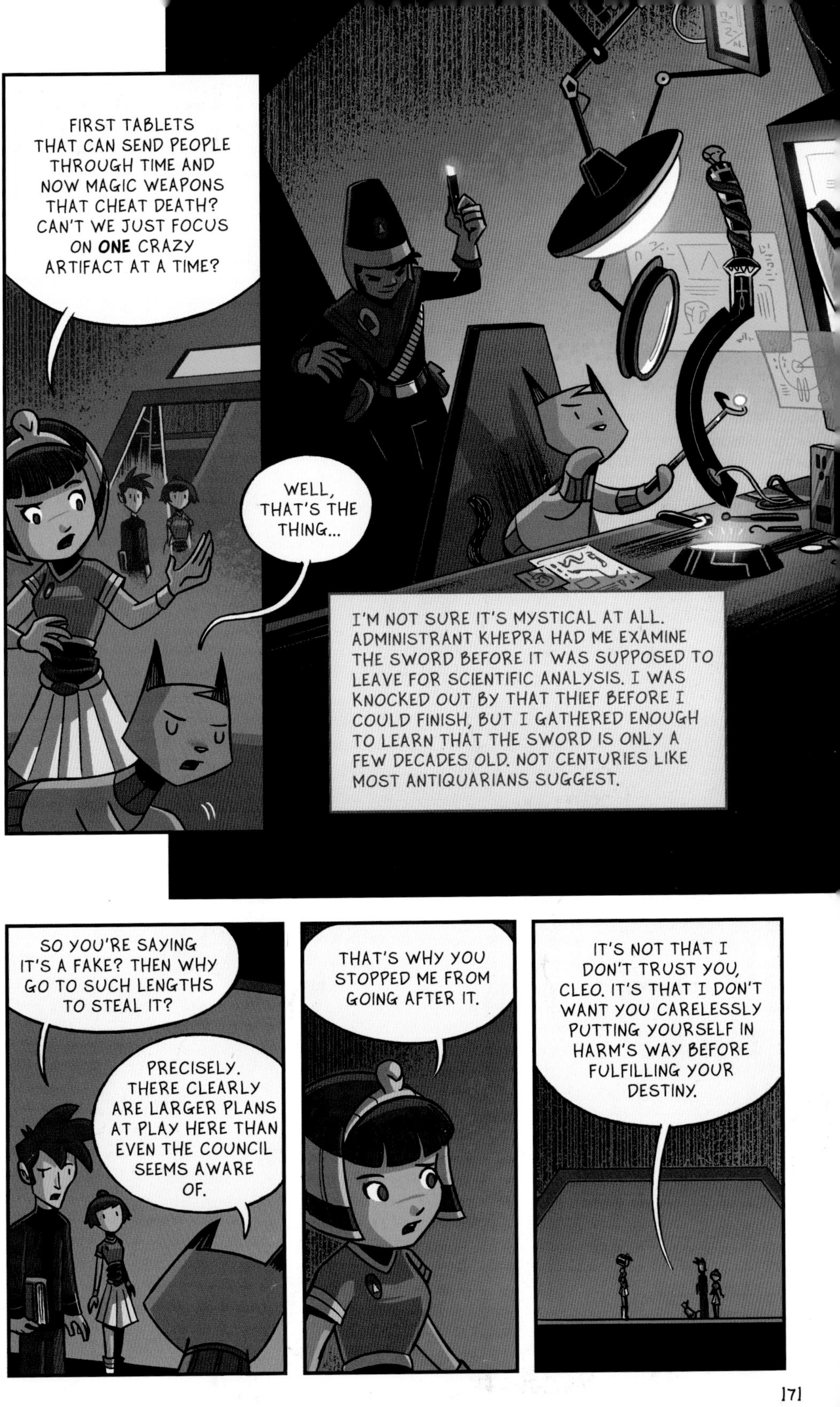
FIRST TABLETS THAT CAN SEND PEOPLE THROUGH TIME AND NOW MAGIC WEAPONS THAT CHEAT DEATH? CAN'T WE JUST FOCUS ON **ONE** CRAZY ARTIFACT AT A TIME?
WELL, THAT'S THE THING...
I'M NOT SURE IT'S MYSTICAL AT ALL. ADMINISTRANT KHEPRA HAD ME EXAMINE THE SWORD BEFORE IT WAS SUPPOSED TO LEAVE FOR SCIENTIFIC ANALYSIS. I WAS KNOCKED OUT BY THAT THIEF BEFORE I COULD FINISH, BUT I GATHERED ENOUGH TO LEARN THAT THE SWORD IS ONLY A FEW DECADES OLD. NOT CENTURIES LIKE MOST ANTIQUARIANS SUGGEST.
SO YOU'RE SAYING IT'S A FAKE? THEN WHY GO TO SUCH LENGTHS TO STEAL IT?
PRECISELY. THERE CLEARLY ARE LARGER PLANS AT PLAY HERE THAN EVEN THE COUNCIL SEEMS AWARE OF.
THAT'S WHY YOU STOPPED ME FROM GOING AFTER IT.
IT'S NOT THAT I DON'T TRUST YOU, CLEO. IT'S THAT I DON'T WANT YOU CARELESSLY PUTTING YOURSELF IN HARM'S WAY BEFORE FULFILLING YOUR DESTINY.

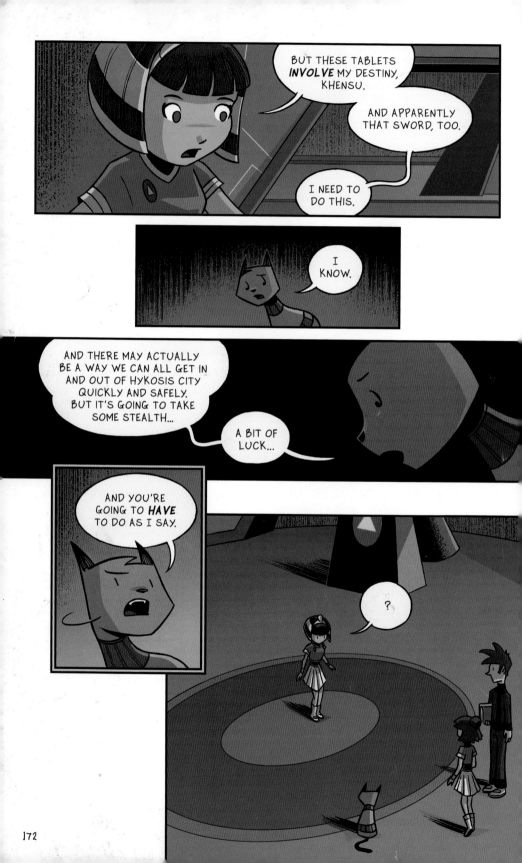

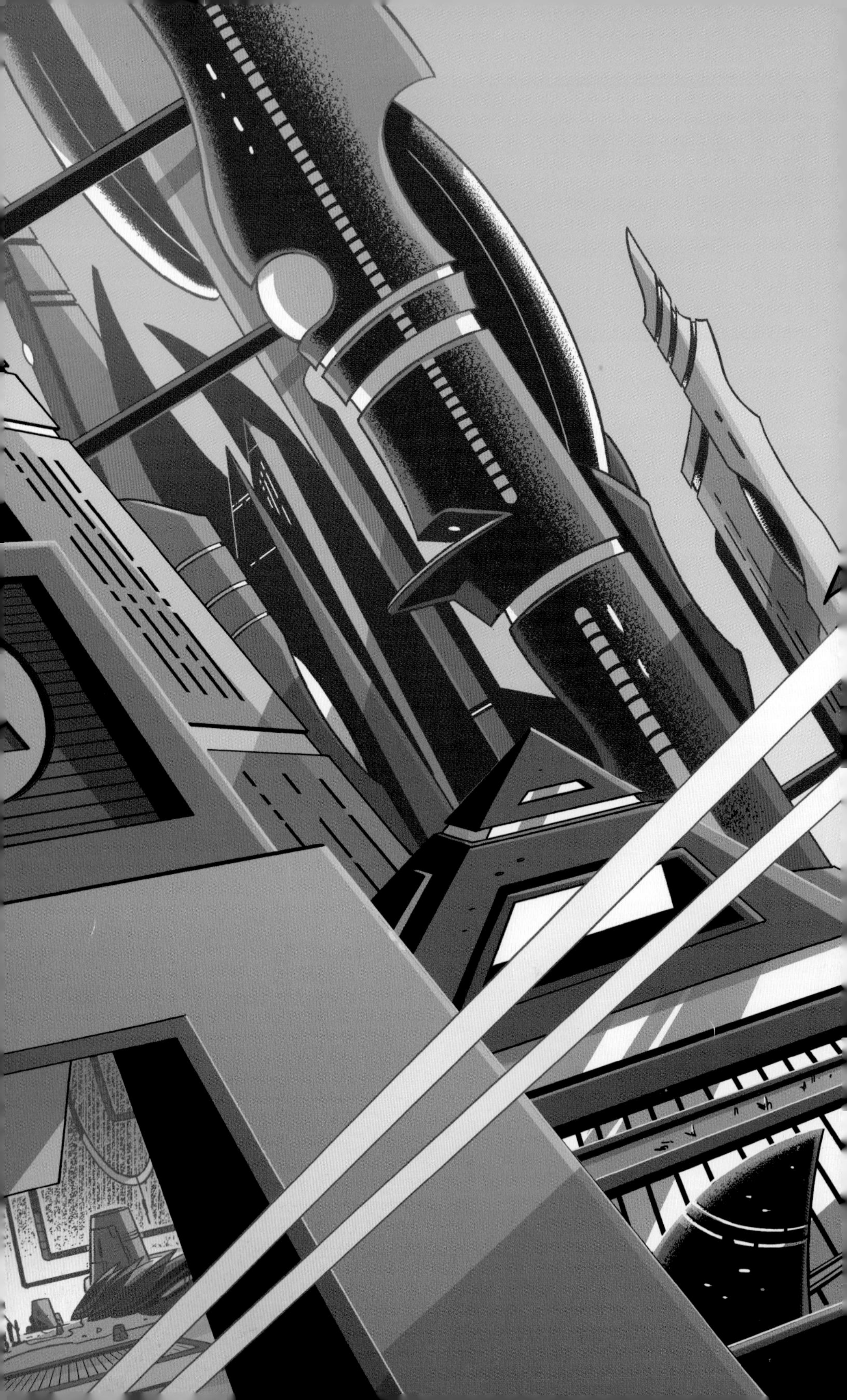

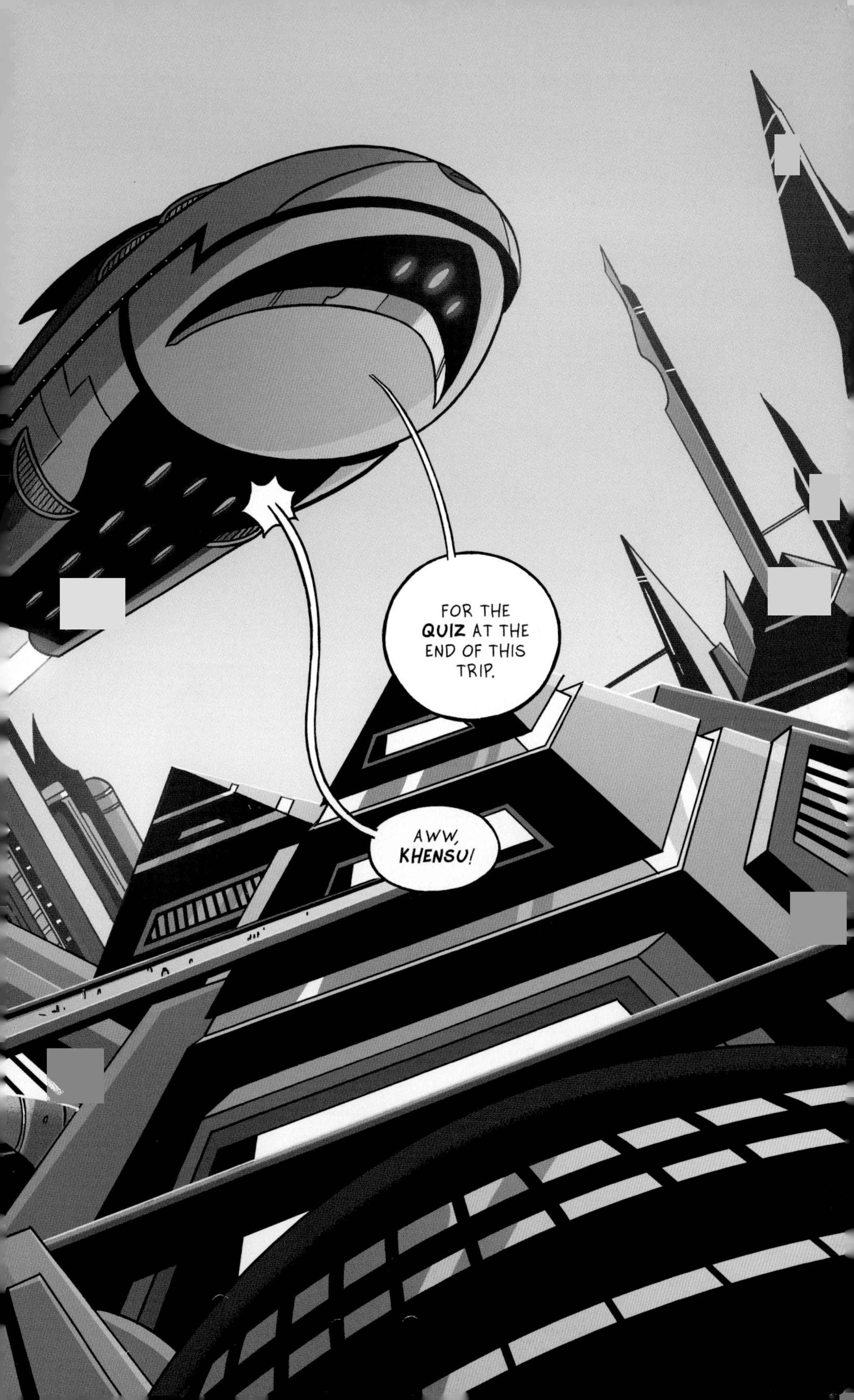
FOR THE QUIZ AT THE END OF THIS TRIP.
AWW, KHENSU!

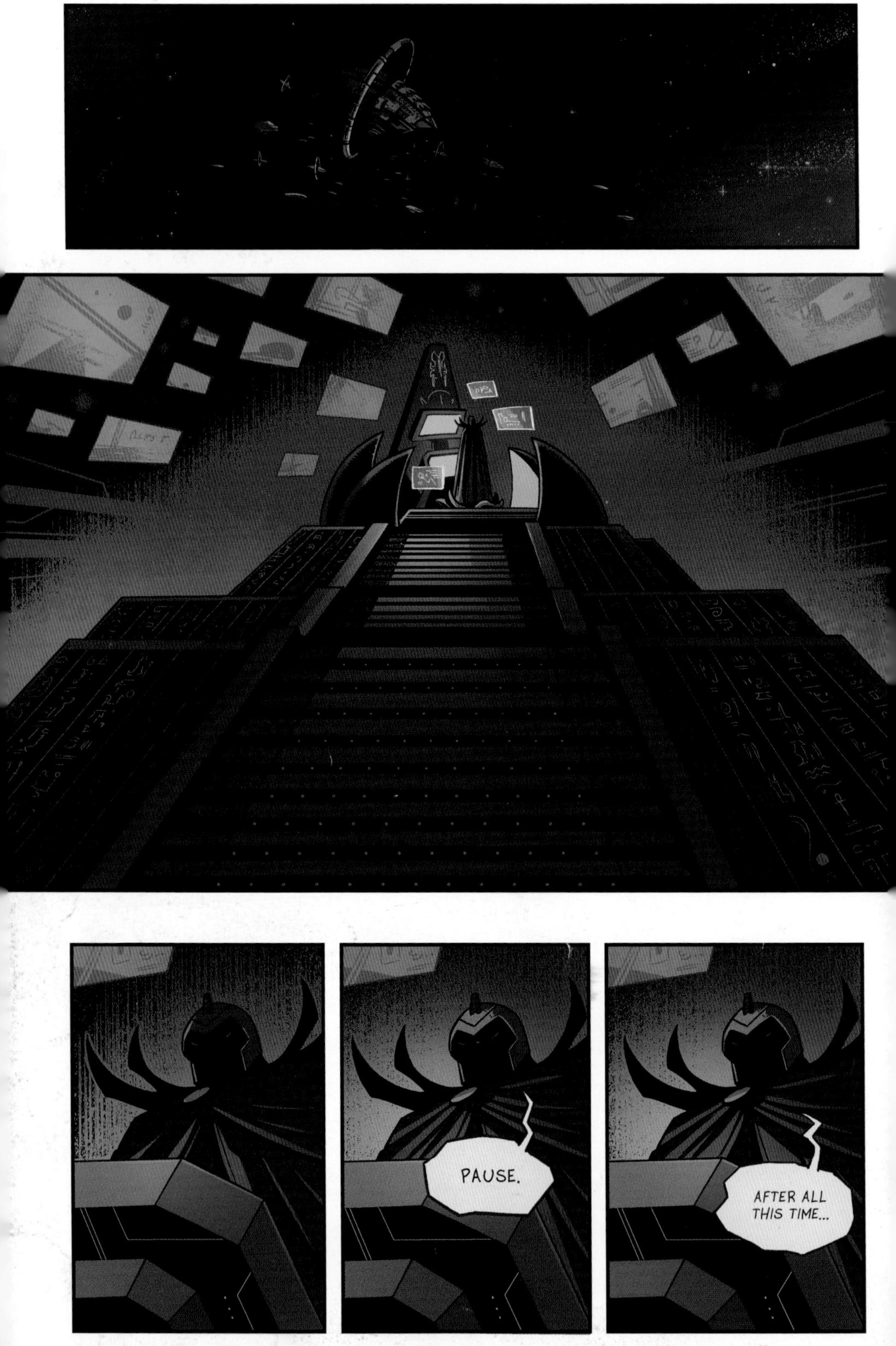
PAUSE.
AFTER ALL THIS TIME...

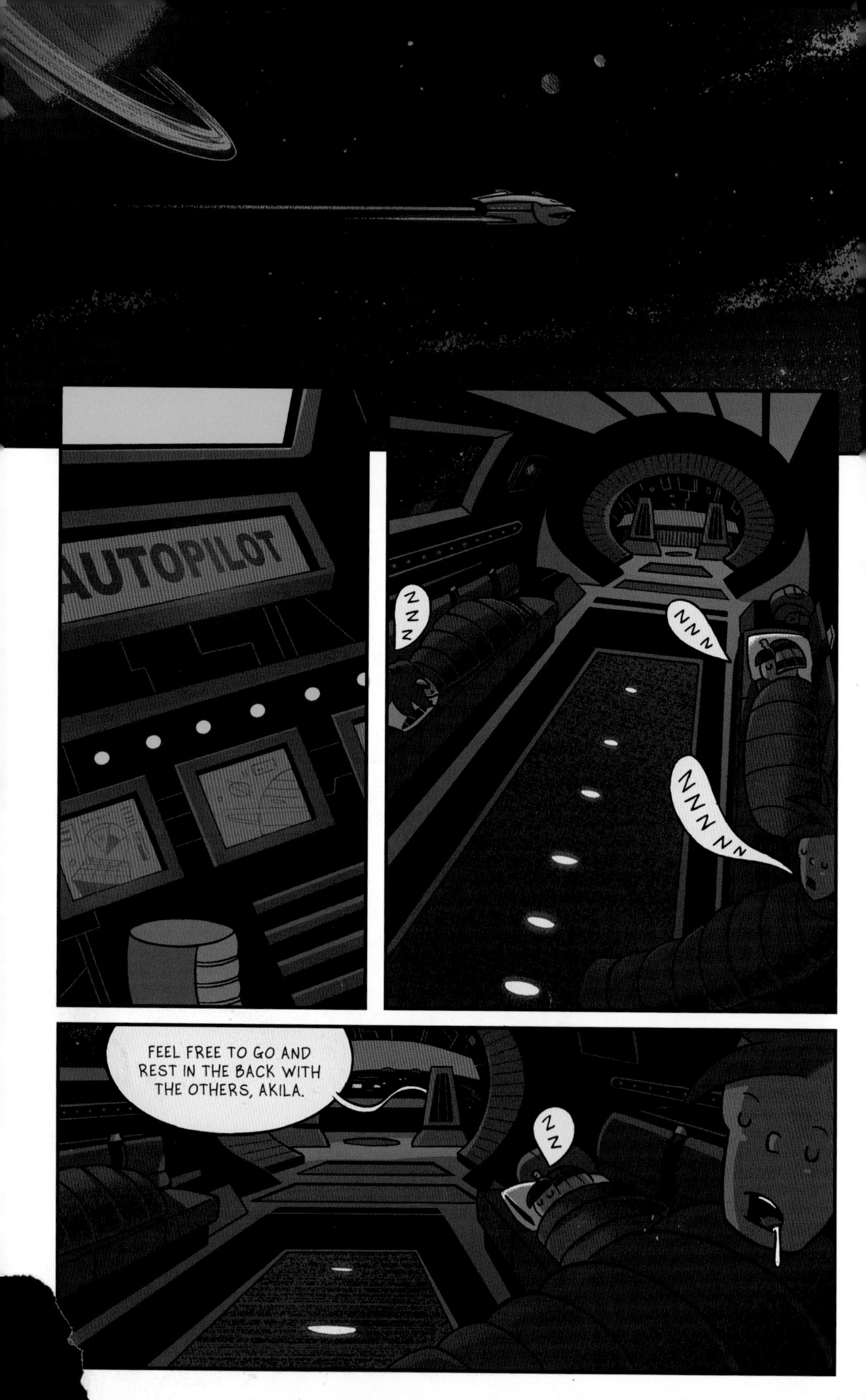
AUTOPILOT
ZZZ
ZZZ
ZZZZZ
FEEL FREE TO GO AND REST IN THE BACK WITH THE OTHERS, AKILA.
ZZ

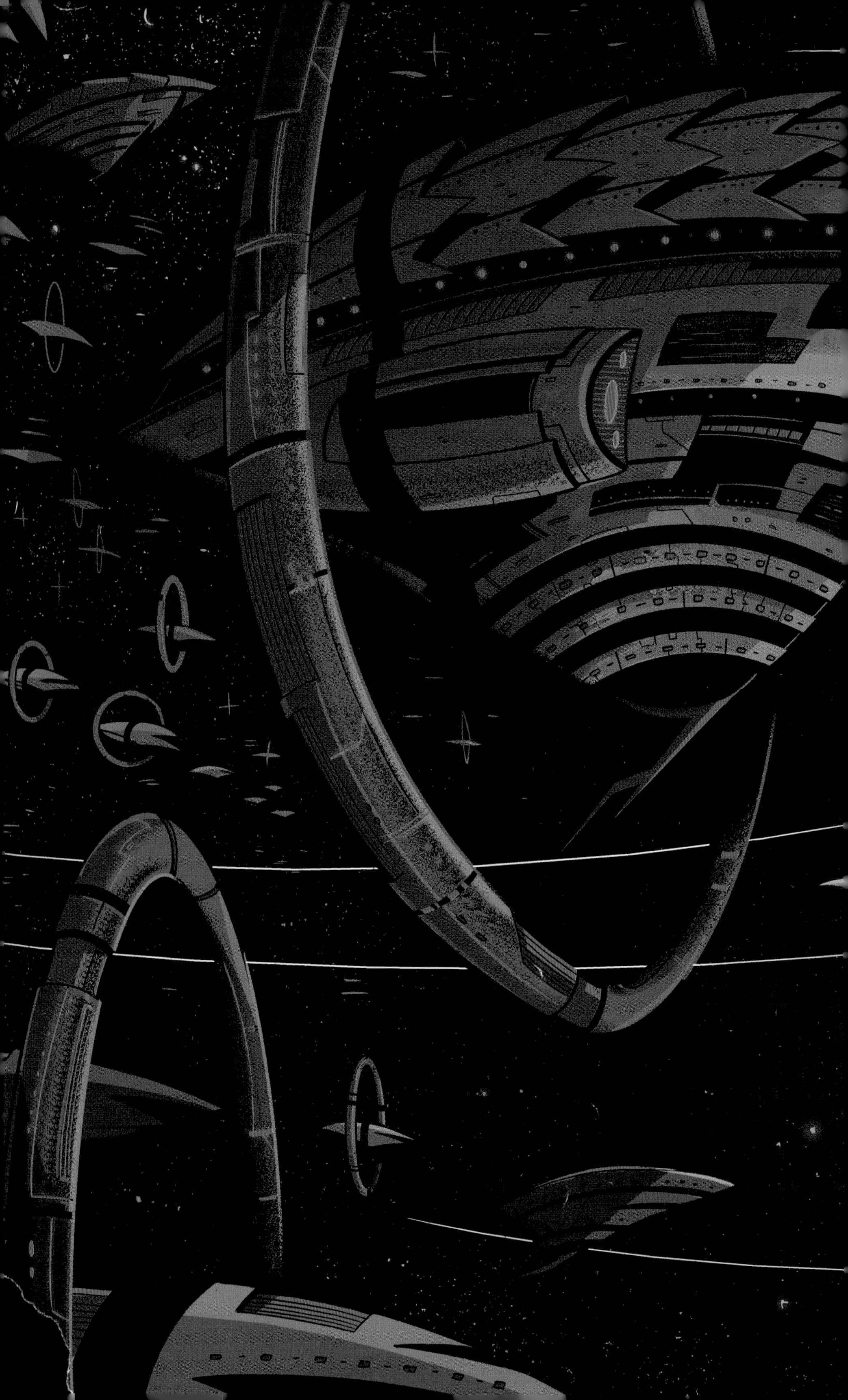

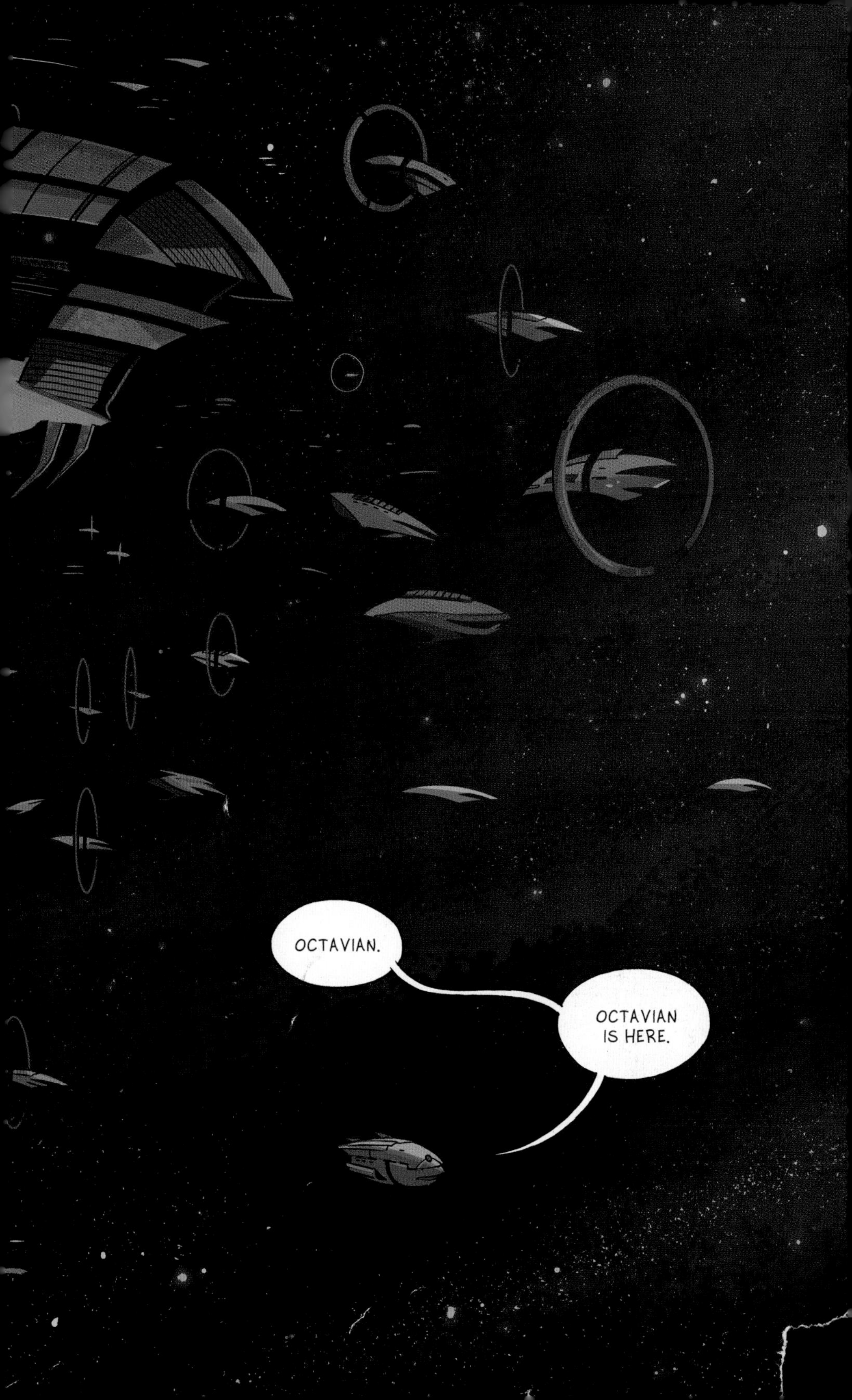
OCTAVIAN.
OCTAVIAN IS HERE.

ABOUT THE AUTHOR

A graduate of the Columbus College of Art & Design, Mike Maihack spends his time drawing pictures of cats, superheroes, space girls, and just about anything else he can think of that might involve a ray gun or two. He is the creator of *Cleopatra in Space, Book One: Target Practice* and the popular webcomic *Cow & Buffalo*; illustrator of the all-ages card game *Goblins Drool, Fairies Rule*; and has contributed art and stories to books like *Parable*; *Jim Henson's The Storyteller*; *Cow Boy*; *Geeks, Girls, and Secret Identities*; and the Eisner and Harvey award-winning *Comic Book Tattoo*. Mike currently lives in Tampa, Florida, with his wife, son, and two Siamese cats.

Visit Mike online at www.mikemaihack.com.

SPECIAL THANKS TO:

My amazingly supportive family: Jen Maihack, Sam and Barb Maihack, Brian and Jill Maeda, Patrick and Kim Tally, John and Darci Roberts, Chad and Jen Roberts, KeAli'i and Lindsey Rozet, Randy and Janice Meade, and — what the heck — my cats Ash and Misty (let's be more useful on the next book though, you two).

My wonderful Scholastic family (including but not limited to): Cassandra Pelham, David Saylor, Phil Falco, Lizette Serrano, Sheila Marie Everett, Tracy van Straaten, Bess Braswell, and Denise Anderson.

Judy Hansen, my literary guide through this tumultuous world of book publishing.

To all the teachers, librarians, booksellers, parents, and readers out there who have supported Cleopatra in Space thus far!

Last but not least, to Christ, my best friend and constant companion, who made certain I put as much love into every page of this book as He showed me every day I was making it.